Waldwick

Waldwick...King of Hearts

Kenneth Linde

Waldwick Books
www.waldwickbooks.com
McHenry, Illinois

Waldwick...King of Hearts

Copyright © 2022 Kenneth Jon Linde

Waldwick Partners, Inc.
dba Waldwick Books
www.WaldwickBooks.com

July 3, 2022

Printed in Wisconsin, United States of America

ISBN: 979-8-9852613-1-8

ISBN: 979-8-9852-6131-8

9 798985 261318

One can only
determine where they
are going once they
realize
where they have
been.

THE PATRILINEAL HISTORY OF THE TERRILL FAMILY

1. Carolus de Menapii	Born: 65 BC	Died:32CE
2. Menapius de Menapii	Born: 44 BC	Died: 19
3. Valerius de Menapiii	Born: 02 BC	Died: 49
4. Carolus de Menapii	Born: 49 AD	Died: 78
5. Priapus de Menapie	Born: 67 AD	Died: 114
6. Carolus de Menapie II	Born: 89 AD	Died: 137
7. Julius de Menapie	Born 115	Died: 172
8. Octavius de Menapie	Born: 144	Died: 212
9. Valardius de Menapie	Born: 179	Died: 236
10. Valeriues I Godefroy de Menapie	Born: 210	Died: 250
11. Vuercius de Menapii	Born: 250	Died: 290
12. Antsard de Menapii	Born: 290	Died: 315
13. Martisindes de Menapii	Born: 315	Died: 347
14. Toxandre de Menapii	Born: 335	Died: 378
15. Ansygius de Menapii	Born: 355	Died: 410
16. Carolus Lii de Menapii	Born: 400	Died: 450
17. Austrapius de Menapii	Born: 440	Died: 508
18. Carolus IV Nazon Hesbaye von Haspengau	Born: 480	Died: 516
19. Charles V Nazon de Hesbaye	Born: 515	Died: 558
20. Carloman of Landen	Born: 547	Died: 645
21. Pepin I le Vieux de Landen (Pepin de Elder)	Born: 580	Died: 640
22. Saint Arnoul Bishop of Metz	Born: 582	Died: 640
23. Ansegisel de Metz	Born: 610	Died: 662
24. Pepin le Gros (Pepin the Great)	Born: 635	Died: 714
25. Charles Martel (Charles the Hammer)	Born: 688	Died: 741
26. Pepin the Short	Born: 714	Died: 768

27. Charles the Great (Charlemagne)	Born: 747	Died: 814
28. Childebrande d'Autun", "de Perracy"	Born: 765	Died: 826
29. Nibelung II de Perracy, count of Autun	Born: 815	Died 879
30. Terric de Tirel Autun	Born: 875	Died: 890
31. Waleran Chevalier de Tirel	Born: 900	Died: 965
32. Walter de Tirel	Born: 920	Died: 995
33. Ralf de Tirel	Born: 940	Die: 1050
34. Lord Foulques "Fulke" Tirel	Born: 963	Died: 1050
35. Sir Gauthier (Walter) Tirel seigneur de Poix II	Born: 1010	Died: 1068
36. Sir Gauthies (Walter) seigneur Tirel II	Born: 1055	Died: 1136
37. Seigneur de Poix Gauthier (Walter) Tyrrell III.	Born 1075	Died 1135
38. Sir Hugh Poix Tyrrell	Born 1100	Died 1159
39. Hugues de Pois Tyrell	Born 1159	Died 1199
40. Sir Roger Tyrell of Avon	Born 1175	Died1230
41. Sir Edward Tyrell of Avon	Born 1210	Died 1315
42. Sir Galfried Lyonell Avon Tyrell	Born 1233	Died 1250
43. Sir Edmond Edward Tyrell	Born1250	Died 1290
44. Sir Hugh Tyrell of Avon	Born 1288	Died 1377
45. Sir James Tyrell of Buttsbury	Born 1290	Died 1380
46. Sir Thomas "The Younger" Tyrell	Born'1315	Died 1382
a. Brother of Sir Walter Tyrell of Heron Hall		
47. Sir Walter Tyrell of Avon	Born1348	Died 1406
48. Sir John Tyrell MP Speaker House of Commons	Born 1382	Died 1437
49. Sir Thomas Tyrell of Heron	Born 1411	Died 1476
50. Sir William Tyrell of Ockenham	Born 1465	Died 1510
51. Sir Humphrey Tyrell	Born 1500	Died1548
52. Sir George Tyrell of Montagu	Born 1530	Died 1571
53. Lord William Edward Tyrell Lord of Bruyn & Ockendon	Born1570	Died 1595
54. Robert Tyrell	Born: 1594	Died: 1643
55. John Terrill	Born: 1615	Died: 1700

56. George Terrill	Born: 1665	Died: 1731
57. Stephen Terrill	Born: 1712	Died: 1774
58. Stephen Terrill of Troon	Born: 1749	Died: 1831
59. Stephen Terrill of Troon Moor	Born: 1776	Died: 1846
60. John Terrill	Born:1803	Died: 1887
61. William Terrill	Born: 1847	Died: 1925
62. Mabel Terrill Harris	Born: 1885	Died: 1958
63. Dorothy Harris Linde	Born: 1911.	Died 1975
64. Kenneth Linde	Born 1946	

Author's Preface

This book is both historical non-fiction as well as fiction. This means the author has researched those in the Terrill history to the best of his ability. In so doing, he has created his interpretation of real events and people except for the final scene and contemporary characters and locations which are figments of his imagination. In so doing, the information contained is intended to provide helpful and informative material on the subjects and events addressed and has been written as an interpretation of his learning. It does not guarantee accuracy and is intended for both education and entertainment.

All of the ancestors were researched and the connection between each generation was done to the best of the author's ability. There is a wonderful town called Mineral Point, Wisconsin where the author visited numerous times during his childhood that was filled with magical moments and marvelous memories. There is also a village called Waldwick that remains nearby that is the birthplace of the author's immediate ancestors.

There are many Terrill's in the area who are the author's relatives and he hopes he has done the family name justice by what he has written for they are the kindred spirit upon which our country was created. There is no reality to the fictional names used to weave the story as they are all of consequence of his imagination.

This book was written as a tribute to Hazel Harris Stuart who spent years collecting information on the Wisconsin Terrill family and the generations who followed from whom the author learned the value of integrity, honesty and the joy of acceptance that only comes from an open heart and a profound sense of decency emanated with each breath so that we might all call this great land "home".

Chapter 1 – Who Am I

Death…as one gets older and nears that juncture where they are only referred to in the past, they have no choice but to ponder its consequence. Is death a point of infinite finality or one of transition? As a historian, who is 73 years old and recently lost his wife, I hope and pray it's a point of transition.

The Greek philosopher, Lucretius concluded that human beings should simply conquer their fears and accept the fact that they and all things they encounter, are temporary and transitory… composites of energy, temporal in nature…that consume energy until that day when they too become an energy source for something else. In so doing, people should embrace the beauty and magnificence of the world NOW, where a world in motion is a world not rendered insignificant but made more beautiful by its transience, energy and ceaseless change where the sum was, is and will always be the same…zero!.

What I am about to share covers the lives of 60 generations of people…all genetically connected…all living and dying, laughing and crying, loving and hating until that last breath when they learned who was right. This is the story of the Terrills, whose descendants inhabit what many of us consider to be heaven on earth, the Driftless Zone in southwestern Wisconsin and the town of Mineral Point.

My name is William Terrill. I'm named after my great grandfather and am the retired Professor Emeritus of History at the University of Wisconsin in Madison where I served as the Dean of the Department for my last twelve years. As Dean, I was honored to lead the entire team as we developed a program rated as one of the top ten History Departments in the United States. I'm most proud of the fact that under my watch, we matriculated nearly 150 undergraduates each year, 15 more earned Master's degrees and nearly twenty more earned their Doctorates. As an educator my specialty was ancient and medieval European history that transcends both early modern and late modern European history but that's what this story is all about.

I got into the history business because of my interest in our family genealogy which is simply the study of family ancestors with pertinent data such as birth, marriage and death dates. Through my employment, I was blessed with being able to expand the genealogy to include our family history and create in-depth summaries of our family lineage with greater emphasis and clarification of some of my ancestors' life stories.

Before you yawn and close the book, let me assure you what you're about to read is full of all sorts of drama, intrigue and passion. You'll learn about knights, barons and kings and relive some of the events and circumstances that affected not only their lives but ours today. Like any good story, there are episodes of love, betrayal and more than one murder, that will rock you, sock you and keep you on your toes when you find out who dunnit and what it all meant to them and even us.

During my career, one profound thought constantly permeated my mind and that was the fact that history and politics are simply a tangle of lies and intrigue. As I took it upon myself to learn the history of our family, I quickly found out the web of history and politics certainly held true. Whether it was lives and love lost, fortunes gained and power grasped, in the end, so much of it was based on that jumble of yesterday that created tomorrow.

Who are the Terrills you ask? From a genealogical perspective, in 1990 the U.S. Census Bureau reported there were 162,253 different last names recorded 100 times or more. Of these one of the names is Terrill, of which there are four iterations, representing 124,511 individuals, who all could be descendants from the same beginning. Of the four iterations 83,226 spell their name Tyrrel. For those spelled Terrell, another 35,408. For Terrills, like us Wisconsin cheese heads, there are 5,641 and then there are 236 Turill's who probably all live down South.

Genealogy can be an arduous process. However, like a jigsaw puzzle, it can be very rewarding when a piece of information finally fits allowing you to add another layer to your family story. Technology has eased the burden of looking back, as yesterday melds into today, so that we can believe in our tomorrow. For me, my greatest genealogical thrill was being able to go all the way back to before the birth of Christ and touch base with Alpha One where the story begins.

History on the other hand, is simply a term comprising past events as well as the memory, discovery, collection, organization, presentation, and interpretation of those occasions that affect the path of society, culture or any form of existence. While some dismiss its relevance, I sincerely believe that without history, you could have no future. History is the reference point and the culmination of what we all call 'now'.

To properly share the story, we need to 'split' the Terrill history into two segments - aristocracy and commoners and then epochs that are highlighted by the rich and famous and how they affected the rest of us. Fortunately for me, I had a cousin named Hazel Stuart who was a self-taught sleuth who traced the Terrill family name back and did so in the 1940's, 50's and 1960's, in a time before computers and heritage software. Poring over documents, letters, notes and articles, my cousin pasted together the Terrill family history. In her quest, she generalized a pre-history that goes back over 2,000 years by manually doing what technology can now do with a faster and more finite representation of those who lived and died and came before and after her painstaking dedication.

Hazel told a story of visiting the Camborne, Cornwall, England Parish House Church and visiting with the rector upon which she was set down with two published volumes of the births, marriages, deaths and baptisms for the Church prior to 1837, when the civil authorities commenced recordkeeping and maintaining the files in the Somerset House in London. I can only imagine the time it took and the patience – something so many of us have lost along the way.

Camborne was the seat of the last of the Cornish Terrills before they emigrated to America. The Church books are filled with all kinds of Terrills, Vivians and Richards. The Terrills seemed to be village folks from places whose names they added to become 'Terrills of Beacon', 'Terrills of Troon' and 'Terrills of Treswithian' that were all villages where the mines are now long gone. All the villages were located near Camborne and became blended together to be entitled by some as the 'Terrills of Waldwick'. It seems my ancestors were all strong when it came to Biblical names as you find numerous Terrills called Elizabeth, Mary, Anne, John and Stephen which makes genealogy that much more of a challenge.

In the story I'm about to tell, I'm going to go from 'back-to-front' - in other words from the distant past to 'just' two hundred years ago. Along the way, I hope and pray I got it all right and if I didn't, I simply ask for your forgiveness.

In looking through the Church records, my cousin discovered a reference to why John Terrill, baptized on December 6, 1803, the son of Stephen and Elizabeth Terrill, fits into the entire Terrill puzzle. There was also reference to a Mark Terrill, baptized on November 12, 1808, whose parents were named Steve and Lizzy, which makes me assume that John and Mark were brothers and the rector couldn't spell. A little further down, Hazel found reference to the marriage of John Terrill to Elizabeth Vivian on March 31, 1831 who emigrated to Mineral Point, Wisconsin in the fall of 1835 as some of the first settlers. This is the story of how the Terrills lived in the shadows of absolute power, rose to a pinnacle of dominance and then simply receded into anonymity, lost in the abyss of being neither too great, nor too ghastly, to be nothing more than a memory. While many generations are not filled with historic people or events, those that are, actually shaped history and allowed this story to be told. However, this book is dedicated to all those who came before, who only had one wish - that their lives were filled with love and happiness and when it was their time to depart, they'd lived a good life, resulting in being fondly remembered and truly missed.

The story takes place in today's, Belgium, France, England, Cornwall and finally Mineral Point, Wisconsin where I was born and lived nearby my entire life. My wife, Margaret, whom everyone called Peg, and I traveled the world extensively seeking answers to many questions. My life has been full of joy and accomplishment and yet I've retained a secret for so long I fear it will be lost forever if I don't share it with someone.

Chapter 2 – Heaven's Waiting Room

When we were young, Peg and I bought some land outside Mount Horeb, Wisconsin that gave us the country living we enjoyed. The 'ranch' as we called it, was on Highway JG and had a small stream running through it. We built a nice brick house and raised our son and daughter there. Over the past several years we watched our small town become a suburb of what they now call the 'Metroplex' around Madison.

For nearly 40 years I commuted to Madison to teach and would still be living there if Peg hadn't passed away. When Peg died, I just couldn't keep up the house and yard. Finally, I came to the conclusion that living alone and trying to subsist on my own cooking wasn't the best way for a person to live and decided to move 'home', which meant back to Mineral Point, and away from the hubbub of the Metroplex.

I started looking around Mineral Point and decided to have lunch at the Red Rooster on High Street one day. As I walked in the front door, I looked across the counter and saw a friendly face who waved and beckoned me to join him. Like me, his last name is Terrill. His dad and mine were brothers. His name is Henry but we all call him Hank. Hank had become somewhat of a local hero that everyone knew to the point that some folks even asked him to run for mayor but he declined.

A few years ago, Hank's first wife, Ann, passed away in a horrific car accident out on the road to Darlington. Seems she hit a deer, lost control and hit a tree. I remember Ann's funeral. It was a really sad day for all us Terrill's as Ann was a good wife, mother, relative and friend. Hank was devastated, as any loving husband would be, to the point that he sold his half of the family farm to his brother, Tom, and simply walked away from what he'd done his entire life. Hank always said that, without Ann he just couldn't do it anymore, which has happened to a lot of folks in the area.

Their old farm house needed a lot of work and was filled with too many memories, so Hank moved into town and was actually living in the apartment above the Red Rooster all alone and I'm certain as lonely as I am now. It was 1969 and, after nearly two years since Ann's passing, Hank decided to go on vacation and flipped a coin – heads was east and tails meant west. Heads it was and so Hank went to Washington D.C., Philadelphia and New York City.

Story is that, in Washington, he met this really nice lady named Katherine, who everyone calls Kat. They did one of those long- distance romances for nearly two years and then got married. To say Hank fell in a pile of doggie dew and came out smelling like roses would be an understatement. Kat is one of the nicest ladies I've ever met. No matter where you go in town, everyone knows her. She's easy with her smile and generous to a fault but then most folks in Mineral Point seem to be that way. It doesn't seem possible that Hank and Kat have been married just short of twenty years. It's been good for both of them and you can tell by the smiles on their faces and the warmth in their hearts, that they love each other very much.

When you live in a small town, rumors do fly and the one about Kat was she had a lot of money. You could always tell by the way she dressed that it was probably true. Nothing flashy mind you but a lot nicer than the everyday clothes most of us wear. The story is Hank proposed while Kat was in the hospital after she was in a car accident. The story also goes that Hank wouldn't get married until he had one of those pre-nuptial agreements to make certain that everything that was Kat's, remained hers. He didn't want people to think he was marrying her for her money.

Over the years, I've met Kat dozens of times and she's kind, sincere and humble, while also an incredible artist, who has worked wonders for Mineral Point. Besides sitting on the Board of Directors at the Chicago Art Institute, Kat puts on the annual Mineral Point Art Fair that brings some of the country's top artists to town each summer. While some folks would limit their involvement, Kat and Hank are also involved in just about everything in the community – sponsoring this, scheduling that - trying to make Mineral Point one of the premier art centers in the Midwest.

Kat and Hank also invested a lot of money in Mineral Point by buying some of the older properties and fixing them up. First was the old hotel they turned into an upscale restaurant when Pendarvis closed. Next, they bought the brewery that our great, great grandfather built out on Shake Rag and converted into an art studio. Finally, they started buying buildings on the south end of High Street and even a couple down on Commerce Street by the railroad museum. In each case, they restored, remodeled and rented the buildings to artists of all types to the point there are over 25 active art studios in town.

That day, Hank and I sat at the Rooster and talked family as we shared a piece of Madge's apple pie. Neither one of us needed it and we could only justify by 'sharing a slice' as Hank called it. I got out my wallet to pay for lunch and Hank eyed Madge and told her to put it on his bill. Seems he still had the same deal he'd had twenty years ago when he lived in the apartment upstairs and paid the Red Rooster at the end of the month along with his rent.

The story goes that when Madge's husband Frank needed hip surgery up in Madison, Hank and Kat paid the bill beyond Frank's insurance and also hired a temporary cook so that the Rooster could stay open. That's the kind of people they are. As we were sharing the pie, Hank asked what brought me to town and I told him I intended to move back to Mineral Point. Hank sat and listened and smiled and noted that it could be my lucky day. Now, Hank always did have a gift- for-gab and so I sort of let it go in one ear and out the other.

Hank got a serious look on his face and lowered his voice and noted that that he and Kat were building a combination condo/apartment/assisted living center half-way between Mineral Point and Dodgeville. Located across Highway 18-151 from the Dodge-Point Country Club and WDMP 'Outlaw Country' radio, whatever that meant. It was going to be quite swanky.

"You mean where the feed lot used to be?" I asked.

Hank agreed, adding, "Now, all the bullshit will be coming from the tenants complaining about this or that, when there's nothing wrong."

I laughed, as Hank's sense of humor was always there and asked him how long it would be until the complex would be completed. Hank said they'd broken ground and poured the foundation and figured it would be open in about six months.

I told him I'd think about it.

Hank whispered, "Word's spread and units are renting and selling fast". As first cousins, I'd known Hank my entire life and knew he was telling the truth and not giving me a bunch of sales malarkey.

Hank looked at me and noted. "If you're interested in seeing what we've got planned, I've got the drawings down at the house.

"Sure!" I replied. "What the heck?"

We said goodbye to Madge, went out the Rooster's front door and walked down Chestnut Street hill to Hank and Kat's house on Fountain Street. One would think that with all their money, they'd be living in some fancy place. Mineral Point has three famous houses, the Moses Strong Mansion and the Gundry House, both of which were historical landmarks that the tourists ooh and aah about and then the third, which is a small brick house built by William Tregray, that Hank and Kat live in. The house was built in 1844 so it's in the National Register of Historical Places. The Tregray house has a lot of 'character' as Peg would say. Hank assured me that he and Kat were quite content there, particularly because it was filled with memories and still had Mrs. Gordon, our high school history teacher's famous flower garden out back.

Word has it, Kat and Hank still have Kat's home in McClean, Virginia that's supposed to be really swanky and a condo in Chicago on someplace called the Gold Coast. Since they got married, Hank and Kat have traveled the world, including one of those 'round the world' cruises for their honeymoon that took nearly a year. I'm not jealous, just really happy for Hank because he's a good guy and would give you the shirt off his back if you needed it.

The walk is but two blocks and we entered the house through the unlocked side door that went into the kitchen. While small, the house had been professionally decorated and was stunning with cream colored walls and burgundy trim. Hank had some sort of fancy audio system installed with a keypad that let him play his $2,000^+$ record albums without all those Columbia House records in the house.

Hank had his office in one of the upstairs bedrooms and went to get some papers. I stood and walked to the open back door where I admired the glass roof solarium on the back of the house with a brick floor and small waterfall with lots of plants, where Kat did her drawing. When Hank returned, we went where most folks in Mineral Point sit - at the kitchen table, as Hank pulled out the plans entitled, 'The Dodge-Point Living Center' with one of those fancy logos that had the letters DPL inscribed above the design.

"Wanna beer?" Hank asked.

It was just after lunch and so I said, "No."

Hank showed me the exterior design of the center that was done in fieldstone and cedar and was in the 'Prairie Style' made famous by our cousin, Frank Lloyd Wright. Cousin Frank, as we called him, grew up in Richland Center. His dad was a minister named William Carey Wright who married Anna Lloyd Thomas, who was a teacher and came from our family tree a few generations back.

Hank pulled the papers out of a carboard tube and showed me the drawing of the exterior that included a large, central chimney and massive walls of windows that Hank indicated would be facing west. I had to admit, it was impressive, especially with the view of the rolling hills out back that I had admired my entire life.

Hank noted, Kat thought it only right they emulate the Prairie Style that Cousin Frank made famous, especially with his Taliesin studios just up Highway 23 in Spring Green. Hank also said Kat wanted the same look and feel that only comes by having the structure married to the ground, with the Wright style of having all the vertical elements hidden beneath long, horizontal, cantilevered roofs.

I shook my head and smiled. It looked like some fancy resort and not some apartment complex as Hank unrolled the plans for the first floor that had the grand entry with a huge fieldstone fireplace and a general meeting area that also served as the dining room. In addition, the plans called for an exercise room and library, along with what Hank called 'the cozy room' that had another smaller fireplace and space for a few tables where you could simply sit and chat or watch the sun go down.

I shook in agreement and could actually envision me living there as Hank added that the interior was going to incorporate a lot of hand-wrought woodwork and fancy glass that Kat and her students were creating, such that the windows would serve as living art to highlight the rolling hills to the west. Hank also noted that much of the furniture was going to be designed and permanently put in place and the public rooms would be adorned by natural woodwork to allow the beauty of the woodgrain to shine through in their pure form, so that the furniture could also be admired.

Hank continued. "The gathering room is going to include the casual and dining space highlighted by the stone fireplace. We're going to have an optional meal service plan where you can eat in the restaurant if you want to. What I really like is that, instead of creating a floor plan based on an exterior layout, Kat and the architects designed 'The Center' such that it's being built from the inside out, so that there will be an intentional visual flow from inside-out, regardless of the time of year."

I was truly impressed and appreciated the thought and detail Hank and Kat had put into the building. This wasn't going to be just another apartment complex but a statement of their love and passion for art, music and the natural beauty of Mineral Point and the Driftless area.

Hank looked at me and smiled and said, "Impressive." With that, Hank pulled out the floor plan showing the assisted living facilities on the second floor that consisted of smaller units with a bedroom and bathroom.

I looked at him, feebly flexed my muscles, smiled and said, "Not yet."

Next, Hank unrolled the blueprints for the apartments on the third floor that expanded the square footage and included a small kitchen and I politely look at the details. Next, Hank unrolled the design for the fourth floor, pointing out that the top floor apartments were all deluxe units with added noise insulation, built-in sound systems and ten-foot ceilings with one of those solar tube skylights in the living room and another in the master bath. He looked at me and noted that all the apartments on fourth floor were one-bedroom units except the ones on each end that were two bedrooms, which not only had a different floorplan than those in the middle but were much larger.

Hank asked if I was interested in a one bedroom or two and which floor. I thought for a moment and said the top floor and I thought the extra bedroom would be nice and then he began telling me about the two-bedroom apartment. "You'll be farthest from the elevator and have the least amount of hall traffic." This sounded appealing to me after living in the country for so many years.

"When you walk in the front door there will be a walk-in closet and large living room with a natural gas, two-way fireplace that's also opens to the master bedroom. Both the living room and master suite will have huge glass windows that look out on the valley to the west with no decks to obstruct your view."

I was already imagining the apartment and the view and loving it as Hank continued. "Immediately to the right, there'll be a kitchenette with a built-in eating area. We're including an under- counter Subzero refrigerator and freezer along with a Bosch dishwasher. The custom cabinets and hardware will match the woodwork in the other rooms and the both the kitchen and bathroom countertops will be quartz."

They were going first class and I liked what I heard as Hank continued. "The master bedroom has a walk-in closet while the master bathroom has been designed to include a huge shower and also include a Miele washer and dryer. The second bedroom will be up to you but we're willing to panel it to match the woodwork in the meeting room if you like."

I looked at the plan and smiled. I really liked the two-way fireplace with Hank saying all you needed to do was flip the switch in either room to turn it on or off. I liked the idea of huge windows. The one regret we had in Peg's and my house was that the windows were too small.

Hank noted that both rooms would have motorized floor-to- ceiling drapes. He had me when he said that there was outdoor parking but the two-bedroom units apartments came with double parking stalls in the heated, drive-in basement, thereby providing a larger storage room along the front of the stalls as well.

Hank looked at me and added. "Finally, the rent also includes weekly maid service. We figured we needed to clean the assisted living floor and so we might just as well have them do the premium apartments as well, where the contract calls for the crew to vacuum, dust and clean the fixtures."

I just shook my head in disbelief. All I'd need to bring were dishes and furniture as I envisioned the apartment, while taking the small bedroom and getting one of those fold-down beds and bookcases to let me use the room as my library. It's amazing how many books a teacher collects over the years.

I asked Hank if I could put bookcases in the small bedroom. Instead, he indicated that he would ask the contractors to panel one wall and build floor-to-ceiling bookcases in front of it if I wanted.

Hank knew I was interested just by my smile. To close the deal, he showed me the landscape designs for the grounds that included a BBQ area, one of those walk-in, outdoor swimming pools and a Jacuzzi and so it was like being on vacation at some fancy resort.

Hank noted, "If the day comes, you need to be in assisted living, all you'd do is move down to second floor. Same building, same neighbors and same friends." This made real sense to me.

I just shook my head and realized that he and Kat had thought of everything. Hank said almost all of the apartments on third floor were rented or sold. He noted that they'd 'saved' the two end apartments on the top floor and I inferred that's where I wanted to be. I didn't want anyone walking on my head and the fireplace sure sounded neat as it was the one thing Peg and I couldn't afford when we built our house.

Hank asked whether I would prefer buying or renting. Being so old, I thought renting was the best way to go. No sense putting the kids through the trouble in a few years. After looking at apartments in Madison and seeing what they cost to rent, what Hank quoted seemed like a bargain and I decided right then and there to take the top corner unit, which brought a smile to Hank's face.

I asked about lease papers and the security deposit. Hank looked at me and frowned, saying all I needed to do was say, "Yes," which I did. We shook hands and the deal was done but then that's the way folks in Mineral Point always did things, especially amongst family.

It was time to go and I stood and Hank gave me a brochure and drawings of the floor plan of my new apartment. That night, I called the kids and asked if they could meet me sometime so I could show them the design of my new digs. We scheduled it for a week later and I could hardly wait. With both of them living in the Metroplex and having been to Mineral Point countless times, all I needed do was remind them that they used to play 'Dibs on Those Horses' and 'There's the Water Tower' whenever we were between Dodgeville and Mineral Point, which made them smile. Moving 'further away' seemed logical, simply because it was less than an hour to either house which meant I was close enough to see them often but far enough apart that it was still a special trip. As for the rationale of selling the house, I offered "Self-sufficiency, near where I grew up, better food on the meal plan and an area filled with family, friends and memories."

At first, the kids seemed somewhat apprehensive, particularly with the traffic on the highway, until they saw the plan and shared my excitement and then were both in favor of my decision, asking if the grandkids could use the pool in the summer. I said I'd find out and was told that Sunday was family day and everyone was welcome.

I didn't know when to put my house on the market and asked Hank for advice. He thought it would probably take about three months from listing to close and offered to let me live with he and Kat if need be. I felt that would be an imposition and didn't want to either be a visitor or live alone and so, when I hired the realtor, I put our house a little lower than the market price with the stipulation that it would be available on a certain date. It would be six months until the center was finished and so I had time to prepare. Phase One consisted of getting rid of so many memories, where the kids took what they wanted and we had an 'estate sale' to get rid of all the things that wouldn't fit in the new place.

I wanted a 'fresh start' and went to Steinhafel's Furniture and ordered new bedroom and living room furniture. The only thing I kept was my leather 'easy chair' that took me years to get just right. For some reason, the saleslady talked me into one of those king-sized beds you could raise up and down. I went to American TV and bought two of those big TV's. One for above the fireplace in my bedroom and one for the study. If I was going all out, I was going ALL OUT!.

We put the house on the market and sure enough, it sold for the asking price to the first couple who looked at it. With closing and all, it worked out just right. Moving day came and there really wasn't much to do as the furniture had already been delivered and the TV's were installed.

With my kids and I all driving mini vans, we took the back rows of seats out and I'd arranged everything in the garage so that I could get the old house professionally cleaned for the new owners. With that, we made the move in one trip, with all my books, clothes and memories back home to Mineral Point. As I handed the new owners the keys, I'll never forget taking one last walk through the house Peg and I had lived in and the memories of each room and, yet, I also knew Peg would have approved.

When we got to the center, my kids really liked what I'd done, or at least that's what they said. That first weekend, just about everyone moved in and it reminded me of going to Madison as a student in the dorm, except everyone had gray hair or none at all. It only took two hours to get me settled as The Center even had some of those six-wheel hotel luggage carts you could hang your clothes on and simply put them in the closet when we got to the apartment. With several people moving in on the same day, Hank and Kat even hired some Mineral Point high school kids to help and our only cost was tipping the kids as the center donated several hundred dollars to the school's general fund.

With the clothes in the closet, my picture of Peg on the nightstand and boxes in what I was calling the library the entire move was done. We all drove separately to Dodgeville and I took the family out to dinner at Thymes, with the kids heading back to Madison and me to my new home. That night, I pulled into the new garage for the first time and it sure seemed different. I got on the elevator and thought about stopping on the first floor but knew there'd be plenty of time for that. Instead, I put away the rest of my clothes, set up all the pictures and started organizing my library. At first, I've got to admit, it sure seemed strange and then, as I settled in, I began to feel as if I was 'home' and starting a new life.

After the 'joys' of suburban life, residing in an apartment took time to get used to and all the excitement began to wear off as a sense of permanence began to settle in. After having five acres, the biggest challenge was having people so close and, like any other social situation, there were those I liked, those I tolerated and some I shied away from, while there were others whose company I truly enjoyed. The other thing was riding an elevator. I hadn't done that at school and so it took time getting used to riding with other people and not knowing whether you were supposed to talk to them or not.

It didn't take long for the routine to settle in. I'd eat breakfast in the apartment and then check the dinner menu 'downstairs'. If it sounded appealing, I'd eat down there. If not, I'd drive into either Mineral Point or Dodgeville and eat somewhere else.

One of the few advantages of being old is that you have plenty of time others are required to allocate to the necessities of life. Peg and I had saved our money and I have a good pension. Peg and I both had life insurance and then selling a nice house on five acres of land in one of the fastest growing areas in Wisconsin, all combined to make sure I didn't have any financial worries for at least fifteen years, as long as I didn't go crazy.

The idea of fancy trips didn't cross my mind as Peg and I had been virtually everywhere. However, I did feel I needed something to look forward to every now and then and so, I began planning annual trips somewhere. My daily routine saw me turning to my books and then writing what you're about to read. For many in their 80's, the thought of learning probably seems worthless, when all will be lost the second they close their eyes and simply cease to exist. Sadly, many wile away their hours watching television or doing whatever. When you spent your life teaching and sharing the joys of learning, I continue to read, sharing sixty years of knowledge and leading an active life and this is what has made me sure I made the right decision.

Chapter 3 - Reverend Mike

A month later, Hank and Kat had a 'Welcome to the Center' BBQ out by the pool and we were all invited. They prepared name tags with our room numbers printed on them and Hank served as MC. As he went around the group, each of us had to stand as he introduced every single person without using a single note card, telling the assembled group who we were, which apartment we were in and where we came from. It was amazing how many old people were there and how many of them I already knew.

Hank announced that it would be an annual event and indicated there was an open bar which are two of the finest words spoken in Wisconsin. The herd wandered towards the two bartenders where I expected cheap booze. Wrong! I glanced at all the top shelf stuff including Korbel brandy, Crown Royal whiskey and Spotted Cow beer. I was in Badger heaven!

As I stood in line, the fellow behind me tapped me on my shoulder and said, "Hello neighbor." I turned around and saw that it was Reverend Mike Thomas who'd rented an apartment down on third floor and just moved in.

"You just get here?" I asked.

"Just moved in. Had to wait until I closed on the house and that was Thursday," he replied.

While walking with a slight limp due to another knee replacement, Mike was still in pretty darn good shape and sharp as a tack. He and his wife, Virginia, were at the Congregational Church for nearly 40 years and built the congregation up by making it an integral part of Mineral Point, participating in virtually anything and everything to help the community and that's how Mike and Ginny got to know Hank and Kat.

While so many other religious people are tightly wound around their church, Reverend Mike was actually wound around the community by being involved in virtually everything from the school board to the cemetery committee and Chamber of Commerce. Ginny and Mike not only supported Mineral Point's American Legion baseball team, Mike played ball in the senior softball circuit with the rest of us old fuddy-duddy's either to stubborn or too naïve to realize we periodically made fools out of ourselves.

"I think you're going to like it here," I offered. "Lot's to do, if you want to and nothing to do if that's your choice."

"How about you?" he asked.

"I'm staying busy reading and leaving the asylum every now and then."

Mike laughed at that, asking, "What don't you like?"

I looked at him and made certain no one could hear me as I whispered, "All the ladies".

He had an incredulous look on his face as he asked, "Why?" "You'll find out soon enough."

"How's that?" he asked.

"The ratio is about six-to-one and they all want to get their claws in you," I added.

"Really?"

"You'll see."

With that Gladys came up and said hello, sizing up the two elderlies as if we were sides of beef. Mike politely nodded as Gladys said, "We've got room at our table if you want to join us."

Mike smiled and said that he would be honored but would like to take a rain check, as he'd just moved in and was going to retire for the evening. With that Gladys sauntered away, turning back to see if we were watching her.

"My God! Is it like that all the time?" Mike asked. "Pretty much so," I offered.

"What do you do about it?"

"Smile, nod and get another drink, especially when Hank's paying for them."

With that, Mike moved next to me at the bar and I told the bartender to give my friend whatever he wanted and put it on my tab.

Mike laughed and shook his head, "All the time?" "Yup."

"Sure wasn't like that when I was in high school!"

"Nope!" I replied as we clinked glasses and I said, "To your health!"

"Can we get out of here?" Mike asked.

"Not tonight! The warden won't let you," I replied nodding at Hank, who was busting a gut laughing at us, to which we walked over to him to thank him for the nice party.

"Having a good time?" Hank inquired.

"I feel like a porterhouse steak in the butcher shop," Mike replied, to which I thought Hank was going to spit out his Korbel.

"That bad?" Hank inquired.

"His first night," I answered, while adding, "He'll get used to it," with a chuckle.

The party lasted all the way to eight o'clock and then some of the folks had to excuse themselves as it was nearly their bedtime. I looked at Mike and asked him if he was unpacked and he said hardly.

"Want to come up and have a drink?" I asked. "Sure, what the hell," he replied.

'My God, a swearing minister! My kind of guy!' I thought as we formally said goodnight to Hank and Kat and made our way to the elevators.

As we stood there, Mike just shook his head. As we entered, I punched four and he said, "Ahh, up in the high-rent district!"

I looked at him and replied, "I had my choice between a studio apartment in Madison or the fourth floor here for the same rent," which seemed to take the wind out of Mike's sails a little bit.

We walked down the hall and I punched the keypad lock and the door opened and we walked in.

"Holy shit!" Mike exclaimed. "You really are in the high rent district."

I looked at him and justified my decision by saying that Peg and I had done all right for ourselves...had paid for the kid's college educations, weddings and down payments on their first houses and this was my reward.

We went to the kitchen and I asked Mike what he wanted to drink and he inquired if I had any scotch. "Coming right up!" I poured four fingers in a water glass and took him on the ninety second tour of the apartment.

"Nice digs"

"Thanks"

"No wonder why all the ladies are after you. They think you've got money!"

"They can keep thinking that!" I replied.

"We sat in the living room and drank our drinks and I filled him in on all the ladies and what I thought of most of them. I knew Mike's wife, Ginny, had been an elementary school teacher in Mineral Point and they had three kids…all grown and moved away. Unfortunately for Mike, they didn't move to the Metroplex like mine and so seeing his kids and grandkids wasn't as common, even though I was certain Mike loved his grandchildren and enjoyed watching them grow.

Mike asked me what I did with my time as that was his biggest worry. I told him I read a lot and tried to find people to play cards with. Mike asked what kind of cards and I told him cribbage and he lit up like a little kid at Christmas.

"You don't need to look any further, my friend. It's my favorite game."

We both had one more for the hallway and then Reverend

Mike slurred, "Good night," as the eight ounces of scotch on top of the Korbel hit home. With a strong handshake, Mike headed for the door, before stopping and asking "How's the food here?"

"Not bad," I replied.

"Guess I'll get used to it. I can't cook, nor even drive for a while. I just had my knee replaced."

"Tell you what, I'll meet you at 8:30 for breakfast and we can play a game of cribbage if you like."

"That's sounds good," as Mike started weaving towards the elevator, with me wondering if he'd remember not only 8:30 but even his apartment number. I just shook my head and smiled at my drunk minister and whispered, "Peg, I don't know if I'll be coming up to see you or not."

Next morning, I was up at sunrise as usual and didn't put any Cheerios in the bowl. Sure enough, when I went down to the 'Cantina' for breakfast, my new good buddy was standing there with four ladies ogling him.

"You made it," I said with a devilish grin on my face.

"Yup!" was all I got, as the ladies pondered each word he elicited.

"How do you do this?"

"Simple, Agnes will come and take your order and they just add it to your rent at the end of the month."

"What about a tip?" the good Reverend inquired.

"They add 18%."

"Fair enough!"

Mike ordered oatmeal, orange juice, two pieces of whole wheat toast and a cup of coffee which was more than I'd eat in an entire day. The oatmeal sounded good and so I had that with brown sugar and raisins. Agnes brought the food and we ate in somewhat sequestered peace.

I looked at Mike and inquired what his plans were for the day and he said he was unpacking. I offered to take him on in a game of cribbage when he wanted a break and he thought that would be great. We agreed to meet at two in the quiet room and sure enough, he was there right on time, saying he needed a break.

As I shuffled the deck, I asked Mike what he wanted to play for. He looked at me and inquired, "You mean gambling?" I simply smiled, as if to agree, which caught him by surprise.

Mike put his hands to his mouth and reluctantly asked, "What do you normally play for?"

I looked him in the eyes and seriously responded, "Normally we play to see who has to go and get the drinks from the free soda machine. If it's really intense, we play for a beer. When things are really extreme, we even play for lunch."

I saw the relief in his eyes and could tell he wasn't a gambler as I responded, "Tell you what, let's play for who gets to decide where we go for dinner tonight but it's Dutch treat?"

A smile crossed his face and I knew that the bond was beginning between us. We cut to see who was going to deal first. I won and bam, the game started. I was on fourth street when he was on second. I threw two fives in the blind and he threw a king, ten and we pulled a queen. This was like taking candy from a baby, except he wasn't crying. I won and chose Culver's in Dodgeville and that's where we went for dinner.

The days rolled by and the games got more intense. I didn't mind losing almost all the time simply because each day I learned a little more about my new friend and the more I learned, the more I liked.

Chapter 4 - The Geezers

One day I ran into Hank in the lobby and waved hello. He came over in his affable way and asked how things were going. I replied, "Great." I was really enjoying my new apartment.

"Are the ladies leaving you alone?" Hank asked.

"Pretty much so but you can only eat so many homemade cookies." I replied.

"Any new friends?" he asked.

This was my entre into sharing how Reverend Mike and I had bonded as I replied, "Mike Thomas and I have become good friends. He's a couple years younger than me but at my age, what's a couple of years?"

I told Hank it seemed funny to spend so much time with a 'man of the cloth'. Perhaps it's God's way of getting me ready for the day I hoped to be with religious people all the time. Hank didn't get it and so I added, "Angels," which got a slight grin.

I shared with Hank, "What's crazy is that, other than Sunday mornings, when he presides over Church services here or fills in for ministers on vacation, he's just another old guy like me."

The more I learned about my beer drinking, card playing buddy, the more people told me why they liked him. First, he was that he was down to earth. Second, he was never preachy. Finally, he never judged another person where his well-worn saying, "He who casts the first stone, needs to make sure he's not looking in the mirror," was famous in Mineral Point.

One morning I was going solo when Agnes from the kitchen came out and asked where Mike was. I told her it wasn't my day to watch him. She just smiled and said she'd been a member of his church and reported, "Mike never judged folks on their race, religion, ethnicity or even their orientation for that matter, before that became so popular, by simply saying, 'We're all God's children'.

I affirmed Agnes summation as she continued. "Mike's 'different' from most ministers in that he had a unique perspective on what his job was all about. Sure, it dealt with birth, baptism, marriage and death and reminding people every week about good and bad but Mike's also a person who allowed his own religious shield to be penetrated so that his humanity could shine through."

I was learning to respect Mike even more as people told me what a great guy he was. Besides that, I sure enjoyed his company, even if it was costing me a couple of bottles of Spotted Cow each week.

A few weeks later, Kat was in the lobby and I said hello, as it was good to see her. She asked. how things were going.

I said, "Fine".

Kat noted that she'd heard Mike and I were boozing buddies, to which I simply concurred that she was right, feeling that was better than being bosom buddies.

Kat noted that all the ladies had a crush on Mike and I simply smiled, glad it was him and not me. Insightful as ever, Kat added, "I think for the first time in his life, he's finally feeling free."

I didn't know what she meant by 'free' and it must have shown on my face as Kat added. "Ministers are usually trained in the art of 'religious isolation' that allows them to separate themselves from the emotions of the events at hand. It can really be a burden when it comes to their 'regular' lives."

I guess I never thought of it that way but it made sense as Kat added. "It's a form of defense that protects ministers from the parishioner's pain and suffering. Sadly, however, that shield can also be a burden. It prevents them from truly reaching out to members of the parish or their own family emotionally. When this happens, it inhibits them from broadening and deepening their own world - a world, I believe, that's no different than those they steward. Mike's a great guy and I'm glad you two have become good friends."

Kat looked at me and I could feel the sincerity in her heart as she added. "I remember when Virginia died. Mike never cried and he should have. Yet, because of the emotional shield around him, he couldn't let go. I really felt sorry for him and hope the two of you can sustain the friendship you're building."

I looked at Kat and realized what a wonderful person she was, even if she was my landlady. Kat looked at the floor and scanned the entry and finally added, "I've often asked myself, don't all people of the cloth, at some time, experience the same emotions as their parishioners and what minister, priest or rabbi isn't plagued by haunting fears, worries, doubts and feelings of sadness? Many times, they reference the word of God and, yet, I've always wondered if they actually ever hear God talk back to them."

I looked at Kat without an immediate answer but knew she realized Mike's and my friendship was deepening to the point of complete trust in each other. I paused for a moment considering her overview before realizing it was spot-on. I then replied, "He's becoming a good friend and my goal is to help remove the shield if he wants me to. I care for him as a friend and a man who, like me, is somewhat alone in the world. There's no ulterior motive except to enjoy the days we have left, doing so through friendship, fellowship and comradery."

Kat smiled and gave me a hug. What a wonderful, decent, woman!

Chapter 5 – The Hunters

Due to the fact that I was still driving and Mike's right knee replacement was in the recovery stage, the two of us made a good pair who began calling ourselves 'the Geezers'. We'd go out to dinner or complain about the food in the 'mess hall' as we called it, go to Badger football and basketball games and enjoy each other's company. We even came up with one of those 'Mission Statements' that's so popular these days. Ours says, 'The Geezers are old men who love sports, playing cribbage, beer, brandy and life, whose only goal is to enjoy life to the fullest.' For being a retired minister Mike's an all- right guy. And, unless he tells you, you'd never know what his career had been.

It wasn't long until the entire center was full, including the assisted living floor. The main dining room became the social center for everyone, as it was designed as a multipurpose facility with that over-sized fireplace and fake logs, one of those big TV's on the wall and plenty of tables where some were designed for up to eight people and others just for four or two. There are also the same huge windows like those in my apartment, that face west providing the same wonderful view of the hills and dales that the Driftless area of Iowa County is famous for.

How nice is it?

A lot of folks simply sit and watch the sun go down.

Some people call the center 'Heaven's Waiting Room' and a few months after we all moved in, the first 'vacancy' sign went up, as one of the fellow residents 'departed', reminding the rest of us that our apartment could be next. I'm certain there are others in the center that feel the way I do, where we're all just waiting until it's 'our time'. With each vacancy sign, I'm reminded, you can't ignore death, nor deny it, and that death is a just part of life - not the end, simply another portion.

As I looked at the vacancy sign I thought of Ivan Ilych from Tolstoy's 'The Death of Ivan Ilych' and his famous question as he nears death, "'What if my whole life really has been wrong?'" I wonder if others, besides me, ever ask themselves that question.

As noted, I continue to read and to stay fluent in my adopted French tongue. I began reading some of the works by the French philosopher and essayist Michel de Montaigne entitled 'Wake Me Up'. In his book Montaigne reveals that his life was filled with death around every corner, including his father, closest friend, uncle, brother and two infant daughters, who all died within ten years of each other, while Montaigne was enveloped in the morbidity of thousands of Frenchmen killed in the religious civil wars of the time.

I found it interesting that Montaigne's first thoughts paralleled my initial beliefs when he said, 'With such frequent and ordinary example passing before our eyes, how can we possibly rid ourselves of the thought of death and the idea that at every moment it's gripping us by the throat?'

As Montaigne continued to survive and age, his attitude about life and death changed just as mine has too, and once again he says it so much better than I, when he observed. 'J'aime la vie deux fois plus que les autres, car la mesure du plaisir dépend de l'attention plus ou moins grande que nous lui prêtons. Surtout en BC moment, quand je m'aperçois que le mien est si bref dans le temps, j'essaye de l'augmenter en poids; J'essaye d'arrêter la vitesse de son vol soit la vitesse avec laquelle je le saisis. Plus ma possession de vie est courte, plus je dois la faire profondément et pleinement,' that means, 'I enjoy life twice as much as others, for the measure of enjoyment depends on the greater or lesser attention that we lend it. Especially at this moment, when I perceive that mine is so brief in time, I try to increase it in weight; I try to arrest the speed of its flight by the speed with which I grasp it. The shorter my possession of life, the deeper and fuller I must make it.'

Finally, Montaigne wrote, 'Si nous avons su vivre avec constance et tranquillité, nous saurons mourir de la même manière' or 'If we've known how to live steadfastly and tranquilly, we shall know how to die the same way.'

Each night as I prepare to go to bed, I look at the photo of Peg and me on our 50th wedding anniversary that sits on my night stand and tell her I love her. I then ask her to wait for me, as I repeat what I would say each day as I left school. "I'll be home soon," realizing it now had a completely different meaning.

I often think of Ilych, who had been in a coma for three days and was awakened by the feel of his son kissing his hand. At this point, Illych felt sorry for others instead of himself simply because, in that instant, he was freed from his fear of dying. As Tolstoy said, 'His burst of love, which is human and/or divine, had freed him from his fear and had freed him to face – and embrace – his death, with a feeling of joy.'

As I awaken each morning and realize 'I'm still here', I feel a lot like Ilych in that I'm ready when God wants to take me. If I still have quality in my life, I'll fight like hell to stay. If, however, I become a burden to others, I hope to be able to simply close my eyes and reopen them again with my Peg standing there - arms open wide, smiling at me and saying, "Welcome home."

I feel this way simply because I've finally begun to accept that Peg's departure didn't mean the end of my love for her, simply a different version, no longer filled with today and tomorrow - just yesterday. My own demise is no longer fearful, simply because in loving, I feel that I'm a part of something greater than myself and that's joy - those feelings of great pleasure and happiness that envelope me and fill my heart with gratitude for all that I've been given in life.

Chapter 6 - The Family Tree

I keep up on my French because it plays an important role in my current research project consisting mainly of European history and how it parallels the Terrill family, whose story entails an extended period of time in Belgium, France, England and Cornwall. It's really interesting to be able to tie them together and imagine how my ancestors lived and reacted through times of change.

From my passion for history, I've also become quite interested in anthropology, genealogy and the study of family history, while tracing the Terrill lineage and learned that our great, great grandfather came from a Cornish area called Camborne. In learning this, Hazel began corresponding with the librarian in Camborne, who introduced Hazel to a fellow genealogist by the name of Sybil Tyrrel. Sybil did the research in Cornwall and determined that she was in fact, our relative. As important, Sybil was able to 'connect-the-dots' with the past and determine that the Tyrrel heritage went all the way back to Charlemagne and his ancestors.

When both Hazel and Sybil passed away, I picked up the genealogy 'bug' and have continued the work they began. In so doing, I've been able to move Sybil's research back to 65CE or 65 years before the birth of Christ. None of this would have been possible if it weren't for Charlemagne, as he is the key that allowed me to trace our family history back over 2,000 years. While there are a great number of aristocrats in the Tyrrel lineage, it was Charlemagne, or 'Charles the Great' that allowed me to learn so much about us.

It's exciting to know one's own heritage. However, one can't get too excited about being related to a king, when they learn that Charlemagne was married at least four times, had three illegitimate sons and also numerous children with his concubines, all of which resulted in probably millions of people today who could say that they are a descendant of him. Unfortunately, I always believed the word 'great' referred to his leadership skills until I learned about his paternal acumen.

Chapter 7 – Spirituality

Madison is the state capital of Wisconsin and home to around 260,000 people with another 240,000 in the suburbs. The city is one of only two in North America that's located on an isthmus (the other is Seattle). Madison is home to fine dining, theater, and a thriving night life, as well as five lakes and plenty of bike-friendly areas. Many college students graduate and then continue to reside in Madison because the city is home to the University of Wisconsin-Madison. It has the feel of a college town combined with the benefits of a metropolitan area, yet a short drive out of the city gives travelers access to the countryside.

After commuting there for forty years, I'd forgotten a lot about the city and, for a change, Mike and I drove there for lunch, visited the Monona Terrace Convention Center, the incredibly beautiful State Capitol and then went to the Humanities Building on campus where I took Mike on tour of my old digs.

I'd mentioned once that Frank Lloyd Wright was a shirt-tail relative of mine and that motivated Mike to ask if we could possibly go by the Unitarian Meeting House, which was designed by my cousin and completed in 1951. We made our way to Shorewood Hills, just west of the University, parked the car and walked inside. I'd worked on campus for over forty years and never once thought to visit this world-renowned building that had all the Wright characteristics including wide overhanging eaves, a low and unobtrusive entryway, large fireplaces and a concrete floor, while its most distinctive feature remained the soaring glass and wood 'prow', on its southern exposure, which Wright said symbolized aspiration.

On our way, Mike outlined the fact that Cousin Frank's parents were founding members of the congregation and Frank was a long-time member of the First Unitarian Society. Mike noted that Unitarian Christians believe that Jesus was inspired by God in his moral teachings, is a savior but not a deity, nor God incarnate. Mike added, "Unitarianism is also known for the rejection of several other doctrines including the doctrines of original sin, predestination and the infallibility of the Bible."

I looked at Reverend Mike and asked if he felt 'odd' when he went inside a Church of a different denomination. Mike just shook his head and smiled and noted, "Will, if we wanted to go to Minneapolis, other than walking, how many different ways would there be to get there?" I shook my head at not only providing a reasonable answer but inquiring the reason for the question.

Mike glanced at me and said "Besides walking, there are four different ways to get from Madison to Minneapolis - by bus, train, car or plane. The question isn't how you get to Minneapolis, just that you get there."

At first, I had no idea what Mike was referring to and then he added. "As a pastor of the First Congregational Church, I have deep convictions based upon the Word of God. What's different from many other religions is my belief that every person has the right to interpret that Word according to the dictates of their conscience - in other words, how to get to Minneapolis - under the enlightenment of the Holy Spirit and not by mandate or decree, which is what I hope attracts people of genuine conviction, adventurous faith and gracious regard for each other's sincerity."

"Since every Congregationalist possesses full liberty of conscience in interpreting the Gospel, we are a diverse group of people united under Christ. We believe there is strength in diversity and by it, there are unending opportunities to learn from each other and to grow in faith. There's a wide variety of thought and practice among our member Churches. This, in itself, reveals an essential aspect of Congregationalism, where each Church uses Scripture as its foundation and is then guided by the Holy Spirit to determine its faithful forms of worship, governance and belief. This naturally leads to diverse worship practices, beliefs and Biblical interpretations among all the Congregational Churches."

"What about Jesus?" I inquired. "Which one?" Mike responded.

"What do you mean, which one?" I inquired, not knowing what Mike was referring to as he added, "There are several different versions, not only based the different religions, including the Muslim faith then there's the commercial Jesus, whose birthday has been turned into a marketing event to sell everything from mattresses to new cars."

As we were leaving the Unitarian Meeting House, we stopped for a moment and Mike asked me, "What about you?" knowing that I hadn't been a regular Church goer.

I replied, "We went to the Methodist Church when I was growing up and then when I got into the history business and learned about all that the Church did – both good and bad - I sort of gave up on organized religion. Today, I believe that Jesus was a prophet but don't know about the Virgin Mary and Jesus being the only son of God."

Mike inquired "Do you believe in the Bible?"

"I believe some of the messages in the Bible, such as the Ten Commandments and how it paints Jesus the same way as Buddhists represent Buddha and Muslim's Mohammed in that all three were prophets who personified four great characteristics – humility, generosity, compassion and forgiveness."

We stopped walking as Mike looked at me and smiled and offered. "And so, you have the basic tenants of being a Congregationalist."

"I guess so," I responded. "But there's more." "What?" Mike inquired.

"I believe that in the center of each person's universe lies themselves and we must protect and defend the 'self' and sustain it physically, mentally and spiritually. I sincerely feel what's right is that which makes one happy while what's wrong is anything that makes either oneself or others unhappy."

There was a bug splattered on my windshield and I pointed to it and asked Mike, "What does this small spec represent to you?"

"A very unlucky bug?" Mike replied with a smirk.

"Is it a black dot on a clear surface or a clear surface surrounding a black hole of death?" I added in all seriousness. "With only one point, there's simply no reference! No direction! Virtually no meaning! Add another dot and the entire thought process begins to change. Now there can be direction and the dots become the point of reference. Connect the dots and you have a line from the beginning until end. Such is life! We all have two dots - our birth and our death. It's the life path we follow between the dots that matters and our belief in the consequence of our existence. Along that path, we all need to develop many things - a concept of self, in terms of our relationship with others, along with concepts of right and wrong, good and bad, permanence and temporal existence and finally the concept of death, which is where spirituality really comes in."

I felt Mike was impressed and so I continued. "I was a history professor and the one thing I learned was that today's generation is not unique in this! As long as man has been able to escape his here- and-now in both time-and-space, the questions of who, what and why have lingered. There's a plethora of varying ideas ranging from profound belief in an omnipotent being, to the belief that there is nothing beyond this instant. Like everything else, there are extremes for a few and the middle for the rest of us."

We were pulling into the apartment garage and you could almost feel the relief on both of our parts. I hoped we hadn't gone too far and climbed in too deep with the religion stuff. Mike was becoming my friend and I certainly didn't want to risk that friendship on philosophy – history maybe but not philosophy.

Chapter 8 - Pips

Beside the family tree, my second passion, which keeps me socially connected, consists of the board games in the Quiet Room. Revolving around chess, checkers and cribbage, I like the Quiet Room simply because you're not supposed to talk above a whisper and it's a great place to concentrate.

Checkers is an obvious game and last on my list. Chess is incredibly complex. The American mathematician Claude Shannon, developed what's called the Shannon Number which is a conservative lower bound of 10^{120} possible moves based on an average of about 1,000 possibilities for each pair of moves that consists of one move for white followed by one move for black. A typical game lasts about 40 such pairs of moves or around 45 billion different possibilities, which can make chess incredibly complex. This leaves cribbage and, if you really get into it, it's just fun. The game was created by the English poet Sir John Suckling in the early 17th century, as a derivation of the game 'Noddy' which is where the term "sucker" originated as those who have mastered the game of 'Noddy' can sucker just about any first-time player.

There are two distinct scoring stages consisting of the 'play' where you add the sum of the cards played and then the 'show' that has a unique scoring system that includes points for groups of cards that total fifteen. While it probably sounds complicated, it's really not. However, NEVER gamble when you're first learning to play. You WILL lose your shirt, or several bottles of spotted cow, if your opponent has experience.

The game is fast paced and can be decided by only a few — or even a single point — and the edge often goes to an experienced player who utilizes strategy, such as calculating odds and making decisions based on the relative position of the opponent on the board. You need to know a little math but if you can learn to count to fifteen and understand combinations, the game's a breeze.

One Wednesday, after breakfast, Mike and I were bored and agreed to 'one quick game' of cribbage that had the potential of an all-day affair if we let it. We took our dishes to the kitchen, got out the cribbage board, went to the Quiet Room and, sat at our favorite table by the window overlooking the valley next to the center. While Mike and I had talked family, women, sports and health during the past year, other than the Madison trip, he'd really never got into the religion stuff and I appreciated that. Today was going to be a little different!

As I got out the pegs, Mike pulled the cards out of their case and asked me what I knew about a deck of cards. Before I could answer, he told me the entire story and left me dumbfounded by all he shared as it opened up what I'm about to tell you.

Reverend Mike exclaimed, "So many things in life have meanings we don't understand, simply because they were either never explained to us or have been forgotten."

With that, he took the deck and spread them out in a fan shape and flipped one end as they all became face-up as he looked at me while reciting. "If they're allowed to, playing cards can make one rich or poor, happy or sad and make life good or bad, just like your dreams. However, let's look at playing cards and see if there isn't greater meaning, just as there was a long time ago."

Holding the folded cards in his hands, Mike said. "The deck is a unit and thereby represents the oneness of God. There are four different suits to the cards, just like there are four seasons to our life. Not only in terms of the weather but in terms of people themselves - babies, children, adults and elderly, each with a different perspective on today, tomorrow and yesterday."

"The cards also represent the Quadrature of the Great Pyramid of Gizeh and when you look at any obelisk, such as the Washington Monument, you will see the four sides represent Iminium, Nour, Ruach, and Iebschah, which mean water, fire, air and earth."

Mike continued, "There are 52 cards to the deck, just as there are 52 weeks in a year and yet some of the cards have more value, while others less, just like life."

"There are 13 cards in each suit representing the total number of people in the Golden Circle of Christ and his 12 disciples. The thirteen, plus the joker represents the number of generations from Abraham to David in the Bible. Sometimes, you'll find two jokers. Why? Because there were fourteen generations from David to the deportation of the

Jews to Babylon and then fourteen from the deportation to Christ. The total face value of the complete deck is 365, which parallels the days of the year."

I sat profoundly mesmerized. Something I'd never thought about had so much more meaning than I could have imagined.

Reverend Mike continued by pulling the tens from the cards. "There are four tens that represents the ten expressions or emanations of God, in the creations of the heavens, earth and all that dwells therein. These are found in the first chapter of Genesis, in which God said, 'Thereby, He spoke the world into existence. There were also ten generations from Adam to Noah and ten from Noah to Abraham. In addition, in the Bible, Abraham was proven with ten trials and there were ten plagues in Egypt."

Mike spread the deck face up again and pulled out the face cards saying, "The Triads are three in number - jack, queen and king - representing the ancient thought of mind, matter and product and also the Trinity of Father, Son, and Holy Spirit."

"Today's 52 card deck preserves the four original French suits developed in 1480 and used around the world: clubs, diamonds, hearts, and spades. The graphic symbols, or 'pips,' that fascinated 16th-century Europe and probably represent astronomy, alchemy, mysticism, and history that are still present."

"Other historians have suggested that suits in a deck were meant to represent the four classes of Medieval society. Cups and chalices (modern hearts) might have stood for the clergy, swords (spades) for the nobility or the military, coins (diamonds) for the merchants, and batons (clubs) for peasants."

"While 'Pips' were highly variable, courtesan cards. What we call 'face cards' today, they have remained virtually unchanged for centuries. British and French decks, for example, always feature the same four legendary kings, while Queens have not enjoyed similar reverence, where Pallas, Judith, Rachel, and Argine have variously ruled each of the four suits, with frequent interruption."

"While designs have changed, numbers added and styles modified, the one thing that has remained constant are the kings. David was the King of Israel and is represented the King of Spades, Alexander the Great is the King of Clubs and either Caesar Augustus or Julius Caesar depending on who you talk to, is the King of Diamonds. Finally Charlemagne is represented by the King of Hearts." Mike continued. "Charlemagne's King of Hearts, offers another curiosity as he is the only king without a mustache who appears to be killing himself by means of a sword to the head. Before one questions why, there is an easy explanation that's much less dramatic. As printing spurred rapid reproduction of decks, the integrity of the original artwork declined. When printing blocks wore out, card makers would create new sets by copying either the blocks or the cards themselves that amplified previous errors to the point that Charlemagne's sword simply disappeared."

Mike paused for a moment and then added. "The ace rose to prominence in 1765, which was the year England began to tax the sale of playing cards, and the ace was stamped to indicate, the tax had been paid. In jolly old England, forging an ace was a crime punishable by death."

"Years later, card makers added corner numbers, which told the cardholder the numerical value of any card and its suit. This simple innovation was patented during the Civil War and has been a benefit simply because it allows players to hold their cards in one hand, tightly fanned as they play while providing values for each card within a suit." "Standard card decks normally contain two extra 'wild' cards,

each depicting a traditional court jester, that can be used to trump any natural card. Jokers first appeared in printed American decks in 1867, and by 1880, British card makers followed suit as the Joker can stand with any one of the suits, as he pulled the joker from the beginning of the nonface cards. "Called the 'odd card,' the Joker represents the missing link in life and can also represent leap year as the 366th value."

Mike handed me one of the Jokers and continued. "Some believe that the Joker is the 'capstone' of the temple or the head stone of the corner, as symbolized by the coni al ha that's associated with the Joker. There are two schools of thought regarding when and why the Joker was added. Some people believe the Joker came about during the transition from Tarot cards to the playing cards of today, where he was known as the fool and had the numerical value of zero, thereby representing the Alpha and Omega or beginning and ending of the cycle of life and death."

"Other scholars construe that the Joker actually began in Germany and the game Euchre while the German name of the card was 'Juker', which evolved into Joker. If we take the Tarot interpretation, the Fool or Joker can denote folly, eccentricity and poorly considered actions. He can also represent originality, or the beginning of an adventure or quest. The Joker is an independent spirit, complete within himself, guided by the forces of nature and wisdom of the Universe."

"What's important is the fact that the Joker has no meaning without association with the other cards and therefore can represent life itself, where the life of no one has meaning without others and, depending on which suit it's associated with, or which style of life, and with whom a person is associated, can be happy or sad, good or bad. With the joker, there are actually five and not four suits, just as in the first five days of creation, where all things were created."

Mike leaned back in his chair and offered. "As you can see Will, a simple deck of playing cards can mean so much more when you look at them carefully and each deck has components where each card gives the full deck its meaning. Remove just one component and the remaining cards mean nothing."

I sat shaking my head. Mike had filled me in and made me realize the true meaning of a deck of playing cards. As the game ended, I bowed my head in disappointment over his two-point victory, resulting, once again, in that I had to go get the coffee.

With the tutorial completed, I knew the time had come to finally share my secret with someone - a secret I'd held within me for over sixty years that no one, including my wife, ever knew. I'd never shared the Terrill family history with anyone and thought it was about time I came to mention what I knew. I looked at my friend and quietly announced. "Charles the Great was born on April 2, 748 and became King of the Franks in 768 at the age of twenty. After he consolidated a number of independent Germanic tribes into one unified force, the Franks migrated from what's now Belgium and Western Germany to an area called Gaul, which is now France, during what has become known as the Carolingian Dynasty. In fact, the name France comes from Latin Francia ('land of the Franks') and originally applied to the entire empire, extending from southern France to eastern Germany."

Mike looked at me quite surprised that I could go into such detail about Charlemagne as I continued. "In 774, at the age of twenty-six, Charlemagne conquered and took control of an area that represents most of today's Italian Peninsula and also became 'King of the Lombards'. Because Charlemagne was a devout Catholic, who had unified virtually all of Western Europe under his leadership and therefore Catholic influence, Pope Leo III bequeathed the title of 'the Emperor of the Romans' on Charlemagne in 800 when he was fifty- two years old, thereby recognizing Charlemagne as king of Western Europe - a position he held until his death on January 28, 814 at the age of 66."

Mike sat back in his chair with a frown on his face and inquired, "Why do you know so much about Charlemagne?"

To which I replied, "I not only taught Medieval history for forty years but Charlemagne is one of my relatives."

Mike looked at me with a smirk as if we'd both had too much Korbel brandy and questioned, "Really?"

I smiled and slightly shook my head as if to say 'yup'. "You're not pulling my leg?"

"Nope."

"You're really a descendant of Charlemagne?"

"Not a direct descendant but a cousin and there's a lot more to the story, if you want to listen."

"Tell me!" Mike responded excitedly.

I lowered my voice to a softer whisper and said, "I've got something to share with you that I don't think you're going to believe. Yet, what I tell you is totally true. It's going to take a long time to fill you in on all the details and so first, I need your word that what we share is between only you and me and that you'll have patience to let me tell you something I've never told another person in my life."

Mike looked into my eyes and could tell I was sincere. We agreed that sitting in the Quiet Room was still not the place for private conversation and agreed to meet in the lobby and 'go for a drive'. We went to our respective rooms, got light jackets as it was early October, and reconvened in the lobby.

As we rode down in the elevator Mike asked, "Where are we going?"

"Out to the family farm." I replied. "Are you up for walking?" "Sure, it might do my knee some good."

"Great!"

"What's this all about?"

"I'll tell you when we get there."

Chapter 9 - Relativity

As we were driving out to Waldwick, I turned to Mike and stated. "You must give me your word, what I'm about to share with you stays between the two of us. If I had a Bible in the car, I'd make you place your hand on it and agree."

Mike looked at me in total disbelief, assuring me I had his word. "Promise me and let's shake on it." I knew that over the years he'd heard just about everything but nothing like what I was about to share with him.

I took a deep breath and began as I peered out the window on Highway 23, before turning left on Rock Branch Road towards the farm. "Mike, what I'm about to tell you, I can't explain, other than to say it was either blind luck or providence that no one else seems to have endured. It took me several years to try and figure out what was going on and I'm still not sure I've got it right but here's what I think happened."

Mike looked at me with a frown, wondering where the conversation was going as I continued. "For some reason, I've been chosen to travel through time and space to visit the Terrill family ancestors. While I'm certain right now, you think I'm either no longer telling the truth or completely off my rocker, let me assure you, I'm neither.

My days left on this earth are numbered and I need to summarize my travels and experiences so that you and, hopefully, someday my family has insight into where we came from and what our destiny shall be. This is what I'm writing for my kids but want to share with you."

Mike looked at me in total disbelief, which was what I expected as I clarified things by adding, "What I'm about to share will seem so incredible that I spent my entire life trying to figure out what happened and why."

I could see the buildings of the farm but, needed to finish laying the groundwork as I explained. "I taught a grad-level history class that included Einstein's theory of relativity simply because history is simply the past, with all of its complicated choices and events that begins and ends with a relationship to and measurement of time. As the semester progressed I would throw in a lecture on the consequence of Special Relativity, where matter and energy become interchangeable via the equation $E = mc^2$, which means that because the speed of light is such a big number, even a tiny amount of mass is equivalent to, and can be converted into, a very large amount of energy, which is why atomic and hydrogen bombs are so powerful."

I parked the car, shut off the engine, looked at my friend and said, "I hope it's not too much but it's required for what has transpired in my life."

Mike looked at me with a very serious expression on his face as I announced, "I've traversed the time/space shield that was in effect and, to my knowledge, reserved only for me."

Mike's mouth dropped open in disbelief.

I concurred and added. "The details I'm about to share are so profound and 'unique' that it's been the beacon of my existence to the point that, since the first time I was affected, it has controlled my destiny, my life and even where I live today."

I opened my car door and looked at the still-in-shock Mike saying, "Come on and I'll share with you all that has happened but remember I've never shared this with anyone and I want you to come with me with hope that maybe, you'll have the answers I can't seem to find."

I paused as Mike had yet to reach for his door handle. Instead, he looked at me and asked, "Have you ever heard of the term 'synchronicity'?"

I shook my head 'no' as Mike continued by stating, "Synchronicity is a concept first introduced by a German analytical psychologist named Carl Jung, whose theory was that events are simply 'meaningful coincidences' if they occur with no causal relationship, yet, seem to be meaningfully related. If there's no causal relationship then, taken one step further, there can be synchronicity, which represents an invisible network that connects everyone and everything, no matter where it or they are in the universe."

I must have had a questioning look on my face as Mike added. "Most people believe in some form of universal causation, which is simply the proposition that everything in the universe has a cause and is therefore an effect of that cause. Every cause and effect in science and philosophy stop when you get to God and that's where religion comes in and where Jung's theory of 'meaningful coincidences' and interrelationships also come to an end, as no one can explain where God came from or what causes him to exist."

Mike had me and I was now truly glad I was sharing all that was going on. We both opened the car doors and looked at each other. In the twenty-minute ride we'd discussed the foundations of both of our careers and beliefs and it was incredible to see how they were actually tied together, where Mike's career actually began at the point where mine left off.

Chapter 10 - The Forest

Mike and I began our trek, stopping first at the family cemetery where I explained all the residents and how they were related. Next, we made our way past the orchard and I explained how the original trees came to be as the Native Americans picked apples in Upstate New York threw their discarded cores they into the field. Finally, we made it to the edge of The Forest and I explained the importance of the small enclave buried deep within a valley and the spring-fed stream that traversed the land.

I noted. "Mike, we've always called it 'The Forest' and each generation has honored the sanctity of the area by leaving it as a natural habitat, other than the small spec where our one-room school house named 'Skunk Hollow' was built."

Mike squinted and smiled as he remembered hearing of Skunk Hollow and me discussing how my cousins had gone to school there while I went to the Mineral Point elementary school. We stopped for a moment to give Mike time to recover as I could tell his knee was bothering him and I continued my expose. "For many, The Forest is nothing more than a group of trees and then the springs. For others, including me, it's an area of profound majesty and mystery where I've gone throughout my life to find peace and tranquility in times of woe."

I looked Mike in the eyes and reported. "To explain the feeling I, and others as fortunate as me, experience whenever we go into The Forest is extremely difficult. Yet, without sharing what happens, you would never understand why the area is so important. When I enter The Forest, my internal subjective state that consists of my moods, emotions and/or feelings immediately begins to change, regardless of where they have been. As an example, if I'm experiencing fear, anger, disgust or sadness, they'll be compensated for and my mind will enter a period of profound tranquility that allows my body to simply relax and experience the majesty of totality. If, on the other hand, I'm in a realm of joy, trust or anticipation, The Forest takes away the edges and allows me to absorb my feelings by enhancing the sensations and positive emotions that I am experiencing. Regardless of my feelings when I arrive I become more introspective, experiencing the consequence of both within my soul." "While the trees of The Forest demarcate the boundaries, the springs give it meaning. The crystal-clear water bathes my soul in a sense of sincerity, decency, purity and innocence. Unlike anything I feel elsewhere, the springs do so to the point that match my beliefs that our current world is flawed and can be replaced by a better place and existence, if only given a chance."

Mike looked at me with a totally different expression on his face. He was realizing that his beer-drinking, card-playing buddy had a different perspective on life that basically paralleled what he'd been preaching for over 40 years. Mike saw a side that he'd never seen before that was more aligned with his own ecclesiastical persona and we were more alike than he had initially perceived. While he'd been 'the man of cloth', I was the one who had pondered all forms of existence and done so in a non-structured manner that actually didn't align with the truisms pontificated by any formal religious structure.

I continued. "To me, The Forest is not a concept but an existence related to but differing from, concepts of heaven, afterlife and the Kingdom of God, where heaven is simply another place or state, and afterlife is an individual's life after death. I believe the Kingdom of God can be anywhere as long as the traveler is willing to give of themselves and accept humility, generosity, compassion and forgiveness, as the goals by which they must live."

Mike looked at me and smiled, slowly shaking his head, accepting that he was a 'man of the cloth' and I hadn't been to church since God knows when. Even so, his beliefs and mine paralleled each other in many ways as he summarized, "In other words, Will, The Forest for you, is where the positive energy is so great that the synchronicity can be felt, transmitted and processed into both emotions and behavior."

I smiled in agreement and relief, realizing he understood what I was talking about as Mike added. "For some people, like you, the feelings are profound because the energy is positively linked to your soul. For others, there is little or no feeling and, therefore, no emotion. No matter how strong the feelings, the connections are still there and that's why your family respects all that there is."

I smiled and added. "While visiting The Forest the experience can be an opportunity that profoundly affects a person. Unfortunately, this is limited to a very few people and I hope and pray you will be one of them. That's why I've brought you here. I know of no other person besides myself who's gone beyond being affected and transcended into another realm that has changed me, challenged me and controlled me since I was a child."

With that, we followed the path and I showed him the remnants of the foundation of Skunk Hollow School consisting of nothing more than a few boulders and a lot of memories. We stopped and I added. "I'm named after my dad, who went to school here. Because my dad came home blind in the First World War, we lived in town, up on Madison Street, and dad would sit on the front porch and listen to the cars go by in the summer or to the radio. Not once did he ever feel sorry for himself and, yet, we all knew he regretted his handicap, not because of how it limited him but because of the limitations it put on the family and what we could do. Not once did he ever complain. However, I knew he would have loved watching me play sports or see my sister in the plays she was in."

Dad had been gone a long time and so Mike could only accept my summary, having never known him. From the remains of the school there was a deer path to the springs and then the bog beyond. I motioned Mike to follow me and we walked the path I'd traversed so many times before. As we were but twenty paces, Mike held up his hand and beckoned me to stop. I thought he was having trouble with my pace or perhaps his knee. Instead, Mike looked at me and whispered, "We're someplace special. I can feel it Will, I've never felt like this before."

"Do you want to turn around and go back?" I inquired.

Mike firmly shook his head no and replied. "Just the opposite. I'm being bathed in goodness and it's a feeling that has transpired only a few times in my life when I sincerely felt I've done good."

"Should we continue?" "Yes, please!" Mike replied.

I slowed the pace to ensure that Mike was able to traverse the path. Once again, Mike stopped. I turned around and saw tears streaming down his face as I asked, "Are you OK?"

Mike shook his head 'yes'.

The silence was deafening and yet I sensed I shouldn't speak and began slowly walking again. When we'd gone twenty more paces, Mike stopped, took a deep breath, exhaled and took another deep breath and closed his eyes.

"Are you sure you're OK?"

Another soft smile pursed his lips as Mike opened his eyes. "Will, I've waited my whole life for this moment. I've always thought it would only take place when I entered Heaven. Yet, for the first time, there is profound peace within my soul and the goodness of simply 'being' has overcome me. When you're a minister, your efforts can be very lonely and the sense of satisfaction fleeting. To come here and feel all that I've dreamt about and hoped for, is simply beyond anything I could have ever imagined."

Tears welled in Mike's eyes as he continued. "For the first time in my life, I realize that what I've done has been the right thing and the feelings I have right now are simply God's way of giving me what I hope I've given to others. While theirs came in small doses, God has given me a profound sense of what heaven will be like when the time comes and he calls me home."

I stood for a moment and let Mike bathe in the majesty of serenity that accompanied him. As the spell broke and a broad smile returned to his face, we continued our journey, finally reaching the point where the spring trickled from beneath the rocks.

I motioned my hands in the form of a cup and gestured to Mike, instructing him to drink from the springs. Mike knelt down and slowly cupped his hands and placed them to his lips. For a moment there was nothing and then Mike's body began to quake as he looked skyward. Mike arose and looked at me and simply shook his head. "God is here, Will! God is here! I can feel him unlike no other time before. Perhaps, this is what the disciples felt like when they met Jesus. Perhaps, this is what Jesus felt like when he was baptized by John the Baptist."

Mike looked at me and said. "Will, you've given me one of the greatest gifts I could ever receive. You've shown me that my life was worthwhile, where all the times I wondered if what I was doing, what I was giving, what I was preaching was worth it. Now…right now…I see and feel that they were justified."

Mike smiled another gentle smile adding "This is a place of worship unlike any I've been before. Not created by man but by God! Not as an interpretation of what we THINK heaven will be like but an exclamation of the goodness He has created. I'll never forget today and all that's transpired, nor will I ever be able to thank you for bringing me here and giving my life meaning."

I was humbled as we stood there and allowed the 'spell' to dissipate. It was then that I looked across the shallow stream and into the bog and saw 'him', the great buck who had traversed time and remained immortal. I whispered to Mike 'look' as I glanced over my right shoulder. With that, Mike's eyes slid across the horizon as the big buck simply bowed his head and quietly walked away.

Mike inquired, "What's that?"

I responded. "He's the buck that appears when someone has seen the beauty of goodness. He'll only stay for a moment and then be gone. He's been here as long as I've been alive, if not before and is where my story actually begins. I don't have any idea what's going to happen to you but I wanted you to come to see if you were the one I could share my story with. I needed to see how you would feel once you were here. I needed to make certain that what you felt was strong enough so that you would accept what I want to share with you as the truth."

Mike's expression assured me that it was all right to continue as I added. "I don't know if you'll ever come again or have the same feelings. I've heard that, for some, it's a one-time thing. For others like me, the sensations come and go, as they react to my own emotions. However, I believe they're always here and that's why I keep coming back."

Chapter 11 - The Hunt

While looking across the little stream and into the bog, I began "When your family comes from a farm, you look at all things as potential food, something you either raise or grow, simply to be eaten or sold. While this primarily consists of domesticated plants and animals, it extends to other plants and animals as well."

"Throughout my childhood and even today, there is talk of 'him' - the great antlered deer you just saw, who appears and disappears into the memories of those who've seen him. Perhaps he exists. Perhaps he's an illusion. Normally living somewhere between six and twenty years, the deer in question has lived for as long as anyone can remember and, yet, he never changes. When he enters your life, it's always the same. He'll stop and look at you until you make eye contact and then, simply walk away. Perhaps there will be a nod, perhaps there won't. No matter what, he will have touched your life."

I turned and looked at Mike. "My dad wanted me to do all the things a father and son would normally do. However, a blind man can't go hunting and so, at the age of twelve, my Uncle Mont began taking me, as he taught me hunting safety and all about respecting the land and 'God's creatures' as he called them. Pheasants, squirrels, rabbits and ducks were all part of our collective hunting experiences where the idea was not sport but cooperation and sustenance. Uncle Mont would carry the shotgun and I'd follow along, learning from him the nuances of tracking and hunting, hoping for the day when I would be able to be more and do more than just follow the leader."

"At the age of fourteen, Uncle Mont gave me a hunting bow and twelve arrows and taught me how to string the bow as he set up two bales of hay for me to practice shooting out behind the barn. As my aim got better, I was given permission to go hunting on my own and it felt good to be trusted. At first, my rate of success was minimal with more than one animal escaping our dinner table that night."

I looked back across the small stream and continued. "It was a late October Sunday when I made my way into The Forest with my bow and quiver filled with the twelve arrows. As I made my way past the school house, I saw him – the big buck – who turned and looked at me. My imagination ran rampant. To bring home the elusive buck would enhance my position as a man and the trophy above the fireplace would make my friends envious."

"The buck saw me and slowly made his way down the path towards the springs. I followed, doing everything I could to ensure he didn't notice me. For every step he took, I took one as well. Each time he paused, I paused too. When he looked up, I froze, doing my best to blend in, as I held my breath hoping not to alert him of his intended demise."

My head couched down as if to act out what happened as I continued. "Slowly the hunt continued with each step taking us closer and closer and closer to the springs. As the buck neared the bog, with the water gurgling from beneath the rocks, he paused to take a drink. This was my opportunity, my chance to become a man. Slowly, I crouched down and pulled an arrow from my quiver. Pulling it forward, I inserted arrow's base into the nocking point on the string and slid the shaft silently onto the arrow rest. Quietly, I turned the bow from a horizontal position to vertical, such that the upper and lower limbs were above and below each other just as Uncle Mont had taught me."

I looked at Mike and added. "I took a deep breath as I studied my prey and took my two fingers and slowly began pulling the serving back beneath my chin. As the buck's head dipped one more time for one last drink, I released my fingers and let the arrow fly. I was certain he was mine! I was ready for the thrill that comes with achievement, especially of such a magnificent animal."

"The arrow flew straight and direct and when it reached its destination, the arrow didn't penetrate the deer. In fact, it was as if he wasn't there at all. Instead, the arrow continued on a path beyond the stream, beyond where I'd ever been before, into the bog where no one had ever dared travel. With that, the buck looked up, stared at me and simply walked away, as I stood in awe and dismay. I asked myself, what happened? How could it be? The arrow had flown directly into the side of the animal and yet, there was nothing! No penetration! No death! Nothing!"

"I stood for a moment in total shock before reality swallowed my insistence and made me come to my senses. I shook my head and realized that one of my arrows was gone and I needed to find it. I knew I needed to walk into the bog and retrieve what had been meant to be an instrument of death."

"Slowly, I walked to the springs, set down my bow and scooped the water into my hands. Putting it to my mouth, its cold refreshment cascaded into my body and with it, the guilt of almost killing the noble beast who had done nothing more than stop for a drink of water. I closed my eyes and thanked God he was still alive."

"Picking up my bow and quiver, I proceeded into the bog oozing into the mud and muck which had served to restrain others from following. My boots protected my feet from the cold as I reached a small bush and began my search, wondering how far the arrow could have flown."

"Before me, lie a patch of fog from a small area of evaporating water that had just escaped from Mother Earth. I proceeded until I was at its edge when I thought I heard a noise coming from within. How could it be? It sounded like voices and crying. I asked myself, how could it be on a cold October day that others were with me in a place I'd never been? I paused for a moment and took a deep breath and stepped into the fog."

"As the fog cleared, I stood amazed. I was no longer in our forest, no longer in the time and place where I'd been. Where was I? How did I get here? Whose voice did I hear?"

"I turned to go back but there was no return. I'd been enveloped in the fog and there was no direction. I tried to comprehend where I was and where I needed to go and took a few more steps. Beyond me, it looked like the sun was shining and so I proceeded into a part of the forest I'd never been before."

Mike looked at me and simply shook his head. I felt he'd had enough for one day and so I stopped right there. We headed back to the center and little was said until we reached the garage when Mike asked, "What happened?"

I looked at him and replied. "It's a long story and so I'll fill you in each time we leave Heaven's Waiting Room," with all its rules and regulations and so many old people that made it truly seem like it was the last stop before heaven.

Chapter 12 - Bingo

The next week Mike and I decided to take a trip to the Hochunk Casino in Wisconsin Dells. Known as "The Waterpark Capital of the World" the Dells offers a range of attractions and accommodations to meet every waterpark lover's needs. There are over 21 water parks, water-skiing thrill shows and super-mini-golf courses. Now two old fat guys sliding down a water filled tube wasn't quite what we were after. We knew if we went in the afternoon we could go to Hochunk, get free drinks and play blackjack for little or nothing. It's about a ninety-minute drive and so I continued the story of what happened after the fog.

I once told Mike I felt there were three things that affected the evolution of mankind. Time and distance were the first two. As we headed towards Dodgeville I added, "The third component is the environment that has shown cyclic patterns of warmer and colder periods where, in the last 750,000 years, there have been eight major cycles, with many shorter episodes between."

"During colder periods, the Arctic and Alpine ice sheets expanded and sea levels fell. Some parts of southern Europe probably weren't affected very much but the advance and retreat of the ice sheets and accompanying glacial environments had a significant impact on northern Europe to the point that, at their maximum advance, they covered most of Scandinavia, the North European Plain and Russia."

"Because of the changes, human occupation wavered but continuous settlement north of the Alps required a solution to the problems of living in extremely cold conditions and with it, different societies and cultures developed with their own beliefs, traditions and languages. As the tribes increased in size, it's logical to think their territories would have become smaller, while the increasingly harsh environments of the last glaciation required appropriate strategies for survival in terms of not only food but apparel and lodging. Anthropologic studies have determined that these precursors to modern man reflect social and economic strategies, which allowed most of the population to stay at one location for long periods while others left to procure food. The challenge came when one group competed with another for the same food source, as the entire concept of structured battle and war began to develop."

"With life, comes death and anthropologists have determined that tribes began instituting deliberate and careful burial, sometimes with elaborate treatment of the dead. As an example in Sungir, Russia and Grotta Paglicci, Italy, the dead were buried with tools and ornaments were left, indicating a respect for their identity or status. Personal ornaments, especially bracelets, beads, and pendants made from a wide variety of materials, including animal teeth, ivory and shells. What's really interesting is the fact that the ornamentation not only shows an evolution of the meaning of clothing as a social barometer but may also have been used as a means of indicating individual and tribal identities."

"The last really cold era was called the Pleistocene glaciation that began to change about 13,000 BC as temperatures slowly rose. Limnologists and climatologists have determined that the Scandinavian Ice Sheet started to retreat northward around 8300 BC and the beginning of agriculture about a thousand years later resulted in the birth of cultural change. As the ice sheets retreated, resettlement began in the once-covered areas. However, the melting ice produced a rise in sea levels that flooded large areas of land in the Mediterranean and especially in the North Sea basin, including Belgium during the 7th millennium."

I hadn't had this much rapt attention in years and it was quite gratifying and so I continued. "One would think that to be able to trace your family back to 65 BC would be far enough. Yet, the yearning to go further back in time and learn more was and remains quite strong and extremely frustrating because I can't find anything before 65 BC."

"65 BC?" Mike incredulously repeated.

"Yup, that's where I get stuck on trying to learn more about the origins of the Terrill family."

"Most people can't do their great grandparents and you're going all the way back to 65 BC? How many generations is that?"

"Sixty."

"You're back sixty generations into your family history?" My loquacious self, responded "Yup!" .

"Incredible!"

"I hope this doesn't sound like one of my lectures, I offered." Mike, being such a good guy, would have let me read the telephone book to him and never complain and so I began.

Chapter 13 - The Gallic Period   65CE - 480

1. Carolus de Menapii	Born: 65 BC
2. Menapius de Menapii	Born: 44 BC
3. Valerius de Menapiii	Born: 2 BC
4. Carolus de Menapii	Born: 49 AD
5. Priapus de Menapie	Born: 67 AD
6. Carolus de Menapie II	Born: 89 AD
7. Julius de Menapie	Born 115
8. Octavius de Menapie	Born: 144
9. Valardius de Menapie	Born: 179
10. Valeriues I Godefroy de Menapie	Born: 210
11. Vuercius de Menapii	Born: 250
12. Antsard de Menapii	Born: 290
13. Martisindes de Menapii	Born: 315
14. Toxandre de Menapii	Born: 335
15. Ansygius de Menapii	Born: 355
16. Carolus Lii de Menapii	Born: 400
17.	Born: 440

	Austrapius de Menapii	

Chapter 14 – The Menapii

As we were driving,

I handed Mike a sheath with some maps in it as I continued. "My area of greatest interest lies in what's now Northwest Belgium and a tribe called the Menapaii. Members of that tribe had a first name and then 'de Menapii' which simply meant 'of the Menapii tribe'. The Menapii were a Belgic tribe of northern Gaul in both pre-Roman and Roman times. Their territory stretched north to the mouth of the Rhine and along the west bank of the Scheldt River (Scaldis) in an area called Belgica."

"Located in the southwest corner of Germania Inferior and along the coast of the Septentrionalis Ocean that's today called the North Sea, the Menapii area included the headwaters of the Scheldt River in what's now northern France and just north of Saint Quentin as it flows through the territory of the Nervians and Menapiens and passes by the cities of Chambray and Valenciennes, where the waters of the Selle river empty into it.

"I could take you back through all the different metal ages but won't bore you with that. Instead, I'll start with the Iron Age which is seen as the time of the appearance in history of the European peoples, the 'barbarians' as they were seen by Rome."

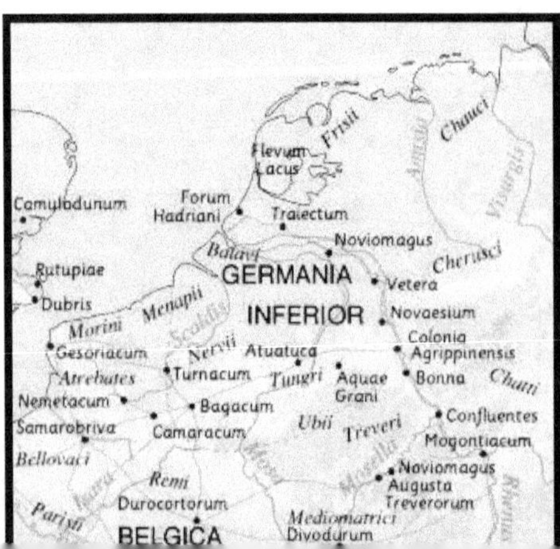

"These people included a number of different tribes and groups. While the configurations changed over time, they all had more or less obvious common roots in the Bronze Age. It was during this period that individually named people appeared elsewhere for the first time, such as in Greece. The names of kings, heroes, gods, and goddesses have become known through legendary writers, such as Homer. What's exciting for me is the appearance of Carolus DeMenapii in written history, and, therefore Alpha One and the first known Terrill ancestor that I have reconstructed to provide a road map from the distant past until the early 1800's."

"While there's a lot anthropologists don't know, they've learned that the people were close to the same height as people living today and were of a similar build."

"You mean, short and fat, like you and me?" Mike countered. "Let's call it vertically challenged and slightly rotund, if you please!" I offered with a smirk, and continued.

"In some areas, people of different racial characteristics were buried in a similar manner within one cemetery, suggesting that the population was racially mixed and it's quite likely that such racial interaction was common in many areas, suggesting that the cultures corresponded to social structure rather than ethnic or racial ones."

"The mortality rate was high, and the average life expectancy was about 30–40 years, with high infant mortality and few very old members of society. Women would give birth at an early age and their lower life expectancy was likely due to death in connection with pregnancy or childbirth. Generations would have been short and the nature of society was, therefore, drastically different. As an example, the estimated census of one group suggests it consisted of 30 to 40 people of which half of them were children. This would have influenced social life, kinship systems and subsistence activities while their discovered remains often show signs of heavy, physical labor and the wear on their bones suggests that many activities took place in a squatting position."

"Initially, social divisions of labor and resources simply didn't exist but this changed with time. The males of some clans, or leading families, had more access to animal products than any of the other members of the community, while the women generally had a more restricted and homogeneous vegan diet. With the advent of the Iron Age, the Menapii society had become so differentiated that some people lived a life without hard labor and physical toils, while others worked extensively and had a poor diet."

"Throughout the Metal Ages, humans were victims of various diseases, such as rheumatism and arthritis, which complicated life and crippled the body. Tuberculosis was also present and many had dental disease and bone tumors. Some of these diseases caused joint changes and deformities which resulted in restricted working and even walking capacities for the individual concerned. Badly crippled and handicapped people often survived and were taken care of by other members of their community. There is also evidence that people took great care in their appearance. Hairstyles were often quite sophisticated with braids, hairnets and ornaments used by women or their hair cut straight at the shoulder. Manicure equipment was also common in the Late Bronze and Early Iron Ages and rudimentary mirrors a favored object."

"In addition to how the people looked, there is also evidence of the clothing and ornaments they used. There are a few scattered wool textiles from the Neolithic Period but the first well-documented evidence of wool textiles dates from the Bronze Age. At times the textiles themselves have been found. However, more commonly it's the equipment used in textile production, such as spindle whorls, loom weights and combs, that show weaving as a household task performed in any settlement."

"With the Iron Age, new weaving techniques developed and embroideries, dyes, and more complicated designs were introduced, as were textiles of materials such as linen, made from flax, and silk. At this point, it also became common to have specialist weavers. The increase in textile production meant the raising of sheep intensified in many regions. In the Aegean area this transformation happened early. In other parts of Europe, it took a little longer. Toward the end of the Bronze Age changes in the fleece of sheep in England demonstrate how substantially the use of sheep had increased."

"There's all kinds of evidence that humans no only changed with the environment but did so in a haphazard degree based on the available resources. As an example, as the reindeer moved north, so did some human groups. Others adapted to new animal and plant resources such as wild cattle, deer and pigs, as well as many types of birds. Fish were also caught, including river species such as salmon, carp and many sea species, along with shellfish. The role of plant foods is difficult to estimate but there's evidence that many species of plants including hazelnuts and various berries were part of the main diets of those who lived in the different regions."

"When agriculture and non-nomadic existence came to be, stone tools increasingly took the form needed to accomplish specific tasks such as small blades for the tips of arrows and spears, hooks, nets, and traps for fishing, birch bark for containers and clothes made from plant fibers along with canoes and paddles."

"Human occupation expanded throughout most of Europe with base camps occupied by all members and small sites used for harvesting of some particular resource. We know that wide social networks existed simply because of the long-distance exchange of some raw materials such as special types of rock."

"The goal of the time was primarily food gathering and it appears as if mobility was important to ensure there was enough. However, some environments, such as the coastal regions of the Baltic including Germany and Belgium, allowed for more permanent settlement and that's where my story begins."

"What about your time travel?" Mike inquired.

"As I noted, when I came out of the fog from the forest, I realized there was a time and space transfer and I began to realize I was no longer on our farm but really didn't know where I was. I looked to my left and there was nothing familiar. I looked to my right and it was the same. Through the trees, I saw people – a man and woman and three children with long hair and definitely from a different time. I quietly crept closer and examined their attire. I was amazed at what they were wearing. Clothes that had been roughly sewn together from hides, bones and antlers, all tied with belts made of strips of trees, covering leather leggings made of goat hides."

Chapter 15 – Rocks on My Head!

I shook my head and exclaimed to Mike. "Perhaps it was my innocence. Perhaps my interest. Whatever it was, I'd thrown caution to the wind and the next thing I felt was a dull pain as someone hit me in the back of the head as I came tumbling to the ground. For a moment, I lay totally numb, in shock and concerned, totally confused. Where was I? How did I get here?"

"As my eyes cleared and I regained focus I looked up at a bearded man with a club in his hand. Before he could strike me again, I raised both arms in protection and pleaded, 'Stop'."

"The interloper stood shocked. While I spoke in English, he understood what I was saying. What was really crazy was that, whatever language he spoke, I understood, when he asked, 'Who are you? Why are you in our camp?' Once again, while he spoke in some strange language, I completely understood."

"I raised my hands to show there was no intended harm and replied, 'My name is William Terrill and I mean you no harm.'"

"How did you get here?"

"'I don't know,'" I replied. "'I don't know'".

"The elder took my bow and quiver and looked at them with a frown upon his face while asking, 'Roman?'"

"I looked at him and replied, 'Made in America,' to which he had no reply. As I stood, I felt the blood on the back of my head and became dizzy. The next thing I knew, I was waking up in a small tent made of hides covered with some sort of blanket. With that, I looked out and saw the man and what appeared to be his wife and children sitting around a fire. I stood and made my way out to them."

"'I'm sorry,'" the man offered. "'We didn't know who you were. Are you Nervian, Batatvite or Morin?'"

"I just looked at him with a perplexed expression and asked, "'Where am I?'"

"'What do you mean?'"

"'Where am I?'"

"'You're in Belgica.'"

"'Belgica?'"

"'We are members of the Menapii tribe.'"

"'Menapii?'" I asked, totally confused.

"The elder spoke, 'We are part of the Belgic confederacy called the Bataves. We are separated by the Scheldt River with the Nervians in the direction where the sun rises, the Atrebates where the birds fly in the darkness and the edge of the great sea where our brothers, the Morins, live. Together, the Belgica land reaches to the mouth of what they call the Rhine River and along the river called the Siene, as well. Beyond us are the Aquitani and Gauls, with whom we live in peace each with our own customs, laws, and language'."

I looked at Mike and clarified everything by saying, "We were studying European history in Mrs. Gordon's class and had just learned that the Menapii lived in the forests of the Scheldt River estuary on the North Sea in today's Belgium. With that tidbit of knowledge, I reached down as my hands crumbled the sandy soil between my fingers and noticed that even in the forest, the landscape was very flat and the area seemed to consist of farms, fields and hedges. I inhaled deeply and could smell the ocean and remembered there were islets, swamps and marshland where the Scheldt River emptied into the North Sea."

"Luck? Coincidence? God's intervention?" Mike asked.

"I really don't know," as I glanced at Mike and then the road and continued. "As my education focused on European history, I began to put the pieces together and later realized that the elder was a farmer who subsisted on animal husbandry and agriculture. Like the first Terrills of Waldwick, these people were living in scattered hamlets or alone with few, if any cities. When there was danger the Menapiins bonded with the neighboring tribes. When there was flooding, courtyards were half buried and constructed at the top of clay or sand mounds, called 'Donken', or river dunes."

"I remember that instant as if it was yesterday, as the man stood and looked at me and proudly stated. 'The Menapii are the oldest tribe and we have lived in peace on this land for over 500 winters. My father's father and those before him were seafarers and traders who established colonies and settlements along the coasts of Britannia, or so it's called by those pigs, the Romans'.

'Over 150 winters ago, we developed the Menapii community in a place now called Ireland. These people are known as the Fir Bolgs. Many of our people live there today.'"

"The elder looked at the ground and then at me and sadly continued. 'Today, we see the Goidels or Gael replacing our ways and language in a land so far way and we hear the Romans are nearby, wanting to conquer us, taking away our young boys to live as slaves, as we are subjected to Roman rule. No matter where we are, we have enemies that want to take away our way of life. How can I give my son tomorrow when I cannot save him from today?'"

"Even at the age of fourteen, I understood the man's passion, frustration, concern and disappointment. I'd come from the future and my only hope was to make sure they survived. My fear was their demise would be my demise…their end, my end and their death my death."

"I still had no idea when it was, I knew I was somewhere in Belgium or Germany but needed to find out the time and asked, 'You said something about the Romans. Where are they?'"

"The elder spoke. 'They are nearby and have killed many people. For the Romans, we are nothing but sheep. They think we have no might and they can control us. They are wrong! We've heard rumors and stories from Rome and our counsel is making plans for the day when they come to make war with us and we will be ready.'"

I shuddered to think they had any idea of the power and might of the Roman legions or their brutality, as the elder continued. 'We've heard about the three Romans who believe there will be tremendous advantage of power, wealth and fame by expanding the Roman empire. We've heard of the man called Gaius Julius Caesar."

"They don't think we know but we do!' With that, the elder spit on the ground to show his disgust."

"The elder looked at me with a level of confidence and continued. 'We have those who keep us informed. We hoped there would be peace. However, the Roman Republic governorships have awarded Caesar command of an army consisting of four legions of 20,000 men he will use to invade our land and destroy our peace.'"

"The elder shook his head with great sadness and added. 'Even the Roman Senators fear this man allowing Caesar to ignore all Roman rules, as he uses his military might to conquer Gaul and invade Britain and do so without authorization of anyone.'"

"The elder stirred the flames as sparks flew into the night and continued. 'The Romans are great soldiers but not great warriors. When a man is fighting for his land, life and family even the might of the legions will not stop him. Caesar and the Romans will only go as far as the Rhine River. Until then, we are afraid that Caesar's army will destroy the inhabitants of all the land, including ours where, through wars and battles, insurrections and defeats, Caesar intends to eliminate anyone and everyone who gets in his way. This man has no soul and the Gods must cry in shame as all he wants is to change the history of Rome and the world forever. We must fight and fight we must. It will be through bravery that we will win.'"

I looked at Mike and offered. "I knew better. I knew the might of the Roman legions was simply too strong for a group of untrained, uncoordinated farmers. I took a deep breath and wondered, what I, a fourteen-year-old kid, could do to help them and more importantly protect the beginnings of the Terrill family and how could I ever get back home again?"

"For some reason, the elder appeared to trust me and for that I was grateful. I looked in the eyes of Carolus and wondered – 'Is he my first ancestor? Do I need to protect him against harm's way? If I fail, will the entire Terrill legacy simply disappear? I shook my head and realized that only a few hours ago, all I wanted was to simply show the world I was a man and shoot a deer. My God, things had changed."

Mike and I were crossing the Wisconsin River in Sauk City as I continued. "I had a glimpse of the past which would control the future and realized I needed to return home and study my history if I was going to save my ancestors and therefore myself from the ravages of the Romans. The questions became how did I get here? How could I return home? If I did and wanted to come back, would I simply walk back into the bog and look for the fog? I sat with Carolus and wondered where he came from and why did the entire Terrill story begin with him? I looked at his hands and his index fingers and realized his fingernails were fan-shaped like mine - the common genetic Terrill thread that has prevailed in all of our family, was there! I looked at the elder and motioned towards Carolus and simply noted, 'Your son has a lot to learn before he becomes a great warrior.'"

"The elder looked at me in a suspicious way and inquired, 'How do you know he will be a great warrior?'"

"I quickly realized that to speak of the future would be a terrible mistake, as those with whom I was in contact would not only question my wisdom but consider me a warlock, someone who could cast evil spells on those with whom I came in contact. I replied, 'He has the hands of a warrior, broad and strong and carries himself with the honor and dignity of a great leader'."

"The elder seemed appeased as he replied 'His father was a great warrior who helped save the Menapii from the Germanians and gave his life so that our people could live in peace. Carolus has been with us since he was a baby and is considered one of our family. With that, I knew the genealogical answer regarding why my research would someday hit its dead end and why the Terrill story began with Carolus de Menapii and couldn't go back any further.

"For two weeks, I remained in camp, teaching the elder and Carolus how to use the bow and arrow and, just as important, how to create their own. I knew the day would come when the weapons would mean the difference between life and death, not only for them but the entire Terrill family."

Mike sat shaking his head as if to tell me it was a wonderful fairytale as I continued. "At the end of the two weeks, I asked the elder to take me to the spot where he found me. When he asked why, I told him I had other weapons he could have. He believed me and took me to the spot in the woods where I saw the fog and walked in. As if in an instant, I was back home in the bog, not knowing if time had continued or I was simply dreaming."

"I turned and saw the great buck slowly nodding his head as he walked back towards the spring with me following. When I reached the springs, I realized that the only thing that had changed was the loss of the bow, arrows and quiver, as the buck simply eroded into The Forest that lie ahead."

"I walked back to the house and Uncle Mont inquired about my weapons. I didn't know what to say and remained silent until he looked down at my hunting pants and saw the mud.

"You were in the bog, weren't you?" Uncle Mont asked. "Yes."

"Will, strange things happen in there, I don't recommend going again."

"What kinds of strange things?" I asked.

"It goes back to the Indians who called it the land of the KaKaKa or 'little people' who live forever. The Hochunk legends tell tales of warriors who disappeared without leaving a trace."

"A bolt of fear ran through my body. Chills overcame my nature and yet I was so intrigued, I knew I needed to see if I could return once again."

I took a deep breath and looked at Mike as we were pulling into the casino parking lot and smiled. Mike just shook his head in disbelief and said, "There's no way you could be making this up".

Chapter 16 - The History Paper

Mike and I had a good time at the Casino. Pleasantly, the afternoon had a total cost of less than twenty-bucks each which made us feel like winners. I mean…somewhat free drinks, little tiny sandwiches and all the excitement of an afternoon of blackjack, what else could an old man ask for?

As we got back in the car, Mike urged me to tell him what happened next and so I began. "The Monday after my hunting trip, I went to school with my mind a whirling dervish. Normally, I was a very serious student and never got into any trouble. I think the teachers appreciated the fact that I always did my homework and handed it in on time. While chemistry, physics and math were my favorites, I worked hard in my other classes, as well."

"Fifth hour was World History with Mrs. Gordon. We all joked behind her back that she was so old, she probably experienced a lot of the ancient history herself. It was mid-term and we were given a choice of taking an exam or writing a paper. Normally, I'd take the exam and be done with it. However, after my encounter, I elected to write the paper, giving me the impetus to learn about the beginning of our family and the challenges that stood before them."

"At first Mrs. Gordon was reticent. However, she finally approved, without ever knowing what had transpired or realizing my goal was to learn as much as possible in case I could return and save my ancestors and, therefore, myself from oblivion."

Mike looked at me and smiled. With that, I had Mike open the car's glove compartment and pull out some old, hand-written, yellowed sheets of paper with tattered corners and curling Scotch Tape intended on saving them from shreds with Mrs. Gordon's letter A$^+$ written in red ink across the first page. It was my world history report I'd put in the car so that Mike could have a better understanding of what was going on. Here's what the report said.

Winning the Gallic Wars

World History
William Terrill

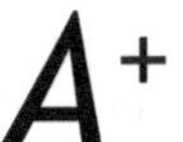

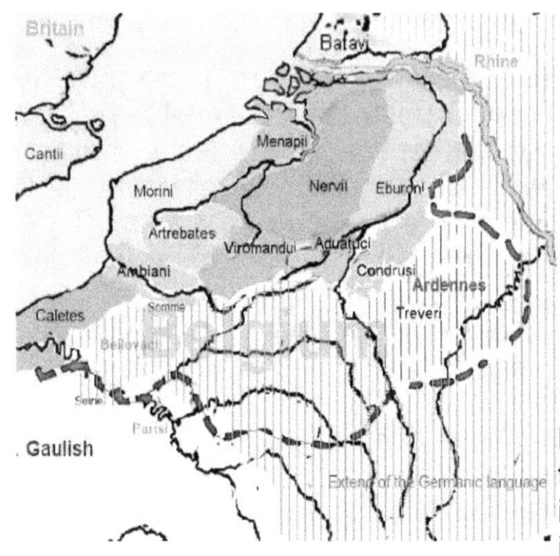

The Roman Empire was one of the greatest and most influential civilizations in world history. It began in the city of Rome in 753 BC and lasted for well over 1000 years. During that time, Rome grew to rule much of Europe, Western Asia, and Northern Africa. Of critical importance was the period from 58 BC to 50 BC and what was called the Gallic Wars that saw Rome invade what has become Western Europe with the defeat of all but a small portion of the land south of the Rhine River.

Rome's domination in battle centered around a centuries-old strategy called acies triplex, which incorporated a three-tier strategy in terms of both manpower and specialization of the soldiers into three lines, or layers of soldiers. In this formation, the first line attacked with thrusting-spears. The second line consisted primarily of javelin throwers and archers. The third, normally consisting or two legions, or 10,000 men, were either on horses or experienced swordsmen.

In a typical battle, the opposing forces would meet in an open field and be in position. The Roman archers would let fly a barrage of arrows and then the first line of Romans would attack, followed by the archers. As the battle ensued, the Roman cavalry and swordsmen would then attack in hand-to-hand battle. Through the combination of domination and specialization, the Romans defeated numerous opponents that resulted in their power and might become one of the most feared in history.

In 60 BC, Gaius Julius Caesar concluded that his rise to power would only come through the conquest of the area called

Gaul. To achieve his goal, his strategy was to align himself with those of supplemental power to create what was called The First Triumvirate, consisting of Caesar, Crassus, and Pompey that melded Pompey's military might, Caesar's political influence, and Crassus' money, allowed for Caesar's election as consul in 59 BC. With these moves, the various Republic governorships awarded Caesar command of an army consisting of four legions, or approximately 20,000 men.

Caesar's tactics were quite simple - divide Gaul into 'regions' and systematically invade, conquer and pacify the populous under Roman rule through domination and intimidation, stopping only at the Rhine River out of fear and respect for the power and tenacity of those inhabitants of the area called Germania. The Gallic War consisted of many chapters—overlapping and colliding, that saw Caesar advancing relentlessly, almost always to violent and heartbreaking endings.

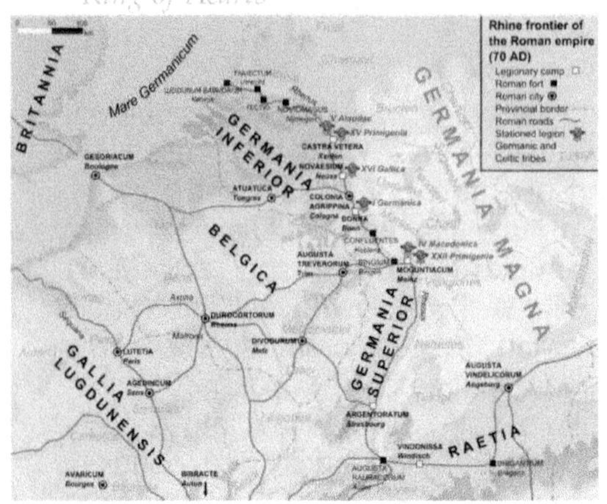

Caesar's strategy was to strengthen Rome's influence on the area by invading from the Southeast and eventually invading the area called Belgae that was home of eight different tribes located in the north and west in what is today, the country of Belgium. In doing so, Caesar not only identified but divided individual tribes, while attacking and destroying

Within the Belgic confederacy, one tribe was called the Menapii, whose neighbors to the north were the Bataves to the east whose territory was separated from the Menapii by the Scheldt River. To the south of the Menapii were the Nervians. The Atrebates were southwest while, near the coast, were the Morins. While all were proud people willing to fight and die for their land, the Menapii eventually represented the most persistent opponents of Caesar's conquest of the entire area.

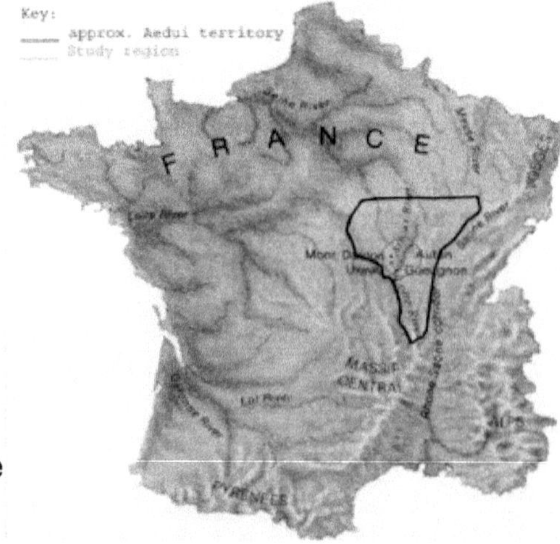

There primary four-year to be better   were three battles in the war that need outlined to understand

how Gaul fell and became unified under Roman rule. The battles began in 58 BC with the invasion of the area in what's now Switzerland where a confederation of five related Gallic tribes called the Helvetti lived on the Swiss Plateau. In July, 58 BC Caesar defeated the Helvetti in the Battle of Bibracte, when he sent his cavalry and four legions into battle with two in reserve.

The Romans easily threw back the Helvetti counter-attack by using javelins and spears. Their onslaught was so intense that many of the Helvetii warriors had spears sticking out of their shields and threw them aside to fight unencumbered, thereby making them more vulnerable to the superior swordsmanship of the Romans. The battle lasted for hours and thousands died on both sides and only ended when the Romans captured the Helvetic baggage train.

According to Caesar, 130,000 enemies escaped, of which 110,000 survived the retreat. Unable to pursue, Caesar rested for three days, before he resumed following the fleeing Helvetii. The Helvetti survivors managed to reach the territory of the Lingones. However, Caesar had pre-warned the Lingones not to assist the Helvetti thereby trapping the Helvetti, prompting them and their allies to surrender and come under Roman rule, at the expense of over 20,000 lives lost.

In September 58 BC, Germanic tribes called the Suebi, crossed the Rhine River, seeking a home in Gaul where they were met by six of Caesar's Roman Legions and were soundly defeated in the Battle of Vosges, also referred to as the Battle of Vesontio, as another segment of what had been an independent nation, came under the auspices of Roman law.

The Roman pressure continued in 57 BC as rumors arose that the Belgae tribes were forming a union to thwart possible Roman interference in their affairs. The union included the Bellovaci, Suessiones, Nervii, Atrebates, Ambioa, Bellovaci, Suessiones, Ambiani, Morini, Caleti, Veliocasses, Viromanduci, Condrusi, Eburones, Caeroesi, Paemani and Me

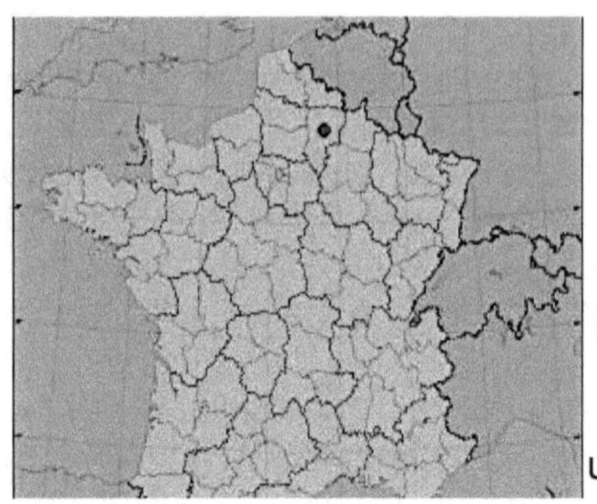

In Spring, 57 BC, Caesar increased the size of his army to eight legions totaling 40,000 men, where it's strength would remain until 54 BC. With that increase, Caesar sent one legion into the territory of the Nantuates, Seduni and Veragri while Caesar's army moved north to battle the Belgic army near Bibrax in the territory of the Remi. Shortly thereafter Caesar moved further north against the Nervii and Aduatuci. His legionnaires were instructed to kill, capture and destroy anything in their way to show the wrath of Rome and succeeded by defeating the forces of the Belgae in the Battle of Axona in May.

Dismayed by the attack and their consequent inability to either take the camp by storm or blockade the Romans from crossing the river, the Belgic forces withdrew and immediately retreated, returning to their home territories where they felt they might better be able to engage Caesar's invading army.

In July Caesar was informed that the Belgae were amassing on the far side of the River Sabis, which today is called the Scheldt River. The Nervii persuaded both the Atrebates and the Veromandui to support them as the battle commenced. Unfortunately for the Belgae, the Aduatuci who did not arrive in time to take part in the battle.

The Nervii intended to use a military tactic called force concentration which remains the practice today, concentrating a military force in one specific area. This created overwhelming pressure against a portion of the enemy and did so to the point that the disparity between the two forces alone acted as a multiplier in favor of the concentrated forces.

sAs the battle ensued, four Roman legions pushed their opponents back while the front and left sides of their camp were left undefended, thereby creating a gap in the Roman line. A compact column of Nervii, rushed through the opening. However, part of Roman column turned to encircle the Nervii as the remainder of the Nervii forces continued to attack the higher part of the camp.

At this point in the battle, it's clear that Caesar's opposition had little hope of survival, being pushed closer and closer into a dense pack surrounded by Caesar's men. Using slings, javelins and archers, the Romans unleashed a barrage of missiles at the closely packed Nervii that rained death and destruction upon the surrounded soldiers with such intensity that the last of the Nervii attempted to catch the Roman javelins and throw them back.

Caesar's report back to Rome spoke of an inspiring image of the last of the Nervii standing atop a mound of corpses of their own warriors, shouting in defiance, fighting till their last breath and went on to say that the Nervii had outstanding courage, for they launched a surprise attack, crossed a river, climbed its banks and did so with a fighting spirit. Perhaps when one is fighting for your land, your family and your life, it's not bravery that motivates but hope – hope that you will endeavor to see another day – hope that your family is safe – hope that your dreams of nothing more than living in peace will come true – when in reality, all around you is death, mortifying in its finality.

The Nervii elders, described by Caesar as 'senators', came out of hiding and surrendered. They said their council had been reduced from 600 men to three and that, of 60,000 fighting men, where barely 500 were left. Imagine 59,000 dead in one battle! Imagine the loss, the tears, the sadness, the emptiness! There's no way to know if any of them were from Menapii. Caesar gave no indication of his own casualties and so there's no mention of those left behind without father, brother and son, so that the scheme of three could continue its relentless journey.

The retreated Aduatuci turned as soon as they heard about the defeat and were subsequently defeated by Caesar with 53,000 men sold into slavery. The consequence of one battle, was the fact that the Veneti, Unelli, Osismii, Curiosolitae, Sesuvii, Aulerci and Rhedones were all brought under Roman control, thereby allowing Caesar and his men to move ever-closer to the Menapii.

In September 57 BC, the siege and capture of Aduatuca took place, which today is in the city of Tongeren, Belgium. Following his successful campaign against the Belgae, Caesar set out for Illyricum. However, once he departed, war flared up again, triggered by the Seventh Legion sending scavenging parties into the territories of the Cariosvelites and Esubii. The Veneti revolted against this infringement with the neighboring tribes rapidly following their lead, including the Ambiliati, Diablintes, Lexovii, Morini, Namniti, Nannetes, Osismii and the Menapii.

In 56 BC, the Veneti sent for auxiliaries from their cousins in Britain. Upon hearing this, Caesar rushed back to northern Gaul and the North Sea, where a fleet was being prepared for him at the mouth of River Loire. Initially, the Veneti and their allies were well prepared, having fortified their towns, stocking them with food, while gathering as many ships as possible for their armada. Knowing that the overland passes were cut off by estuaries and a seaward approach was difficult for their opponents, the Veneti planned to fight the Romans using their powerful navy in the shallows of the Loire River.

The land campaign by the Romans was protracted and when Veneti strongholds were threatened the populous was evacuated by sea, forcing the Romans to begin again. Eventually the Veneti fleet was cornered and defeated in the Battle of Quiberon Bay on the west coast of France. After the defeat of their navy, the Veneti strongholds were stormed and much of the Veneti population was either captured, enslaved or butchered, thereby dismantling the confederation. Roman rule was firmly stamped upon the region in all areas south of the Rhine River, except for that of the Menapii and Morini, who both refused to succumb to Roman domination. Caesar wasn't done! Against Roman counsel, he built bridges across the Rhine River and crossed the English Channel into Britain causing Pompey and Crassus to turn against him and complicate an already strained relationship.

Sensing achievement in conquering Gaul, Caesar looked south and directed his arm to cross the Rubicon River and invaded Italy, thereby triggering what was either called Caesar's Civil War or the Great Roman Civil War that began as a series of political and military confrontations between Caesar and Pompey with battles fought in Italy, Illyria, Greece, Egypt, Africa, and Hispania. This change in focus, resulted in the end of the Gallic War and the demise of literally all tribes on Western Europe except the Menapii who never surrendered, nor suffered the consequences of Roman defeat. Perhaps it was the Menapii's location. Perhaps, their ability to do battle. Perhaps, it was Caesar's change of focus to Italy that saved the

Menapii and its people from the consequence of Roman conquest. The Menapii eventually sued for peace and became citizens of Rome.

Mike folded the paper and slid it back in the glove box as I recapped. "Mike, to me the incredible fact that so many people died and how their death must have affected those they left behind is almost incomprehensible. The times were tough enough without war and yet to learn about the thousands of people being killed simply for defending the right to live is almost beyond comprehension."

Chapter 17 – Breaking Down the Barriers

I paused for a moment, looked at Mike and asked…"Do you mind if I talk about religion?"

Mike looked at me as his smile evaporated and expressed, "Will, religion is nothing more than man's concept of their relationship with God as it outlines our relationship with others. It's usually defined as a social-cultural system of morals, beliefs, worldviews and ethics that are sanctified by places, prophecies and organizations that confirm the deductions of those who created the doctrine's conclusions. While humans have and will continue to 'discover' the secrets of the universe, there has been and will always be one thing they can't explain."

"What's that?" I asked. "Death." Mike replied. "Death?"

"Not just in the physical sense, where death is defined as the irreversible cessation of all biological functions that sustain an organism but the consequence of death concerning one's overall existence. This is what really lies at the core of all religions. If you boil religion down, mortality has to do with the belief by humans that there's an existence after the cessation of the biological functions where the consequence of how we live on earth will determine how and where we're going to end up when we perish. You have to realize that, for millennia, humans had no perception of another form of existence and then, as they advanced, they became more spiritual as you noted when you talked about the items buried with individuals to take to the nether land."

I'd never thought of life, death or religion in that manner and Mike's brief answer was simply profound as I offered, "Go on."

"I can't prove there's a God. All I can do is share experiences that outline why I believe there must be more to life than what we have 'down here'. Thomas Kuhn's book, *'The Structure of Scientific Revolution'*, points out that all humans have a really difficult time dealing with infinity and the universe due to its complexity and profound vastness. What humans do is reduce existence down into smaller segments to the point that we develop theories, structures and opinions of the world that Kuhn calls paradigms or, 'universally recognized scientific achievements'.

'These achievements create problems and then a community of practitioners develop hypothesis and solutions from their basic knowledge at that time.' Such things as a flat world or the earth being the center of the universe were all paradigms that now seem quite quaint. However, when people were burned at the stake for believing in something that wasn't a popular belief, it became quite serious, especially to them."

Mike added. "There were fourteen people who actually began the movement in the name of Christ. It's really important to realize that Jesus wasn't trying to start a religion. His goal was to spread the gospel through the initiation in the belief of one God and the personification of four critical human characteristics…humility, generosity, compassion and forgiveness."

"John the Baptist actually started the entire movement as a Jewish prophet known in Christianity as the forerunner of Jesus who preached about God's Final Judgment and baptized repentant followers in preparation for it amongst whom one of those he baptized was Jesus."

"People have to realize that the power of the time was based on what the Romans believed. It certainly wasn't one God or the four pillars of life, where the consequence of disobedience was death…normally by some form of brutal method that not only killed a person but made a spectacle of their pain and suffering to their end."

"What about today?" I asked.

Mike simply shook his head and garnered a forlorn look. "Anytime you have potential authority, you have people who want to change the rules to make certain they retain the power. We call it politics but it affects virtually any and all human structures…business, government education and religion."

I felt I needed to get off the subject and so I tried to switch back to the Terrill family history but Mike continued on. "The Bible differs from most religions in that there was an absence of an initial state as outlined in the Book of Genesis. Christians believe that we will lie in waiting for the return of Christ. Muslims believe that if you have lived by the faith, you'll go to heaven. The Jewish faith does not believe in the afterlife while Hindu's feel that you'll be reincarnated over and over and over until you lead a good life and that you will be finally freed to go to heaven. Buddha taught that you are reincarnated and are basically good and that it's your errors in life that determine if you need to have a do over."

"What's remarkable is that all the religions seem to teach those same four basic tenants...humility, generosity, compassion and forgiveness, as personified through their apostles...Jesus, Moses, Mohammed, Buddha or whomever. In expanding beyond the 'big five' we see that all other religions follow the same criteria and that death can be compensated for through leading a life that follows the rules of that religion. What's so incredibly profound is how much of our world has come about because of religion, art, music, and architecture. What's also so incredibly profound is how much pain and suffering have come about because of man's self-ordained concepts regarding what they believe is right and wrong, good and bad and the ways to get to heaven."

Mike was deep in thought and I was mesmerized by what he was saying as he continued. "What I learned is that all religions are formalized interpretations laid down by people. There's no direct communication with some form of omnipotent being! Regardless of the faith, almost all religions have as their goal the creation of conscience that teach the consequence of not abiding by the four precepts. Christians, Jews and Muslims have rules about things you should not do such as the Ten Commandments, 'Though shall not covet thy neighbor's wife' while many eastern religions focus on things you should do. In the end, religions were created by humans to interpret how they should interact with other humans and what happens when a person doesn't act that way. In other words... creating a conscience."

Mike stared down at the ground in contemplation and then into my eyes and added. "We've both experienced the physical and mental selves. Yet, to me neither has meaning without the spiritual self. To some, the word spiritual immediately conjures up a vision of religion. If so, which religion? In the troubled history of mankind, more people have unwillingly died simply because they had a different religious concept than for almost any other reason."

"To me, spirituality is not about religion but about our concept of good and bad, right and wrong, proper and improper. Religion is the format by which these elements are formalized but each religion has at its core a fundamental belief that permeates into a series of premises about how we should act towards each other and towards the world in which we live. Religions then summarize the consequences of our thoughts and actions and then, in every religion, there is a personification of those actions."

"While going to church, temple, mosque or any other physical entity serves as a reinforcement of our basic needs, it's really what happens in our daily lives that fulfill that profound need of understanding good and bad, right and wrong, so that we establish a code of conduct and have the ability to properly function within that realm. Mankind inherently knows what it should be doing. It does this to the point that what's right is what makes a person happy but does not impinge upon the happiness and overall wellbeing of other souls. What's wrong is what either makes us unhappy or transcends to other beings...both human and non-human, in such a manner as to make them unhappy."

Mike looked at me and then stared out at the horizon and continued. "While we have the Ten Commandments as a general guideline, you can never forget that these were written by a group of men who had their own perception of good and bad, who then determined the consequence of each. Any time you have men dictating morality, there's room for error and dispute and there's no scholarly consensus over what precisely constitutes a religion. The biggest disappointment for me as a pastor was the irrational attitude some people had that I was too sanctimonious...too uptight... too... too religious to be normal. My goal was to help people, not cure them! Not condemn them and certainly not judge them!"

"I got into the profession because it was a way for me to take my compassion for others and structure it. I know and accept that the problem with power is corruption, whether it's financial, political or religious. I'd attend church meetings and see all the ass-kissing and realize that religion was just like every other organization, you had those who coveted power and prestige and those who had it and how they did everything they could to either get or keep it and that wasn't for me."

"I had offers of larger congregations. I had offers of more money. I had offers of greater authority but that's not why I got in the game. We stayed in Mineral Point because I was too small, too insignificant and too independent to matter and people left me alone to do what I wanted and how I wanted to do it and that gave me the one thing those others never got and that's satisfaction."

"Being a preacher is NOT an easy job. Between what's expected of you socially, morally, ethically along with the politics within the congregation, it's hard to maintain your own persona, then throw in all the ditties and problems you hear about and it's no wonder why so many ministers have issues themselves. When Ginny and I started dating, I asked her if she could accept the fact that there would be three men in her life and not one? She asked me what I meant and I replied…the public me, the private me and God. The public me had to carry on in a certain way that didn't always coincide with the private me. When there was a dichotomy, Ginny needed to understand that, like an actor, I needed to play my role. She also needed to accept that I have a profound belief in God and that the belief in Him would affect both the public and private person she was asked to live with."

"Did this mean she was always second?" I inquired, hoping for the answer I needed.

"Heaven's no!" Mike retorted. "To me, God's a supreme being and creator of all things who is with us at all time. He's omnipotent, omniscient, omnipresent, omnibenevolent and eternal. Man-made God is judgmental and done so for those who define Him for their own edification to create their concept of morality from whence good-and-bad, right-and-wrong were created with consequences for not following the rules that man has put in place. While many of the rules are just, there are others that have come and gone, been implemented and eliminated simply because they had the ability to create or sustain man's biggest flaw…greed…not only financial greed but power, prestige and dominance."

"You need to remember that when Carolus was a child there was no religion in Western Europe, just a bunch of beliefs based more on a lack of knowledge where most of the rituals were based on the fear of death. To understand the centrality of the role of the Church in western Christendom we have to go back to Roman times. The Christian Church had its origins dating back to the beginnings of the Roman empire, in the ministry, death and Christians believe, the resurrection of Jesus of Nazareth."

"Until the 4th century, religion was virtually an underground organization often persecuted at a local level, and sometimes it was the target of state-sponsored, empire-wide attempts to destroy it altogether. Under such circumstances, there could be no overall, tightly-knit organization. Each congregation formed its own cell, meeting in the house of one of its members and electing its own elders and pastors. The different congregations elected an overall leader, or bishop. Some bishops became more prominent than others, mostly depending on the size and importance of the cities in which they were based."

"Bishops of Antioch, Alexandria, Rome and Carthage came to be seen as having special prestige and authority in the debates of the Church and became known as the 'patriarchs' which comes from the Greek word for 'fathers' of the Church."

"The questions of right and wrong constituted continuous debates over the centuries as church leaders hammered out what they believed was permissible. Not what was necessary to believe or not believed. These debates took place in councils which occurred from time to time. Also, the bishops frequently corresponded with one another and, out of all this discussion came the idea of what the "orthodox" beliefs of the Church were."

"The conversion of the emperor Constantine to Christianity, resulted in the Church no longer fearing persecution. Quite the reverse, it began to enjoy imperial favor. Emperors and empresses, landowners and high officials showered the Church with treasure and land, and it became profoundly wealthy. In 380 the Church received a further boost when it was made the official religion of the Roman empire."

"Was everything the original church professed right? Is the world flat? Is the sun the center of the universe? They made mistakes... of which none has been greater than judging others for beliefs that differed from their own."

"What about you? What happens when someone has a different belief than yours?" I asked.

"In public, or in the realm of the church?" Mike asked. "Is there a difference?"

"There's a profound difference. In public, I simply brush it off as having a different background and therefore a different perspective on life than me. Within the church? That's where it always got a little dicey as we were a congregation who vowed to uphold the basic premises of our faith. Differences can be good as they allow for positive change. Differences can also be profoundly bad when they are intent on shifting the power base for the benefit of a few at the expense of others. There'd be times when I'd come back from a conference all lathered up about this or that and want to explode and Ginny would walk me up to our church and sit me down in one of the pews and ask me what I saw and felt. She had a way of calming the savage beast within me."

Mike looked at me and had an incredibly sincere expression on his face I'd ever seen as he continued. "What kept me going when things were bad was my belief that, if organized religion can be structured in such a way that it brings out the worst in human nature, it can also be organized in such a way that it brings out the best. Even with all its faults, religion can provide a space for us to face evil head- on. It's a space in which we not only curse the darkness but light a candle, following the example of the One who faced the darkness himself and did not run away from it but overcame it by the offering of his life."

'Holy shit!' I thought. This guy was more like me than I could have ever imagined. Did it mean I could let my guard down or would the cloak always be there? I wanted…make that, yearned for a friend...an equal… devoid of an ever-present definition where I didn't need to measure each word as if it in some way offend him by what I thought, said or construed.

A broad smile crossed my face as I realized that the man who sat across from me, truly offered someone to share so many things bottled up inside me. Perhaps, just perhaps God sent him to allow the pain and agony of my little secrets slowly be exposed so that the pieces of my life that had been sequestered for so very, very long could finally escape and I'd have internal and hopefully eternal peace.

Mike stared out the window and, with a softer tone to his voice simply said, "Through it all, one thing has remained somewhat constant and that's the Bible. While there have been additions and iterations, it was and remains, a collection of 66 books written by around 40 different authors over a period of 1600 years. While those in power either politically or religiously, took it upon themselves to slant the Bible one way of another, even with all the editing, the main message is still the kingdom of God."

"Mankind has this aggrandizing precept that he knows everything. In the end, we really know so little. Ask someone to define the universe and they can't. Yet, what we perceive as the universe could actually only be a spec in the megaverse. As an example, what happens if we find a black hole that opens up into another one of our limited universes? In the end, it all had to start somewhere and then have it end and that's where God comes in. For all mankind, we've worried about death. Generation after generation that's mystified humanity until we got to the point that we had to define it, modify it and quantify it to fit our perception of forever. Along comes a guy named Jesus…an incredible person…an individual said to be God's son. Who knows? Was He? Is He? Or is He simply one of the great prophets who all taught and personified those same four great things…humility, generosity, compassion and forgiveness?""By personifying those traits and then having Jesus die on the cross, mankind created a reference standard…something to look up to, something to revere, something to give us hope that there's more than nothing after death."

Mike looked at me and I could feel the sincerity in his heart as he concluded. "Who knows? No one! Yet, those of us who believe in Christ do so simply because he stands for what's good and what we need to have in our lives that will allow us to accomplish the one thing we all seek and that's happiness."

WOW!

I'd been taught never to talk about politics, religion or money. Mike brought up religion and I wanted to add my two-cents worth about politics and added. "I think American government is structured a lot like the Catholic church. The President is the Pope, the Senators are the Cardinals, the Congressmen represent the Bishops and the Priests your local authorities. Sadly, Americans are losing faith in the government where they hope for thing to be better and then find out that campaign promises are rarely kept to allow someone to either gain or retain power, authority and the perks that come with both. They both have a lot of great people trying to make things better."

"In government, a lot of people are upset by all the laws and regulations. However, many of them have been implemented for two reasons… to keep those in power, powerful and to respond to someone or something that has violated the sanctity of trust in others by cutting corners, cheating or sadly, to be so Narcissistic that all that matters to them are themselves. Tragically, no one trusts anyone anymore and we are seeing cracks in the dignity of democracy where the concept of we, has become the mantra of me. We no longer have heroes, only celebrities and politics has become nothing more than Hollywood for ugly people."

Mike let out a nervous laugh as if in agreement. We'd established the platform of what was wrong with America and yet both of us knew and admitted there wasn't much we could do about any of it.

Chapter 18 – The Menapii and the Gallic War

After my high school report and our discussion on religion and politics, I felt like Mike had asked me what time it was and I'd provided other instructions on how to build a watch. Needless to say, I was relieved when Mike looked at me and said, "Tell me about the Menapii."

I smiled and went into my dissertation. "The Menapii were the oldest traceable Celtic tribe in Europe. As early as 500 BC they were seafarers and traders who established colonies and settlements along the coasts of the British Isles. By 216 BC they had developed a major community in Ireland. In Belgae, the Menapii lived in the forests of the Scheldt River estuary on the North Sea. The soil was generally sandy and the landscape very flat, the area consisted of farms, fields, hedges, forests and islets in the swamps and marshland where the Scheldt River empties into the North Sea. The Menapiins of Caesar's time were farmers who subsisted on animal husbandry and agriculture. They lived in scattered hamlets or alone with few if any cities, which impeded Caesar's ability to extinguish them with typical Roman power and precision. When there was threat of violence, the Menapiins bonded with the neighboring tribes."

"It's the Year of the Consulship of Cotta and Torquatus, or year 689 Ab urbe condita, today identified as 65 BC. The Menapii and thusly Terrill story begins with the birth of the first recorded member of the tribe named Carolus de Menapii, where the last name 'de Menapii' simply means 'from the area of the Menapii'."

"In 58 BC, Carolus was just seven years old when Caesar's initial purge of the Menapii began. In that year Caesar became proconsul or provincial governor and led six legions, consisting of approximately 30,000 members of the Roman army, into Gaul, deploying auxiliaries as part of this army including slingers, archers and Celtic/Gallic cavalry."

Chapter 19 - The Spoils of War

Mike and I decided to go to Dubuque for a change and wound our way down Highway 51 through Belmont and Platteville. Being the historian, I reminded Mike that Belmont was founded in 1835 by land speculator John Atchison and was the original capital of the Wisconsin Territory. I pointed out that the name Belmont comes from the French for 'beautiful mountain', referencing the three hills within the village and asked Mike if he wanted to stop at the original territorial capitol building outside of town. He said he'd been there and done that and so I kept driving. I remember once driving through town and they were having a 'gas war' and it was eleven cents a gallon. I didn't need gas but at that price, who could pass it up? The old Buick took a little over three gallons and I gave the attendant a half-dollar and told him to keep the change.

We arrived at the Mississippi River and a slight smile crossed my face. The Eagle Point Bridge was still in use that scared the be- Jesus out of me as a kid. First, it was a very narrow two-lane automobile bridge that connected Iowa to Wisconsin. Second, it was a toll bridge that cost a dime each way that you paid on the Iowa side. Third, it was made of thick steel mesh and you could actually look right down through the bridge at the Mississippi River below. I don't know what scared me more, driving across the mesh, paying the dime or going into Iowa.

We drove around and went to the casino and played the slots. All of a sudden, the dime toll didn't seem that bad as Mike hit a big one and offered to buy lunch.

On the way home, Mike asked for more of the Terrill story and so I began as he offered. "Even in high school, you really knew your history stuff but what about your ancestors?"

"You have to remember, I'd been there but really didn't know what was going on. When I got back to 'now', I realized I needed to learn more and then figure out how I could help the Menapii survive."

"You went back?"

"Yes!" I looked at Mike and was hesitant and then began again. "Of greatest concern to me was Carolus and the fall of the Menapii under Roman rule. The Roman legal tradition made it clear that capture in war resulted in the loss of freedom. The sale of freshly seized enemy combatants and civilians was standard practice and stood as the engine that provided the economic growth and stability of Rome while providing the necessary funds needed to finance the legions."

"Slavery was an ever-present feature of the Roman world. Slaves served in households, agriculture, mines, the military, workshops, construction and many other services. Slavery was so imbedded in Roman culture that slaves became almost invisible and there was certainly no feeling of injustice in this situation on the part of the rulers. Inequality in power, freedom and control of resources was an accepted part of life and went right back to the mythology of Jupiter overthrowing Saturn."

"It was believed that the freedom of some was only possible because others were enslaved. Slavery was, therefore, not considered evil but a necessity by Roman citizens. The fact that slaves were taken from battle was simply a helpful justification and confirmation of Rome's belief in cultural superiority and the divine right to rule over others, exploiting those conquered for absolutely any purpose whatsoever."

"How massive was the infusion of slaves? Usually, wars resulted in tens of thousands of new slaves for Rome. As most of the wars were with Greece, naturally, the majority of Roman slaves were Greek with the first great influx happening when the Macedonians were defeated at the battle of Pydna in 168 BC Next, about 250,000 Carthaginians were enslaved in 146 BC when their city was destroyed. Another large influx occurred after the Mithridatic Wars in the 80s BC. However, none of these wars could break the record of Julius Caesar's conquest of Gaul where about 500,000 Gauls were enslaved."

I looked at Mike and continued "No one's sure how many slaves existed in the Roman Empire. As many as one-third of the population in Italy and one-fifth of the Roman empire were slaves at one time. In comparison, at its peak 18% of the population in the United State in 1790 were slaves. Like the States, this foundation of forced labor created the entire edifice of the Roman state. A rich man might own as many as 500 slaves and an emperor usually had more than 20,000 slaves at his disposal."

Mike simply shook his head in disbelief as I added. "When it came to Caesar and war, to support his army of 30,000 men took a great deal of money and the fastest way to generate cash was selling new slaves to wholesale dealers at the location of conquest. Fight them! Capture them! Sell them! Julius Caesar once sold the entire population of a conquered region of 53,000 people to slave dealers and did so on the spot. Bam! Your life was over as you knew it!"

"There was a regular system developed for the capture and sale of slaves and their relocation to Italy. Upon rounding up the combatants and their families, negotiations took place between the Roman victors and wholesale dealers regarding value and price of the captives. Here, the normal method of delineation was to segregate the captives into different classes based on both the wholesaler's perceived ability to sell the slaves and their anticipated market value."

"Terrible!" Mike stated.

Not wanting to offend Mike but also wanting to make certain he realized it was a significant component of the times, I offered. "Isn't it true that, without exception, biblical societies were slaveholding societies?" I'm not an expert on the Bible by any means but the Bible outlines a myriad of diverse cultures and in every one of them, people owned the rights to others."

Mike's forlorn look and slight nod, indicated he knew what I was referring to as he added "The Original King James Version of the Bible had two mentions of the word slave consisting of once in each Testament. The New King James Version has 46 occurrences."

"I'm not saying it was right but when all of society believes it's OK, how is it wrong? Today, we only think of those who were captured, put on a boat and brought to America to be sold like chattel but there were so many different ways that people were enslaved throughout antiquity. Beyond War Slaves, there were Blood Slaves who were born into it, Debt Slaves who owed so much money they literally 'sold' themselves as a form of payment, Marriage Slaves who married a slave, became chattel and finally the slave trade we know so much about. In the end, all but America, seemed to have some form of manumission where a slave could gain their freedom."

I took a deep breath and continued. "Adult soldiers were normally considered the highest value because of their ability to do manual labor while those with skills such as cooks, blacksmiths or doctors came next. Young males with a trade could fetch quite a sum of money simply because they not only had a trade but their youth meant they could last for quite a number of years where the average time in slavery was around 20 years. The next group in terms of value were pre-pubescent-to-teenage boys and girls, not only because of their probable length of tenure but as 'breeding stock' to expand the slave holder's family and for other purposes."

Mike and I stopped for a moment as I looked at the ground and then continued. "Anthropologists have noted that the average life expectancy in the first century BC was normally 30-40 years and children normally represented more than 50% of most tribes. At the end of a conflict, the ability to literally 'harvest' children and transport them to Rome was quite prevalent during Caesar's time. Carolus was only twelve when the war was over and was of prime age for abduction, enslavement and physical abuse and that had me worried." "Captured slaves would be transported to Rome in 'cage wagons' and were sold at public auction or sometimes in shops. Private sales also took place concerning the more valuable slaves. Slave dealing was overseen by the Roman fiscal officials called Quaestors. At auction, slaves stood naked on revolving stands with a plaque describing their origin, health, character, intelligence, education and other information pertinent to purchasers hung around their necks."

"Because the Romans wanted to know exactly what they were buying, the dealer was required to offer a warranty and take a slave back within six months if they had defects that were not manifest at the sale and make good the buyer's loss. Slaves that were sold with no guarantee were made to wear a cap at auction and then it was up to the buyer to make the decision concerning ability and durability."

"The price of a slave normally ranged between 2,000 sestertii ($4,400) for an unskilled male worker to 25,000 sestertii ($55,000) for a pretty girl. To put it in perspective, the average worker in Rome earned about 1,000 sestertii, or $2,200, per year and so the cheapest slave cost an average of two years wages and the most, literally a lifetime."

"Once purchased, a slave was a slave for life and could only earn their freedom if it was awarded by their owner or the slave was able to purchase it. To buy freedom, the slave had to raise the same sum of money their master had paid, which was virtually impossible. If a slave married and had offspring, the children automatically became slaves. Slave babies were sometimes killed by their parents rather than have them become slaves."

"How horrible!" Mike offered.

I continued. "A logical assumption is that slaves led poor lives simply because they were slaves. However, a good master looked after a good slave simply because an equal replacement might be hard to acquire – or too expensive. A good cook was highly prized, as entertaining was very important to Rome's elite as families tried to outdo each other when banquets were held."

Mike just shook his head in dismay as I continued. "Because of economies of scale and the fact that enslaved people were forced to work longer and harder than free Romans, slavery helped increase the economic expansion of Rome and support further development of the country by creating demand for greater supplies of agricultural products. Some Roman owners of large farms even switched from growing staple grains to high value crops, such as olives and grapes, or raising animals, which was not an option for small family farms. With this structure, the Roman Republic expanded its influence, while its political institutions proved both resilient and adaptable, thereby allowing it to incorporate the diverse populations throughout its area of influence."

"When Caesar was incurring the Menapii, I was profoundly afraid that Carolus could fall victim as he was the right age and had the right features to make him a valuable commodity. To this end, I explained the 'Roman way' to the elders who hid Carolus and others of his age, thereby protecting them from battle and possible demise. Thank God they did for both Carolus and the Terrill lineage or our family wouldn't exist today."

Chapter 20 - 32186

The first Iowa County Fair was held in 1851 in Dodgeville and moved to Mineral Point in 1856. I think I remember that! (Just joking but not by much). It's the highlight of the year for our little town, providing agricultural, educational and entertainment for everyone. While not a farmer myself, I don't think I've ever missed going. As a kid we went for the candy, rides from the tilt-a-whirl to the scrambler, snow cones and cotton candy. As a teenager, we went to meet girls. Whenever we went, we'd always make a day out of it.

Mike and I decided to go as I'd never missed and didn't plan to until I was their 'next door neighbor' at Graceland Cemetery. As we walked the midway I realized just how many people Mike knew who'd all stop and say "Hi," tell him they missed him in church or extend their condolences about Ginny.

Now I'm not much of a gambler. In fact, I couldn't remember the last time I bet anything more than what Mike and I played for which certainly wasn't that much. As we were walking down the midway we saw a crowd looking at this Winnebago Chieftain motor home. Now it was really swanky and I was wondering what in hell it was doing on the grounds as I thought it had to belong to some rich entertainer or something.

Instead, as we stopped, we saw a sign that said it had been donated to the Iowa County 4H by Clyde Downing and they had a picture of Clyde and Helen sitting outside the Winnebago that was taken before he passed away. It seems they were having a drawing to convert Clyde's gift into cash they could use to serve the 500 or so kids who belonged to the 4-H and FFA.

For a dollar you could tour the inside of the bus and there was a line. For ten bucks you could get the tour and a ticket for a chance to win the Chieftain. Mike and I agreed and took the ten-dollar tour. I think we did it more to make the donation than anything else as I'd never been inside one of those big busses in my life. To say the inside was neat was an understatement. It had fancy blue velour seats, a kitchen with a stove and microwave, bedroom, television and even a bathroom with a shower in it.

As we were about to exit the bus, I saw a sign in the window stating the vehicle had cost Clyde nearly $50,000 and only had 11,534 miles on it. Seems Clyde thought he and Helen would do some traveling and then she got sick and died and the bus only made it to the Southwest once or twice before he joined her.

With no kids Clyde willed it with the idea they could sell it and use the cash for something else. Well, I learned the market was glutted with lightly used motorhomes simply because so many people had dreams like Clyde that never came true and the best way to get the most for the bus was to make it someone else's dream through the raffle.

Now I never expected to win and thought my ten bucks was more of a donation than anything else, as they told me to write my name and phone number on the back. I almost didn't do it but thought 'What the heck' as they tore off the other half and handed it to me.

Mike and I finished looking at the cows, chickens, ducks, lambs and pigs and had corn dogs and lemonade for dinner before making our way back to Heaven's Waiting Room. I thought nothing of the money I felt I'd donated to the kids.

The night the fair ended they had a drawing and announced they'd earned $47,416 between the tour admissions and raffle and the winning number for the bus was 38126. Yup, the winner was one Will Terrill. They called and I almost fell off my chair. Jesus, Mary and Joseph! I'd won a Winnebago Chieftain M-27RC motor home. 'What in hell was I going to do with it?'

They told me, I had to get the bus out off fairgrounds the next morning. Jesus! Next, some reporter from the Democrat Tribune wanted to take my picture and run some kind of story in the paper. I thought, 'What the hell, perhaps it would help the kids.'

Next morning, Mike drove me out to the fairgrounds and was laughing his butt off as he watched this old codger try to back the bus out of its parking place at the roaring speed about ten feet per hour. The roustabouts taking down the tilt-a-whirl and scrambler just stood and watched and got their laughs as I slowly and I mean slooooowly edged the bus in-and-out, in-and-out of what had been the midway, all the time thinking, 'Couldn't they have another drawing?'

The three-mile ride from the fairgrounds to Heaven's Waiting Room took over a half hour with a whole caravan of pissed off people on Highway 51 trying to pass me on their way to wherever. We finally pulled into the parking lot and all the 'blue hairs' as Mike and I began calling the ladies, wanted to see my latest contraption and go for a ride. No way Jose! I was nervous enough with just me inside, let alone a flock of cackling old hens.

I let the fellow inmates take the tour and called my cousin Tom out at the farm and told him the good news. He said he'd already heard, as had the whole town. I asked if I could keep the damn thing out in the equipment shed and offered to let him use it instead of me paying him rent. I knew it would be a cold day in hell before he'd ever go on a trip. Dairy farmers have around 150 mistresses that come a mooing twice a day and a motor vacation just isn't in the cards or would that be curds…tee hee.

All the excitement settled down and just when things were getting back to normal, I almost pooped my pants when I received a letter from the Internal Revenue Service. It seemed I had to pay taxes on my winnings. Not a small amount of taxes but a whole hell of a lot! Here's what the IRS wrote to me.

Dear Mr. Terrill

We have been informed that you recently participated in a fund-raising raffle and are the winner of a 1989 Winnebago Chieftain motor home. In general, a raffle is considered a form of lottery. As such, a raffle generally refers to a method for the distribution of prizes among persons who have paid for a chance to win such prizes, usually determined by the numbers, or symbols, on tickets drawn. Generally, an exempt organization must report raffle prizes if (a) the amount paid reduced, at the exempt organization's option, by the wager (the amount a person paid for the chance to win a prize), is $600 or more; and (b) the payout is at least 300 times the amount of the wager. The organization uses Form W-2G for this report and has dutifully submitted it.

A person receiving gambling winnings must furnish the exempt organization a statement on Form 5754 made under penalties of perjury stating his or her identity and the identity of any others entitled to the winnings (and their shares of the winnings.) When the person receiving winnings is not the actual winner, or is a member of a group of two or more winners on a single ticket, the recipient must furnish the exempt organization information listed on Form 5754, Statement by Person(s)

Receiving Gambling Winnings, and the organization must file Forms W-2G based on that information. The organization must keep Form 5754 for four years and make it available for IRS inspection. (See the specific instructions for Form 5754 for more information.)

The exempt organization must file Forms W-2G with the IRS by the last day of February of the year after the year of the raffle. Use Form 1096, Annual Summary and Transmittal of U.S. Information Returns, to transmit Forms W-2G to the IRS. The organization must also issue Forms W- 2G to prize recipients by January 31 of the year after the year of the raffle. Pursuant with the above IRS rules and regulations, we have determined that the fair market value of the prize you have won is 34,363. In so doing, you are responsible for payment of said value and need to include this amount on your 1990 income tax report. '

Sincerely.

James E. Jones
James Jones Auditor
Internal Revenue Department

I realized my ten-dollar 'winning' was going to cost me over $10,000 in taxes...shit! Then I needed to get a license, registration and insurance. Clyde and I went to high school together and I never really liked him. Now, I really disliked the SOB as I imagined him looking down from heaven and having the last laugh.

Chapter 21 - Road Trip #1

Being a stubborn old fool who could still rub two nickels together and come out with a quarter, there was no way I was going to pay all that money to the IRS and not get something for it. Instead, I started going out to the farm and taking the bus for drives until I got comfortable with its size and felt safe having a passenger with me.

Now, if you've never been to Wisconsin, you really don't know what you're missing. Between the scenery, attractions and the people, there's always some place to go, something to do and people to meet. I went to Keith Mitchell's City Service gas station and got a free map of the State and got a piece of cork at the Ben Franklin to put behind it. My idea was playing a game of darts where the winner of our Wednesday competition would throw a dart and wherever it landed is where we'd go. I mean, other than gas and probably having to pay camping fees, we had all the luxuries we had at home and could not only see things we'd never seen but escape the blue hairs as well.

We were scheduled to get together for our weekly card, chess or checkers game and I got into the quiet room early and set up my map by hanging it on the wall. Mike walked in and frowned asking, "What's the map for?"

"Well, I've got this great big bus that can easily sleep two that has a TV, kitchen and bathroom with a shower that's just sitting out at the farm with the pigeons pooping all over the roof. I thought we could 'play' darts after cards and the winner of the card game could throw a dart and wherever it lands in the state, we'd take the bus and go."

"You serious?"

"Heh, I've paid the IRS, got the license and registration renewed and have insurance. In addition, for the past few weeks I've gone out and been driving the bus and learning that it's really not that hard to get used to.

A smile crossed Mike's face as he realized I was serious. We played chess and as usual, I lost. However, instead of having to get the soft drinks, Mike got to toss the dart. His first shot landed in Lake Michigan.

"Uh…I don't think that would be a great place for our first road trip," I sarcastically offered.

Mike looked at me and whispered. "Smart ass!" "OK, come on, toss again."

Mike took aim and tossed his next dart having it land way up in 'heh der' which is what we all call northern Wisconsin because of the way the folks talk up der in Bayfield County.

"OK, I'll do some research and tell you what we can do and see. I'll fill you in at breakfast if you want."

Here's what I read compliments of the State of Wisconsin tourist bureau. For a small-town experience that's rich in history, tourists should visit Bayfield. Home to only a few hundred people, Bayfield is the main gateway to the Apostle Islands National Lakeshore. There are two museums, Bayfield Maritime Museum and Bayfield Heritage Museum, and a few art galleries but the town's biggest attraction is the yearly Apple Fest in October.

"The Apostle Islands draws in hikers, water sport enthusiasts and campers. The islands are home to Meyers Beach, Bayfield Headquarters, the Little Sand Bay Visitor Center and Fishery, and the Northern Great Lakes Visitor Center. Visitors should be aware that the only way to the islands is by water."

A lot of people choose to access the islands by kayak but there is a ferry that can take cars to Madeline Island. Stockton Island is home to one of the greatest concentrations of black bears in North America, though bears may be found on just about any of the Apostle Islands. While we're up there we can go to Pattison State Park, home to Big Manitou Falls, a 165-foot waterfall and the tallest in the state. Native Americans were said to believe they could hear the Great Spirit's voice from the falls. The park also has Little Manitou Falls, which is 31-feet high and there's a state park with campsites where we can hook up the bus.

Mike was like a kid waiting for Christmas. We were about to take the first of what would be several road trips simply because the codgers realized there was more to life than Mineral Point and Heaven's Waiting Room. He asked, "What do I need to bring?"

"Well, you might want to bring some ear plugs as me, the verbose one, will try to keep filling your head with history and you won't need to worry about bears at night as I'm certain my snoring will keep them all away."

Mike asked if there was any storage space on the bus and I told him that the M27RC not only had closets but was built a little higher so that there was a huge storage compartment underneath. Little did I know that my best friend had a surprise for me.

We set the calendar to make sure we made it to Bayfield in time for Apple Fest and figured out what we'd need for food and libation as well as cards, chess and the cribbage board. As the day approached, Mike said he had a small present and I was almost floored when we met in the parking lot and he presented two Honda 50 motor scooters that were small enough to slide into the side compartments.

"You didn't have to do that," I offered.

"Gee, let me see, you get a $50,000 motor home and I provide two motor scooters. Who do you think go the better end of the deal?"

"But I only paid ten bucks for the motor home." "Plus taxes, license and insurance," Mike countered.

Mike's reasoning was that with the bus being over twenty-eight feet long, the last thing we'd want to do was drive everywhere. Every time you moved the bus, you needed to re-set the levelers, even though Clyde had bought the deluxe version with all the bells and whistles, including Air Sensiride that would automatically level the bus, when you parked it.

Chapter 22 - Going to War

The day came and it was time for our first road trip. I really don't know who was more excited, Mike or me. We began the drive and it was then that we both realized how far it was. This wasn't like driving to the Dells. It was 383 miles and would take six hours. Wow! At least it would give me time to share a little more…make that a lot more…of the Terrill history as we rolled through central Wisconsin. I waited until the newness of the ride wore off and we'd just crossed the Wisconsin River when Mike stated, "In high school, you paralleled the fall of Rome with what's happening to American society today, and even then it shows you really knew your stuff".

I looked at Mike with a smile and added, "That's because I was there."

Another look of disbelief, "What?" Mike added incredulously.

"Yes, I had two weeks to write the paper and decided to see if I could go back in time again, as I quickly saw that the only way I could save the Terrill family was to inform them of the Roman danger and teach them how to fight."

"So you went back?"

"Yup! After school, I rode my bike out to the farm and went into the woods and thought about all that had happened, while concluding the key had to be the buck. I went to the springs and he was there. He looked at me, strode into the bog and I followed. Once again, there was a spot filled with fog and I walked into it. While it had only been three days in my life, it had been four years in Menapii time. As I came to the camp of Anvardic the elder and his family, Carolus was now ten years old and I knew it was 55 BC."

"I was recognized, welcomed and sat with both Anvardic and Carolus and detailed all that had transpired and my observation of the might and determination of the Roman army. I noted that the only way to survive was to use a different method of battle than attacking the legions head-on."

"Anvardic listened and I believe was impressed by my wisdom to the point he suggested I meet with the council of elders and provide my opinions to them. Two days later, Anvardic, Carolus and I walked to a clearing and, as we neared the meeting spot, armed guards began appearing from all sides. Anvardic quietly spoke to a group of men and I was finally motioned to join them. The leader was a man by the name of Ambiorix, who looked at me with great disdain."

"'How could a young man possibly have enough knowledge to teach an entire nation how to do battle against the mighty Roman legions?' Ambiorix inquired."

"Anvardic spoke and told the leaders how I'd appeared from the fog with a new weapon, more powerful than anything he'd ever seen and I'd come from the future and knew many things that would help save many lives of the Menapii."

"After extensive discussion, it was finally agreed they should at least listen."

"I asked the council if they knew how to kill a snake. They looked at me as if I was an idiot and replied, 'You simply cut off its head.'"

"I then asked, 'Where is the venom of the snake located and they said, 'In the head.'"

"I then inquired what would happen if you cut the snake in two by slicing it in the middle or only took off the last few inches? They replied, 'The snake would still die.' I then replied! But you wouldn't have to worry about the venom, would you?"

"The counsel looked at me and wondered why I was talking about snakes but I caught Anvardic's nod of approval, with his slight smile, as we'd discussed a strategy unlike anything the Menapii had considered."

"Because I'd done my homework on Caesar and Roman tactical military strategy, I was able to outline what the Menapii were about to face regarding the Aces Triplex of archers, javelins and legions of well-trained, well-equipped swordsmen. The council sat with false bravado thinking they could over-run the Roman legions but I knew better. I then outlined how, in every Gallic battle, the Romans fought in a very structured way by using archers, javelins and legions in exactly the same manner and did so on open ground and surmised that the Menapii had no chance of defeating up to 30,000 Romans without major losses."

"With that, there was a lot of grumbling about my consideration of their ability to fight until they asked for my suggestion. I looked at them and outlined that their strengths were the Romans' weaknesses. Rome wanted to fight in open land while the Menapii lived in the forest. The Romans wanted to overcome the enemy with shear volume that was concentrated and do so at one time. The Menapii were dispersed over a relatively large geographic area that could not be coerced into one fighting unit. The Romans tactile strategy consisted of arrows first, then javelins and finally swords, all aimed at a concentrated enemy. By simply working in small bands that were dispersed throughout the region and periodically attacking the flanks of the Romans, fewer lives would be at risk and the advantages the Romans normally enjoyed would be neutralized."

Mike just shook his head and muttered, "Guerilla Warfare."

"Vietnam," I replied, as Mike agreed and I continued. "From our meeting, Ambiorix and the elders determined that my strategy was right. They could attack small groups of

Romans with small groups of warriors by enticing the legions away from their formal positions and, therefore, their standard methods of warfare."

"I explained that the keys to victory were enticement, surprise and division, supported by the use of traps with bows and arrows, as the first onslaught. I explained that each type of weapon had advantages and disadvantages which was why the Romans incorporated all three. I noted that arrows were superior to lancers as they could kill from a distance, lancers impeded swordsmen and legionnaires were there for hand-to-hand combat. I also noted that the soft underbelly of the Roman legion were its wagons as they contained food, tents and medical equipment. I asked the council how to stop a Roman legion and they shook their heads. I answered, simply stop the wagons and you'll stop the army."

"'How do you stop the wagons?' I inquired, to which the response was, 'Attack.'"

"I looked at the council and asked, 'What pulls the wagons'?"

"The council looked at each other and then at me and they had their answer, use their archers to put arrows into the lead horses. When there are no animals to pull the wagons, the wagons couldn't move unless they used legionnaires to slowly pull the wagons and legionnaires would then, not have their weapons. With a few arrows from archers, who then blended back into the woods, there would be little risk of lost Menapii lives but would still create the impediment of the Roman army."

"I looked at the council and continued. 'War is not about killing the body, it's about changing the mind. To remove the Roman confidence by making them constantly afraid, you will slow their advancement. When you slow the advances, you create larger targets and can then attack in small battles, which is totally contrary to how the Romans are taught to fight.'"

Mike simply shook his head, realizing I'd assisted in extending the existence of the Menapii and, therefore, the Terrill beginnings.

I continued by indicating it was critical that the Menapii warriors knew the land so they could attack and then disappear into the forest without being captured or killed.

"Ambiorix's opinion was seen to change and the gloom and doom that pervaded the council was transformed into one of positive anticipation as the elders began to see a slight glimmer of hope as the plan was established. I spoke of camouflage and how the Menapii needed to 'disappear' into the woods and showed what and how to create clothing and make-up to hide even the most obvious. I spoke of training their archers to learn to shoot arrows from trees and how to build traps that would kill or maim Roman legionnaires."

"We began developing a summary of the places where the Roman columns would be most susceptible, which consisted of narrow paths instead of broad fields. The idea was to cut the snake into small pieces."

"The final piece of the plan included not only taking the Roman weapons but their uniforms and armor, as well. When asked why this was important I outlined how the Romans would begin spreading their forces and sending soldiers to the crests of hills to confine the Menapii between two flanks. I summarized that with Roman uniforms and armor we would be able to fool the legions into thinking that Menapii warriors had been outflanked when, in fact, those in Roman armor could serve as support for the archers in the event the Romans attacked. In addition, those in Roman clothes would be able to initially get closer to the wagons without any suspicion. However, once the Romans realized what was happening the element of surprise would be lost but the question of whether the man in the uniform was actually a Roman soldier or a Menapii warrior would arise. Their goal must always be to always keep the Romans off guard and never allow them to become comfortable and, therefore, confident".

Mike shook his head in dismay as he knew what the results were as I continued. "The strategy was particularly effective as Roman soldiers would fall dead with arrows in their backs with no enemy for the legions to fight. Traps were set that would impale would-be invaders and either kill or maim the Romans to the point they'd began to lose the one advantage they'd carried with them and that was confidence."

I continued my explanation. "As I trained the Belgic warriors I instructed them that it was better to permanently handicap a Roman than to kill them. Dead soldiers are buried, handicapped require special attention that remove other soldiers to care for them. In so doing the Belgic became experts at removing eyes to make men blind and fingers so that the enemy could not hold a sword, throw a javelin or pull the string of a bow, thereby making them unable to fight."

"Over the next few weeks, plans were put in place and literally hundreds of booby traps were created that would impale or maim unsuspecting Roman legionnaires. Reports would come back of the havoc these were causing and how the Romans were in disarray. I knew this would be temporary and warned the council not to get over confident."

I continued. "The Menapii scouts reported on Roman troop movements and identified an opportunity to attack with maximum results and minimum risk in a narrow path between two areas of marsh that the legions would need to travel through. With so many men and equipment we also knew that hand-to-hand combat would not work. We believed that Roman scouts would scour the area before the legions arrived to ensure safety."

"I asked council where they obtained the fuel they used in their torches and they noted they were made from tree resin that was gathered similar to maple syrup, except resin would burn. The resin was then mixed with damp peat from the bogs not far from where we met. I told them to harvest as much peat as they could and make certain there was adequate resin mixed in. They noted the fire would actually burn hotter than wood if the peat was allowed to dry. I told them we didn't want it to burn. Instead we wanted to spread it along the wet, wooded narrows on both sides of path where the Romans would need to travel."

"At first, they thought I was crazy and then realized my plan, as buckets of peat mixed with resin were spread and then covered with grass and leaves along the sides of the paths that would be used by the Romans. We knew the Romans would send scouts who would be looking for archers, not piles of peat."

"The day came and so did the Romans. Their scouts surveyed the area both on the road and upon the hills. Little did they realize we had over 200 men hiding over the next hill with archers ready to send flaming arrows into the peat."

"As we watched the legion proceed, the signal was given and the archers lit their arrows and let them fly. Whoosh.

Whoosh. Whoosh. The flaming arrows landed in the peat and it began to quickly burn with flames twenty feet high. The Roman garrison was trapped as the dense smoke billowed around them and they could neither breathe nor see."

"As the flames shot up our archers pelted the area with hundreds of arrows on the concentrated Roman forces and attacked from the front and rear. After the first volley by our archers, our lancers and then swordsmen appeared simply slaughtering the blinded, coughing Romans as they attempted to escape the burning inferno. In the end, only twelve Menapii warriors were lost, while the Romans lost over 500 men with 150 more captured, representing one of Caesar's worst defeats of the entire Gallic war."

"There's a saying about winning battles and losing wars. While the Menapii won the battle, Caesar's reputation was threatened and the consequence was almost beyond comprehension in terms of overall brutality and decimation. After nearly two years of hit-and-run warfare, Caesar had seen enough and took the might of the Roman legions and used it to begin burning anything and everything in the forests, including the forests themselves. Gone would be the cover needed. Gone would be the food required. Gone would be the homes of those who remained loyal to the combatants and not to Rome."

"The reaction from the Menapii was to simply retreat further into the forest, where the land was damp and fires could not rage simply because the ground was too wet. The warriors continued their attacks while Rome lost over 7,000 men. As the Romans retreated the Menapii warriors harvested all the Roman weapons and armor to provide equipment for the growing participants of the battle."

"When the Roman senate learned that over 7,000 Roman soldiers had been killed they asked for justification from Caesar to which he complained that the Menapii were the only tribe in Gaul who never sent ambassadors to discuss terms of peace and sustained ties with Ambiorix. The senate voted and directed Caesar to send five legions against the Menapii with a renewed campaign of devastation."

"While our strategy temporarily worked in terms of extending freedom, the size and power of Rome was simply too great for the Menapii to overcome. The turning point was the loss of the Menapii navy, as the Romans captured or sank the

Menapiian's only exit from the onslaught. Then, as the war raged on, reality set in and the surviving Menapii realized further battles were futile and called for a truce."

"Like all politicians, Caesar reported to Rome he had defeated the Menapii. The real truth was the Menapii agreed to stop the guerilla attacks if the Romans agreed to cease all war-like actions including rape, pillaging and taking Menapii slaves. In so doing, the risk to Carolus and subsequently the Terrill lineage was reduced."

"In other words, by teaching the Menapii how to kill, you probably saved the lives of your ancestor?" Mike interjected, to which I affirmed an absolute, 'Yes,' as if to justify my own actions.

I stopped for a minute, took a drink and continued, not out of concern for the truth but because of Reverend Mike's occupation. After getting his permission to be a little 'frank' I continued, "The Romans were quite brutal in the treatment of captured leaders. In order to intimidate their former enemies, while providing a form of 'reward' for the victorious legionnaires, one of the opposing leaders would be brought to trial before counsel. If it was determined that the Romans needed to make an example the captured or defeated army would never forget, a form of dehumanizing punishment would be initiated."

I looked at Mike for a moment to ensure I should continue as he sat waiting for me. "As I noted, in Rome, masculinity was predominantly exemplified through dominance in all ways of life, particularly in sexual activity, where dominance was held in high regard. Contrarily, subservience from an emasculated man was considered a true indication of his subordination. Based on this and Caesar's need to make a statement, it was rumored that one captured Aduatuci leader would be humiliated in such fashion."

"Previously, when what was about to take place happened, a captured leader's teeth would be forcibly removed and he would be stripped of his clothes, forced to his knees and bound with his hands and feet behind a tree or post so that he could not fall to the ground. All surviving legionnaires would then be invited to have the captured leader satisfy them orally to the glee of their fellow infantrymen as witnessed by those who had been captured or detained."

"The captured leader would be warned that, should he fail to satisfy any and all legionnaires or expel what was expended, his throat would be cut and a replacement chosen to take his place. He was also informed that Rome would continue to do so until all the participants had their opportunity to be pleasured. If the leader satisfied all those who came before him, his life would be spared."

"A few days after the truce was signed, Caesar's legion took command of the area and nearly 50 legionnaires were standing in line to be serviced by Anvardic with Anvadic's former troops, along with the elderly Menapii men, women and children present to witness the act."

"While this alone was beyond anything I could conceive, I learned that upon completion, Anvardic would be raised up and two rocks would be used to crush his testicles, while his index fingers would be severed, thereby eliminating his ability to either use a sword or pull the string on a bow and arrow. In so doing, Anvardic would be emasculated, humiliated and crippled, only to be released to the cheers and jeers of the Roman soldiers. Needless to say, the humiliation and brutality of Rome was intended to leave a lasting impression on those in attendance, while serving the purpose of relieving the stress and tensions of battle for Caesar's men who, because of the terms of the truce, were not rewarded with any form of pillage they would normally acquire."

"As Anvardic was led to the post, I stepped from the crowd and faced the Roman Major and asked if the word of Caesar meant nothing. I asked how the Menapii, who had agreed to the truce, could trust any Roman, if they violated the peace agreement that day. I mentioned that I was aware that Caesar had lost over 7,000 men in battle and the leaders in Rome wanted to know why a group of 'infidels' had been so effective. I asked the Major if he thought there had been enough death as I asked him. 'Haven't enough Roman women lost their husbands? Haven't enough Roman children already lost their fathers? Haven't enough Roman mothers and fathers already lost their sons? If you despoil Anvardic, you will have broken the truce signed by Caesar himself and the war that just ended, will begin again.'"

"I looked the Major in the eye and flatly stated, 'If you feel that the pleasure of your legion is more important than their safety, proceed. However, if you've come in peace and prefer the honor, integrity and nobility of Rome, you will treat those who stand before you with the honor and dignity they deserve and we shall all live in peace.'"

"The Roman major looked at me as just a kid and did so with disdain. Instead of shirking, I stared back and said 'You've come to terms of peace and yet, where are the weapons of war that took so many Roman lives? Can't you see that the swords and arrows, lances and armor that were harvested from your fallen soldiers have been hidden and are ready in case the word of Caesar and Rome has no merit?'"

"It was then the Major realized the spectator sport he'd intended could result in the beginning of a new round of guerilla warfare and he personally would be blamed for the lost lives of Roman soldiers when all had been accomplished. It was then I saw him realize that the consequence would be his demise, to which he turned and ordered that Anvardic be released."

"I stuck out my hand to shake in agreement to which the Major simply walked away as I whispered one word, 'Peace.'"

"Wow!" Mike replied.

"Quite honestly, I was scared shitless but knew right then and there it needed to stop or I wouldn't be here today."

"So, there was peace?" Mike asked.

"Not really! The thirst for labor was too great to feed the hungry Roman beast. If a solider or non-soldier committed a crime, many times the punishment was to be sold into slavery where it was common for them to be publicly castrated, simply because the rationale was they couldn't propagate future Roman enemies. After the Menapii truce the Romans didn't try to turn the Menapii into Romans. In fact, for the most part, cities and regions were allowed to maintain their existing cultural and political institutions and few were captured and enslaved. The only major requirement Rome imposed was that the Menapii provide soldiers for military campaigns, where a military victory usually meant a share of the loot taken from the conquered while participating on the winning side offered incentives to Rome's new allies."

"Fortunately, because I'd tutored Carolus in numerous subjects beyond military tactics, as the adopted son of Anvardic, he was included with the elders at a very young age and both the Romans and Menapii considered him too valuable to become nothing more than fodder for the Roman warring machine."

"The Menapii were offered a level of Roman citizenship and elders were given full voting rights. However, because a person had to be physically present in Rome to vote, the extension of those rights didn't drastically alter the political situation. However, the offer of citizenship did help build a sense of shared identity and loyalty to Rome as life went on with Carolus becoming a teenager in a land where he was recognized as a Roman citizen."

I continued. "Although Rome had little interest in managing the daily affairs of the new territories, the area did adapt as Rome's influence spread. One way was through the construction of bridges and roads intended for the Roman military that made the movement of both soldiers and goods easier and faster. For the first time in history, there was a system of transportation that not only allowed for greater interaction but the concentration of people as villages and inns developed along the travel routes. At the same time, the Romans minted coins and introduced a small silver coin called a Denarius, which became the standard unit of currency for much of the Roman period, thereby, creating a somewhat universal form of value for which goods and services could be sold or bartered."

"The standardized currency facilitated trade across the growing Roman world. Coins could be exchanged for any goods or services and were easy to transport. Currency made it easier to relocate and direct resources and this, in turn, encouraged more economic interactions."

Mike looked at me and shook his head, realizing that one full semester of my 40 years of teaching was being condensed into one lecture as I continued. "Rome's economy was based on agriculture, which was incredibly labor intensive. As Rome fought more foreign wars, many small landholders were away serving in the military for longer periods. If they failed to return or their farms went bankrupt in their absence, wealthy Romans bought their land, creating larger farms, known as Latifundia."

Mike sat shaking his head as I continued. "Needless to say, the area of Roman dominance now covered almost all of what's now Western Europe except Germany and

Scandinavia. In order to manage the new territories, the Romans created formal provinces and appointed political officeholders to manage them. Given the distance between most provinces and Rome, these governors often had considerable power and flexibility in dealing with local issues. The Romans tried to create a balance between giving governors enough power to control their provinces, while still preventing them from becoming so powerful they could challenge Rome's authority. In terms of the Menapii, Caesar placed his ally, Commius in control of the area and it was agreed that the Menapii could live in peace, including Carolus."

I looked at Mike and admitted. "I'm both grateful and feel guilty for changing history. I believe I was able to reduce the number of deaths of the Menapii and also protect the person I've labelled Alpha One or Carolus de Menapii, the first in line of the Terrill genealogical sequence, and save him from death or subversion by the Romans."

We pulled into Bayfield, got some dinner, directions and made it to the campground and connected the electricity and septic system. Our 'rent' for the night was $10.00 per night. Mike offered to pay. I told him it was my treat for letting me share the story of our family. I never did figure out who got the better end of the deal.

Chapter 23 - Generations

I wanted to make sure Mike was truly interested and not just being polite and deduced he was actually engrossed by my recollections of our family and so I began again. While I went to The Forest several times, intent on going back in time, the buck didn't appear and I quickly realized that he was the key to my energy transfer to a previous period in time. By 'working backwards' I was able to determine the Terrill lineage from the time they came to America and created typed sheets that summarized the twelve generations following Carolus de Menapii, who represented those with whom I knew nothing other than when they were born, sometimes who they married and the name of their male child.

With the bus in place and our bellies full, I opened my tattered briefcase and handed Mike the typed list of the first 13 generations who covered 900 years. While they all had lives and I'm certain each one had stories to tell, I could only research and highlight those who changed the course of the history.

I noted to Mike. "There's no record of Carolus growth or childhood. However, in 44 BC, when he was twenty-one, Carolus fathered a son by the name of Menapius de Menapii with his wife whose name was never recorded. There is no further record of Carolus including the year or cause of his death, owning only to the fact that he was the first in what's now a lineage stretching over two thousand years. Following a patrilineal sequence, the following generation was the son of the person before them and you can deduce who was whom from father to son then to grandson and great grandson, etc. from 65BC until 347AD."

Mike examined my typed summary, looked at me and asked, "Where did this come from?"

I noted that time, patience and the Library of Congress allowed me to 'connect-the-dots' that took over forty years to accomplish. I also noted that the names were the male offspring of the generations that preceded them. While the death was that of the father simply because I felt this tied the two together in a genealogical chain.

Chapter 24 - Roman Rule

Bayfield and Lake Superior were everything they were made out to be. I mean, what beautiful places! The 'Codgers' as we began calling ourselves, as in 'old codgers', had a grand time in 'heh der' with a lot of sights, laughter and beer. Packing to go home wasn't what I'd call difficult. It meant unplugging the electrical outlet and septic system, pushing the leveling button and closing the door and starting the engine. My 'camping' sure was tough. Tee! Hee!

I'd intentionally laid off the history stuff for both Mike's and my relief during our visit. However, once we headed for home and were headed south on Highway 13 along the Lake Superior shore Mike asked what happened next and I knew it was time to begin again. I think he was really intrigued by my correlation of church and state.

I took a deep breath and offered. "During all this time, the Menapii were under the jurisdiction of Rome. While this was a constant, the variable was all the changes taking place over 1,000 miles away and we need to go back in history to examine the social, political and religious structure of Rome to understand the future of Europe from 800-1700."

"Rome's power hit its zenith in 200 A.D. when its breadth and might entailed over 50 million people while its power to control the political, social structure and religion of what's now Europe and the Mediterranean was absolute. In order to gain and retain that power, the Roman soldiers were required to raise Roman armies to defeat and defend the territory. To this end, the Roman Senate created a system called 'Manorialism', where large landowners were bequeathed lands for conscripting tenants to fight for Rome while consolidating their hold over both their lands and the laborers who worked them. In such conditions, small farmers and landless laborers exchanged their land and/or freedom and pledged their services in return for the protection of powerful landowners who had the military strength to defend them. In this way they were ensured permanent access to plots of land which they could work in return for the rendering of economic services to the lord who held that land."

"Rome had been dominant in Western Europe from 58 BC until the third century, when several major elements arose. Due to expansion the Roman Empire contained various ethnic, religious and language groups, all of whom thought they were the basis for Roman society. The Eastern Empire was vastly different from the West and consisted of the largest and wealthiest cities."

"At its height, the Roman Empire stretched from the Atlantic Ocean to the Euphrates River in the Middle East. However, its grandeur may have also been its downfall. With such a vast territory to govern, the Empire faced administrative and logistical nightmares. Even with their established road system, the Romans were unable to communicate quickly or effectively enough to manage their holdings. Rome struggled to marshal enough troops and resources to defend its frontiers from local rebellions and outside attacks and, by the Second Century, the Emperor Hadrian was forced to build his famous wall in Britain just to keep the enemy at bay. As more and more funds were funneled into the military, upkeep of the Empire and technological advancement slowed and Rome's civil infrastructure fell into disrepair."

"If Rome's sheer size made it difficult to govern, ineffective and inconsistent leadership only served to magnify the problem. Being the Roman emperor had always been a particularly precarious job. During the tumultuous Second and Third Centuries becoming emperor virtually resulted in a death sentence. Civil war thrust the Empire into chaos, and more than twenty men took the throne in the span of only 75 years, usually after the murder of their predecessor."

"The Praetorian Guard, who were the emperor's personal bodyguards, assassinated and installed new sovereigns at will and once even auctioned the position to the highest bidder. The political rot also extended to the Roman Senate, which failed to temper the excesses of the emperors due to its own widespread corruption and incompetence. As the situation worsened, civic pride waned and many Roman citizens lost trust in their leadership."

"Even as Rome was under attack from outside forces, it was also crumbling from within thanks to a severe financial crisis. Constant wars and overspending had significantly lightened imperial coffers. Oppressive taxation and inflation widened the gap between rich and poor. In the hope of avoiding the taxman, many members of the wealthy classes even fled to the countryside and set up independent fiefdoms. At the same time, the Empire was rocked by a labor deficit. Rome's economy depended on slaves to till its fields and work as craftsmen and its military might had traditionally provided a fresh influx of conquered peoples to put to work. When expansion ground to a halt in the Second Century, Rome's supply of slaves and other war treasures began to dry up. A further blow came in the Fifth Century when the Vandals claimed North Africa and began disrupting the Empire's trade by prowling the Mediterranean as pirates. With its economy faltering and its commercial and agricultural production in decline, the Empire began to lose its grip on Europe."

"While the inherent divisions were based on language, beliefs and ethnicity, it began to come to a head in 313 AD when Constantine issued the *Edict of Milan*, while personally accepting Christianity. It was enhanced in 323 when it became the official religion of the Roman Empire and then in 324, when the official capitol of the Roman Empire moved to Constantinople."

"The Menapii family continued to thrive during this tumultuous time with six generations 14-19 surviving." With that, I directed Mike to the next set of names in the binder as I kept on blabbing.

Mike simply shook his head thinking about the time it took to do all the research and the fact that I was able to trace the Terrill family back to before the birth of Christ. What really seemed to impress him was knowing not only who they were but, in many instances, when they married, when they died and how old they were at the time of their demise. We both could only surmise the cause of death of the younger ancestors. Was it murder, famine or disease? No one would ever know.

I needed to share a little bit more about Rome and so as we continued south on Highway 63 and made it past Hayward, I began. "The fate of Western Rome was partially sealed in the late Third Century, when the Emperor Diocletian divided the Empire into two halves— the Western Empire seated in the city of Milan, and the Eastern Empire in Byzantium, later known as Constantinople. The division made the Empire more easily governable in the short term but over time the two halves drifted apart. East and West failed to adequately work together to combat outside threats and the two often squabbled over resources and military aid. As the gulf widened, the largely Greek-speaking Eastern Empire grew in wealth while the Latin-speaking West descended into economic chaos. Most importantly, the strength of the Eastern Empire served to divert barbarian invasions to the West. Emperors like Constantine ensured that the city of Constantinople was fortified and well-guarded but Italy and the city of Rome, which only had symbolic value for many in the East, were left vulnerable."

"The split was most prevalent when it came to religion. Orthodoxy emerged as the primary religious faith, in the East when the citizens refused to acknowledge the Roman pope or pontiff as the supreme head of the Christian Church, vesting authority instead in the Patriarch of Constantinople who was appointed by the emperor. The West ascribed to the 'Latin' Church, which became the Roman Catholic Church, located in Rome. Christianity displaced the polytheistic Roman religion in 391. However, it still viewed the emperor as having divine status and shifted the focus away from the glory of the state and onto a sole deity. Meanwhile, popes and other Church leaders took an increased role in political affairs further complicating governance."

"The attacks on Rome partially stemmed from a mass migration caused by the Huns invasion of Europe in the late fourth century. When these Eurasian warriors rampaged through northern Europe, they drove many Germanic tribes to the borders of the Roman Empire. The Romans grudgingly allowed members of the Visigoth tribe to cross south of the Danube and into the safety of Roman territory but they treated them with extreme cruelty, even forcing the starving Goths to trade their children in exchange for dog meat. In brutalizing the Goths, the Romans created a dangerous enemy within their own borders. When the oppression became too much to bear, the Goths rose up in revolt and eventually routed a Roman army and killed the Eastern Emperor Valens during the Battle of Adrianople in 378."

"Division and invasion would have been enough to bring what had been the world's greatest nation to its knees. However, poor imperial leadership resulted in localized civil war between competing would-be emperors that contributed to the growing weakness making Western Rome more prone to barbarian incursions as Germanic tribes invaded Gaul, and eventually Italy during the Fifth Century. Roman western legions were often composed of barbarian recruits that had no loyalty to Rome, or shared common interests related to imperial goals. As civil government crumbled, the Catholic Church emerged as both the civil and spiritual leader under the auspices of local bishops whose seats coincided with the Roman civitates."

"The Romans weathered a Germanic uprising in the late Fourth Century. However, in 410 the Visigoth King, Alaric, successfully sacked Rome as the Empire spent the next several decades under constant threat before 'the Eternal City' was raided again in 455 by the Vandals.

I lamented for a moment and added. "What's amazing is that one of the greatest popes of all time, Pope Leo the First, was pope from the year 440 to 461, and reigned during the dissolution of the Roman Empire. Pope Leo is best known for writing the celebrated Tome of Leo, which established the doctrine that Christ's natures coexist which he outlined as **'Jesus Christ is God the Son. Jesus Christ is man. Jesus Christ is one person whose divine and human natures cannot be changed, divided, separated or mixed. Jesus Christ was resurrected bodily from the dead'** and his Incarnation reveals that human nature is restored to perfect unity with divinity."

"In one of the most interesting experiences of his life, Pope Leo met Attila the Hun in 452, and successfully convinced the barbarian raider to turn back from his invasion of Italy. Attila was, apparently, so impressed with Pope Leo that he willingly withdrew. After Rome was sacked anyway, by the Vandals in 455, Pope Leo assisted in rebuilding the city."

"One of his most enduring teachings can be found in his 'Christmas Day sermon' where he exhorted 'Christian, remember your dignity,' in which he articulated that fundamental dignity is common to all Christians, whether saint or sinner, and the duty to live up to that dignity lies in goodness, no matter who we are. Pope Leo wasn't interested in power for power's sake. He resolved disputes, and clarified the Church's teaching about the dual nature of Jesus Christ."

Finally, in 476 the Germanic leader, Odoacer, staged a revolt and deposed the Emperor Romulus Augustulus. From then on, no Roman emperor would ever rule from a post in Italy, leading many to cite 476 as the year the Western Roman Empire suffered its deathblow where the invasions and collapse of Roman central authority led to a decline in urban culture and standards of life. The net result was basically there was no basis for institutional trust, official currency or institutionalized system of protection and little in the way of secular culture such as had been known in the Roman period. This fragmentation of power ushered in a new wave of invasions of Northmen, Saracens and Magyars. Locals had to take responsibility for their defense and began to consider that what they defended was their own, while establishing the concept of 'spear won' property, where the conqueror claimed as his own personal property everything won in his name or that of the kingdom."

"Although missionaries like Patrick and Augustine made Christianity hugely successful in the British Isles, there was only one tribe in the whole of mainland Europe who were mainstream Christians until the Merovingian King Clovis 1 married Clotilde in 493 and converted to Catholicism in 496. With Clovis' protection, the Church grew in numbers and influence and became the most powerful institution in Europe, far beyond that of any ruler. While the advent of Christianity standardized religion and led to the development of the interaction between Church and State, it also planted the basic seeds for social structure within Medieval Europe that would affect that structure for nearly 1,000 years."

"Concurrently, Germanic rulers began dividing their kingdoms among their children which was an important variant on fragmentation. With this practice, sons were often unhappy with their share and fought or murdered each other. Division among king's sons meant that each had less to attract support that contributed to further fragmentation, where the key element consisted of individual and private agreements regarding armed forces that promoted increased violence by providing property in return for personal loyalty."

We stopped for coffee in a little town called Cumberland and stretched our legs and when we were leaving town, I began again. "While a lot of what happened to Rome can be blamed on ego, politics and greed, the Justinian Pandemic of 542-546, named after Justinian I, emperor of the Byzantine Empire, also played an important role. The epidemic originated in Ethiopia and spread to Pelusium, Egypt in 520. Located on Egypt's eastern boundary, the city was of immense strategic importance. It was both a departure point for expeditions to Asia and an entry point for foreign invaders attempting to conquer Egypt. During peacetime it was an important trading post and in the Graeco-Roman period it became one of Egypt's busiest ports, second only to Alexandria."

"The plague spread west to Alexandria and east to Gaza, Jerusalem and Antioch. From there, it was carried on ships to both sides of the Mediterranean, arriving on Constantinople in the autumn of 541 where it reached its peak in 542 with an estimated 5,000 deaths per day, wiping out one-third of the city's population."

"Victims were too numerous to be buried and were simply stacked in the city's churches and wall towers because of the Christian doctrine preventing their disposal by cremation. Over the next three years plague raged through Italy, southern France, the Rhine Valley, Iberia and then Denmark and Ireland. By the time it was done between Asia, Africa and Europe it killed nearly 100 million of the estimated 206 million people on earth or nearly one-half of all humanity. The disease permanently changed the political and social fabric of the Western world with food production severely disrupted as seeds for crops were consumed, resulting in an eight-year famine that followed."

"The only positive consequence of the Justinian Plague was a gradual change in the agrarian system to the three-field system of agricultural organization. In the former two-field system, half the land was sown to crop and half left fallow each season. In the three-field system only a third of the land lay fallow, thereby increasing productivity and the availability of grain."

In the West, Muslim attempts to conquer what's today Europe were repelled decisively such as at Tours in 732 by Charles Martel. The consequence was the cohesiveness of the Roman Empire was replaced by that of the Catholic Church which was forced to forge alliances with strong secular rulers. The net result, at least on one level, was the fate of both the Eastern Roman and Western Roman Empires who were directly linked to religion and the role of Christianity."

"In order to understand the social, political and religious structure of medieval Europe, we need to understand the effects of the New Testament of the Bible on society. Written from A.D. 33 to about A.D. 80, the Bible's twenty-seven books were written by nine authors whose works can be divided into Gospels and Epistles. In reading the Bible and then applying it to religious structure, the Church developed a pyramidical system of authority, consisting of God at the apex, followed by one elected Pope, who was supposed to follow in the footsteps of St. Peter and act as a moral role model who led the religious nobility consisting of archbishops and bishops who managed priests, superiors of convents and monasteries and finally friars, monks and nuns who tended to the believers."

"The Church leaders were the most educated individuals in society. They were called upon to help the secular leaders as advisors on political, financial, judicial and military issues in addition to spiritual matters. Most important, the Church with its structure helped legitimize the feudal system structure. The Church taught that God appointed the pope and kings (divine right of kings). This meant that each person was born into their divinely determined position in society. Next, you were bequeathed land, power and prestige and named a prince, lord, duke or earl because 'God wanted it that way!'"

Time was flying by as we finally merged with the Interstate and were able to not only speed up but get rid of all the maniacs behind us who thought I was driving too slow. I took a deep breath and continued. "These princes, lords, dukes and earls had to pledge an oath of allegiance to the king in exchange for land, power and prestige they were awarded. They were required to provide both funds and support in times of need to the king's wishes, where those entrusted with battle were the knights, who governed the serfs, who worked the land operated by the knights, managed by the princes, lords, dukes and earls on behalf of the king."

"You need to remember, this was a time of profound fear of death and its consequence where the Church began preach about heaven, hell and purgatory. The fear of purgatory and hell was so great that land was routinely awarded to the Church by nobles in what were called 'indulgences' that allowed those in power to buy their way into heaven. The practice was so widespread that, by the end of the Medieval period, the Church was the largest landowner in the Europe, owning one-third of the land."

"With that much land, the Church became very powerful and with power, always comes abuse. However, development of a mutual interdependence between Church and state characterized a new order where the Church provided solutions to problems faced by the state - namely monks and clerics, who had the education needed for administration, while the state provided the Church with protection for its missions and property. This interdependent structure is really critical to understanding how the post-Roman social, political and economic structure of Medieval Europe developed and how the entire feudal structure emulated the Church and not the other way around."

"You were there?" Mike inquired.

"Yup, I visited several times, saw the good and bad, and found it interesting and somewhat spooky to meet some more of my ancestors."

"Did you tell them who you were?"

"Are you kidding me? They would have thought I was some sort of nut job or worse yet, a warlock and had me killed. You need to remember, people back then really got spooked easily by anything they couldn't explain."

"How long were you gone?" Mike asked.

"Sometimes a few days. Sometimes a few weeks. Others, a few months in their time."

"What about when you returned?"

"No matter how long I was away, it was usually about twenty minutes in real time."

"Then what happened?"

"That's another story for another day, my friend," I replied.

Things were getting familiar as we turned off the Interstate at the Dells and headed south on Highway 12, regretting we hadn't taken the river road along the Mississippi and vowing we'd do that another time.

It was getting dark as we pulled in the Heaven's Waiting Room's parking lot and realized were only gone a week that seemed like a month. Mike and I walked in the front door and saw that nothing had changed, realizing it was not only good to go but also great to be back home.

The next morning, Mike and I unloaded the bus and I took it out to the farm, cleaned the interior and got it ready for our next trip. With it now early November, I didn't know if we wanted to go up north again or wait until spring. Perhaps Florida! Who knew. The one thing I was totally certain of, I was sure happy I won the bus.

Chapter 25 – Tis the Season

The Carolingians 480 – 814

	B	D
18. Carolus IV Nazon Hesbaye von Haspengau	om: 480	ied: 516
19. Charles V Nazon de Hesbaye	om: 515	ied: 558
20. Carloman of Landen	om: 547	ied: 645
21. Pepin I le Vieux de Landen (Pepin de Elder)	om: 580	ied: 640
22. Saint Arnoul Bishop of Metz	om: 582	ied: 640
23. Ansegisel de Metz	om: 610	ied: 662
24. Pepin le Gros (Pepin the Great)	om: 635	ied: 714
25. Charles Martel (Charles the Hammer)	om: 688	ied: 741
26. Pepin the Short	om: 714	ied: 768
27. Charles the Great (Charlemagne)	om: 747	ied: 814

It was November and the Badgers and Packers were the center of everyone's attention. I don't know what for. The Badgers ended the season with one victory and the Packers only won six. The *wait till next year* mantra had begun in October. Yuk!

Thanksgiving meant all the festivities for those who called our complex home. For me, it meant getting together with the kids who saw the sadness of being alone wiped from my face as I shared the joys of my friend, Mike and all the tales we had about Heaven's Waiting Room.

December 4th it started snowing and it snowed and it snowed and snowed, depositing more than a foot of the white stuff in most places and 18" at the complex. If the snow wasn't enough, we had a slight 'breeze' come through with winds of 60 MPH that created drifts that were seven feet tall against the west side of the buildings. Needless to say, not too many ladies were doing their water aerobics in the pool. While there were hundreds of car accidents and nine people died from heart attacks, Hank and Kat had it all set with plows and then, of course, our heated garage that was kept at a balmy 50 degrees. Gee, I really missed digging out the car and freezing my butt off trying to keep up with Mother Nature while watching the flames flicker in the group fireplace and drinking hot toddies with the blue hairs and not even minding it.

Thanks to having the snow removal equipment, Wisconsin was back to normal in a few days as everyone who had anyone, made plans for Christmas while getting together with family and friends was assured that they would take place. For some of us, it meant the extended family here at the center. It's sad to be so close and yet so far away from your family. They had plans and I didn't want to interfere. One certainly is the loneliest number!

Mike had gone to visit his son in Virginia for a month and arrived home right before New Year's thereby missing the blizzard. I drove to Truax Field in Madison, picked him up and filled him in on everything at the asylum, which was actually nothing, making sure he realized how good it was to see my old buddy.

"Good to be home?" I asked.

"Good to see you," Mike replied.

"What now?" I offered.

"What do you mean?"

"What do you have on the agenda?" I asked.

"Hmm, let's see, unpack and then go stir crazy," Mike replied.

"Want to go to Florida?"

"What?"

"Sure! We can take the bus and go down to Disney World and if it's too cold, keep going all the way to the Keys. I'm going crazy and need a break."

"I haven't even unpacked yet!"

"I know but what the hell, why not?" I replied, forgetting that my buddy had been a minister.

"Sure, why not? Mike replied.

"When do you want to go?"

"I don't know, I'll have to check my social calendar. There, I just did and it's totally blank!"

We decided to wait until after everyone finished winter break and head out in mid-January. That way all the kids would be back in school and Disney World and Florida wouldn't be as crowded.

I took the bus to Mitchell's and had it checked over and then washed the pigeon poop off the roof. Two days before we planned on leaving, I loaded up the groceries, put my clothes in the closet and got all set.

AAA mapped out the route and I realized it was going to take about 18 hours and we would be traveling about 1300 miles. In other words, more time to share with my buddy about the Terrill family history IF he was still interested. The last thing I wanted to do was bore him with details he really didn't care about.

The day came and we jumped in the bus and headed for the Interstate, picking it up in Beloit. We made it past Rockford and decided to head south on I39 and avoid driving in Chicago. That's one place I didn't like to drive a car, let alone a bus.

As we settled in to the flatlands of Illinois, Mike asked, "Are you going to fill me in on some more of your family history?"

I didn't know if he was being polite or really interested and so I asked, "Are you sure?"

Mike smiled, adding, "I don't know a single person, other than you, who can trace their family back to before the birth of Christ and the way you're sharing it keeps me wanting more."

I was happy to hear those words and so I began. "The next eight generations saw my ancestors evolve from spectators to participants in the medieval history of Europe. This evolution is what allowed me to go back and learn so much about where we came from.

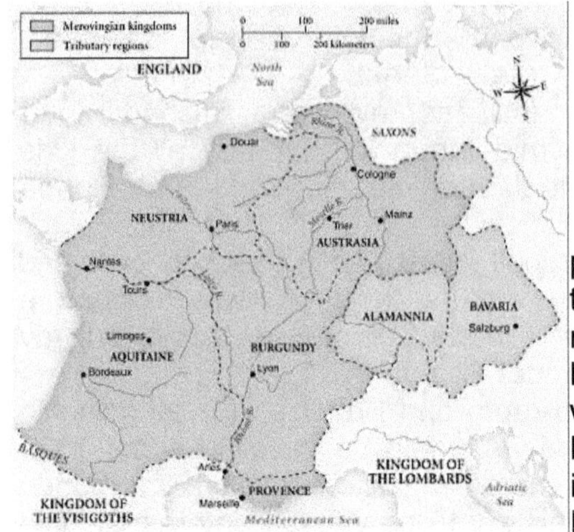

Without the people I was about to share with Mike, none of what I'd been able to learn would ever have been recorded. I call it the Carolingian Period and hope you'll understand why." I directed Mike to the binder in the glove compartment that he opened to the next section and examined the typed genealogical summary.

After a brief pause to let Mike better understand the importance of the names on the sheet, I began. "As the times changed, so did the power within each domain. In the late decades of the 500's, the first mention of the term and role 'maior domus' or Mayor of the Palace in the kingdom of Neustria, comes into play. This appointment allowed non-aristocratic individuals, who gained favor with the king, gain power and authority as head of the royal undertakings and do so without biological lineage and how the aristocratic Terrill family began to exist. I hope you don't mind, Mike but with this group, I need to go into greater detail."

"Go for it," Mike replied.

"Carloman of Landen married Gertrudis Brabant and they had one son, Pepin I le Vieux de Landen, also called Pepin the Elder or Pepin the Old, who was born in 580 and served as Mayor of the Palace of Austrasia."

"Carloman was not the first member of the Terrill family associated with aristocracy, nor would he be the last. In fact, based on the names, it appears as if the pre-Terrills had already been associated with royalty for over 400 years which would continue for well over another millennium."

I instructed Mike to turn the page and he examined the map as I continued.

"Pepin I, served as councilor of the Merovingian king Chlotar II and mayor of the palace in Austrasia. Through the marriage of his daughter Begga with Ansegisel, son of Saint Arnulf, Pepin was the actual founder of the Carolingian dynasty.

Pepin assumed his role serving the families of Merovingian Frankish nobility that continued from the 6th to the mid-8th centuries within the three Merovingian kingdoms of Austrasia, Burgundy and Neustria. The Merovingian dynasty was the ruling family of the Franks from the middle of the 400's until 751. By 509 they had united all the Franks and northern Gaullist Romans under their rule. They conquered most of Gaul, defeating the Visigoths in 507, the Burgindians in 534, and extended their rule into Raetia in 537, while those in Germania, Alemanni, Baravrii, along with the Saxons, accepted their authority."

"Do you think they could play in the NFL?" Mike inquired. "We need a team to cheer for that can win every now and then."

I just smiled and continued. "The Merovingian realm had been the largest and most powerful in western Europe following the break- up of the empire of Theoderic the Great. The first known Merovingian king was Childeric I, who was born in 437 and died 481. Childeric was a Frankish leader in the northern part of what was called Imperial Roman Gaul, who was described as King and received his Roman seal ring."

"Upon Childeric's death, he was replaced by his son, Clovis I, who converted to Christianity. In so doing, we begin to see the initial co-dependence of church and state, as Clovis used the church to help unite the Franks and conquer most of Gaul. With the expanded territory Clovis actually represents the first king of what would eventually become France."

"Upon Clovis I's death in 511, his four sons divided the kingdom between them into areas called Austrasia, Neustria, Burgundy and Aquitaine that remained divided but treated as a single, yet divisible entity."

"At first there was a delicate balance between different rivals and also the Church in what's now called Western Europe. However, with each passing day, the power and authority of the Church continued to grow in a time when religious renewal was gathering momentum. This dynamic added a new dimension to the forces defining, directing, and sustaining the Christian community, while also limiting the processes of the Carolingian dynasty."

Mike had a quizzical look on his face and so I added. "You need to remember that the power of the Roman Empire was so great and so intrusive that its literal existence sustained a world that changed very little during Rome's 1,000-year domain. The fall of the Roman Empire created a void in power that allowed smaller civilizations to flourish of which the Lombards represented one of the more successful nations to take advantage of the voids in authority and leadership. Originally from southern Scandinavia and emigrated into what became Germania around 200 BC, the Lombards represented just one of the fierce groups of warriors Caesar had been so concerned about during the Gallic Wars and times of Carolus de Menapii."

"With Rome in disarray, numerous skirmishes and wars took place, none of which was longer, nor more brutal than the twenty-year Gothic War from 535-554 between the Byzantine or East Roman Empire and the Ostrogoths in Northern Italy. In order to achieve military objectives, King Audoin of the Lombards was obliged to send 5,000 troops to serve under Narses, who was one of the great generals in the service of the Byzantine Emperor, Justinian I, in Italy, to help defeat the Goths on the slopes of Vesuvius."

"To raise such a large army, King Audoin instituted an organization similar to the military system used by other Germanic tribes in which war bands consisted of kinship groups led by a hierarchy of dukes, counts, and other commanders. This group then fought against the Ostrogoths in battles so brutal and comprehensive it virtually left Northern Italy severely depopulated and totally devastated."

"Audoin died around 564 and was succeeded to the throne by his son, Alboin, who recognized an opportunity to settle in an area rich in farmland and well-watered by both the melting snow from the Alps and the Po River that ran to the sea. Alboin, gathered the kinship groups and invaded the area north of the Po River, conquering it almost unopposed, in 569."

"The dukes, counts, and other commanders who had supported both Audoin and Alboin were rewarded not only with plunder but able to acquire the power and resources needed to conquer and occupy additional areas in central and southern Italy as well. In so doing, this established the Lombard Kingdom named Regnum Italicum or 'Kingdom of Italy' that remained in place for over 200 years."

"As Arian Christians, the Lombards believed that the Son of God was not co-eternal with God the Father and was therefore distinct from the Father and subordinate to him. Because of this, they were considered pagans by the Roman Catholic Church and represented a major threat to the Church and its continuing dominance over Western Europe, and this is where Pepin the Short comes in."

Mike shook his head in disbelief, thinking of the Church as a religious entity and not a political organization to which I continued "As you can see, you had three growing forces in Europe…the Franks, the Lombards and the Catholic Church."

"Throughout Pepin's time as king, there were wars of expansion   that continued as he conquered Septimania from the Islamic Umayyads, while   repeatedly defeating Waiofar and Gascon and their troops in the south. One deciding battle took place in 762 when Waiofar's cousin, Count Mantio, supported by a regiment of Gascon troops, lay in ambush of a Carolingian force as it was entering the village of Narbonne, near the Mediterranean Sea. However, in the subsequent battle, they were routed and Mantio and his entourage were killed. The Gascons left the battlefield and fled on foot with Pepin's soldiers taking their horses as spoils of war." "These battles were so decisive that the Gascon and Aquitanian lords saw no option but to pledge loyalty to Pepin, thereby, securing the area now seen as Southern France. Pepin, however,   remained troubled by the revolts of the Saxons and Bavarians, who were loyal to the Lombards, and campaigned tirelessly in Germany. However, Pepin was never able to succeed in defeating them or signing an alliance with the different Germanian tribes."

"Under Pepin, there were other critical changes concerning the Frankish social system. Previously, alliances had been based on kinship ties and bonds that linked war leaders together. This system was being replaced by a structure where weaker landholders committed themselves, along with their land and people, to a stronger force for both protection and economic gain. This secured a larger area that was then enhanced when the war lords formed protection alliances with each other. Under the alliance's realm, the smaller and weaker lords provided warriors and grain in exchange for safety and security."

"In other words, a literal form of taxation?" Mike inquired. "Or, a protection racket similar to what the Mafia did in the States." I replied and continued. "At that time, the entire political structure in western Europe was in turmoil and was being reshaped politically and economically by the decline of the Eastern Roman Empire, which became known as the Byzantines. The Byzantines, had recognized the growing power of the Frankish empire and bestowed the title of 'Patricius' on Pepin, in an attempt to appease him. However, Pepin was being challenged from the north by invaders from what's now Denmark and Scandinavia, from the east by the Slavic world, which included people living in areas such as today's as Belarus, Ukraine, Romania, Moldovia and Russia and from what's now Italy by the Lombards. If that wasn't enough, there were also the Arab forces from the Middle East, who were attempting to spread the Islamic religion across the Mediterranean. In other words, Pepin's relatively secure area, was being threatened from three sides and those in between were scared shitless!"

"Pepin the Elder was selected Mayor of the Palace of Austrasia under the Merovingian King Dagobert who served from 623 to 629 and also functioned as mayor for Sigebert III from 639 until his death a year later. Here we find, the individual named Arnulf comes into play, who represents the first detailed recording of the Terrill lineage that goes beyond simply finding names and dates and does so to the point that it includes the names of spouses as well."

"In other words, Medieval women's lib?" Mike interjected.

Chapter 26 – Saints and Sinners

I just kept going. "We can't discuss Arnulf without also referencing Pepin de' Landen. Arnulf was born to an important Frankish family near Nancy, France which remains a riverfront city in the northeastern French region of Grand Est. Nancy is known for its late baroque and art nouveau landmarks and functioned as the capital of the Duchy of Lorraine around 582. Today it's known as Lay-Saint-Christophe. Our ancestors owned vast domains between the Moselle and Meuse Rivers. As an adolescent, Arnulf was called to the Merovingian court of King Theudebert II where he was educated in Latin Studies by Gondulphe of Provence. Subsequently, Arnulf was recommended to King Theudebert II and placed in charge of the palace government in the province of Moselle."

"Arnulf gave distinguished service as both a military commander and civil administrator and, at one time, had six distinct provinces under his rule. In 596, Arnulf married a noblewoman named Doda, who was the daughter of the Count of Boulogne. Arnulf and Doda had several children, including sons Ansegisel and Clodulf, whom we will talk about a little later.

"This was a period of profound turmoil in a region with numerous wars, where rulers were poisoned, captured, tortured and killed and may be the reasons why Arnulf entered the Church. In 611, Doda took the veil as a nun in a convent at Treves and Arnulf saw it as a sign of God to become a priest and bishop himself, while continuing to serve as the king's steward and courtier."

"After the death of King Theudebert in 612, Arnulf was chosen as the 29th Bishop of Metz and enthroned near the end of that year, a position he held for 40 years, during which time he richly decorated the cathedral of St. Stephen. After King Theudebert's death, the rule of Austrasia came into the hands of Brunhilda, who also ruled Burgundy and did so in the name of her great-grandchildren."

"In 613, Arnulf joined with Pepin of Landen and led the opposition of Frankish nobles against Queen Brunhilda and the subsequent reunification of Frankish lands under Chlothachar II."

"Chlothachar II later made his son, Dagobert I, king of Austrasia, which he ruled with the help of Arnulf and Pepin of Landen, who was named Mayor of the Palace.

In 624 Pepin and Arnulf encouraged King Dagobert to murder Chrodoald, who was an important leader of the Frankish Agilolfings family."

Mike looked at me and commented, "Saints, sinners AND murderers – sounds like the Terrills I know."

I looked out at the highway sign that said 'Welcome to Normal' and wondered if that meant the rest of Illinois was abnormal as I continued. "It's really important to remember that, in ancient times, bishops were elected by the congregations of the cities over which they ministered. Over time, bishops came to be elected by the clergy, who also had the authority to appoint local priests. Because it was so lucrative, it wasn't uncommon for parishes to pass from father to son, and therefore, sustain the power, prestige and wealth that came pouring in. As bishops carried such weight with the people, those in power were often better politicians than they were spiritual leaders. How bad did it get? Ecclesiastical offices were openly bought and sold to the highest bidder."

I think Mike was a bit embarrassed by my knowledge and was beginning to understand my organized religion reticence.

"St. Arnulf played a large role in the Edict of 615 which laid out two fundamental laws that did away with the outright permanence of hereditary land, stating that nobles had to continue to actively manage the lands to continue their ownership, while also decreeing that bishops were to be elected by the faithful and not appointed by the king."

"Arnulf also played an important role in the politics of his time, being a close advisor to King Dagobert, while participating in the councils of Paris in 614, Metz and Reims in 625 and Clichy in 627. Arnulf became tormented by the violence that surrounded him and feared he played a role in the wars and murders that plagued the ruling families. Obsessed by these sins, Arnulf went to a bridge over the Moselle River, took off his episcopal ring and threw it into the water, praying to God to give him a sign of absolution. Several years later, a fisherman brought a fish to the Bishop's kitchen in which they found the ring in the fish's stomach and

Arnulf considered it a sign from God and immediately retired as bishop."

"Legend has it that the moment Arnulf resigned a fire broke out in the cellars of the royal palace and threatened to spread throughout the city of Metz. Arnulf stood before the fire and said, 'If God wants me to be consumed, I am in His hands.' He then made the sign of the cross at which point the fire immediately receded."

"After resigning as bishop, Arnulf moved to a mountain retreat near Remiremont where he built a chapel and became a hermit for the remainder of his life. While there, Arnulf sheltered lepers and other social outcasts. His reputation attracted men who wanted to live a solitary religious life but Arnulf directed them to his friend at Romary's Monastery near Remiremont."

"Arnulf lived alone and died on August 16, 640. Romary conducted his funeral and buried him at Arnulf's mountain chapel. Goery, the Bishop of Metz, Tiffory, the Bishop of Toul and Paul, the Bishop of Verdun, led a procession to Metz in July, 642 during a very hot spell to recover the remains of their former Bishop."

"The members of the procession had very little to drink and the terrain was inhospitable and they were about to leave Champigneulles, when one of the parishioners by the name of Duc Notto, prayed, 'By his powerful intercession, the Blessed Arnulf will bring us what we lack.' The story goes that, immediately a small remnant of beer at the bottom of a pot multiplied in such amounts that the pilgrims' thirst was quenched and they had enough to enjoy the next evening when they arrived in Metz."

"Due to the miracles of the episcopal ring, burning palace and flowing beer, a Declaration of the Sovereign Pontiff was beatified for Arnulf in Metz. Arnulf was held in such high regard that the Congregation for the Causes of Saints accepted proof that two miracles had taken place, thereby, deeming Arnulf as a saint, entitled to the full honors of the altar of Metz. Canonization then was celebrated in Saint Peter's in Rome, where a solemn novena was made."

"For this reason, Arnulf - also known as Arnold - is the patron saint of beer and brewers owing to a pious legend about the saint. Arnulf was reburied at the Abbey of Saints Apostles which later became the Abbey of Saint

Arnulf. Unfortunately, the abbey was destroyed in 1552 by the Duke of Guise during the siege of Metz. However, the relics were saved and returned to the abbey where their tower was named after Saint Arnulf, or today, known as Saint Arnold." I actually got serious for a moment and added. "Pepin of Landen was perhaps, the most important and powerful person in the empire during his age. As Duke of Brabant and also mayor of the palace for kings Clotaire III, Dagobert and Siegebert III, Pepin determined much of the policy of the Franks and established laws concerning social structure that carried on for over a thousand years." "From a descendance perspective, Pepin of Landen was the husband of Blessed Itta, or Ida, who was the daughter of Arnulf. Together they had two daughters who grew and dedicated their lives to the church and were canonized as Saint Gertrude of Nivelles, Saint Begga of Ardenne, and one son named Grimoald who became mayor of the palace. After Pepin's death, Ida built a Benedictine double monastery at Nivelles, Belgium under the leadership of her daughter,

Saint Gertrude."

Mike got serious for a moment. "You really did have some incredible ancestors, didn't you?"

"I'm proud to say, I did. Pepin also worked to spread the faith throughout the kingdom, defended Christian towns from Slavic invaders and did his best to minimize graft and corruption amongst those who coveted power. He was described as a lover of peace and defender of truth and justice though it may not seem that way at first glance. Probably the most important aspect was the marriage of Pepin and Ida's daughter, Begga, to Arnulf's son, Segislius and grandfather to Pepin of Herstal, who became the first ruler of the Carolingian dynasty of France. Pepin de Landen was buried at Landen but his remains were later moved to Nivelle where they are enshrined with Ida and their other daughter, Gertrude."

"Was Pepin canonized?" Mike asked.

"Not by the Catholic Church but he is listed in some of the old Belgic martyrologues and also in a litany published by the authority of the Archbishop of Mechlin."

"Did you and Peg ever visit where he's buried?"

"We did and I was also there for his funeral." I replied.

Mike got serious for a moment and offered. "You really do have some saints in your family."

"I'm very proud to say they were my ancestors."

I paused for a moment for it all to sink in as Reverend Mike simply shook his head and said, "So you're the descendent of a saint?"

I had a sheepish grin on my face as Mike looked at me, smiled a wicked smile and added, "And a whole bunch of sinners."

I laughed at the man I now adeptly called the 'Sinister Minister' and added. "The entire story of Arnulf is important because it represents the first written collection of the life of the Terrill ancestors. It becomes more important due to Saint Arnulf's second son, Ansegisel who was born in 608, matured and married Begga, daughter of Pepin I, also called Pepin de' Landen, thereby making Arnulf grandfather of Pepin of Herstal, great-grandfather of Charles Martel and great, great grandfather of Charlemagne."

"Lucky guy!" Mike interjected.

"Ansegisel had a son he called Pepin le' Gros, or Pepin the Great, who was born in Herstal (Héristal), Belgium in 635 who was also called Pepin von Heristal, as well as Pepin II and Pepin the Middle. Pepin matured and married Plectrudis von Herstal that united the houses of the Pippinids and the Arnulfings."

"It created what would eventually be called the Carolingian Dynasty, where Pepin le' Gros was named the Frankish king and ruler of the Carolingian Empire. Pepin had several children including Grimoald, Drogo, the aforementioned Charles Martel, who was born in 688, and a daughter named Childebrande."

"Pepin le' Gros embarked on several wars to expand his power and united all the Frankish realms by the conquests of Neustria and Burgundy in 687. In foreign conflicts. Pepin increased the power of the Franks by his subjugation of the Alemanni, Frisians, and Franconians and also began the process of evangelization in Germany. Pepin's statesmanship was notable for the further reduction of Merovingian royal authority and the acceptance of the undisputed right to rule for his family. Therefore, Pepin was able to name his grandson, Theudoald, as heir. This wasn't accepted by Charles Martel, which lead to a civil war after Theudold's death, where Charles Martel emerged victorious."

I added. "An example of a ducal appointment consisted of Pépin maior domus of Neustria and Austrasia who vested his son, Drogo as dux or duke of Champagne in 688 and the Burgunds around 697 and appears to be the source that allowed for the creation and maintenance of the genealogical records of the Terrill family both forward and back in my research."

I looked at Mike and said, "Without Drago none of the preceding history or nothing that followed would have made sense simply because Drago allowed me to 'connect-the-dots' for the first 765 years, when little was written and even less saved."

"During that final century of Merovingian rule, the kings were increasingly pushed into ceremonial roles with actual power increasingly in the hands of the mayor of the palace. The traditional view of the maiores domus at the Merovingian courts was that they assumed a dominant role in the kingdoms of Austrasia and Neustria, and relegated the kings to a subservient position, which justified the general nickname 'les rois fainéants' - the lazy kings - which has often been applied to these monarchs. The one power most kings retained was establishing titles of dux or duke that were normally awarded for bravery, loyalty and success in defending the power and authority of the king. It also set a precedent that continued for the next one- thousand years."

I didn't know if I should broach the subject of the Church but thought, 'What the hell?', the worst that could happen is Mike would stop the bus, get out and I'd lose a friend forever and so I proceeded with caution.

"Quietly the Roman Catholic Church continued to increase its dominance within all of Europe. Religious practice was dominated and informed by the Church. The majority of the population was Christian, and 'Christian' at this time meant 'Catholic' as there was initially no other form of religion."

"The Church regulated and defined an individual's life, literally, from birth to death and was thought to continue its hold over the person's soul in the afterlife. The Church was positioned as the manifestation of God's will and presence on earth and its dictates were not to be questioned, even when it was apparent that many of the clergy were working toward their own interests other than those of God."

"The Church claimed authority from God through Jesus Christ who, according to the Bible, designated his apostle Peter as 'the rock upon which my church will be built' to whom he gave the keys of the kingdom of heaven.

Mike interjected, "Matthew 16:18-19."

I continued, "Peter was therefore regarded as the first Pope, head of the church and all others, as his successors were endowed with the same divine authority."

I paused and Mike added. "The Church maintained the belief that Jesus Christ was the only begotten Son of the one true God as revealed in the Hebrew scriptures, and agreed with this point of view, which became the Old Testament of the Bible that prophesied Christ's coming. The date of the earth and history of humanity was all revealed through the scriptures which made up the Christian Bible – considered the word of God and the oldest book in the world – which was consulted as a handbook on how to live, according to divine will, and gain everlasting life in heaven upon one's death."

"The Church felt that interpretation of the Bible, was too great a responsibility for the average person and so the clergy was a spiritual necessity. With this structure, in order to talk to God or understand the Bible correctly, a person had to rely on their priest who was ordained by his superior who was in turn ordained by another, up and up and up, all under the authority of the Pope who was God's representative on earth."

"The Church hierarchy also maintained the social hierarchy. One was born into a certain class, followed the profession of one's parents, and died as they had. Social mobility was extremely rare to nonexistent since the Church taught that it was God's will one had been born into a certain set of circumstances and attempting to improve one's lot was tantamount to claiming God made a mistake. People, therefore, accepted their lot and made the best of it."

It was my turn to add to the religious discussion. "Mike, all my studies indicate that the lives of the people of the Middle Ages revolved around the Church. People, especially women, were known to attend church three to five times daily for prayer and at least once each week for services, confession and acts of contrition for repentance. The Church paid no taxes and was supported by the people of a town or city. Citizens were responsible for supporting the parish priest and the Church facility through a tithe of ten percent of their income. Tithes paid for baptisms, confirmations and funerals as well as saint's and holy day festivals such as Easter celebrations."

"The teachings were absolute and there was no room for doubt or questions. One was either in the Church or out of it. If one wasn't a member of the Church interactions with the rest of the community were limited. Jews for example, lived in their own neighborhoods, surrounded by Christians and were regularly treated quite poorly. Muslims in Europe were rare outside of Spain as were the traveling merchants conducting trade. A citizen who didn't belong to either the Church or was Jewish, had to adhere to the orthodox vision of the Church in order to interact with family, community and even make a living. If one found they couldn't do so, or at least appear to do so, the only option was a so-called heretical sect which was defined as a religious opinion contrary to church dogma and normally characterized by heresy which later on in history could result in death."

"The center of a congregation's life in a small-town church or cathedral was not the altar but the baptismal font. This was a free- standing stone receptacle/basin used for infant or adult baptism and was often quite large and deep that also served to determine a person's guilt or innocence when one was charged with a crime. To clear one's name, a person would submit to an ordeal in which one was bound and dropped into the font. If the accused floated, it was a clear indication of guilt and if the accused sank, it meant innocence but the accused would often drown."

Mike added. "Gee, I never thought to do that in Mineral Point. We could have used the swimming pool. However, instead of drowning, the results would be whether or not you froze to death in the spring water."

I just kept going. "The church exercised exclusive jurisdiction over a wide range of matters including incest, bigamy, finances, failure to perform oaths and vows, matrimonial cases and legitimacy of children. All these were dealt with according to Canon Law and not secular courts. In addition, all churchmen enjoyed immunity from secular courts freeing them from the same social, financial and ethical limitations placed on the masses."

"Critical to controlling the populous was the Church's teachings on purgatory where souls remained trapped until they'd paid for their sins. This generated enormous wealth for various clergy who sold writs known as indulgences, promising a shorter stay in purgatory for a price. Relics were another source of income, and it was common for unscrupulous clerics to sell fake splinters of Christ's cross, a saint's finger or toe, a vial of water from the Holy Land, or any number of objects, which would allegedly bring luck or ward off misfortune. Incredibly, the church literally had control of the individual from birth to death and even in the hereafter."

I paused for a moment to see how Mike would respond to my elocution.

"You've got it spot on," he responded, thereby, giving me a great deal of relief.

"I hope there's more," Mike urged, as I continued.

"King Childebert III acceded to the throne in 695 and died in 711 as the ducal appointment system continued to reduce the Merovingian rulers to what their Carolingian successors dubbed 'do nothing' kings. The real power belonged to the Carolingians who continued to claw their way to dominance by utilizing the office of Mayor of the Palace and relationships with the church to establish control over the royal administration while acquiring the resources and support necessary to build a following strong enough to fend off rival Frankish families seeking comparable power."

"During the 700's the key Carolingian mayors were Charles Martel and his son, Pippin III, also known as Pippen the Short, who was born in 714. The two of them increasingly turned their attention to activities aimed at checking the political fragmentation of the Frankish kingdom. Due to the weaknesses of the kings they continued to wield real and effective power to the point that the kings were reduced to simply performing ceremonial functions as little more than figureheads."

"The English Terrills have a patrilineal lineage through a gentleman by the name of Childebrande, of which there are three possibilities regarding his parentage. We know his father was Pepin' le Gros but history isn't quite certain who his mother was."

"Aha! And so now I know where your wandering eye came from!" the sinister minister evoked.

I totally ignored his smart-ass comment, realizing my roving eye preceded me when I thought I'd been so clever hiding my observations. Instead, I continued. "First, it may have been a woman by the name of Alpaida, Pippin's mistress, who bore Childebrande. Second Childebrande was Pippin's son borne by his second wife Chalpais thereby making Childebrande Charles Martel's brother. Third, he was the son of Chalpais by an earlier marriage and therefore Charles Martel's half-brother. Regardless of who the mother was it has been attested that Childebrande was a descendant of Pippin le Gros, thereby, making him an uncle to Pippin the Short and great uncle of Charlemagne. No matter what, the Terrills of England were at least cousins of Charlemagne and descendants of Pepin le Gros."

Chapter 27 – Do You See Tennessee?

As a member of AAA, I ordered what was called a Trip-Tik that segmented maps and directed us due south and then along the Gulf Coast. No sense driving through Chicago, Indianapolis and Atlanta. I was the pilot and Mike the navigator and each little map meant a demarcation that part of the trip was completed.

After five maps, we made it into Tennessee and it was getting late. I saw a sign for a rest area and we agreed to stop for a break. Even with a motor home, you need to stretch your legs. I pulled in, shut off the engine and it hit me…exhaustion. I'd been driving for ten hours.

One would think that being the Interstate Highway, all the states would have the same rules. Nope! Some states allow weary travelers to sleep in their vehicles as long as needed. Other states place a time limit on how long you can stay. Just outside of Chattanooga, it seems that Smokey the Bear was looking for someone to make his night. Both Mike and I were sleeping and around three in the morning, there was a rap on the door that woke me up to the sight of red and blue lights flashing. I stumbled to the door, opened it and there stood a State Patrol officer. By now, Mike was awake and came to the door as well.

"What can I do for you officer?" I asked. "Camping is not permitted in any rest area."

I looked around as if to inspect the inside of the bus and replied, "Camping is generally defined as setting up a tent or sleeping outside your vehicle and so we're actually, not camping, officer. We were tired and for safety's sake pulled in the REST STOP."

Mike added, "I read the rules in our AAA Trip-Tik and it said sleeping in your RV is not considered camping."

Now the cop was becoming impatient. "This is Tennessee and there's a two-hour limit and no overnight parking or camping."

Mike was back at him. "Officer, we're both old men. We drove for 10 hours and stopped to rest and fell asleep. Would you prefer that we continue driving and fall asleep?"

"This is not an RV camp. You should have thought of that when you left Wesconsin."

"Officer, why don't we do this? Why don't we just leave? You have duly notified us that we've stayed too long and we're willing to abide by your directives and depart."

"What are you, one of them fancy damn lawyers?"

"No officer, I'm a retired minister and my friend here is a retired History Professor. We're a couple of widowers. Just two old men trying to enjoy life. Until now, this is the first time I've ever had any form of altercation with a police officer. I've had some officers as members in my parish and worked with several others over the years when they needed my assistance to notify the next of kin because someone was too careless or too tired when they should have stopped and rested. If it's important that we leave your rest area, consider it done. We can be on our way and out of Tennessee as soon as possible."

"Minister, huh?" "Yes."

"Which religion?" "Christian." "Baptist?"

"No, Congregational." "Believe in Jesus?" "Of course."

"Well, you know, I've got a job to do and we get folks who think they can break the rules and stay all night. If you feel like you need to rest some more, that's OK with me. I'm sorry to have bothered you."

"Thank you, officer. We're both wide awake and I think we'll be leaving now, if you don't mind."

"Again, I'm sorry I bothered you two fellas."

"It's Ok, you were just doing your job. You know officer, you might want to suggest putting up a sign that says you're only welcome to stay two hours."

"That's a good idea."

With that, we got back in the bus and headed south. I didn't need sleep. The adrenaline was flowing and our next goal was Florida.

Chapter 28 - Charles The Hammer

As we escaped the clutches of the law in Tennessee, I continued the story as if I'd only stopped to catch my breath. "It had been sixteen years since my journey to visit Carolous. I'd married Peg and the kids were born. I felt the days of adventure were over as life centered around Mount Horeb and Madison, with little time for Waldwick or Mineral Point. One day the urge was there and for some reason I went to the farm and the Forest. I walked the path to the springs and the Buck was there. He looked up as if to say. 'The time has come.'"

"I caught the Buck's eye and he mine, as he wandered into the bog and I followed. I wondered if I was going to transcend and if so, when and where I would end up. With fourteen years of studying and teaching European history I'd become quite attuned to the social, political and geographic dynamics of the Continent."

"As I entered the bog the fog that shrouded my first encounter appeared and I walked directly into it. There was no fear or trepidation. I was confident my linear time would stand still and I'd find a way back home. In an instant I transcended and found myself in what appeared from the topography to be Northern France. I had no idea the year but from the garb worn by the peasants, it appeared to be in the 700's or over seven hundred years since my previous visit."
"While I'd traversed the time and place, my attire was that of the 1930's, namely a white-shirt and tan trousers, while still wearing my Timex wristwatch, set on Wisconsin time. Needless to say, I stood out amongst those clothed in hopsack and it wasn't long before two magistrates came to my side. Once again, there was no difficulty understanding the magistrates as they asked, 'Who are you?'"

"I looked at them as they peered at me and responded. 'My name is William Terrill and I've come to visit.'"

"'Visit who?' was the inquiry."

"I shrugged my shoulders and replied. 'Anyone, everyone.'"
"Are you loyal to Pepin or Carloman?"

"It was then I knew that I'd arrived at another apex of history and one wrong word could mean both my and the entire Terrill lineage's demise as I replied, 'I have come at the behest of Charles Martel'".

"With this, both men grabbed my wrists, asking me how I knew the self-proclaimed Duke and Prince of the Franks, Mayor of the Palace."

"Looking at the two of them, I replied, 'The Duke has summoned me to his council and should you not unhand me, I'll make certain the Duke's officers are aware I've been mis-treated.'"

"My ruse only worked to the point that my hands were freed but swords were drawn as I was led to the palace. "

"Teaching European history and learning French taught me that the name Charles Martel meant 'Charles the Hammer' who was a man of tremendous self-confidence based on his enviable skill when it came to battle. I also knew that the Merovingians effectively ceded power to the Mayors of the Palace. These descendants of Carolous de Menapii were my ancestors who were actually ruling the Frankish realm of Austrasia in all but name, simply because they were controlling the royal treasury, dispensing patronage, granting land and privileges, all in the name of the figurehead king."

"This structure continued until 737, when King Theuderic IV died and Charles Martel, his Mayor, began ruling the kingdom. While Charles the Hammer had a reputation as a cunning warrior, it was his father, Pepin of Herstal, who was able to unite the Frankish realm by conquering Neustria and Burgundy who was the first to call himself Duke and Prince of the Franks."

"Quickly my mind was challenged, why was I here and what threat was there to the Terrill lineage? Then it came to me, I'd been beckoned because there was to be a battle between Pepin and his brother Carloman, to determine who would control the Frankish Kingdom. I quickly realized that, should Carloman win, the history of not only Europe but the Terrill family, would be profoundly different, not because of the brothers but because of one of their offspring and I was sent to ensure Charles' victory. My objective was to convince Charles Martel to select Pepin and not Carloman as his heir. The questions were, first, how did I get to meet him and, second, what did I do to convince Charles Martel."

Mike looked at me and simply shook his head as I continued. "I was escorted to the castle and the guards really didn't know what to do. People gawked at my funny clothes and had no conception of my wristwatch, which immediately caught their attention."

"As they pondered my demise I turned to them and reported that I'd come from the future and could therefore use my time machine to share what was about to happen and I needed to warn the king. I was led into the castle and entered a large hall. One of the magistrates departed and Boniface, a priest, appeared looking quite concerned as he inquired, 'Who sent you?'"

"I replied that I'd come from both the past and the future and my 'time machine' allowed me to counsel those in times of peril. I outlined the Gallic wars and how the Menapii used a different military tactic than those used elsewhere and had been initially successful in repelling the Roman legions. I indicated that I had a message only for the King to which Boniface scoffed and said it was impossible. I looked at him and outlined the life of Charles Martel in terms of not only his lineage but the battles and the fact that Charles had escaped from prison in 715 and been acclaimed mayor by the nobles of Austrasia." "I outlined the 716 Battle of Cologne and how it represented Charles' only defeat. I summarized the Battle of Ambleve that same year, where Martel attacked the enemy as they rested at midday by splitting his forces into several groups. I asked about the Battle of Vincy, the following year and how it aligned the support Charles needed in order to rule."

"Boniface seemed unimpressed until I told him I knew the day that Charles was going to die and had come to warn him and provide information that would allow him to prepare. Still Boniface remained reluctant until I offered, 'Is it not true that last year Pope Gregory III begged Charles for his aid against Liutprand but Charles was reluctant to fight his onetime ally and friend and ignored the Pope's plea?' This had been confidential information that few outside Charles and Boniface knew and I could tell by the look in Boniface's eyes that he was beginning to believe."

"I looked at Boniface and noted that he was born in 680 to a noble family in Devon, Town of Crediton, in Wesex, England and that his name had been Wynfrid. I outlined how he'd been educated in the Benedictine Abbey of Adescancastre and became a Benedictine monk in 710, moved to Frisia, which I knew was today's Netherlands in 716, where he attempted to evangelize the Frisian Saxons but was rebuffed by King Radbod."

"I continued. 'That year, you returned to England to learn your abbot had died and you'd been elected in his stead. Instead of accepting, you attempted your second career as a missionary and in 718, led a group of pilgrims to Rome where you were entrusted with a mission east of the Rhine with a goal of converting the Germania pagans.'"

"Boniface looked at me with both a frown and scorn. I knew too much and it concerned him as I added, 'Is it not true that Pope Gregory II asked only that you use the Romany formula for baptism rather than the Celtic and to consult with him personally should you have any problems?'"

"Boniface was beginning to see I knew more than could be learned as I also added, 'Was it not true that the Pope changed your name to Boniface and consecrated you a missionary bishop? Didn't the Pope also provide you with a collection of canons and ecclesiastical regulations and the letter of recommendation to Charles Martel that secured your passage and introduction to master of the Frankish kingdom? You also made certain that Martel's two sons were properly educated, where they received ecclesiastical education from the monks of St. Denis?'"

"I looked at the man and continued. 'If, and it's a very big if, you and I can convince the king to split his throne instead of awarding it entirely to Carloman, I can guarantee you that in 747, there will be a reforming council that will encompass the entire Frankish kingdom that will use the disciple of the Church for its laws and do so with the wholehearted collaboration of both Carloman and Pippin.'"

"I felt I needed to tone it down and so I added, 'Father, you are an organizer, educator, and reformer. You've profoundly influenced the course of intellectual, political and ecclesiastical history. Due to the monasteries you've created, those who follow you, including bishops, missionaries, teachers and individuals can live in the peace of God, while under the leadership of Rome. This is why I've come to assist you in making the right decisions so that your legacy will be such that, someday, after you've joined God in Heaven, you'll be canonized and known throughout history as Saint Boniface'. This caught Boniface off guard and, yet, I could still see his reservation simply because all I had done was express events from the past."

"I stared at Boniface and asked how many people knew that he was called the proconsul of the papacy. 'I know of your organizing genius, your missionary zeal and that your first calling was to Frisia where you would like to someday return. You are respected within the Church because you have brought the works of the missionaries under the direction of Rome and not those in Ireland, and have done so, not for your own grandeur but simply because of your zeal for unity of the faith."

"Boniface stood stunned as I continued, 'I've read your letters, which I think are called Epistolae along with several of your sermons and poetry and find them quite interesting.'"

"Boniface's mouth dropped open as I offered. 'Charles trusts you and only you and does so because it was you who converted Charles to Christianity. If you assist me, upon Charles' death, Pope Zacharias will make you legate and charge you with the reformation of the entire Frankish Church. You'll succeed and be named Bishop of Mainz but it will only be a temporary position as we both know your passion is to build another mission in Frisia, in the land fronting the North Sea, including the Frisian Islands. If you assist me, it shall be done.'"

"I'd shared enough. I didn't want to tell Boniface when, or the fact that the mission would mean his demise in 754, at the hands of a band of pagan Frisians, who killed him as he was reading the Scriptures on Pentecost Sunday. However, I did share with him that, in order for this to happen, there needed to be peace and together we needed to gain the support of both Carloman and Pippin. Finally, I never mentioned that failure to do so would probably mean the demise, not only of the Terrill family but the entire unification of what's today Western Europe under Charles' grandson, Charlemagne."

"There was a pause, and then Boniface asked, 'Why do you need to see the king?'"

"'I need to share with him his fate and work with him to ensure that his legacy is filled with dignity and honor and beg him not spread upon the land of the Franks, the turmoil of confusion, in hope that they will be one, united and strong.'"

"As one more gesture, I took paper and quill and wrote October 22, 741."

"'What's that day?'" Boniface asked." "'The day, Charles Martel will die.'"

"Boniface excused himself and returned a few moments later indicating that Charles Martel would see me. For the second time in my life, I was about to meet one of my ancestors. I entered the court and examined both the room and the King, where I realized that the pallor of death had already arrived and it was simply a matter of time." "Boniface introduced me and requested to show Charles my time machine. Charles examined my watch with great interest asking

numerous questions as I outlined how it worked and what it kept track of to the point that, I sincerely believe, it was my watch that convinced Charles my suggestion was correct."

"In our meeting I outlined the need for unity and, if he chose to award all land to one son and nothing to the other, his decision would divide the nation and potentially cause it to fail, just as many of Charles' predecessors had done before."

I continued. "Charles realized his time was near and my watch seemed to be enough to earn his trust to the point that I spent the next several months working with Boniface and the king's court in deciding who was going to be awarded what."

"On October 22nd, the bells tolled and Boniface looked at me from a different perspective as Charles Martel died the day I'd predicated. We had succeeded in convincing Martel and made a death decree which divided the rule of the Frankish kingdom between Pepin III and his elder brother, Carloman, who were Martel's sons by his first wife Rotrude. With the decree, Carloman became Mayor of the Palace of Austrasia and Pepin III became Mayor of the Palace of Neustria."

"Being well disposed towards the Church and papacy, Pepin III and Carloman continued their father's work in supporting Saint Boniface in reforming the Frankish Church and evangelizing the Saxons. The brothers were active in successfully suppressing the Bavarian, Aquitanian, Saxon and Alemanni revolts in the early years of their reign. Carloman, who was intensely pious, became frustrated with war and retired to religious life, allowing Pepin III to become mayor of all the Franks."

"Needless to say, not everyone agreed. However, because I knew what was about to transpire, I went to Father Boniface, who then warned Pepin of pending revolts, first led by his half- brother Grifo and then by Carloman's two sons, Drogo and Grifo."

Mike laughed..."Drogo? I hope they taught him how to fight.

What a horrible name."

"So, you'd rather be called Grifo?" I asked.

"Drogo and Grifo! It sounds like a tumbling act to me."

"You want me to continue or should we laugh some more about the crazy names back then?"

"Ok! Ok Drogo. Keep going!"

Chapter 29 – Pepin III

We hit the Florida/Alabama border and so we high-fived. We'd been snacking on potato chips and root beer for breakfast while having a belching contest to determine both the loudest and the longest and, needless to say, it was time for lunch. We stopped at a Stuckey's and had what Mike politely called 'grease burgers' with some of their not-so-famous fudge for dessert. I paid, feeling it was the least I could do for a guy who had to listen to me babble. Mike left the tip and made sure the sultry waitress understood her service was terrible. We got back in the bus and headed for Orlando, as I continued my history lesson.

"As mayor of the palace, Pepin III was formally subject to the decisions of King Childeric III. While Pepin III had control of the magnates, he soon realized he needed the Church to gain and retain his domain and sent word to Rome that he wanted to depose King Childeric III. By traversing the right channel, I grew in stature until I was providing counsel to Pepin III. I knew it was critical for Pepin III to have an alliance with the Church and was also aware that the Church was hard pressed by the Lombards. I suggested and Pepin III agreed, while offering his support to Pope Zachary who welcomed this move to end an intolerable condition and lay the constitutional foundations for the exercise of royal power. Pope Zachary replied that such a state of things as those under Childeric III, 'Were not proper and, under these circumstances, de facto power was considered more important than the de jure authority.'"

"Pepin III realized the importance of the potential alliance with the Church but also knew there would need to be some sort of mutually agreeable structure. To this end, Pepin III was assisted by his friend, Vergilius of Salzburg, who was an Irish monk, and used a copy of the 'Collectio canonum Hibernensis' which was an Irish collection of canon law, to advise him."

"Pepin III was elected King of the Franks by an assembly of Frankish nobles, supported by a large portion of his army, who were loyal to him. I knew that this was in the best interests of the Franks and convinced Pepin he needed the Pope's approval to depose Childeric III so that he could receive royal unction from the Church as well. In so doing, I felt that Pepin III would officially be recognized by the magistrates, his army and the Catholic Church as king. Fortunately, I was right."

"Anointed a first time in 751 in Soissons, Pepin's first major act was to go to war against the Lombard's King Aistulf, who had expanded into ducatus Romanus, or the area surrounding Rome itself. After a meeting with Pope Stephen II at Ponthion, the war counsel suggested that Pepin force Aistulf to return the Seized property. In so doing there would be a re-confirmation of the papacy through the provision of possession of Ravenna, which was an area on the east coast of Italy, near the top of the boot and also Pentapolis, which consisted of five coastal cities south of Ravenna, which history has bequeathed the name 'Donation of Pepin'. In so doing, the first Papal States were established and the temporal reign of the papacy officially began who went from solely being a religious organization to a political one, as well, by creating laws, establishing defenses and collecting taxes."."

Mike offered, "You really know your stuff".

I replied. "It's hard not to when you're there. In 752, Pepin III turned his attention toward Septimania and headed south in a military expedition down the Rhone valley where he received submission of Eastern Septimania. After securing Count Ansemund's allegiance, Pepin went on to capture Narbonne in what's now Southern France which had been the main Umayyad stronghold. However, Pepin III was unable to capture territory from the Iberian Muslims until 759, when they were driven totally out to Hispania, or today's Spain." "For his success, in 754 Pepin III added to his legitimacy as

king when Pope Stephen II traveled to Paris to anoint him for a second time in a lavish ceremony at the Basilica of St Denis. Now I've been to all sorts of fancy shindigs but nothing like that. From the food, to the flowers, to seeing lions, elephants and tigers, it was something way beyond Ringling Brothers. At the ceremony Pope Stephen bestowed the additional title of 'Patricius Romanorum', or Patrician of the Romans, which is the first recorded crowning of a civil ruler by a Pope in history, as European politics and religion moved ever-closer together."

I looked at Mike and continued. "With the nature of the times in terms of battles, disease and unexpected death, Pepin III wanted to ensure family continuity in terms of authority and requested that Pope Stephen also anoint Pepin's sons, Charles, who was 12, and Carloman II, who was 3, as patricians as well, which the Pope agreed to do. In so doing, Pepin and his sons became rulers 'by the grace of God', where the Church imposed new, yet somewhat undefined sets of powers, relationships and responsibilities concerning authority, responsibility and control by the Vatican. Pope Stephen and Pepin not only inaugurated and legitimized the Church within the Carolingian dynasty but recognized Pepin as the sole Mayor of the Palace and dux et princeps Francorum which meant the Duke of the Franks which has been used for three different offices, where the word 'duke' always implying military command and 'prince' implying something approaching sovereign or regalian rights."

"And you returned home?" Mike inquired.

I shook my head no and stated it was only the beginning of my journey for two reasons. First, because this was the most important chapter in the Terrill history and second, because I couldn't locate the spot where I'd entered the time zone and was afraid I'd be forced to remain in the 700's forever.

"I think some of our neighbors at Heaven's Waiting Room would have been your neighbors even back then." Mike cackled with an enormous guffaw.

I looked at Mike and continued. "With threats on three sides and the Vatican's awareness of the Arab presence, Pepin created an alliance with the Church and was able to expand his territory into Italy, while remaining the King of the Franks. He did so by building up the heavy cavalry his father had begun and maintaining the standing army his father found necessary to protect the realm. In so doing, he was able to contain the Iberian Muslims by driving them out of what's now France, while holding the Lombard's area of dominance in Italy in check and capturing the Italian areas I mentioned earlier that he turned control of to the Vatican

"As important, Pepin managed to subdue the Aquitanians and the Gascons after three generations of clashes, thereby opening the gate to central and southern Gaul and Muslim Iberia. At home, he continued his father's expansion of the

Frankish Church in Germany and Scandinavia and expanded the institutional infrastructure of feudalism that would become the backbone of medieval Europe."

I looked at Mike and added, "Pepin died during a campaign of 768 at the age of 54 and was interred in the Basilica of Saint Denis in Paris. Pepin and his wife Bertrada had seven children that included Charles, Carloman I and Pepin, but then, that's a story after we stop and stretch."

Chapter 30 – Disneyworld

We got on the Florida Sunshine State Tollway that we quickly began calling the Screway. My God they are bold when it comes to taking money from tourists who use their roads. It was fun and yet still frustrating, checking the signs regarding how many miles to Kissimmee with a heated discussion as to how you pronounced the name of a town. Was it Kiss-A-Me or Kiss-Sem-Me? When that discussion terminated Mike got out the Trip Tik to determine how many more toll booths we would stop at, drop coins in the bin and listen to "ya all have a fine day now, hear".

Thanks to AAA, we had reservations at Sherwood Forest RV park which was located four miles from Disney World and we had a shuttle to the park. It even had mini golf, shuffleboard and a pool. The sign said "Pets are welcome" and so I told Mike he was welcome too. We parked the bus, leveled it and thought whoopee… summer is here and we were in the Sunshine State. Can you say fog…rain… thundershowers… fog…rain…50 degrees…40 degrees… how about 35 degrees? Brrr! This isn't what the brochure said when we packed shorts and tee shirts. Damn, it was cold!

When the kids were young, we made the obligatory trip to Disney World one spring break. It was magical! It was mystical! And it was affordable! I remember staying at the Contemporary Resort Hotel and 'upgraded' with a room overlooking the park for $44.00 a night.

Back then, it cost $3.50 for Peg and I and a buck each for the kids for a grand total of $9.00 for general admission. Then we bought the eight-adventure book for $5.40 for Peg and I and $4.40 for the kids or another $19.20 for the day, which included use of Walt Disney World Transportation, Magic Kingdom admission and eight attractions in the park. With eight tickets, we had to have serious discussions about how to use our A-B-C and D tickets on Mainstreet USA, Adventureland, Frontierland, Liberty Square, Fantasyland and Tomorrowland. Because we stayed for three days, the kids got to each pick the rides for each day and it all worked out.

When you haven't done something for nearly twenty years, you don't realize how things have changed. First, Mike's and my ride selection was certainly going to be different than the kids and we agreed no 'Small World' as that damn tune still rattles around in my head. We agreed not to go near the Dumbo ride for fear little ones would get us mixed up with the ride and be unhappy when they couldn't climb on board. Due to our advancing age, we knew we wanted to spend some time in the park and spend most of our time in Epcot. We didn't realize that tickets had increased in price…not just a little bit…they'd gone through the roof costing both of us $100 each for the four-day pass. Imagine $25.00 for a day in Fantasyland!

With our 'Courtesy' $10.00 ride from Sherwood Forest to the park, the Disney representative filled us in on Epcot. Here's what he had to say. "EPCOT…which stands for *Experimental Prototype Community of Tomorrow*…was a personal vision of Walt Disney and one of his last great ambitions. It was to be an actual city where people would work, live, and play. The city would highlight the best of urban planning and new technologies and the highlight of the "Florida Project" (which came to be Walt Disney World). In fact, Walt only intended to build a Disneyland (which came to be the Magic Kingdom) in Florida to help finance EPCOT."

"After Walt Disney's death, the company opted against building a city. Without Walt's creative vision, the company leaders felt too uncertain about the project. However, many of the principles and ideals of EPCOT did guide the creation and layout of Walt Disney World, particularly in terms of the transportation network and creation of the Reedy Creek Improvement District and Lake Buena Vista, which are both entities effectively controlled by The Walt Disney Company."

"In terms of the park itself, while many Disney fans consider it one of the most ambitious and greatest creative successes of any theme park, EPCOT Center was dramatically different than Walt Disney's personal vision. The park's highlighting of emerging technologies and general sense of optimism in Future World drew from the themes of what he envisioned the future would be like. The World Showcase of different nations was designed as a permanent World's Fair of sorts, which had always been of particular interest to Walt Disney. I didn't realize that each country in the real world had a gift shop when you left it. Anyway, you could say that EPCOT was guided by Walt's vision to a degree."

"Opening in 1983, the original 'Journey into Imagination' was my favorite of EPCOT attraction. A long dark ride that truly showcased the power of imagination, science and the arts, Journey into Imagination truly pushed the envelope and resonated with guests, especially youngsters like me."

"EPCOT's Carousel of Progress - Horizons, is considered by many to be the greatest Disney World attraction of all time. Horizons is an elaborate attraction dedicated to humanity's future, with the mantra: *'If we can dream it, we can do it."* It opened one year after EPCOT Center on October 1, 1983.'"

"Spaceship Earth has a theme concerning communication. In addition to being an attraction, Spaceship Earth is an 18-story geodesic sphere that serves as the main entrance to Epcot and its marketing symbol like the castle does for the Magic Kingdom."

"EPCOT's Center pavilion called The Land, focuses on agriculture, horticulture, food and human interaction with the earth. While 'The Land' has seen a great amount of changes in the pavilion over the years, it's arguably the pavilion that remains the truest to its opening day message with two restaurants and three attractions."

"The Living Seas pavilion, with Sea Base Alpha, was added to EPCOT Center in 1986 where the Living Seas strives to do more than other pavilions by attempting to convince guests they were actually descending to Sea Base Alpha when they 'boarded' the Hydrolators." To me it was all just a bunch of bubbles.

"Although World Showcase has been part of EPCOT Center since that pivotal day when the models for two separate parks were pushed together to form what we know today, World Showcase has changed over the years. It's changed a lot less than Future World, and much of what you can see today could also be seen by guests who visited in 1982. Still, there have been additions and changes over the years."

With the four-day pass and the monorail, we rode all the rides we wanted to, saw all the different countries and displays in Epcot and froze our asses off. At least we knew why the park was empty. No one in their right mind would have tolerated the rain, fog and damp cold the way we did all bundled up in double Disney sweatshirts that cost us twenty-bucks each.

As our days ran out, so did we and needed to decide where to go. "I want some sun and warm weather" I offered and Mike agreed. "Next stop, the Florida Keys!"

Chapter 31 - The King of Hearts

We got up early, checked out and heard "Ya all come back now," one last time and headed down the Sunshine Screway. More than once I thought of telling the toll collector to put the money where the sun don't shine but remembered I had the minister riding shotgun and we were in the sunshine state. A few miles after we pulled out of Orlando I asked Mike if he was ready for more of the Terrill family history and he said, "Go for it." I looked out at the passing highway rolling beneath our wheels, realizing that it was quite true, 'You'll always find a beautiful girl just over the next hill in Florida,' simply because it's so flat it even made Illinois seem mountainous.

I took a deep breath and began the Terrill lineage again and so I began. "Pippin's son, Charles, who would come to be known as 'Charles the Great' or 'Charlemagne' is probably the most famous person of the Middle Ages. Without him tracing the entire Terrill legacy would have stopped. Because of him I was able to go back to Carolus de Menapii."

Mike leaned back in his seat as he realized how important one man was to solving the riddles that allowed me to go back further than literally anyone else in genealogical time.

I peered ahead and began the daily dissertation. "While little is known about Charlemagne's youth, other than the exploits of his father and the fact that he was educated in a Catholic monastery, the results of his adulthood suggest he received practical training in leadership by participating in the political, social, and military activities associated with his father's court."

"Charlemagne's early years were marked by a succession of events that had immense implications for the Frankish position in the contemporary world. As I mentioned in 751, with papal approval, Pippin the Short seized the Frankish throne from the last Merovingian king, Childeric III."

"When Pippin died in 768 his realm was divided, according to Frankish custom, between Charlemagne and his brother, Carloman. Almost immediately the rivalry between the two brothers threatened the unity of the Frankish kingdom. Seeking advantage over his brother Charlemagne formed an alliance with Desiderius, king of the Lombards, accepting as his wife, the daughter of the king, and did so to stabilize the agreement that threatened the delicate equilibrium that had been established in Italy by his father's alliance with the papacy. The sudden death of Carloman in 771, of which rumor had it, was at the hands of Charlemagne, ended the mounting crisis and Charlemagne, disregarding the rights of Carloman's heirs, took control of the entire Frankish realm."

Mike looked at me and commented, "Nice guy!"

I just shook my head knowing that 'sudden death' was quite common, where today we normally call it murder. "Charlemagne assumed rulership at a moment when powerful forces of change were affecting his kingdom. By Frankish tradition he was a warrior king, expected to lead his followers in wars that would expand Frankish hegemony and produce rewards for his companions. His Merovingian predecessors had succeeded remarkably well as conquerors but their victories resulted in a kingdom similar to that of the Roman Empire, made up of diverse peoples over which unified rule grew increasingly difficult. Complicating the situation for the Merovingian kings was not only the insatiable appetite of the Frankish aristocracy for wealth and power but the constant partitioning of the Frankish realm into smaller and smaller segments. This evolved from the custom of treating the kingdom as a patrimony to be divided amongst all the male heirs surviving each king."

"As had been the case with the Romans back in Carolus' time, Charlemagne's initial strategy was one of military conquest and then absorption of the conquered area and its people under his realm. In so doing, the 'buffer zone' around his home base located in today's Aachen, Germany, became that much wider and Charlemagne felt safer and more secure."

"What changed?" Mike asked.

I smiled and knew it was time to outline my presence in the time and place of Charles the Great. "While others such as Charles Martel and Pepin the Short aged, I did not. For this reason, along with my knowledge of the past, which was still the future, I was considered somewhat of a soothsayer and held in high regard to the point that I became a member of Charlemagne's council who he would look to for advice. I knew I needed to be careful and yet, I also realized I had the opportunity to actually change history for the better. Knowing both the past and future, while understanding the decline and fall of the Roman Empire, I believed I could assist Charles the Great in developing a plan that would endear him to not only his current subjects but those whom he conquered."

"You met Charlemagne?" Mike asked incredulously.

"Yup, and got to know him quite well."

"When I returned to the present, I wrote a brief summary of the man I not only met but worked with. I thought I'd write a book but never got around to it. Here's what I wrote" as I had Mike pull another Manilla folder from my battered and beaten leather satchel.

Charlemagne was large, strong and, for the times, quite tall. The upper part of his head was round. His eyes were very large and animated. His nose was a little long and he had light brown hair that was turning gray. He had a natural smile and his range of emotions were such that most people considered him almost merry, unless, of course, you raised his ire and then there was a totally different side. All-in-all, his appearance was always stately and dignified, whether he was standing or sitting. Because I saw him in his later years, his neck was a bit thick and he had a slight double chin. His belly was rather prominent but the symmetry of the rest of his body concealed these defects. Even though he was in his late sixties, his walk was firm and his whole carriage was manly. The surprising thing was that his voice was clear but surprisingly thin and not what you would expect from a man of his size or stature.

"'His health was excellent until four years before he died when he frequently suffered from fevers and limped a little. Even then he followed his own inclinations rather than the advice of doctors who were always frustrated because they wanted him to eat boiled meat instead of roasts.'"

"'For his rank and power, one would have assumed he would be regaled in finery but he wasn't. Charlemagne always kept to the traditional Frank dress consisting of a linen shirt and trousers, as underwear, covered with a silk-fringed tunic and trousers tied with bands. His shoes changed with the seasons to protect him from the cold. In winter he always had an otter skin coat over his shoulders. When it was really cold, over the otter skin he would wear a blue cloak and always wore a sword, usually one with a gold or silver hilt and belt. Depending on what was happening that day the sword could be a very basic design or sometimes jeweled but then only on great feast days or when he was entertaining foreign ambassadors.

Charlemagne was moderate in eating and particularly in drinking and would have a facial expression of disdain if they had too much to drink as he hated drunkenness in anybody, even more so in himself. His doctor's premise for recovery from any illness was fasting but Charlemagne couldn't abstain from food too long and often complained that fasts were detrimental. He very rarely held banquets, except on great feast days but when he did he would invite a large number of people. His meals usually consisted of four courses, one of which would be what his huntsmen would ceremoniously bring in on a spit which would elicit a huge smile as he loved this better than of any other dish. At meal times he would listen to reading or music where the readings were stories of the old days, particularly St. Augustine's writings and especially 'The City of God.' He was so moderate in drinking wine that he rarely allowed himself more than three cups in the course of a meal. In summer after lunch he would eat some fruit, drink a single cup of wine, undress, and rest for two or three hours. I was told he'd awaken and get up from bed four or five times during the night."

"Gee, that sounds familiar," Mike interjected with a smile.

When Mike was done reading, I continued. "While he was dressing and putting on his shoes, he not only gave audience to his friends to the point that, if the Count of the Palace told him of a case requiring his judgment, he had them come to his room and would judge the case as if he were at his court and perform the day's duties right then and there."

"Sounds like Lyndon Johnson, who sat on a different throne." Mike added.

"At council, I witnessed the political pressures applied by those whose only goal was to enhance their position with the king and, therefore, their power and holdings simply by advocating brute force. Instead, I inquired as to why almighty Rome failed and members of council could not answer. Instead I asked, 'Which is easier, to guard against insurrection simply because the conquered have been given no rights and opportunities or develop new territories and citizens by providing them with more than they had before?'"

"Some of the war council said that the only way to control the masses was through fear. One example was in 782 and defeating the Saxons at Verden, Germany. Charlemagne had 4,500 of them beheaded for refusing to convert to Christianity. Charlemagne expected, make that demanded loyalty in return for his generosity. While he made men rich and powerful he also expected them to defend and support his reign. When one failed to do so the consequences could be catastrophic."

"With this in mind, while others pondered my question, Charlemagne looked to me for an answer to which I replied, 'What is it that you have conquered when you succeed in battle?' The council looked at me as if I was an idiot. However, I held my ground and remembered what Mrs. Gordon taught us in history. I looked at council and then at Charlemagne and responded, 'A battle is simply a small part of a war, while a war is made up of several battles that aren't only fought with swords, arrows and axes but for the hearts and minds of those who are not warriors simply because war isn't just about land but attitudes and beliefs as well.'"

"There was a snide look of disdain from part of the group as I continued. 'Normally, the outcome of a battle does not decide the winner of a war, simply because war is an intense armed conflict generally characterized by extreme violence, aggression, destruction and mortality. The true winners of war are those who garner the willing loyalty of the citizens. This cannot be achieved by force and fear. However, they can be created by providing things they covet that were not there before. Then and only then will there be true peace and complete loyalty, as those who were conquered become soldiers for the common good of their former enemies.'"

"The War Lords shook their heads in disagreement as Charlemagne pondered my words and inquired, 'And what do you propose?'"

"I looked at him and indicated that we needed to identify what he could provide that the conquered didn't already have including social, financial and political structures that would indicate Charlemagne's way of life was better than what they had before."

"Examples, please," Charlemagne responded. "What's the one thing that everyone wants?"

"There was a pause and then I answered my own question, 'Short term… safety, security, land ownership and a sense of justice. Long term… a better life for their children' to which every member of council agreed as I continued. 'Upon conquering an area, laws and regulations must be posted that outline the citizen's rights and freedoms and also the pledge of safety and security, including theft of property, right to trial along with safety and security for the women and children from any form of forced physical contact.'"

"Again, the council concurred as I added, 'Second, is the establishment of an educational system for all children and even those adults who so desire, allowing them to learn to read and write, including the provision of books and school materials.'"

"'Third, is the development of a fair and equitable form of taxation, where a portion of what is collected is returned to that community to help build better roads, wells, schools and churches so that those who have paid can see something for what they contributed.'"

"'Fourth, there must be a way for all citizens to have the opportunity to earn partial ownership of their land, such that they begin to feel accomplishment and commitment to the point that their sacrifices are seen as something they have invested in for the betterment of themselves and their family.'"

"'Finally, there must be an impartial judicial system that states what the penalties are for crimes against each other and the government. When the laws are broken an impartial judge from outside the community, should hear the trial and the accused be given the right to speak, from which the judge, and only the judge, shall make a decision of guilt or innocence.'"

"I looked at the council and reiterated, 'With these five components, you will give the conquered something they did not have and that is hope - hope that tomorrow will be better than today and not as good as the next. From hope comes belief and from belief comes loyalty, not forced and not coerced, but earned without threats and violence. Do we all not want to live in peace and feel that we are safe because those beyond our realm will stand with us and defend what they feel is theirs?'"

"'What about those disloyal to the king?'"

"'Those who lie, steal or attempt to usurp the authority of the king must be made examples of to the point that no one, and I mean no one, can believe they are above the law or the integrity that comes from honesty and loyalty to the king.'"

I looked at Mike and added. "Charlemagne stood and looked at his council. They all knew that once he stood, his decision was made and further discussion was fruitless as he decreed, 'We shall follow the proposal put forth. While there will still be many battles, we shall not seek control by oppression but by inclusion.'"

I continued. "And so, it began, unlike the Romans, Charlemagne's military campaigns were focused on securing an area and then having the conquered willingly come under his rule. This transformation wasn't to be done through domination but through an awareness that, under his auspices, new citizens would have protective rights, including not only military defense but opportunities not seen before. Also, unlike the Romans, Charlemagne did not condone the brutalization of the citizenry as a show of power."

"Charlemagne abided by the covenants set forth as he truly understood that lasting peace came through cooperation and respect and not through domination and intimidation and, to sustain this, it meant a strong alliance with the Church. While there was peace amongst the conquered, Charlemagne continued to wage a bloody three decades long series of battles against the Saxons where he sustained his ruthlessness. While battles were brutal, when they were over his goal was to integrate the conquered land into his realm and gain the local populous' support and in most instances, he did."

"The rules he established for the conquered were nothing more than those already aligned. In fact, he demanded a level of propriety amongst those who fought with him that exceeded what he required from those he conquered. One example dealt with a campaign into southwest France where one of Charlemagne's soldiers took it upon himself to take advantage of a young girl. When Charlemagne learned of the event, he held a public trial in front of the recently conquered citizens where it was determined that the event did take place."

"As a penalty, the soldier was taken to the center of the village and a pole was put in place to which the solider, whose hands and feet were bound, was lifted off the ground by an ever-tightening leather strap that had been looped around his genitals. Literally hanging there, the soldier was made an example of. When the weight was not enough to cause his body parts to separate from his torso, rocks we added to his arms and legs until separation took place and the soldier was left to bleed to death. In so doing those who were under Charlemagne's command recognized his intensity for civility, while those who had been conquered realized their new ruler was a man of peace, whose only goal was unification and not domination."

"The distinguishing mark of Charlemagne's reign was his effort to honor the age-old customs and expectations of Frankish kingship while responding creatively to the new forces impinging on society. His personal qualities served him well in confronting that challenge. The ideal warrior chief, Charlemagne was an imposing physical presence blessed with extraordinary energy, personal courage and an iron will. He loved the active life…the military campaigning, hunting and swimming…but was no less at home at court, generous with his gifts, a gregarious host at the banquet table and adept at establishing friendships."

Mike looked at me and responded, "In other words, the consummate politician".

I smiled as if to agree and continued. "Never far from his mind was his large family that included five wives, several concubines and at least 18 children over whose interests he watched carefully."

I continued. "Although he received only an elementary level of formal education, I quickly saw that Charlemagne possessed considerable native intelligence, intellectual curiosity and willingness to learn from others, along with a profound level of religious sensibility, which were all attributes that allowed him to comprehend the forces that were reshaping the world around him."

"Charlemagne was fluent in speech and could express whatever he had to say with the utmost clarity. However, he was never satisfied with speaking in just his native language and so he learned foreign ones as well. He was a master of

Latin and could understand Greek but was challenged when it came to speaking it, which would frustrate him immensely."

"If one didn't know better, he might have passed for a teacher of eloquence as he was keen on the arts and held teachers in great esteem, while numerously conferring great honors on them. As an example, Peter of Pisa, who was also known as Petrus Grammaticus, was an Italian grammarian, deacon and poet who originally taught at Pavia, Italy. In 776, after Charlemagne's conquest of the Lombard Kingdom, Peter was summoned to the Carolingian court simply to teach Charlemagne grammar."

"While Petrus, as I called him, was influential, one of the most important people in Charlemagne's life was Alcuin, who was an educator from England who taught Latin. As well as being a poet and cleric, Alcuin met Charlemagne in 781 in Italy where the king was assembling the leading English, Irish and Italian scholars to create a school for himself, family and friends."

"Alcuin introduced the teaching methods of the English into the Frankish schools as he systematized the curriculum, raised the standards of scholarship and encouraged the study of liberal arts for the better understanding of the spiritual doctrine, particularly humanism. This centered on the development of human virtue, in all its forms and to its fullest extent, by not only understanding benevolence, compassion and mercy but also more assertive characteristics such as fortitude, judgment, prudence, eloquence, and even love of honor."

"In his 'spare time' Alcuin made important reforms in the Roman Catholic liturgy and left more than 300 Latin letters that have been a valuable source on the history of his time. He was also responsible for the introduction of the Irish Northumbrian custom of singing the creed and arranging votive masses for particular days of the week in an order still followed by Catholics. Alcuin also re-edited the Latin Vulgate, and wrote a number of works on education, theology, and philosophy."

"Latin was established as the standard language of scholarship, allowing the exchange of ideas between the diverse ethnic groups brought together for scientific, religious and political texts that persisted well into the 17th century. To this day, it's Latin that allows those in science and medicine to communicate regardless of their native tongue."

I returned to my train of thought and added. "We talked of what Charlemagne could do to transform his role from Warlord to Exulted Ruler and lead by respect instead of force. I expressed my value of education and he followed through on opening schools, teaching anyone and everyone who wanted to learn how to read and write. Through the efforts of his council, and particularly the priests, he incorporated a style of writing that we call cursive, that's still used in a modified form today."

"In addition, Charlemagne took some of the tax money and did as I suggested and built churches and libraries, where those who wanted to, could continue to learn. While also concerned about the beauty and sanctity of the churches in his realm, he would also provide workmen and materials needed to ensure that all churches remained houses of God."

"Evolving from Warrior King to Regal Leader allowed Charlemagne to combine his persona with his generosity and make him a figure worthy of respect, loyalty and affection, much like Washington and Lincoln of our nation.

True leaders are capable of making informed decisions, willing to act on those decisions and skilled at persuading others to follow them and have the good of the people as their primary consideration and not themselves and Charlemagne certainly had all the necessary attributes."

"Like many nobles of the time, there were numerous attempts on Charlemagne's life of which one of the most famous represents his mindset. Aachen was known for its hot springs which Charlemagne enjoyed immensely. When noble guests would visit, Charlemagne would periodically invite them to join him in the baths.

"One such incident found Charlemagne in the company of what he considered an ally. As they were partaking in the bath, the ally slipped poison into Charlemagne's drink when he wasn't looking. Previously alerted to the planned indiscretion, Charlemagne pretended to drink the poison and continued with the bath and events of the afternoon with no consequence."

"Charlemagne arranged for a large banquet in the honor of his attempted murderer. At the event, a special meal was prepared for his guest consisting of rare meat that

Charlemagne reported had been acquired by his huntsman. The delicacy was served in a wine sauce that his guest consumed with great indulgence, not realizing he was eating the testicles of four of the attempted murderer's guards who were castrated for the event."

"Upon completing the meal, Charlemagne announced he'd ordered special entertainment for the guest consisting of an enormous captured Bohemian who was confined to a cage who would ravage a victim for his guest's pleasure. Charlemagne then asked his guest if he preferred watching the Bohemian violate a young maiden, young boy or a wench. In observing his guest's facial expression Charlemagne determined that the choice was the young boy and watched the horror on the face of his would-be murderer when the naked child was brought forth and the would-be murderer realized it was his own son."

"The tale says that the would-be murderer begged to have the event stopped and Charlemagne inquired whether his guest would like to make another choice, at which, both the guest's wife and daughter were presented as the Bohemian raged in anticipation of conquest. Again, the attempted murderer begged for mercy!"

"Charlemagne then provided the vial which had been hidden in the baths and offered the guest the option of watching one of his family members be violated or consuming the contents of the recognized vial, thereby providing his potential murderer with the option of taking his own life or the loss of a family member. Unbeknownst to the guest, the contents of the vial had been replaced by a harmless potion."

"The guest was distraught – take his own life and save that of his family, or allow one member to die a punishing death. There was a long pause and the guest drank the vial and waited for his own demise. When it didn't happen, there was relief, as Charlemagne informed him that he, who had once been an ally, had become a traitor and for that reason had been spared."

"Charlemagne notified his guest that he was to be sent in exile with nothing but his family and done so naked of all clothing and possessions except the four neutered guardsmen whose index fingers were severed so that they could use neither sword, nor bow and arrow. With that, the ceremony ended and Charlemagne exited the banquet hall, leaving his remaining guests to ponder the value and consequence of loyalty to this powerful man."

Chapter 32 - Manorialism

I looked at Mike and simply asked "More?" Mike shook his head yes as I thought, 'What a glutton for punishment!' We had just passed the Port St. Lucie exit and still had over one hundred and fifty miles to the Keys and God only knows how many more tolls and so I continued.

"The first three decades of Charlemagne's reign were dominated by military campaigns, which were prompted by a variety of factors that included the need to defend his realm against external foes and internal separatists. Wars cost money and so there was always a desire for conquest and booty to pay the soldiers. Finally, there was always a keen sense of opportunity offered by changing power relationships enhanced by the profound urge to spread Christianity."

"As the victories increased so did the size of the area of dominance and it became apparent that one centralized government couldn't control everything. To this end, Charlemagne developed the initial form of feudalism that consisted of awarding huge tracts of conquered land to the warrior nobility who had been victorious in battle in return for specific obligations in terms of providing resources to Charlemagne. These obligations consisted, not only of goods and money but pledges of total support to the defense of entire regions and participation in the continuing expansion of the area of dominance."

"The system allowed Charlemagne's power and subsequent authority to grow, while the obligations also expanded to include all three components of the social realm - the nobility, the clergy and the peasantry - that were bound together by a system called 'Manorialism'. Depending on the area and the degree of loyalty, the designated area normally included a large, sometimes fortified manor house where the lord of the manor and his dependents lived and a population of laborers working the surrounding land to support themselves and the lord, too. These laborers fulfilled their obligations with labor or a portion of the crops they grew and later by a form of taxation."

"While many conquests were quite easy, Charlemagne's most demanding military undertaking pitted him against the Saxons, in an area called Saxony, whose conquest required more than 30 years of campaigning, beginning in 772 and ending in 804. Saxony consisted of the area between the Rhine and the Elbe Rivers and was critical for Charlemagne's protection by its location and proximity to his beloved home in Aachen, only seventy miles away. Without getting into too much geography, one needs to know that the Rhine River flows from the Alps of east-central Switzerland, northwest through today's western Germany to the North Sea, while the Elbe River runs from today's Czech Republic through central Germany and also the North Sea."

"The Saxons weren't easily defeated and their conquest represents Charlemagne's longest skirmish marked by pillaging, broken truces, hostage taking, mass killings, deportations and draconian measures to compel acceptance of Christianity, along with occasional Frankish defeats. In the end, Charlemagne did what Caesar couldn't do and that was conquer the area held by the Saxons for well over 2,000 years, with the Frisians, who were Saxon allies, living along the North Sea east of the Rhine, also being forced into submission."

"While the vanquish of Saxony was in progress Charlemagne undertook other campaigns. As soon as he became sole king in 771, he repudiated his Lombard wife and alliance with her father, King Desiderius. Soon after, in 773–774, he answered the appeals of Pope Adrian I, whose reign required military protection. He did so by leading a victorious expedition into Italy, which ended with his assumption of the Lombard crown and annexation of northern Italy under his realm. During this campaign Charlemagne went to Rome to reaffirm the Frankish protectorate over the papacy and confirm papal rights to the territories conceded by Charlemagne's father."

"Concerned with defending southern Gaul from Muslim attacks and beguiled by promises of help from local Muslim leaders in northern Spain, who sought to escape the authority of the Umayyad ruler of Cordoba, Charlemagne invaded Spain in 778. This was an ill- conceived venture that ended in a disastrous defeat of the retreating Frankish army by the Gascon, or Basque, forces in the Battle of Roncevaux Pass."

"Located in the Pyrenees, on the present border between France and Spain, Roncevaux Pass is a high mountain valley. As the Franks retreated across the Pyrenees and back to Francia, a large force of Basques ambushed the rear guard of Charlemagne's army. In so doing, they cut off the Frankish lords who stood their ground but were wiped out in retaliation for Charlemagne's destruction of the city walls of Pamplona which was the Basque capital." "Among those killed in the Battle of Roncevaux was Roland, a Frankish commander whose death elevated him and the Paladins, or Twelve Peers, who were the foremost warriors of Charlemagne's court to a point of veneration. This served as the reference for the stories of King Arthur and the Knights of the Roundtable while personifying Christianity and its battle against the Saracen or Muslim invasion of Europe. The tale of bravery by the Frankish lords influenced the code of chivalry in the Middle Ages and also the birth of the belief in the Crusades that took place from 1095 – 1291."

"Chivalry defined the way in which a knight was supposed to behave and the ideas were developed in France during the Eleventh through Thirteenth centuries before coming to England. The knight was to show loyalty, morality and generosity. In other words the knight should always support his king or lord and be prepared to put his life on the line to protect him. The knight should always do the right thing and be prepared to provide his time and energies for free. These prescribed values became so engrained in society that all the sons of the nobles either became members of the orders of the knights or members of the church."

"Knighthood was a long and difficult process. At the age of seven, boys were sent by their family to the home of a wealthy noble where the training would begin. The boy would serve as a page and improve his fitness and skills by playing sports and doing structured exercise. At the age of fourteen or fifteen the boy would become a squire, looking after the lord's armor and horses and possibly accompanying the lord into battle."

"At the age of twenty-one, the young man would become a knight. In a ceremony held in the presence of the lord and other knights of the order, he would swear an oath of loyalty and bravery to defend God, the church and ladies. Finally, kneeling before his lord, the lord would place his sword on the new recruit's shoulder and declare him a knight and be awarded the title of 'sir'."

"Despite this Battle of Roncevaux setback, Charlemagne persisted in his effort to make the frontier in Spain more secure. In 781 he created the subkingdom of Francia Occidentals, which means 'West of Francia', of which Aquitaine represented the southwest section of today's France. In medieval history, it represents the earliest stage of the Kingdom of France, lasting from about 840 until 987, which emerged from the partition of the Carolingian Empire in 843 under the Treaty of Verdun, and did so following the death of Charlemagne's son, Louis the Pious. From that base, Frankish forces mounted a series of campaigns that eventually established control over the Spanish Marsh, which was the territory lying between the Pyrenees and the Ebro River."

"Back in what's today Hungary and Italy additional campaigns were required to incorporate the Lombard kingdom fully into the Frankish realm. However, an important step in that process came in 781, when Charlemagne created the subkingdom of Francia Orientalis, or East Francia, ruled by the Carolingian dynasty until 911 with Charlemagne's son, Pippin, ordained as king."

"In 787–788 Charlemagne forcibly annexed Bavaria, whose leaders had long resisted Frankish rule. That victory brought the Franks face-to-face with the Avars who were Asiatic nomads who had formed an extensive empire largely inhabited by conquered Slavs living on both sides of the Danube. By the 8th century, Avar power was in decline and successful Frankish campaigns in 791, 795, and 796 hastened the disintegration of the Empire. Charlemagne captured a huge store of booty, claimed a block of territory south of the Danube in Carinthia and Pannonia, in what today is part of eastern Germany and opened a missionary that led to the conversion of the Avars and their former Slavic subjects to Christianity."

"One of Charlemagne's classic battles against the Avars took place at the Iron Gates on the Danube River between Serbia to the south and Romania to the north. The Iron Gate valley is about 2 miles long and 530 feet wide with towering rock cliffs on each side that make it one of the most dramatic natural wonders of Europe and also an ideal place for an ambush. Located near the town of Sip, there is a large rock reef called Perigrada that obstructed nearly the whole width of the river until the construction of the Sip Canal in 1896."

"Charlemagne followed the Avars and captured several of their warriors and appeared to be retreating back to Aachen for his winter respite. Instead of having the Avar warriors killed, he had them blinded by hot pokers, as his strategy had always been that a wounded man required more attention than a dead one and that meant fewer combatants."

"A lesson from the Menapii!" Mike offered, making me appreciate the fact that he was actually listening to what I was saying. I continued. "Because it was an exceptionally cold winter, there was a layer of ice on the Danube. It had begun to snow and yet Charlemagne was intent on ending the winter battle once and for all and directed his men to soak the dried pith of the rush plant in fat or grease, normally used for their torches and create a large circle on the ice near Perigrada. With snow falling, Charlemagne then took the blind warriors, tied them together and placed them on the ice, bonding them together so that they couldn't move and continued his march up the frozen Danube."

"The Avar warriors saw Charlemagne's entourage and followed up the river. Seeing their comrades, they elected to come to their rescue. As they approached, the pith was torched on both sides and the Saxons were encircled in flame, as the ice around them began to melt. They were trapped as the ice gave way and they fell into the fast-moving river where over 100 Avars drowned."

"Charlemagne's military successes resulted in an ever-widening frontier which needed to be defended. Through a combination of military force and diplomacy, he established relatively stable relations with a variety of potential enemies, including the Danish kingdom, several Slavic tribes inhabiting the territory along the eastern frontier stretching from the Baltic Sea to the Balkans, the Lombard Duchy of Benevento in southern Italy, the Muslims in Spain and the Gascons and the Bretons in Gaul."

With my summary, Mike appeared to be realizing that Charlemagne literally unified all of today's Western Europe.

I continued. "The Italian scene was complicated by the Papal State, whose boundaries remained problematic and whose leader, the pope, had no clearly defined political status relative to his Frankish protector. Charlemagne's relations with the papacy, especially with Pope Adrian I, were positive, which brought him valuable support for his religious program and praise for his qualities as a Christian leader. The expanded Frankish presence in Italy and the Balkans intensified diplomatic encounters with the Eastern emperors. This strengthened Charlemagne's position with respect to the Eastern Roman Empire that had been weakened by internal dissension and threatened by Muslim and Bulgar pressure on its eastern and northern frontiers."

"Charlemagne also established friendly relations with the Anglo-Saxon kings of Mercia and Northumbria and the ruler of the Christian kingdom of Asturias in northwestern Spain and enjoyed a vague role as protector of the Christian establishment in Jerusalem. By boldly and resourcefully combining the traditional role of warrior king with aggressive diplomacy, based on a good grasp of current political realities, Charlemagne elevated the Frankish kingdom to a position of ultimate leadership in the European world."

We finally made it past the last toll booth and onto Highway 1, just south of Homestead as both of us simultaneously yawned as we saw the sign reading "Key Largo Twenty-Seven Miles" and the first of many signs for a KOA campground that promised Camping, RV Parking, Pool and Dive Shop."

With my train of thought still on Charlemagne, I wanted to wrap it all up before we stopped for the night and so I continued. "While responding to the challenges involved in enacting his role as warrior king, Charlemagne was always mindful of the obligation of a Frankish ruler to maintain the unity of his realm. While language, writing, education and re-investing a portion of the taxes helped, the burden was complicated by the ethnic, linguistic, and legal divisions between the populations brought under Frankish domination in the course of three centuries of conquest, beginning with the reign of King Clovis."

"As a political leader, Charlemagne was not an innovator. His concern was to make more effective the political institutions and administrative techniques inherited from his Merovingian predecessors. Regardless of what people think or write, the central directive force of the kingdom remained the king himself, whose office, by tradition, empowered its holder with the right to command the obedience of his subjects and punish those who didn't."

"For assistance in asserting his power, Charlemagne relied on his 'palatium', which was a shifting assemblage of family members, trusted lay and ecclesiastical companions, and assorted hangers-on, which included me. They constituted an itinerant court following the king as he carried out his military campaigns who sought to take advantage of the income generated from widely scattered royal estates. Members of this circle, some with titles suggesting primitive administrative departments, performed various functions decreed by the king related to managing royal resources, conducting military campaigns and diplomatic missions, while others produced written documents needed to administer the realm, or undertook missions across the kingdom to enforce royal policies, render justice, conduct religious services, and counsel the king."

"In other words, like America today," Mike replied.

"You got it!" I answered and continued, "A critical component of the king's effectiveness and a matter of constant concern was the army in which all freemen were obligated to serve at their own expense when summoned by the king. Increasingly important in maintaining the military establishment, especially its armored cavalry, was the king's ability to provide sources of income consisting normally of land grants, that enabled his subjects to serve. The resources required to sustain the central government were derived from war booty, income from royal estates, judicial fines and fees, tolls on trade, obligatory gifts from noble subjects and, to a very limited degree, direct taxes."

"Yup, nothing's changed!" Mike interjected.

I continued. "To exercise his authority locally, Charlemagne continued to rely on royal officials known as counts, who represented royal authority in territorial entities called 'Pagi'. Their functions included administering justice, raising troops, collecting taxes and keeping peace. Bishops also continued to play an important role in local government. Charlemagne also expanded clerical involvement in government by increasing the use of royal grants of immunity to bishops and abbots. This freed their properties from intervention by public authorities. This privilege indirectly allowed its recipients or their agents, to rule over those inhabiting their property as long as they enjoyed royal favor. The effectiveness of this system depended largely on the abilities and loyalty of those who filled offices at the local level. Charlemagne recruited most royal officials from a limited number of interrelated aristocratic families who were eager to serve the king in return for the prestige, power and material rewards associated with royal service."

"Still sounds like our country today!" Mike interjected.

I concurred and continued. "Charlemagne relied on these alliances for protection and in turn, would assist the landowners in maintaining order whenever there was a problem. For this he expected loyalty as well. Whenever there was an uprising or an ally that chose to disregard the alliance, Charlemagne would make certain they paid a huge price, not only to quell any insurrection but show others that a violation of peace would result in dire consequences."

"In one such instance, a lord who had been loyal, elected to steal from Charlemagne and attempt a coup. The King of Hearts learned of the plan and sent his men. When the lord awakened one morning he found the heads of 250 of his loyalists stuck on posts surrounding his castle. Needless to say, the lord realized that the consequence for violating trust could be monumental."

"Ouch!" Mike offered.

"Charlemagne's most innovative political measures involved strengthening the linkages between himself, his palatium and local officials where he made full use of the traditional Frankish annual assembly and the mustering of those called to military service. This generated the common bond needed and the willingness to follow their leader into war. Charlemagne expanded the function of these meetings to make them an instrument for cementing the king's personal ties with counts, bishops, abbots and powerful magnates. At these assemblies, he heard their complaints, accepted advice, gained their approval for his policies and delivered, in his own words, commands for ruling his realm."

"The network of families from which Charlemagne selected most of his officials provided important channels through which pressure could be applied to assure that royal commands were executed locally. In addition, Charlemagne required all his free subjects to swear, under oath, to obey the king and conduct themselves in ways that contributed to peace and accord. Especially important in strengthening the king's hand politically was Charlemagne's practice of establishing personal ties with powerful figures by accepting them as royal vassals in return for benefices in the form of offices and land grants for their personal benefit as long as they remained loyal."

"Charlemagne integrated the central and local administrations by standardizing and expanding the use of 'Missi Dominici' who were royal agents charged with making regular circuits through specifically defined territorial entities to announce the king's will, gather information on the performance of local officials and then correct abuses. The greatly expanded use of written documents as a means of communication between the central and the local governments allowed for greater precision and uniformity in transmitting royal orders and gathering information about their execution. Among these documents were the Royal Capitularies, which were quasi-legislative documents dispatched across the kingdom to set forth the king's will and provide instructions for enacting his orders."

"Charlemagne's reign also indicates his awareness of new developments affecting economic and social conditions. Although scholars are divided on the import of his actions, evidence suggests that he was concerned with improving the organization and techniques of agricultural production, establishing a monetary system better attuned to actual exchange operations, standardizing weights and measures, expanding trading ventures into areas around the North and Baltic Seas and protecting merchants from excessive tolls and robbery. Royal legislation also sought to protect the weak against exploitation and injustice."

"While Charlemagne helped clarify the incipient lord-vassal system and utilized that form of social contract to promote order and stability, his economic and social initiatives were actually motivated by his moral convictions. These measures gave modest impetus to movements that eventually ended the economic depression and social instability that had gripped Western Europe since the fall of the Roman Empire two-hundred years before."

"Charlemagne's effort to be an effective ruler was given fresh impetus and direction by a change in the perceptions regarding the purpose of government and role of monarchs. That change led to the grafting of a religious component onto the traditional, somewhat narrow, concept of royal authority. Drawing on the Old Testament and teachings of St. Augustine of Hippo on the nature of the 'city of God', Charlemagne and his advisers, progressively saw his position as bestowed by God for the purpose of realizing the divine plan for the universe. Sovereignty therefore, took on a ministerial dimension, which obligated the ruler to assume responsibility for both the spiritual and material wellbeing of his subjects entailing a vast expansion of traditional royal authority and a redefinition of the priorities that his government should serve."

"Mike, if you look at the initial concept and structure of the U.S. government established by our founding fathers, you'll see that a great deal of it came from 1215 and the British Magna Carta that declared the sovereign to be subject to the rule of law. In addition, it also sustained the purported liberties held by free men regarding individual rights in Anglo-American jurisprudence."

"In so doing Charlemagne's basic configuration served as the foundation, structure and theory for the U.S. Constitution, albeit prior to the brilliance of adding Amendments that allow our laws to be a dynamic treatise that is both structured and malleable at the same time."

The day's history lesson was over. I believe Mike was impressed, not only by the depth of my knowledge but the magnitude of what transpired. We found the KOA and pulled in. Unlike Sherwood Forest, the place was more like a gravel parking lot, with a store, small pool, volleyball court and dive shop. After the drive, neither of us cared. Above all else...it was sunny and warm...hoorah!

Chapter 33 – The Coral Grill

We hunkered down at the KOA and met snowbirds from all over the country. Within a few days it was like being back in Mineral Point without the snow and pasty but plenty of gossip. Mike and I sauntered over to the dive shop and met Kenny and his wife, Laura, who ran the place. We found out there was an underwater state park nearby called John Pennecamp   encompassing nearly 70 nautical square miles where Kenny and Laura took people on snorkeling or dive tours for twenty-bucks a pop.

We thought 'What the heck,' and signed up for the tour the next day and, boy, were we in for a treat. It was Mike, Kenny, Laura and me. We took a look at the scenery, including Laura in one of those tiny, barely-there, string bikinis. I looked at Mike and he at me and both sets of eyebrows rose in approval. Needless to say, we didn't have that back in Heaven's Waiting Room.

Kenny took us to see the mangrove swamps and tropical hammocks in hopes of seeing Myrtle, the park's Manatee, then we headed out to the coral reefs. Some visitors go for the glass bottom boat ride. We went snorkeling and saw hundreds of fish. Laura was our snorkel guide and neither Mike nor me wanted to stop looking. I know! I know! Dirty old men. Tee! Hee!

While that would have been enough, Kenny wasn't aware that Mike was a retired minister and took us for a cheap thrill as we slowly passed by the nude beach on the way back to the KOA. I looked at Mike and he just grinned, making sure I didn't let on what he'd done for a living. Needless to say, seeing a bunch of naked old people isn't nearly as erotic as one would think as it brought back memories of the folks back home…sagging bottoms, wrinkles and all, including the men. Yiikes!

"You ever been skinny dipping?" Mike inquired. "Out at the farm, we did it all the time." I replied.

"Me too, except Ginny and I'd go over to the Arboretum and Lake Wingra in Madison and do it there." Mike reflected with a shy grin on his face.

"When you were in college?" I inquired somewhat incredulously.

"Most certainly! We'd park the car in Lost Village and walk over through the woods. There was this tree that leaned out over the water and we'd slip out of our clothes and go into the lake and have our fun."

My mind wandered back to Peg and I going out to the pond and doing the same thing. I guess you never think that ministers would be prone to such until you realize that, only in America is the naked body considered obscene. I'd forgotten about the times in the South of France when we'd 'join the crowd' and think nothing of it. Those were the good old days!

"Did you wear a fig leaf?" I joked.

Mike laughed and said. "Hardly."

Laura overheard our jocular bantering and pointed out that her degree was in Art History and, before meeting Kenny worked at the Wilzig Art Museum in Miami that she said housed an incredible collection of art from around the world. She noted that inside were ancient Roman antiquities, pre-Columbian artifacts, and Japanese shunga illustrations including artists such as Salvador Dalí, Robert Mapplethorpe and even Rembrandt, as they were props from films like *'A Clockwork Orange'*.

As we were slowly making our way back to KOA, she noted, "I really feel sorry for the poor fig leaf that shielded famous biblical figures and nude sculptures for centuries. How would you like to be a plant synonymous with sin, sex, and censorship?

"Mike probably wouldn't but some of it doesn't sound too bad to me," I offered.

Laura was being very serious as she leaned back and, over the hum of the engine, added. "In large part, we had a dark period in art history where the artists determined to portray nudity as beautiful art even when it was considered taboo. Take Michelangelo's famous sculpture David. Here you had a muscular, starkly naked depiction of its namesake biblical hero that scandalized the artist's fellow Florentines and the Catholic clergy when unveiled in Florence's Piazza della Signoria in 1504. At the direction of Pope Julius the Second, good old David's 'privates' were girdled with a garland of bronze fig leaves by authorities."

"I think they were just jealous," I snickered.

Breaking some of the intensity, Laura got a wry grin and added. "Sixty years later and just months before Michelangelo's death, the Catholic Church issued an edict demanding that 'figures shall not be painted or adorned that would excite...lust.' The clergy began a crusade to camouflage what they considered vile in artworks across Italy. Their coverups of choice? Loincloths, foliage, and—most often—fig leaves and that became known as the 'Fig Leaf Campaign,' one of history's most significant acts of art censorship."

"The plant's cultural significance can be clearly traced back to the tale of Adam and Eve. According to the men who wrote the Bible, the duo was shamed by their nudity after eating from the tree of knowledge, 'sewed fig leaves together and made themselves aprons.' Early artistic depictions of the purported events show the once-nude figures sheathed in leaves that obscure their genitals, subtly represented original sin and a fall from grace while communicating to the religion's flock that nudity was shameful."

"By the medieval era, art commissioned by the Catholic Church mostly represented nudity and was used to depict people who'd been sent to hell. That began to change in the 1400s, when Italian artists—thanks to a mounting interest in antiquities and excavation, rediscovered classical Roman and Greek art forged in a time when the chiseled nude body represented honor and virtue, as opposed to immorality and vice."

"I knew there was a reason why Peg kept wanting to go out to the farm. It was me!" I exclaimed.

Laura just shook her head and continued. "This idea inspired artists like Donatello, who started in 1440 to honor the nude body in all its glory in Florence, where the Catholic Church wielded vast power. His bronze rendition of David has been cited by scholars as the first known sculpture depicting a completely naked figure since antiquity."

"Michelangelo, even after receiving criticism for his own version of David, continued to incorporate nudity into his work. Sadly, as, Michelangelo's artistic career developed, Pope Paul III and the Catholic Church's crackdown on 'lasciviousness' also intensified. This had everything to do with accusations of corruption against the Church being made by Martin Luther. Fearful of losing its flock Pope Pius IV and the

Vatican began ordering reforms across the church, including censorship of nudity in art. Even so Michelangelo received an abundance of commissions from popes and other powerful clergymen during his life, most notably the ceiling of the Sistine Chapel."

"Periodically, the Vatican called him out for crossing the line of decency. As an example, in the 1540s, he pushed his luck, yet again—this time for a wall fresco in the Sistine Chapel depicting the Last Judgement. Traditionally, that subject had been illustrated with figures clothed according to social rank but Michelangelo stripped them of both their status and clothing, showing everyone in the buff. Certain powerful figures in the Vatican weren't happy, calling the paintings fit 'for the public baths and taverns' rather than a chapel. These passionate criticisms effectively launched the Fig Leaf Campaign. Instituted by Pope Pius IV and formalized at the Council of Trent's 1563 decree banning 'all lasciviousness' in religious imagery, nude sculptures across Italy, and especially in Rome, soon sported carefully placed metal fig leaves with many of the plaster and marble phalluses were even chiseled off."

"The discretion campaign didn't spare paintings, either. Areas of Michelangelo's 'Last Judgement' deemed unsavory were painted over twice in the 1500's, and then again in the 1700's by Pope Clement XI, Innocent the XIII and Benedict XIV with little swaddles and loincloths added. The trend also transformed 15th Century frescoes in Florence's Brancacci Chapel and in the 1600's an unknown artist painted fig leaves over its nude figures, namely a depiction of Adam and Eve being ousted from Eden. Between 1758 and 1759, Pope Clement XIII swathed even more sculptures in the Vatican's collection with fig leaves."

Laura looked at Mike and I in earnest and continued. "The fig leaf phenomenon spread beyond Italy's borders, too. When the Grand Duke of Tuscany gifted a cast of Michelangelo's David to Queen Victoria in 1857 a large leaf was promptly sculpted to 'spare the blushes of visiting female dignitaries.' Luckily the leaf was created so that it could be removed easily. Today, the sculpture stands completely nude, while a small vitrine next to it houses the leaf."

"Over the last twenty years Masaccio's Adam and Eve and Michelangelo's Last Judgement have been restored. In order to honor the artists' original visions, some of the painted loincloths and leaves have been painstakingly removed from their original surfaces. Still, censorship and the moral dilemmas nudity inspires still rage on."

While the snorkeling was interesting, and the 'saggers' as we called them funny, Laura's passionate explanation of censorship was by far the most intriguing part. Beyond the discussion and learning that Mike and I had one more thing in common what made the snorkel trip a complete success was that Kenny invited us to go "shrimping" that night along the canal walls.

Mike and I hoped Laura would be wearing the same attire but she wasn't…darn! We learned that shrimp hang onto the canal walls at night for security and when you flash a light on them they freeze. All you need do is scoop them off the walls and dinner is served…well, after you boil and peel them, that is.

It sure was fun and wasn't long before we had a bucket full. Laura offered to cook them the following night for dinner as Mike and I took our Honda scooters down to the Winn Dixie and bought a couple bottles of wine.

As we shared our histories, we asked Kenny where we should go for dinner. Kenney replied, "the best place by far, is the Coral Grill in Islamorada. They've got a fifty-foot long spread and on Fridays have all you can eat Grouper for $9.95."

I looked at Mike and he at me and we knew we'd skip breakfast and make pigs out of ourselves. Kenny offered to drive and sure enough the buffet was fifty feet long with all kinds of fruit, vegetables, seafood and then about twenty different types of dessert. Mike and I snarfed down enough Grouper until we thought we couldn't eat anymore and then headed back to the desert bar and had the best Key Lime pie you could imagine. With as generous as Kenny and Laura had been, Mike pulled out his wallet and new American Express card and said the meal was on him. Politely, Kenney said no but I knew there wouldn't be any other way.

Mike and I agreed that, if you visited the Keys, you needed to make it all the way to Key West, acclaimed to be "America's Southern Most Point". However, the idea of driving the bus or riding our scooters 113 miles each way wasn't my idea of fun. Kenny, suggested that we rent a car from rent-a-wreck for $19.95 and drive down. It made sense to me and so the next morning at 7:00 AM and the minute they opened, two old Badgers were standing there waiting to rent a wreck.

Sure enough, you could rent a car for $19.95 but I didn't think we'd be getting a Rollscarardly… which was a car that rolls down one hill and can hardly make it up the next. The kid behind the counter talked us into a bright yellow 1985 Ford Mustang Convertible with 'only' 176,000 miles on it for 'just' $29.95 for the day.

We went out and inspected the vehicle and thought 'Why not?' and so off we went, down Highway One, across the Seven-Mile Bridge, which is actually only 6.8 miles according to Mustang Sally's odometer, then through Marathon, until all the teaser billboards for Key West started showing up and we began to get all jittery with excitement.

There it was, the last town in America. A cheap thrill! We drove around and found Hemingway's house and then the actual end of America where we took our pictures next to the sign to prove we were there. Next, we went into town and, well, it was a little different than we thought it was going to be, as there were a lot of guys holding hands. Mike just shrugged and said, "They're God's children too."

After a couple of hours of looking in the stores and drinking a couple of beers, it was time to head back to Key Largo. As we headed up the road from whence we came (*I've always wanted to write that*) I glanced to the west and saw some cumulonimbus clouds. As we continued north, those clouds got closer and closer and darker and darker and then all of a sudden it started pouring and I mean raining like a cow pissing on a rock!

We tried putting up the convertible top only to learn it didn't work. We had our choice, keep driving and getting wet, stopping and getting wet or getting wet. We chose getting wet and kept driving, laughing our asses off at how stupid we must have looked but not really caring.

As we got to Tavernier the rain stopped and we saw a Dairy Queen in the middle of the road. Well not actually in the middle of the road per se'. Highway One split and the Dairy Queen was on an island in between. You would have thought it was the end of a rainbow as far as we were concerned as two old farts sloshed their way indoors and ordered Peanut Buster Parfaits as the water trickled down onto the floor to the sounds of squish, squish, squish with each step we took.

The two drowned rats made it back to rent-a-wreck and the kid gave us a ride back to the KOA, dropping us off by the 'guest center'. Arnie, the desk clerk, beckoned us inside and in we sloshed. It seems that the folks who owned the KOA wanted to ask Reverend Mike if he was still 'working' and he'd said, "once a minister, always a minister" noting he filled in for the sick or vacationing ministers back home.

I added, "But just a little more sinister than before", from which the official title Sinister Minister hit home and stuck.

"Reverend Mike, could you possibly do a non-denominational service in the morning?" the warden…err, clerk, behind the counter asked, never blinking at our still soaked clothes.

Mike being Mike said, "Sure," and so one of the two drowned vermin had a job the next morning.

Chapter 34 - Religious Reform

I hadn't been to church in a long time and thought it might do me some good. Being the Keys and the congregation from who knows where, I'm certain most folks thought it would be one of those boring Sundays. Boy, were they in for a surprise!

We went to the volleyball courts at 9:30 or about a half-hour early and Mike went to work greeting those who were setting up chairs and those who'd come early. I think the combination of the gentle smile and the warm handshake before services put everyone at ease.

With it being a vacation location, Mike looked out at the crowd of mostly elderlies like us and simply smiled. Whether it was two or two-hundred, wouldn't have made any difference. I sat and watched my beer-drinking, card-playing buddy scope out the audience and then he began.

"Good morning and thank you for letting me come and talk to you today. I'm the retired minister of the Congregational Church in Mineral Point, Wisconsin. Now you've probably never heard of Mineral Point but I'm here to tell you, you're really missing a great place to visit the next time you're looking for some place special to go."

"A few months ago, I moved into one of those fancy 'adjustment' complexes in Mineral Point. You know, you start out with an apartment and then get transferred to assisted living and then the nursing home and finally they put you in a box and take you out and plant you in this great big yard filled with all kinds of people who were probably strangers or, perhaps, even some friends."

Mike paused for a moment to let the snickers subside and then continued. "When I moved into my new digs a former neighbor of mine, when my wife and I had our house, knocked on my apartment door, carrying a large box."

"After a little small talk, I welcomed him in and motioned toward the box."

"What's this?" I asked. "It's a box of old Bibles."

Mike walked to one side of the volleyball court and leaned against the pole for effect and continued. "I must have had a frown on my face as my former neighbor noted he was going to move into our complex, was cleaning out his house and didn't know what to do with all the Bibles that had been in his family for generations. He noted he wasn't very religious. In fact he said he hadn't been to church since he served in Vietnam. He knew I was a pastor and thought maybe I'd want them."

"It was a kind gesture. Yet, I felt uncomfortable as I didn't have any place to store them."

"'You don't want them?' I asked. 'How about your kids.

Wouldn't they want to keep them in the family?'"

"No," he said. 'Like you, my wife passed away and my kids aren't interested in them. They don't read the Bible, and neither do I. If I throw them away, God might strike me dead or something.' I almost laughed but realized he wasn't kidding. He honestly thought God would punish him if he threw away the Bibles."

"I looked at my former and future neighbor and said, 'Tell you what, I'll take all but one and I'll only take the rest of them if you'll simply open the one you choose to any page and read that page to me."

"My former/future neighbor really didn't know what to think as he pondered my offer. After a moment he agreed and so he looked through all the Bibles and finally selected one that seemed a bit older and a little more worn than the others."

"This old man sat on my couch and opened the book in his hands to Psalm 119 and read aloud... 'Blessed are those whose way is blameless, who walk in the way of the LORD! Blessed are those who keep is testimonies, who seek him with their whole heart, who also do no wrong but walk in his ways! You have commanded your precepts to be kept diligently. Oh, that my ways may be steadfast in keeping your statutes! Then I shall not be put to shame, having my eyes fixed on all your commandments. I will praise you with an upright heart, when I learn your righteous rules. I will keep your statutes; do not utterly forsake me!'"

Mike looked at me and continued talking to the congregation as he continued "I opened my hands as a gesture to my former/future neighbor and asked him to select another page. He simply slid his finger to another passage and came upon Matthew 6:14-15. 'If you forgive other people when they sin against you, your heavenly Father will also forgive you. But if you do not forgive others for their sins, your Father will not forgive your sins.'"

Mike paused, took a deep breath for emphasis and added, "My former/future neighbor just sat there…mouth agape. Words he'd chosen at random were directed at him. A tear welled in his eye as he looked at me and simply asked, 'Do you mind if I keep two more for my kids?"

According to Guinness World Records as of 1990, the Bible remains the best-selling book of all time, with an estimated 5 billion copies sold and distributed. Five billion! Who's the author? It's estimated that there were 40 different contributors and the good book took 1,600 years to write. While many of you enjoy a good book while on vacation, I don't see too many people sitting on their chaise lounges reading the Bible and that's too bad. Regardless of your faith, there's something in there for everyone. Instead, you read above love and hate, acceptance and denial, war and deceit but isn't that what the Bible's all about?"

"As pastors what are we to do with people who possess more Bibles than ever but have little interest in reading them? More important, how do I motivate you to simply open a Bible and engage yourself in a few passages in a way that leads to your own encounters with God. Don't read the Bible for information, guilt or pride. Read it to meet and know God. When you know Him, you will fill your heart with love and joy unlike any you've ever felt before."

"We all have questions we cannot answer. Who made me? What's my purpose? What will happen to me when I die? These are pivotal questions that, in life, we hardly take time to ask and answer. They define who we are, and the answers we provide serve as both the guideposts on our road to heaven and anchors in the rough seas of existence we all have. Vacation is the perfect time to make friends with our souls. It's a time to perk ourselves up, open our eyes, ears, and hearts and seek God's presence in the simple moments between here and there. God IS with us! Ask God to grant you a deeper appreciation for His presence and always remember, you are special. Not only to God but the ones your love."

The folks sitting in the rapidly warming sun were stunned. Those who would have been half asleep on any other Sunday had mouths agape, including one old man who'd forgotten the majesty of the spoken word when given with compassion.

As services ended and the obligatory hand-shakes and thankyou's subsided, we walked back to the bus, started the engine and headed for home. At first there was profound silence as the magnitude of the message was overwhelming. Finally, I broke the silence by simply saying one thing. "Mike, I have one regret."

"What's that?"

"I didn't have the honor to come to your church and hear you preach. Perhaps if I had, the black hole in my heart that has been dug so deep by reading about the other side of religion wouldn't be there."

Mike stared out the windshield and recited. "Will, all the holes can be filled in. Those in the heart can be filled with love and kindness and that's what's good about faith. Yes, there were those who took advantage of the situation! Yes, there has been hypocrisy! But, beneath it all, there is profound goodness sullied by the weakness of man for his own wellbeing. If you have faith in God and then in yourself, that hole will close. I promise you that."

I looked at Mike and simply asked, "Who's the neighbor?"

A slight smile came across Mike's face as he replied, "Simply a friend."

We decided to head back home on I-65 through Atlanta. Along the way we kept seeing signs for Cracker Barrel restaurants. We'd see them along the road and vowed we should stop. Finally we did. I parked the bus on the side lot and we walked in to a virtual cornucopia of stuff we'd never buy in a million years, except for the candy that is.

We were led to our table and perused the menu and the chicken and dumplings caught my eye, bringing back memories of Peg and how she'd make them with Bisquick. I smiled and ordered as did Mike. As we sat waiting for our meals, the couple behind us were talking loud enough for even me to hear. Unfortunately, it wasn't very pleasant with him accusing her and she accusing him of this and that. Perhaps they were tired! Perhaps they were tired of each other. We didn't know.

The food came and it was quite good. Unfortunately, the conversation behind us didn't get any better. The waitress came and delivered the check and instructed us to pay the cashier. We stood and Mike caught the eye of the young man who had been the instigator of the dialogue.

"What are you looking at?" The young man questioned.

Mike just looked at him for a moment and then tilted his head down as if to ponder whether he should speak or let sleeping dogs lie.

"You heard me, gramps! What are you looking at?"

Mike had enough and went to the side of the table and said. "My friend and I stopped here for a meal and a little relaxation. Unfortunately, you and this young lady felt it was proper to share your troubles with the world. Now we all have problems but most of us keep them to ourselves or at least until we're in private. From your conversation it appears one of you doesn't think much of the other and that's too bad."

The kid just glared at Mike and was about to get up when Mike splayed his fingers and continued. "You sir, said…'It's not that I want you to do it. It's that I want you to want to do it.'"

"So?"

"Well, young man, your wife or girlfriend has either said something similar to you or you've said it to her before. If either of you haven't said it, you've probably wanted to and it's likely you had a big argument where you danced around the sentiment with those exact words flashing in your brain."

I looked at the young girl and saw her head nodding as Mike continued. "The issue never really matters much. It could have been anything and yet it caused disagreement and frustration that I could hear and feel as we sat eating our dinner. Now, I'm certain a few miles down the road, we'll have forgotten what was said and continue on with our lives but how about you two?"

The bravado in the young man was gone as Mike questioned. "It looks to me like you love each other, correct?"

Both responded in the affirmative as Mike added. "Whatever the reason for your disagreement, underneath and at the heart of the matter, are the sacrifices we all need to make when we're together and care for someone. That's because the real question is, '*Am I with a person who will make sacrifices for me?*' It's only when we are vulnerable that we learn how to love. This means that our love become authentic when it's born of heartache, pain and turmoil which is a part of all of our lives."

Mike paused for a moment and then continued. "Relationships aren't easy. In fact, no matter how far you go back in time, it's where humans have always had the most problems. The point is not who wins the argument. The question is who's willing to *'carry the cross'* which means, who's willing to make the sacrifices, simply because they love the other person enough to say, *'I'll do it for you, simply because I love you.'*"

"I'm a retired minister. I've talked with dozens of young couples like you. I don't know if you're religious or not and a few minutes from now I'll be out of your life forever. If I can leave you with just one thought, that I sincerely believe will solve the riddles between you, it's this. 'God doesn't care that much about what we have to offer. He cares about the strength to offer what we have. God bless you. May His light shine upon you. May the peace of the Lord be with you and that you find the love you have for each other and realize love is about dedication and compromise."

The young couple simply sat there. They'd been dressed down in a way that allowed them to feel our frustration without any anger. Once again, I saw the majesty of my friend. Once again, I saw his brilliance and compassion and was honored to have him ride with me into the sunset. We got into the bus and heading back to reality. As I began driving, there was silence and then, as if nothing had transpired, Mike inquired, "What happened to Charlemagne?"

The spell was broken and so I offered. "Charlemagne's military conquests, diplomacy, and efforts to impose a unified administration on his kingdom were impressive proof of his ability to play the part of a traditional Frankish king. His religious policies reflected his transition from warrior king to sovereign and also his capacity to respond positively to forces of change in his world. He was fervently devoted to Christian principles, which had been instilled from infancy. He built the beautiful Church at Aix-la-Chapelle, which he adorned with gold, silver and lamps with rails and doors, made of solid brass. He had church columns and marble floors brought in from Rome and Ravenna and worshipped there constantly, going morning and night, besides attending mass."

"Charlemagne made sure all services were conducted properly in every way and often warned the sextons not to let anything improper be brought into the building. He provided many sacred vessels and so many clerical robes that even the lowliest doorkeepers never had to wear their everyday clothes in church. Charlemagne took great pains to improve reading and singing and was well skilled in both, although, I never heard him read or sing, except quietly along with the congregation."

"Charlemagne's military conquests, diplomacy, and efforts to impose a unified administration on his kingdom were impressive, while his religious policy reflected his capacity to respond positively to forces of change working in his world. With considerable enthusiasm he expanded and intensified the reform program instituted in the 740's by his father and uncle, where his goal was to deepen spiritual life and make it a prime concern of public policy and royal governance."

"Charlemagne's program for meeting his religious responsibilities was formulated in a series of meetings with both clerics and laymen. These meetings considered the agenda set by the royal court from which all laws were established concerning the interactions of people to people, people to those with authority and people to the Church, that royalty and members of the Church were expected to enforce. As it applied to the Church, the reform focused on strengthening the Church's hierarchical structure, clarifying the powers and responsibilities of the hierarchy, improving the intellectual and moral quality of the clergy, protecting and expanding ecclesiastical resources, standardizing liturgical practices, intensifying pastoral care aimed at general understanding of the basic tenets of the faith and improvement of morals, while rooting out paganism."

"As the reform progressed so did the efforts of Charlemagne to discipline clerics, assert control over ecclesiastical property, propagate the faith and define an orthodox doctrine. Despite extending his authority over matters traditionally administered by the Church, Charlemagne's aggressive moves in directing religious life won acceptance from the Church, including the papacy, and in so doing, the balance of power within Europe shifted in his favor. While one might think this was because of the belief in what Charlemagne was doing, in reality, he controlled the appointment of bishops and abbots and was the sole protector of the Papal States."

"Finally, Charlemagne was heir to a long tradition that measured a king by his success at war. This established a precedent that required him to devise means of governance capable of sustaining control over an increasingly divergent population. However, it was his association with the Church, along with the implementation of a basic feudal system, that allowed for the blending of so many different cultures into one somewhat cohesive unit."

We took our time and a few days later, got back to Mineral Point. That night, there was soft knock at my door and it was Clarence Larson. He'd moved in a few months past and we'd said hello but nothing more.

"What can I do for you, Clarence?" "I have a gift for you, Will."

With that Clarence offered a book that wasn't already on my shelf and I knew right then who the former/future neighbor Mike had referred to had been. I looked down at the book and then at Clarence and offered, "This looks like it's been part of your family for a long time."

"It has."

"But why now and why me?"

"I'm going to be leaving soon and heard you might like it." "Are you going on a trip?" I inquired.

"Yes. I'm going to be with Grace and I'm looking forward to the journey."

My eyes opened wide in that I knew that Clarence's wife, Grace had passed away.

"Clarence, what are you doing tomorrow?" I asked.

Clarence just shrugged his shoulders indicating that he, like so many others, had more time than anything else.

"Would you like to take a trip with me? There something I'd like to share with you."

The next morning Clarence and I went out to Waldwick and the farm. I helped Clarence make our way into the forest, down the deer path and to the springs. At first, there was no response beyond the majesty of silence and then a soft smile crossed Clarence's face and I knew the feelings were within him.

I took the old tin cup and filled it will the purity of innocence and offered it to Clarence. He took a sip and his body began to quake. He looked at me with soulful eyes as tears trickled down his cheeks. I took his trembling hands in mine and felt the energy traverse from his body into his soul.

"Can we go home now?" Clarence offered.

Slowly we made our way back to the car and then the complex. Nary a word was spoken. As I pulled into my parking place, Clarence looked at me and simply said "Thank you. I'm ready to go now," which caught me totally off guard, as it had no meaning.

When I got back to my apartment Clarence's gift was still sitting on my kitchen counter. I opened it to Genesis and began reading the first three books - Genesis, Exodus, Leviticus - as I became flush with guilt that something so great had been disdained for so long.

A few days later Mike called to let me know Clarence had passed away. It seems he had cancer and his time had come. On his kitchen counter was a note thanking Reverend Mike and me for all we'd done. I felt guilty, as all I did was take a lonely old man for a ride and shared with him, the purity of innocence.

We had a memorial service in the big room at the complex and Reverend Mike said a few words. Mike asked me to speak. Instead I stood and simply read Psalms 119 as tears glistened in everyone's eyes.

Religion is a funny thing. For those who study the past it can be harrowing because all we learn about are the exceptional ones…both good and bad. For those who look at it from the perspective of the humans who maintain it they can see all the warts that have taken so many people away from what its intent really is. When a person comes along who shows you what it can be and does so without trying to convert you, the majesty of belief in something greater, something better, and something more gratifying that can result in something profound. One Sunday in the warm, Florida sun in January! A few spoken words! A little old dying man! Each one placed a droplet of love in the hole in my heart and made me begin to feel alive again.

After the memorial, Mike and I had the afternoon 'off' and so we went out to the farm and down to the springs. Mike stood in complete silence as the purity of innocence enveloped his soul. After a long pause, Mike opened his eyes and said, "Clarence made it. He's with Grace and all is well."

I looked at my friend and could see both peace and yearning deep within his soul. Peace in knowing that there was a place beyond here and now and he was yearning to go and be with

Ginny. Selfishly I guess, I hoped he had the patience as I really didn't know what I would do without him.

Chapter 35 - Charlemagne's Cultural Revival

Spring had sprung and the grass had riz and the warmth of friendship was what it is. It was one of those rare spring days when it felt good to be alive. Hank and Kat already had the chaise lounges out by the pool even though it was still covered.

It had been quite a long time since my last elocution of the Terrill history as Mike asked, "Is there some reason why you haven't kept going on your family history?"

"Not really, I just wanted to make sure you weren't just being polite."

"Polite? For the first and probably the only time in my life, someone is sharing the entire history of a family that goers back over two-thousand years. How could I ever be bored?"

I don't know if it was true but it certainly made me feel good…someone who was actually interested in what I learned, what I said and how I felt. Loneliness has a way of scraping away the joy of life until all that's left is yesterday.

"Let's see, I think we were discussing Charlemagne, weren't we?"

Mike rolled his eyes and nodded yes.

"Let me see if I can't tie his realm into how it affected the religious structure of medieval times."

"Sounds good," Mike replied with a generous smile.

"A notable feature of Charlemagne's reign was his recognition of the implications for his political and religious programs of the cultural renewal unfolding across much of the Christian West during the 8th century. He and his government patronized a variety of activities that together produced a cultural renovation that was later called the 'Carolingian Renaissance.' The renewal was given impetus and shape by a circle of educated men in the 780's and 790's who were mostly clerics from Italy, Spain, Ireland, and England to whom Charlemagne gave prominent place in his court."

"The interactions among members of his inner circle, in which the king and a growing number of young Frankish aristocrats and I often participated, prompted Charlemagne to issue a series of orders defining the objectives of royal cultural policy. Its prime goal was to be the extension and improvement of Latin literacy, viewed as essential to enabling administrators and pastors to understand and discharge their responsibilities effectively. Achieving that goal required the expansion of the educational system and production of books containing the essentials of Christian Latin culture."

"The circle played a key role in producing manuals required to teach Latin, expound the basic tenets of the faith and perform the liturgy correctly. It also helped create a royal library containing works that permitted a deeper exploration of Latin learning and the Christian faith. A royal scriptorium was established, which played an important role in propagating the Carolingian minuscule, which was a new writing system that made copying and reading easier. In experimenting with art forms the minuscule was also useful in decorating books that could transmit visually the message contained in them. Members of the court circle composed poetry, historiography, biblical exegesis, theological tracts and epistles, along with works that exemplified advanced levels of intellectual activity and linguistic expertise."

I sat as a withering old man, getting somewhat excited thinking about my time in Aachen and the electricity in the air. I remembered regretting being there for a short period of time, while feeling profoundly constrained simply because I couldn't impart more knowledge than I could, due to the risk of changing history.

I looked east at the harrowed rows and realized that in a few weeks the corn or soybean seeds would come forth and a new year, a new season and a new cycle of birth, life and death would begin as I continued. "Aachen was the center of a tremendous building program that included the Palatine Chapel, which opened in 804 that represented a masterpiece of Carolingian architecture and served as Charlemagne's Imperial Church. Although the palace itself no longer exists the chapel was preserved and now forms the central part of Aachen Cathedral that Peg and I visited several times."

Mike smiled and sensed my enthusiasm as I continued. "Royal directives and the cultural models provided by the court circle were quickly imitated in cultural centers across the kingdom as bishops and abbots, sometimes with the support of lay magnates, sought to revitalize existing episcopal and monastic schools and start new ones. Some schoolmasters went beyond elementary Latin education to develop curricula and compile textbooks in the traditional liberal arts. The number of scriptoria and their productive capacity increased dramatically and the number and size of libraries expanded, especially in monasteries, where book collections often included classical texts whose only surviving copies were made for those libraries."

"Although the full fruits of the Carolingian Renaissance emerged only after Charlemagne's death, the consequences of his cultural program began to appear during his lifetime. These advances included improved competence in Latin and the expanded use of written documents in civil and ecclesiastical administration. In addition, it included advanced levels of discourse and stylistic versatility in formal literary productions. These enriched liturgical usages and variegated techniques and motifs that carried over into architecture and the visual arts."

"If one examines the critical societies that affected middle ages and even today, one needs to first look at Greece. Their culture developed the basic concepts of democracy, the alphabet, library, Olympics, science and mathematics, architecture, mythology, as well as the lighthouse and even standardized medicine, trial by jury and the theater."

"Ancient Rome also had a lasting legacy on world history by covering a vast amount of land at its peak and existed for almost 1,000 years, whose structure is still felt today in our culture in areas such as government, law, language, architecture, engineering, and religion."

"Charlemagne took what he culturally inherited and modified it. While the brutality of the times continued his realm structured a society and a culture that existed for nearly 900 years that defined leadership and enhanced the role of the church in everyday life."

Chapter 36 - Emperor of the Romans

The sun was shining and even in March we could feel its warmth, that was only superseded by the warmth of friendship I felt from the man who had become my best friend.

"Go on!" Mike urged.

"Charlemagne's prodigious range of activities during the first 30 years of his reign were a prelude to what some contemporaries and many later observers viewed as the culminating event of his life. On April 25, 799, during a Roman procession, Pope Leo III was physically attacked by assailants who accused him of misconduct. It was learned that their ultimate plan was to blind Pope Leo and remove his tongue, thus disqualifying him for the papacy. Instead, he escaped and fled across the Alps and met Charlemagne at Paderborn, Germany."

"Charlemagne listened to the pope's plea and provided both the political and military power needed to restore Leo III to the papal office. After extensive consultation in Francia Charlemagne went to Rome, himself, in December of 800 to face the issue of personally judging the Vicar of St. Peter and restoring order in the Papal States. After a series of deliberations with Frankish and Roman clerical and lay notables it was arranged that, in lieu of being judged, the pope would publicly swear an oath purging himself of the charges against him. Two days after Leo's act of repentance, while Charlemagne was attending Christmas Mass in the basilica of St. Peter, the pope placed a crown on Charlemagne's head and proclaimed him 'Emperor of the Romans.'"

"Given the pope's tenuous position and Charlemagne's penchant for bold action, it seems highly likely that Charlemagne and his advisers made the key assessment involving a new title, leaving it to the Pope to arrange the ceremony that would formalize the decision. The new title not only granted Charlemagne the necessary legal authority to judge and punish those who had conspired against the pope, it also provided suitable recognition of his role as ruler over an empire of diverse peoples and guardian of orthodox Christendom, while giving him equal status with his rivals in Constantinople."

"On the assessment of Charlemagne's years as emperor historians don't all agree. Some see the period as one of emerging crisis, in which the activities of the aging emperor were increasingly constricted."

"Because Charlemagne no longer led successful military ventures the resources with which to reward royal followers declined. At the same time, new external enemies appeared to threaten the realm, especially the Vikings and Saracens."

"In retrospect, there were already signs of structural inadequacy in Charlemagne's system of government. The largest challenge was constantly taking on new responsibilities without the necessary increase in resources. We all could sense a growing resistance to royal control by both the lay and ecclesiastical magnates who began to grasp the political, social, and economic power that could be only derived from royal grants of land and immunities. Within this larger context, there were other developments that suggest that the imperial title meant little to Charlemagne. In 802, when he first formally used the title 'Emperor, Governing the Roman Empire,' he also retained his old title of 'King of the Franks and Lombards.'"

"To validate this conclusion, all one needed to do was see that Charlemagne continued to live in the traditional Frankish way, eschewing modes of conduct and protocol associated with imperial dignity. He relied less on the advice of the inner circle who had shaped the ideology that led to the revival of the Roman Empire and more on his own intuition. Indeed, Charlemagne seemed oblivious to the idea of him being a unified political entity that came with the imperial title which really came to light in 806, when he decreed that, on his death, his realm would be divided amongst his three sons."

Mike appeared confused and so I continued. "After 800 Charlemagne's religious reform program stressed changes in behavior that implied membership in the Imperium Christianum that required new modes of public conduct. In addition, Charlemagne challenged the circle to bring greater uniformity to the diverse legal systems prevailing in the Empire concerning both the terminology and symbols employed by the court. At the same time an attempt was made to establish standard policies and artistic motifs that would reflect one unified ideology throughout the entire region."

"By 810 age and illness were beginning to affect our beloved leader. His robust appearance began to take on a pallor and he began walking with a slight limp but none of it stopped him from his goal of acceptance throughout all of the Christian world. While many historians have minimized the relationship of Charlemagne to his official title, evidence indicates that the title was important to him to the point that he engaged in a long military and diplomatic campaign that ended in 812 when he gained recognition from Nikephoros I, who was the Byzantine Emperor at that time."

"In 813 Charlemagne assured the perpetuation of the imperial title by bestowing the imperial crown on his son, Louis the Pious. The coronation in 813 suggests that Charlemagne believed that the office had some value and he wished to exclude the papacy from any part in its bestowal. In its entirety the evidence leads to the conclusion that Charlemagne saw the imperial title as a personal award in recognition of his services to Christendom, that could be used as he saw fit to enhance his ability and that of his heirs to direct the Imperium Christianum to its divinely ordained end."

"Toward the close of 813 Charlemagne was limited by ill health and old age and summoned his son, Louis, King of Aquitaine. Charlemagne gathered together all of us in the inner circle along with the chief men of the entire kingdom in a solemn assembly where he appointed his son, Louis, with our unanimous consent, to rule over the entire kingdom and made him heir to the imperial title."

"It was the last time I saw Charlemagne alive, as he spent the rest of the autumn hunting and in January came down with a high fever. As had been his practice, as soon as he became sick, he abstained from eating, hoping that the disease could be driven off by fasting. Instead, after receiving holy communion, he died on January 28th 814, at the age of 72, after reigning for forty-seven years."

"Charlemagne was buried in Aachen that afternoon even though he'd requested to be buried near Paris. What was interesting is how he was buried. Instead of lying down he was buried sitting up with his scepter in his gloved right hand and gold crown upon on his head."

"In 1,000 AD the tomb was opened and his remains were put in a gold sarcophagus. Peg and I visited his museum in

Aachen a few years ago and I got the chills seeing a lock of hair and one of his forearm bones on display in vacuum-sealed vaults. To think I knew him as a man and realized I was looking at the remains of one of my elatives from over 1200 years ago, sent chills up my spine and burned images in my brain that have never been forgotten."

"After the funeral I walked into the woods near Aachen and saw the fog, stepped inside and returned home. What I'd seen. What I'd heard. What I'd experienced remain with me to this day and yet, in terms of real time, I was only gone for twenty minutes."

"I drove back to Mount Horeb and Peg asked me how my day went. I never told her about my 'voyages' as I'm certain she would have thought I was Looney Tunes. I didn't sleep well for a long time as I was so filled with thoughts and emotions that I wanted to outline for my graduate lecture on Charlemagne. To this day, I believe that lecture was the best one I ever gave simply because, not only had I seen so much, I'd also felt so much and realized what a great man he really was.

"Having 'been there' I take umbrage to those who only point out his faults. His efforts to adjust traditional Frankish ideas of leadership for the public good and more contemporary standards in society made a crucial difference in European history. His renewal of the Roman Empire in the West provided the ideological foundation for a politically unified Europe, which is an idea that has inspired Europeans ever since the demise of the Western Roman Empire."

"Charlemagne's feats as ruler served as the standard to which many generations of European rulers looked for guidance in defining and discharging their royal functions. His religious reforms solidified the organizational structures and the liturgical practices that eventually enfolded most of Europe into a single 'Church.' His definition of the role of the religious authority in directing religious life laid the basis for the tension-filled interaction between temporal and spiritual authority that played a crucial role in shaping both political and religious institutions in later western European history."

"Charlemagne's cultural renaissance provided the basic tools—schools, curricula, textbooks, libraries, and teaching techniques—upon which later cultural revivals would be based. The impetus he gave to the lord-vassal relationship and the manorialism system played a vital role in establishing the seignorial system and then the feudal system, in which lords exercised political and economic power over a given territory and its population. The system, in turn, had the potential for imposing political and social order and for stimulating economic growth. Such accomplishments certainly justify the superlatives by which he was known in his own time: Carolus Magnus ('Charles the Great') and Europae pater or 'Father of Europe'".

I took a deep breath and looked at my friend who simply sat in awe realizing that what I had experienced and knew first-hand was evoked in such an emotional manner that was so much more than most people could ever comprehend. We quietly arose and went to the elevator simply knowing we were returning to reality.

Stopping at Mike's floor I did something I'd never done before I simply gave him a hug to express my appreciation for his friendship and for allowing me to share my history and passion and it felt good. My ride to the third floor and my passage to my apartment gave me time to reflect on a day, a friend and an experience that all combined to fill my heart with joy.

"How are you related to Charlemagne?" Mike asked. "Charlemagne's great aunt was my so-many-greats, grandmother and that's what's next if you want me to continue." I replied.

"He truly was the King of Hearts." Mike offered and I realized that what I had said, what I felt and what I wanted to express had been recognized, realized and valued to the same degree as me, for which I would always be grateful.

Chapter 37 – Galena

We'd been to Bayfield, Madison, Florida and the Dells and so I asked if Mike wanted to drive down to Galena. We hopped in and I began driving south on US-151 S to Wisconsin Highway 80 south. Forty-five minutes and forty-two miles later, we arrived in what Mineral Point would have been, had there only been a river - namely a tourist destination filled with shops, selling everything from nick knacks and sweatshirts to homemade fudge.

I figured that, with all my blabbing, the least I could do was buy lunch and so we went to Durty Gurts for some great hamburgers. Sitting out on the patio I began again. "While George Washington is remembered as the Father of Our Country, Charlemagne, for all intents and purposes was the Father of Europe with eighteen or more children sired from his wives and mistresses that included Pippin the Hunchback who was born in 769, Amaudru, 770, Charles the Younger, 772, Adelaide, 773, Pepin of Italy, 773, Adeltrude, 774; Rotrude, 775, Ruodhaid, 775, Lothair, 778, Louis the Pious, 778; Bertha, 779, Gisela, 781, Hildegarde, 783, Theodrada, 784, Hiltrude, 787, Alpaida, 794, Drogo of Metz, 801, Hugh, 802, Richbod, 805 and Theodoric, in 807 who then provided twenty-four known grandchildren."

"I can't believe you can remember all those names." Mike offered.

"It took forty years but I got it down. It's like the McDonalds Big Mac jingle about two all-beef patties, special sauce, lettuce, cheese, pickles on a sesame seed bun."

Mike just laughed that I could remember that as well as I continued. "Following Charlemagne's death, Louis the Pious was named ruler of the Carolingian empire. During his reign Louis had three sons by his first wife, Irmengard, named Lothair I, Pepin, and Louis II, who was also called Louis the German. In Frankish tradition in 817 Louis the Pious divided the empire so that his sons could rule over their own kingdom under the greater rule of their father."

"Lothair the First was established in the Kingdom of Italy whose domain became known as both the Low and Benelux Countries. In addition, his kingdom included the coastal region of northwestern Europe, consisting of Belgium, Netherlands, Luxembourg, Lorraine, Alsace, Burgundy,

Provence, as well as the Kingdom of Italy, which covered the northern half of the Italian Peninsula, along with the two imperial cities of Aachen and Rome."

"Pepin received Aquitaine, located in the western, central and southern areas of present-day France to the south of the river Loire, which had been Louis's own subkingdom during his father's reign. In 822, Pepin married Ingeltrude, daughter of Theodobert, Count of Madrie, with whom he had two sons: Pepin II in 823 and Charles in 825. Both were minors when Pepin died, so Louis the Pious awarded Aquitaine to his own son and Pepin's half-brother, named Charles the Bald. Louis the German received the Kingdom of Bavaria, was entrusted with the government in 825 and began his rule the following year."

"Lothair and Louis the German rose up in revolt against their father to protest attempts to make their half-brother, Charles the Bald, co-heir to the Frankish domains. Upon their father's death Charles the Bald and Louis the German joined forces against Lothair in a civil war that lasted from 840–843 and defeated Lothair at the Battle of Fontenoy in 841, while sealing their alliance in 842 with the 'Oaths of Strasbourg'. These declared Lothair unfit for the imperial throne, after which he became willing to negotiate a settlement that led directly to the breakup of the Frankish Empire assembled by their grandfather. This established the foundation for the Treaty of Verdun that was signed in August 843 where Charles, Lothar I, and Louis divided the western, middle, and eastern parts of the empire respectively. Louis received the territory of the Franconians, Swabians, Bavarians, and Saxons, together with the Carolingian provinces to the east."

"With so many offspring of Charlemagne, virtually every person of Western European lineage is descended from Charles the Great. The real challenge for me was determining how to define an 'heir'. The easiest way is to follow what's called primogeniture, which is simply the first-born child or 'Salic law' which was more prevalent in western Europe, where women didn't count at all."

"For the Terrill family, the post-Charlemagne era began with the Treaty of Verdun enforced by the Germanic-Latin language split that gradually hardened into the establishment of separate kingdoms with East Francia becoming the

Kingdom of Germany and West Francia the Kingdom of France."

Mike simply shook his head, realizing that the egos of three men literally disassembled what Charlemagne spent 47 years creating. Because of them, two countries who went to war seven times from 1701 to 1871 and then two more in the 20th Century, known as World War I and World War II, that cost the lives of over sixty million people including my uncle and the sight of my dad.

I sat back in my chair and inquired as to whether Mike knew which twenty-eight countries were in the European Union. Mike shrugged his shoulders as I handed him a map and continued. "To fathom the impact of Charlemagne, all you need do is remove the eight EU countries – Norway, Sweden, Finland, Great Britain, Ireland, Greece, Spain and Portugal. The twenty remaining were under his domain!"

I looked at Mike and noted, "Well my friend, that's how I was able to trace our family back in history where the life and times of Charlemagne made the difference."

"But how did you get from Charlemagne to mining in Cornwall?" Mike inquired.

We'd been sitting at Durty Gurts for over three hours and the waitress finally gave up and told us to come and get her if we wanted something. I guess it was her way of telling us we'd been there long enough. I excused myself, used the restroom and paid the bill, giving the girl a $20.00 tip. Needless to say, twenty bucks was a nice surprise that I hoped made up for all the lemonade and times she'd come to ask if we wanted anything else.

The ride home skipped any more history as we talked about the Brewers, Badger football and finally the Packers. It was spring but you still needed to mentally prepare for the thrill of victory and the probable agonies of defeat, promising each other we'd make it to one of each before the snow fell.

Chapter 38 - Checkers

It was Wednesday and that meant time for another round of simply getting destroyed at cribbage. I went to the 'quiet room' and saw Mike with a checkers board instead of our normal cribbage board set on the table.

I sat down and asked, "Why the checkers board"?

With that, Mike opened a small box to show the pieces and I realized it wasn't checkers he was going to talk about, it was chess as he said. "We've been talking about love and war and how it played such an important part in the lives of so many of your ancestors, so let's look at a chess board and see how it all fits together."

"Chess was invented in India around the 8th Century and was known as Chatrang. That changed over the centuries as it evolved through the Arabs, Persians and ultimately the medieval Europeans, who changed the pieces' names and appearances to resemble the English court. Throughout its history the structure has remained the same and that's what's really cool about chess, as it has always consisted of 33 pieces."

I must have had a strange look on my face as Mike indicated "Thirty-two pieces and the board. Although technically not considered a chess piece, the chessboard is also a part of the entire set as it's impossible to play the game without it. When closely examined the chessboard consists of 64 squares and resembles a battlefield. Two warring parties fight until one is crowned victorious or there are no more legal moves that can be made, at which time the game ends in a draw. With so many options it's why so much strategy and planning is involved in the game, simply because - just like life – there's a sense of change that's constantly unfolding, where every move is the result of another and the consequence of each move also affects the entire direction of one's life."

Mike took out one of the pawns and placed it on the board. "Each side has 8 pawns and they go in front of the other pieces. There's a debate about whether the pawns are peasants who live outside the castle walls or soldiers protecting the royal court behind them. Either way, they're the first line of defense against invaders. In chess, it's normally the pawn that gets to move first before a full battle ensues."

"Your great, great grandfather, George the First, as you call him, was a pawn, which is not a derogatory statement. Without his first move, the game of life, as you have known it, would never had taken place. We're all pawns in some way or another, moving here, moving there, living life and fighting its battles."

Next Mike placed a Castle, or Rook, on the board and added. "This piece is positioned on the corners of each player's side. As the name 'castle' suggests, this is the protective barrier or wall that guards the higher-ranking pieces and is why they're placed on the sides to symbolize protection over royalty, in the same way, a castle or a tower protects those inside. We all have some sort of protection, some sort of barrier that protects us from others. Whether physical, psychological or emotional, simply because we all have Rooks in our lives."

Mike looked at me and added. "The Knight or Horse pieces are the protective pieces and are shaped like a horse to symbolize what knights rode during battle. They're also protected by the tower because, back in medieval times, knights were affluent and only well-educated and upper-class warriors could be considered knights, protectors of the royal family and the first line of defense in case the enemy breaks through the castle walls."

I looked at Mike and proudly announced. "In the 64 generations of Terrills, there were several knights and even those who rode with Kings into battle during the Crusades."

Mike thought that was pretty neat and, moving the knight with his hand to show me how they could be re-positioned, added. "The Knights also have the ability to leap over other pieces and can do so because of the horses they rode in real life. They're also the only pieces that can start the game instead of a pawn. Why the knight moves in an "L" shape isn't very clear. Many theorize it symbolizes the beautiful and graceful movements of a knight riding his horse."

Next, Mike pulled out a Bishop and said. "The Bishop stands close to the king and queen and represents the Church, which many royal courts held near and dear to their hearts. It's considered the third most powerful piece on the chessboard. This is because, back in the day, religion influenced many people in many, many ways, both good and bad, with and without help of the royal family. Also, the bishop was considered next in line from the reigning king and queen in medieval Europe."

Next, Mike added the Queen on the board and exclaimed. "The Queen is considered the most powerful piece in the game of chess. She's allowed to move in any direction and as many squares as she wants. History has proven that many reigning queens could be ruthless when it came to battles and wars. In fact, if you look back at some of the battles you've talked about, you'll see that the Queen was a commander in those conflicts and is represented as such, simply because she can move freely across the board to the point that many players favor this piece over all others.

Finally, Mike added the King to the board. "The King's not as powerful as the Queen but is considered the most important piece and requires the most protection. Once a King is trapped and no additional moves will allow for other options, the game is over. This symbolizes both the power and vulnerability of the king during medieval times. In battle, if the king was killed or forced to surrender, the battle was over and the opposing party declared victory."

Mike looked me in the eye as a wry smile came across his face, as he pointed out. "Chess, like both life and war, is infinite and therefore not an easily conquered. There are 400 possible positions after each player makes just one move, 72,084 positions after two moves, over nine million positions after three moves and over 288 billion different possible positions after just four moves. In a 40-move game the number of potential moves is greater than the number of electrons in our universe. Like life every action has an equal and opposite reaction. Some are planned and some are unexpected but all of them have a consequence."

With that, Mike took one black and one white piece, put them behind his back and then held them out for me to choose within his palms closed simply because, in chess, white always moves first and actually has a slight advantage. I pointed to Mike's right hand and it was a black pawn. Mike made the first move and an hour later, I gently tipped my King over to signify 'check mate'. Mike had won but also provided a great lesson on life. Just as he had done in cards Reverend Mike had added depth and meaning to a game that so many really didn't understand the significance of, for which I was grateful.

Chapter 39 - Route 66

Mike and I were both getting antsy. Spring has a way of doing that to people in Wisconsin. I knew I wanted to get away (again) and called AAA and asked for Trip-Tiks to Arizona, specifying that I wanted to see some of the country and not just rest stops and formula restaurants.

The nice lady on the other end of the phone asked how long we would be traveling and I told her we were two old codgers who had more time than money and it really didn't matter. There was a pause and then she suggested taking Route 66. I had no idea what she was talking about other than remembering the song from the 40's about 'get your kicks on Route 66'.

The lady noted that U.S. Route 66 or U.S. Highway 66 was one of the original highways, established on November 11, 1926, with road signs erected the following year. She added "US 66 was a primary route for those who migrated west especially during the Dust Bowl of the 1930s and supported the economies of the communities through which it passed. On vacation one year, I read John Steinbeck's novel *'The Grapes of Wrath"* where the highway symbolized escape, loss and the hope of a new beginning where Steinbeck dubbed it the 'Mother Road', while other names included the Will Rogers Highway and the Main Street of America."

"You mean we'll be driving on country roads?" I asked, concerned about the bus on narrow highways.

"No, Mr. Terrill, US 66 has undergone numerous improvements and realignments over its lifetime and was officially removed from the United States Highway System six years ago when it was replaced by segments of the Interstate Highway System that passes through Illinois, Missouri, Oklahoma, New Mexico, and Arizona. The highway, which became one of the most famous roads in the United States, originally ran from Chicago, through Missouri, Kansas, Oklahoma, Texas, New Mexico and Arizona before terminating in Santa Monica, California. If you drive the entire length you'll have traveled a total of 2,448 miles."

"I think we just want to go to Phoenix and then head north up through Las Vegas, if that's OK."

"OK, I'll send you two sets, one for your trip out and then one for your trip back."

By leaving in late March and heading south I felt we'd miss the last of winter. When we returned, spring would be in the air. Mike agreed.

We left on a Monday and drove south into Illinois. As we slid a little east to DeKalb and then went south to Bloomington/Normal where we connected with 66. No sense going into Chicago. Too much traffic just to say we'd been there.

After serious discussions on the Milwaukee Brewers and their pennant chances. We had an in-depth discussion of the design of their new uniforms that Mike and I both agreed were more contemporary. Simply by removing the blue piping and adding a script version of the Brewers logo they seemed like they'd finally made it to the 90's. However, we still didn't understand why they didn't put their names on their backs like all the other teams until the sinister minister thought it was to sell more programs at the game.

Mike finally broke the ice and asked about the Terrill history. I told him to look in my leather case and find a filed named "Normandy" that was a summary called the 'Tirills.' Mike took out the binder and studied the lineage. Little did he realize the consequence of what I was about to share with him on world history.

The Tirils of Normandy 765 – 1055

	B o r n : 7 6 5	D i e d : 8 2 6
28. Childebrande d'Autun", "de Perracy"		
29. Nibelung II de Perracy, count of Autun	B o r n	D i e d

	Born:	Died:
	Born: 815	Died: 879
30. Terric de Tirel Autun	Born: 875	Died: 890
31. Waleran Chevalier de Tirel	Born: 900	Died: 965
32. Walter de Tirel	Born: 920	Died: 995
33. Ralf de Tirel	Born: 940	Die: 1050
34. Lord Foulques "Fulke" Tirel	Born: 963	Died: 10500
36. Sir Gauthier (Walter) Tirel seigneur de Poix II	Bor...	Die...

	Born: 1010	Died: 1068
37. Sir Gauthies (Walter) seigneur Tirel II	Born: 1055	Died: 1136

I began. "History gives a nation its bearing on what it is and how its people are affected by what has happened in the past. For kings and queens its wars, with victories and defeats that mold a nation's culture into the way it views itself in the present. In the same way, a family history presents how a family has survived and come to terms with the great social and cultural experiences of the ages."

I boldly proceeded. "If you remember the name Charles Martel, who was Charlemagne's grandfather, you should also remember that he was a descendent of Carolous de Menapii, where this whole story began. Unfortunately, there's very little primary source material available in tracing the family lineage and this initially caused my genealogy to be based more on location and dates than anything else. I repeatedly searched for the names of those who preceded my ancestors from Cornwall and for years didn't have any luck at all. When you need to begin and come forward it becomes extremely difficult, simply because you really don't know which child was your ancestor and picking the wrong one sends you off on a tangent that can be incredibly far from your actual forbearers. When you work 'backwards' in time, it's much easier."

"In many of the best sources there are inherent contradictions and entire generations are still believed to be missing. However, the people listed did exist and most likely existed in that order and are direct descendants of the Terrill family that can definitely be traced through Charles Martel and his first wife, Rotrude, mother of Carloman, Pepin the Short, Hiltrud and Auda of France."

"I took my eyes off the road for an instant and started. "With so many James, Johns, etc. it was easy to make mistakes that would then shadow all I did from then on. My hope is that it's as close as possible to being accurate. I can say that each name and the events that surrounded them all had something to do with the name Tiril or some iteration thereafter."

"If it's OK, I need to circle back a bit so that you see how we are related and what the consequence was. If it wasn't so darn important I'd skip over it but the following genealogy actually is the foundation of the Terrills of England."

Mike told me to 'Go for it,' and so I continued. "Carloman was born in 713, married Alard the Seneschal and was father of Rotrude, Princesa de Austrasia, who was born in 722, and was the brother of Drago, Mayor of the Palace of Austrasia."

"Rotrude Princesa de Austrasia was born in 754, married Girard, Count of Paris and their eldest son became Count Leuthard of Paris. They also had another son named Beggan (Bego) born in 755 who also, eventually, became the Count of Paris."

"Bego, Count of Paris, was appointed Count of Toulouse, Duke of Septimania, Duke of Aquitaine, and Margrave of the Hispanic in March, 806. Also in 806 William of Gellone abdicated and Charlemagne appointed Bego to take his place in Toulouse and the March of Gothia."

"Bego either married Amaudru, the illegitimate daughter of Charlemagne, or her niece, Alpais, or even Alpheidis, the illegitimate daughter of Louis the Pious and had five children that included Leuthard II."

"Bego didn't succeed his father in Paris but was placed in the comital office that served to eliminate weak cases, disclose key elements of the prosecution's case, identify guilty pleas early in the prosecution process and rehearse the case and clarify issues. Unfortunately, he didn't live long after that."

"Leuthard II, also called Leutaud, Leuthand, Liedrat and Lisiard, was born in 785 in Paris, Ile-de-France and succeeded his father as Count of Paris in 815. He married Grimhildis and became father of Adalard 'le Senechal'. Leuthard II then married Ingeltrude who was a member of the Franks of

Orleans family. They had a son, Gerard II, Count of Roussillon who was born in 810 in Rhone-Alps, France. Gerard II became Count of Auvergne, Comte, de Morvois, d'Ostrevant, de Paris, Duc, de Lyon, Gouverneur, Régent, de Provence, Count of Paris."

"Try putting all that on your driver's license" Mike chimed in as I continued, "Gerard II married Ava d'Auxerre and fathered Eve de Morvois, Ava de Roussillon, Theudric and Hucbald Count of Ostrevant before he died in 879."

"Hucbold Ostrevant was born around 830 in Ostrevant, Nord Pas De Calais, France and became Count of Ostrevant - aka – VonOstrevant. He married Heilwig di Friuli and had two sons Guy de Senlis and Rauol Gouy before Hucbold died in France in 890."

"Raoul Gouy was born in 877 in Vexin, Seine Inferieure, Normandy, France and was married to Alpais Carolingian Chimay and Aleidis de Cambrai. He was father of Raoul Cambrai de Cambrai, Gauthier de Dreux [de Guoy], Geoffroi Papabos de Bourges and Humbert de Chartres and Raoul and died in 926 in Valois Oise, Picardy, France."

"Gautier de Dreux (de Gouy), Comte d'Amiens, du Vexin, de Valois et de Dreux was born in 919 in Vexin Normandy, France and was also known as known as 'Walter', 'Gauthier', 'Gautier', 'Count of Amiens Vexin & Valois', 'Gauthier Count of Dreux', 'Walter De Tirel', 'Gauthier Comte en Vexin et Amiens de Tirel.' Gautier was married to Adele de Deux, Lady Eva de Dreux and Adele d'Anjou, Comtesse d'Amiens from whence came Geoffroi du Vexin, seigneur de Chaumont, Ralf de Tirel, Gautier II 'le Blanc de Mantes comte d'Amiens et tu Vexin, de Valois, da Mantes, Guy, bishop of Soissons, Raoul de Vexin and one other unnamed child."

Mike inserted. "Can you imagine being introduced for dinner and having all those titles repeated? Everyone else would be eating dessert by the time you were done telling them who you were."

I smiled at Mike's wit and continued. "The entire Terrill name began with one person, Sir Ralf de Tirel, who was born in 940 and was the son of Gauthier (Walter) I, Comte (or Count) de Vexin, and was a descendant of Pepin le Gros, Charles Martel and cousin of Charlemagne and represents the genetic connection the Terrills have with Charles the Great."

"All those I've mentioned are ancestors of Sir Ralf de Tirel, Count of Amiens Mirepox who was born in 940 in Picardy, France. Sir Ralf is how I was able to tie England to Continental Europe. Because I was able to link the de Tirel's to Pepin le Gros, Charles Martel, Duke of Brabant, Charlemagne and the Dukes of Burgundy even though the orthography, or spelling, in ancient France was Tyrell and Tyrrail and became Tyrrel and Tyrell that morphed into Turold, Turrell, Terrell, Terrill, Tiril and several other variants throughout the ages, it was the puzzle piece I needed."

"Ralf fathered Faulques (Fulke) de Tirel, who was born in 975 in Sauveterre-de- Rouergue, Midi-Pyrenees, France and the story continues. Sir Foulques or Fulke de Tirel married Orielda de Tirel and then Orielda Tryyell and Seigneur de Poix Gauthier I (Walter), Avise de Tirel who, was born in 1,000. Faulke died 1050 in the Northern Cape of South Africa. He married twice, first to a Saxon by the name of Olga and second to his beloved wife Alix, Dame de Fremontiers, who was the only daughter of Richard de Fremontiers. Sir Walter had a son by his first marriage, named Sir Walter Tyrel II. Walter II died young and then Walter I had another son with Alix they named Walter III Tyrel.

In 1046 Walter I and Alix built the Chateau de Poix et de Moyencourt and also the fortress of Famechon and became one of the most powerful lords of the country and founder of one of the most illustrious blood lines in Picardy. Sir Seigneur de Poix Gauthier I (Walter) Tyrell I married Alix, dame de Fremontiers of Normandie and was a Norman lord of Poix-de-Picardie in France and Langham, Essex England. Sir Walter was the first member of the family of Tirel family to go by the name, Tyrell de Poix and was a cousin of Robert, Duke of Normandy, and father of William of Normandy."

Chapter 40 - Break time

Whew! I needed a breather as Mike politely asked, "Where did you get all your information?"

"Mainly from libraries in Madison, the Library of Congress in Washington and then London and Falmouth, Cornwall, where Peg and I would do genealogical research in the morning and go sightseeing or boating in the afternoon and, of course, being there."

"How long were you with Charlemagne?" "In their time seven years."

"Seven years? Wasn't Peg worried that you were gone so long?"

"Peg never knew." "Huh?"

"That was in 'past time' as I called it. In 'real time', no matter how long I was 'there', I was never gone more than twenty minutes." "Incredible! Simply incredible!"

"For all the trips and all the times, there's no way I could explain it and that's the reason why I haven't told anyone."

"Who would have believed me?"

"I didn't want to end up in the Dane County Home in Verona."

"You mean the home for the mentally ill?"

I simply replied, "I drove by it every day on my way to school and that reminded me what they did with people they considered mentally ill."

Another swallow of lemon tea and I was ready to add more. "Sir Walter de Tirel I had a son named Sir Walter de Tirel II, who was also known as 'Gauthier' and then 'Tirel', 'Seigneur de Poix', 'Tyrell' or 'Tiril'. Walter II married Baroness Adeliza de Clare, de Tunbridge who was the daughter of Richard FitzGilbert de Bienfaite, Lord Clare of Tonbridge and Rohese Giffard de Longueville. Adeliza's father was also the Chief Justice of England, Earl of Buckingham, Sherriff of Devon, founder of the House of Clare, Lord De Bienfai, Lord de Clare & Tonebridge, Earl of Clare, Sieur, de Bienfaite, d'Orbec, de Clare, de Tunbridge, de Kent, Régent, d'Angleterre Lord of Clare. If all that isn't enough Richard Fitzgilbert was also known as 'Strongbow' and was the leader of the semi-official, Anglo-Norman invasion of Ireland during Henry II's reign for which he obtained a grant of the lordship of Leinster from the King in 1171."

"Sir Walter II and the Baroness had six children that included Gauthier III Tyrel, seigneur de Poix and Robert Tyrel, seigneur de Bergicourt."

I just shook my head and directed Mike to open my genealogy binder to the correct tab.

"What's this?"

"It's a copy of a report written in 1846 on the beginnings of the Terrill name that might provide some better insight before I get into the specifics."

Mike looked at the paper and began reading aloud which gave me a break… thank God.

'The ancient House of the Tirils came from Normandy and was an issue of the first dukes of Normandy and is a very old and distinguished name. In the charter of the primal Church of Rouen in 1030 Walter Tiril is mentioned, and is stated to be a wealthy nobleman and a close kinsman or cousin of Robert, Duke of Normandy. The Robert, Duke of familiarly known as Robert, the Magnificent and sometimes as Robert the Devil, fifth Duke of Normandy, was the father of William the Conqueror.

English historians of the Tiril Family, provide exact pedigrees of the family from Ralf, the founder, down to the time of this writing. These pedigrees were evidently prepared with great care and based upon information easily accessible in England, which Mr. Tiril regarded as absolutely reliable. In fact, Mr. Tiril provides a list of authorities he consulted in the preparation of the Tiril history that were not only very rare but expensive books which would have made it impossible seigneurial possessions (an institutional form of land distribution) and their high positions in this province and in the neighboring provinces of France.

They possessed many fiefs and were Lords and Princes de Poix, de Brimen, Conty, Fremontiers, Morenil, and de RiM court. They were Viscomtes d'Equennes et de St. Maxent; Barons d' Angles et de Prunget and lords of ninety-four towns in Picardy, Brittany, Berry, Poitou, Touraine, Valois, Vermandois, etc.

The first member of the family to bear the title of Prince de Poix was Hugues, (in English, Hugh), who was a great-grandson of the first Sir Walter and who will be hereafter spoken of. The Hugh Tiril who firmly established the Tiril family in England, was this Hugh Tiril I, Prince de Poix. The family in Picardy, in the male line, died out in 1417 and all its possessions and titles passed from those of that name to the illustrious House of Moyencourt through a female member of the Tiril family, who had married a Moyencourt. When that family ceased to exist in the direct male line in 1510 the titles and possessions passed into the family of de Crequy, also descendants, through marriage, of the Tirils for anyone on this side of the Atlantic to consult. The books include many old French and Norman family histories along with summaries published by archaeological societies, county pedigrees, works on extinct titles, books on heraldry and many of the earliest books published in the English language on genealogy."

Mike stopped and so I added. "According to the pedigree lists, the second son of Ralf, Viscount of Amiens, was Fulk de Tirel, who became the Seigneur of Guemanville and Dean of Evreux. He married Orielda, daughter of Richard I, the third Duke of Normandy. Among the children of Fulk de Tirel and Orielda was Walter, known in history as Sir Walter Tiril I, Lord of Poix, Castellan of Pontoise, and a Baron of both France and England. This was the Sir Walter Tiril who accompanied his cousin Duke William of Normandy, in the expedition which led to the conquest of England, and was present at the battle of Senlac or Hastings. According to M. D'Acy's book, the House of Tiril was prominent both in Picardy and Normandy.

"Wow! You really do have some aristocrats in your heritage," Mike interjected.

I looked at Mike and offered. "Mike, marriages back then weren't for love, they were business mergers intended in sustaining or enhancing one's position, power and prestige. Aristocratic parents often pledged their daughters when they were small children and marriages at ages 12- 13-14 weren't uncommon. While you might think there was a lot of messing around and that's why there are so many multiple wives, the real reason was because about 20%, or one-in-five women, died during childbirth. Through these arrangements, the Tyrells were able to sustain their power and authority and actually expand their influence. For over 600 years the family included a knight in every generation and few other families in history can say that. "

"I glanced to see if I still had Mike's attention and sensed a degree of confusion or boredom setting in and so I asked.

"Do you mind if I go into some of the details? We can stop at the next rest area and I'll bride you with another beer if you'll listen."

Mike just smiled as I saw a sign that said St Louis thirty-five miles and made the McDonald Mega Arch, better known as the Gateway Arch, my goal. I told Mike and he agreed and read the back of Trip Tik that said. 'The 630-foot stainless steel arch is the tallest man-made monument in the United States. The design was determined during a nationwide competition held between 1947-48 that was won by Eero Saarinen's. The foundation was laid in 1961 but the construction of the arch itself began in 1963 and was completed on October 28, 1965 for a total cost of less than $15 million.'

We arrived, and both went "Wow," It was even bigger than we thought it was going to be.

Mike added. "Can you imagine the size of the Quarter Pounder you get from this place? It would weigh a ton. And how about those French fries, they'd be ten feet long!"

"Do you still think you'll get change back from your dollar?"

We took the ride inside on the curving elevator and got the cheap thrill and then headed back to the bus. Before leaving, we each had another bottle of Spotted Cow beer and a toast to the golden arches, which was better than fallen arches. I knew we needed to ration our booty or we'd be out before we hit Oklahoma. Imagine a beer from New Glarus that you had to drive over to see if Dan could sell you, or at least put you on the waiting list.

Dan's a good guy who spent time working for larger breweries. When he and his wife, Deb, started New Glarus Brewing Co. he wanted to try something different. That's certainly evident in the multitude of beers that the brewery turns out after they are wood-aged, blended with fruit, and expertly soured. Some people call Spotted Cow a cream ale but it doesn't fit those guidelines because it's unfiltered. Some people call it a farmhouse ale Dan said "As long as people drink it, I really don't mind what you call it." Mike and I call it 'good' and a special treat when you can get it.

"How much of this stuff did you pack?" Mike inquired.

"Dan was able to rustle up four cases."

We clinked the green trimmed label with the jumping cow and said "here's to Route 66".

"You mean, you've got ninety-six bottles of beer? Mike detailed with a smile on his face.

"Not anymore…just ninety-four."

This got us into singing the ditty - "Ninety-nine bottles of beer on the wall if one of those bottles should happen to fall, ninety-eight bottles of beer on the wall," We sang on and on until we were singing "Two bottles of beer on the wall," which was half way across Missouri. As our rendition ended, we needed to stop and get rid of those first two now-processed bottles we drank in St. Louis simply because I thought one of us was going to pee his pants right then and there.

Chapter 41 - William the Conqueror

After the pause that refreshed us, we got back in the bus, I looked at Mike and noted. "Because William the Conqueror was such an important person in terms of the history of England and subsequently, the structure of America and, finally, the Terrill name, I'm going to expand on who he was and why he was so important."

"English heraldry does get a little complicated. For this reason, I've created the royal lineage so you can understand who all the kings and queens were and how they fit into the Terrill realm, simply because it's the only way to explain how and why the Terrill family was able to be a member of aristocracy and remain so for so many centuries."

"Go for it!" Mike responded.

Before climbing back into the driver's seat I handed Mike a chart entitled 'The Norman Kings' that included the king's name, how long they ruled and the relationship to their predecessor and announced, "Here's the short version and then I'm going to go into details on some of them so that you see how they interacted with and affected the Terrills."

We made our way back into traffic and I began. "William I - also known as William the Conqueror, became King of England by conquest. He married Matlida of Flanders who was a Tiril cousin.

Robert, their eldest son, inherited the dukedom of Normandy from his father. Richard, who was their second son, died and their third son, William Rufus, became King of England. When he was *accidentally* killed, the crown went to William and Matilda's fourth son who became King Henry I.

"All was not as pleasant as it sounds. Henry the First secured his claim to the crown by capturing his elder brother, Robert, and marrying Matilda of Scotland, who was descended from Alfred the Great. When King Henry I died, his nephew, Stephen of Bois, who was the grandson of William the Conqueror, seized the throne."

"Stephen of Bois married Matilda of Boulogne, who was descended from the old English kings. The daughter of King Henry, Empress Matilda claimed the English throne and after several years of conflict agreed that her son, Henry the Second, would become king when Stephen died."

"Got all that?" I inquired.

"Only because you gave me the chart," Mike snickered. "OK, let's get into the details, as it represents how the Terrills got from Normandy to England and why they stayed."

I took a deep breath and began. "Normandy is located northwest of Paris along the coast of the English Channel. Other than Dover, its beaches are the closest landmass to England and has the Seine River flowing through it. For centuries it represented the ideal point of attack for the Viking raiders who attempted to establish their presence in the area between the Rhine, Scheldt and Seine Rivers.

"After centuries of fighting, the Norman dynasty was founded by Rollo, or Hrolf the Ganger, who was a Viking raider chief. He was granted the duchy by Charles the Simple, King of France, in 911, at the Treaty of Saint-Clair-Sur-Epte, in exchange for feudal allegiance and conversion to Christianity. As part of the agreement, Hrolf took the baptismal name of Robert, who fathered a son named, William I Longsword, who, in turn, fathered a son named Richard I the Fearless in 933.

Richard the Fearless married Gunnor and they had four children including Richard II also called Richard the Good. Richard the Good married Judith of Brittany and they had two children including Robert I the Magnificent who was born in 1005. Robert The Magnificent became Count of Hiémois on the death of his father in 1026, while his elder brother became ruler of Normandy, known as Duke Richard III. Robert The Magnificent rose in rebellion against Richard III but was defeated and forced to swear loyalty to Richard. Unfortunately, for Richard he 'accidentally' died one day and Robert The Magnificent assumed authority, also, becoming known not only as Robert The Magnificent as well as Robert 'the Devil', Duke of Normandy."

"Like so many nobleman, Robert had several mistresses including Herleva, who was sometimes called Arlette, daughter of a traveling leather tanner in Falaise. Robert and Herleva had a son named William who was born in 1028 at Falaise Castle. Because of the liaison between Robert and Herleva, William was commonly known by his contemporaries as 'William the Bastard' where the verbal intimidation from so many appears to have affected him greatly and changed history in many, many ways."

"William's mother, Herleva, also had a daughter named Adelaide with Duke Robert. Although they had a long relationship, the gap in Robert's and Herleva's social standing rendered marriage out of the question and Herleva was married off to one of Robert's vassals named Herluin, who was a knight. From this marriage, Herleva produced two additional sons, Robert, who later became Count of Mortain and Odo, destined to become the Bishop of Bayeux and the Earl of Kent in England."

"When Robert The Magnificent converted to Christianity he decided to expiate his sins by going on a pilgrimage in 1034. Since he had no legitimate heir to succeed him, he persuaded his barons to accept William as the future Duke of Normandy. On his return journey from the Holy Land, Robert The Magnificent died suddenly and William succeeded his father with his Great Uncle, then Archbishop of Rouen, serving as Regent.

"The Norman barons exhibited no loyalty toward young William. Instead, William grew up in a very tentative time where he had to learn at a very early age how to survive. To make things worse, several of William's guardians were murdered in succession beginning with Duke Alan of Brittany, Gilbert of Brionne, then Turchetil, and Osbern, the nephew of Gunnor and finally the wife of Duke Richard I, who was killed while actually protecting William."

"One can only imagine the trauma of first being labeled a bastard and then having so many people whose job it was to protect you, be murdered. Because things were so dangerous, William's maternal uncle finally hid William with peasants to literally save his life. To say William was less than stable would be an understatement. However, having seen so many of those who protected him murdered during his savage and insecure childhood, it's no wonder William's personality was molded into the stark and often ruthless ruler he became."

"In 1047 William was nineteen years old when his cousin, Guy of Burgundy, led a rebellion in Normandy and attempted to defeat William at the Battle of Val-ès-Dunes. The battle forced William to seek refuge with King Henry of France, who came to his aid, and together they battled the rebels at Caen. As a result of winning the battle William was able to retain his title and maintain control over the western half of his duchy. At the village of Alencon the burghers insulted William's parentage by hanging 'hides for the tanner' over the walls of the fort to indicate how much they despised William. This didn't work out too well for the burghers. On capturing the town William had their hands and feet cut off and emerged as undisputed Duke of Normandy."

"William needed alliances and stability and so he negotiated a marriage in 1049 to Matilda of Flanders, a descendant of the old Saxon House of Wessex and daughter of Baldwin the Count of Flanders, whose wife Adela was the daughter of Robert II, King of France. Tradition has it that when William sent representatives to her father's court to request Matilda's hand, Matilda retorted by informing the representative that she was far too high-born to consider marrying a bastard. Furious on receiving this response, William rode to the Village of Bruges, Belgium where he confronted Matilda on her way to church, pulled her off her horse, threw her down in the street and rode off."

"Now that's what I call a rough way to start a relationship," Mike retorted.

I continued. "In 1051 William visited his English cousin, King Edward the Confessor, who, along with the King's brother Alfred, were close to William because they'd spent much of their childhood in exile at the Norman Court because their mother Emma was a daughter of the House of Normandy. During William's visit Edward, who had no children, purportedly promised William the crown of England, should 'he die without issue' or with no male heir."

"The true heir to the throne of England was Edgar the Atheling. Edgar was King Edward's great-nephew and grandson of his brother, Edmund Ironside. The problem was Edgar the Atheling was a child who knew little of England having spent much of his life in exile in Hungary."

"Several others coveted the English throne. The chief candidate amongst them was Harold Godwinson, son of the powerful Godwine, Earl of Wessex, whose sister, Edith, was married to King Edward. Harold was unfortunately shipwrecked on the coast of Normandy and found himself the unwilling guest of Duke William when word was received that King Edward was near death. Harold was anxious to return to England to forward his ambitions. However, before William would allow Harold to leave, William required Harold to swear an oath of allegiance to William's claim to the crown of England. With the choice of incarceration or even perhaps yet another untimely 'accident' Harold finally acquiesced."

"King Edward died in January, 1066 and was buried in the foundation of St. Peter's Church in Westminster. It was reported that on his deathbed Edward named Harold his successor, a choice immediately accepted by the English Council of Elders who traditionally elected the next English King."

"Back in Normandy, William was royally pissed and began to build an invasion fleet to take by force what he considered his. The Church got involved and Pope Alexander II personally blessed William, providing a cross banner that was carried into battle. Harold quickly assembled the Saxon form of militia of freemen called the 'fyrd', comparable to our National Guard, in preparation for William's landing. War was on the horizon but no one knew when or where."

"Sensing weakness and division, in mid-September King Hardrada of Norway invaded England, accompanied by Tostig, Earl of Northumbria, who was Harold's discontented brother who had been banished and his earldom confiscated. King Harold marched his army north to meet the Norse invaders at Stamford Bridge in Yorkshire and won a decisive victory over the Viking army."

"Back across the narrows of the North Sea, the winds William had been waiting for turned favorable and he set sail with his massive invasion fleet of somewhere between 4,000 and 7,000 men. News of the invasion was conveyed to Harold who responded by retreating south to meet the opposing forces. In haste, Harold provided his exhausted army little time to recover from the Viking battle. Had Harold rested and reorganized his army, the outcome of the impending battle and English history may have been very different."

"On October 14, 1066 the Saxon and Norman forces clashed in The Battle of Hastings where Harold took up a defensive position on Senlac Ridge, thereby forcing the Norman army to attack uphill, placing them at a disadvantage. Harold's army formed what was called a 'shield wall' along the edge of the hill which rebuffed repeated Norman attacks."

"A rumor arose in the Norman ranks that Duke William was dead, creating panic and desertion by many of William's troops. Seeing an opportunity to win many of the Saxon fyrd pursued the fleeing Normans down the hill. William announced he was still alive. His troops rallied and Harold's brothers, Gyrth and Leofwine were both slain on the lower battlefield."

"The battle continued for most of the day. As dusk began to fall William ordered his archers to fire high into the air and one of the arrows hit Harold in the eye, mortally wounding him. Harold's army began to flee while the Housecarls, who represented Harold's trained professional militia, defended the body of their King to the end. Upon their demise Harold Goodwinson's body was mutilated by the Normans in a vindictive act, in which William supposedly took part. William then proceeded to London and was crowned King of England at Westminster Abbey on Christmas Day, 1066 and that's how William, Duke of Normandy became known as William the Conqueror."

William had chosen his close cousin, Walter Tyrell I, to lead the center column in the first assault on the English lines. For his gallantry, Walter I's name is cited on the 'Cartulaire de St. Martin de la Battaille' which was a list of prominent noblemen who participated in the battle and is also inscribed on the wall of the Church at Dives, at a port in Normandy that was placed there in 1861 by one of the antiquarian societies of France."

"William accepted the surrender of two Saxon Earls named Edwin of Mercia and Morcar of Northumbria, as well as Edgar Atheling. In so doing southern England submitted to Norman rule profoundly affecting language, culture, literature and architecture as well as the social and political structure for the next 700 years. Whereas, resistance in the north was more prolonged, William responded by subjecting the English to a reign of terror to punish and crush the rebellion and strike fear into English hearts. In so doing, he lay waste to vast tracts of Yorkshire while replacing English gentry with his Norman and French followers, including William Tiril I, and did so by distributing the confiscated English lands to them and supplementing the former power structure by adding a French twist to who's who and who got what."

"So you're heritage includes William the Conqueror?" Mike asked, somewhat incredulously.

I just smiled a devilish smile affirmed that he was a cousin and went back on the historical track of this incredibly important period. "Beyond having his name on the registry, the family was awarded land in Essex County, England even though they primarily resided in France."

Chapter 42 – Ch..ch..ch..Changes

"Today Sir Walter Tyrell I's bloodline is represented in France by two principal branches - the Moyencourt and Mouchy de Poix families where the line of Tyrell de Poix figured prominently in the Crusades. They also held high positions of the Court of the kings of France and filled many distinguished posts in the history of France."

"Sir Walter I died in 1068 and was succeeded in title and possession by his grandson, Sir Walter Tiril III seigneur de Poix, who was born in 1035 and built the fortress of Famechon. Sir Walter III became one of the most powerful lords of France when he married Ann (De Clare) De Brionne, daughter of Gilbert (Giselbert) De Brionne, Count Of Eu, and Constance D'Eu, daughter of Guillaume (William) D'Eu and Beatriz De Goz. Giselbert's mother was a half-sister to Richard Fitz-Gilbert De Clare who received more than 100 lordships for his service to King William the First, or William the Conqueror, during the conquest of England."

"The Tyrell family was provided links to north-east Essex and granted the Manor of Langham where the family was based for eight generations until Sir James Tyrell married Margaret the daughter and heir of Sir William Heron and the family moved to Heron Hall in Horndon. The births, deaths and marriages are all recorded in the archives of All Saints Church, East Horndon, and it's really cool to visit the church and see the names listed there."

"While many things changed English Earls were an Anglo-Saxon institution that remained intact and were based on the integration of administrative structures similar to American townships as being part of a county or 'shire' and then part of a state. Around 1014, the shires has been grouped into Earldoms, led by a local leader adroitly called an earl. What was unique is that the same man could be earl of several shires at the same time."

"When William conquered England he continued to appoint earls but not for all counties. Instead, the administrative head of the county became the sheriff. Earldoms began as offices and earned a share of the legal fees in the shire. Gradually, the titles and responsibilities became honorary, with a stipend of £20 a year which would be equal to about $250,000 US dollars today."

"Like most feudal offices the positions were inherited but the kings frequently asked earls to resign or exchange earldoms. Usually there were few Earls in England and they were men of great wealth in the shire from which they held title, or an adjacent one, depending on the circumstances."

"One structural oddity is that there were no dukes named between William and Henry II from 1066 to 1189 in England while both of them were Dukes in France. When Edward III ordained himself King of France in 1327, he made his sons Royal Dukes, to distinguish them from other noblemen, much as Royal Dukes are now distinguished from other Dukes. Later Kings created Marquesses and Viscounts to make finer gradations of honor and delineate ranks above and below that of Earl, respectively. In other words, the body of peers, or titled nobility in England evolved into five ranks, in descending order from dukes to marquess, earls or counts, viscounts and barons."

"In all my studies, I couldn't find any Terrills who became Dukes but there were several that became sheriffs and therein lies the secret to their power and wealth and one reason why many had the title of 'sir' before their name." I looked at Mike and added one more morsel of insignificant facts garnered through my years of teaching. "The term 'sir' was an honorific address for men derived from Sire and was derived from the French word 'Sieur' which meant lord. It was imported to England in 1066 by the French-speaking Normans and now exists in French only as part of the word 'Monsieur' which is equivalent 'My Lord' in English. I know, hoop-de-do!"

"Peace was not at hand! In 1068, Edwin and Morcar rose in revolt of William with the support of Gospatric, Earl of Northumbria. William the Conqueror marched through Edwin's territory and built a castle at Warwick. Walt Disney has done a wonderful job of making a castle seem magical. In reality, castles were actually forts designed to house the military and represent power and authority over the citizens and, in many cases, held torture chambers and jail cells."

"So, I take it no Tinkerbell?" Mike asked.

"Edwin and Morcar submitted but that didn't appease William. He continued to York, built what became his most notorious castle and then to Nottingham, before turning south. On his journey back to London, William began constructing castles at Lincoln, Huntingdon, and Cambridge and placed his supporters in charge of the visible expressions of Norman dominance. Two such supporters were William Peverel, thought to be William's illegitimate son, who was put in charge at Nottingham and Henry de Beaumont at Warwick."

"In 1069 Edgar Atheling rose in revolt against William's rule and attacked York while destroying William's castle. Although William returned to York and built another castle, Edgar remained armed and dangerous and joined forces with King Sweyn of Denmark. The Danish king brought a large fleet to England and attacked not only York but Exeter and Shrewsbury."

"York was taken by the combined forces of Edgar and Sweyn. Edgar was duly proclaimed King of England by his Saxon supporters but William counter-attacked, laying waste to the entire city as he symbolically wore his crown in the ruins of York on Christmas Day 1069. He then triumphantly marched to the River Tees while ravaging the surrounding countryside."

"Edgar fled to Scotland where Malcolm III, King of Scots, who was married to William's sister Margaret Waltheof, Earl of Northumbria, joined the revolt and eventually surrendered to William, along with Gospatric. Both were pardoned and allowed to retain their lands. However, William's vengeance was not satiated and he marched over the Pennines during the winter and defeated the remaining rebels at Shrewsbury before building two more castles at Chester and Stafford."

"In 1070 Hereward the Wake rose in a rebellion against William's rule, which centered on the Isle of Ely. William led an army to Ely where Hereward, joined by a small army led by Morcar, made a desperate stand. Eventually, the Normans bribed Abbot Thurstan of Ely to reveal a safe route across the marshes which resulted in Ely being taken. Morcar was captured and imprisoned while Hereward managed to escape into the fenland to continue his resistance."

I looked at my friend, shook my head and added. "William was a savage and formidable ruler, who, even by contemporary standards, was exceedingly cruel. However, his methods produced the desired results and extinguished the fires of opposition. In the end over 80 castles were built across England to enforce his rule including London's White Tower which was the first building in the Tower of London complex. With a height of nine stories, it's said that the dominating shadow of the White Tower loomed menacingly over medieval London, as a visible expression of William's power."

I leaned back in the driver's seat and continued. "Anglo-Saxon England was radically altered by the Norman conquest. It changed the entire way of life where its laws, aristocracy and Church were altered to parallel the French feudal system but gave rise to the history and prominence of the Terrill family in England."

"As time went on the Anglo-Saxon language was replaced by Norman French as the language of the upper classes and modern English became the outgrowth of both cultures with the roles of the conquerors and conquered still seen in many English words and ways."

Mike was shaking his head in disbelief and I realized I needed to summarize the consequences. "First, you need to understand that the entire social concept was altered. As was the case in Carolingian France, all land in England was deemed to be the property of the king. From this assumption an entire feudal structure was built that was the combination of legal, economic, military and cultural customs transposed from France and Charlemagne."

"This all can be traced back to Aristotle's 'Politics' which was a political definition of 'aristocracy' that he determined to be the rule of the best men. Family background and wealth were understood to contribute to fitness for this public role but did not necessarily define it. A leading family might have unworthy descendants and social newcomers might have the abilities needed for political excellence but neither guaranteed success. This understanding of social status remained during the early Middle Ages that divided society into three orders, first were the clerics who prayed, then the nobles who defended and governed and finally, the commoners who met society's economic needs."

"At its peak there were about two hundred families in English aristocracy that included the Tyrells. Between the families, they aggregately held about one-fourth of the kingdom's land. Political and social influence matched their economic hold. In some regions, aristocrats and gentry enjoyed a near monopoly on high positions in the church, army, and administration. To a significant extent, these intertwining forms of domination and the social, political, economic and ideological justifications that accompanied them defined England and Europe's social order."

"How did the system work?" Mike asked.

"Normally, the king or his representatives would offer a substantial amount of land called a fief in exchange for allegiance and promise of military service to protect and defend the king. This land was awarded under terms and conditions creating what were called 'tenants-in-chief' or lords or barons. In so doing, the recipient would retain total control of who resided on the land, how it was used and, eventually, who would inherit the land at the time of the lord's demise."

"For all intents and purposes, the fief was a form of lease where the baron or lord held the land in fealty, or 'in fee', and did so in return for their allegiance and service to the king along with taxes and fees that were paid to the crown. While the most common form of value was the land itself, anything could be held in fee, including a governmental office, hunting or fishing rights, monopolies in trade and products that were manufactured on the land."

"In broad terms, a lord was a noble who held the land. Next was a vassal who was a person granted possession of part of the land by the lord. At the bottom was a fief. In so doing, the individual who accepted responsibility for the land also accepted a mutual obligation that included military support by knights in exchange for certain privileges."

"In other words, the National Guard," Mike offered.

"You got it! Except you did so without pay and had to bring your own uniforms. Normally, military service amounted to forty days each year in times of peace or indefinite service in times of war. The actual terms of service and duties varied considerably and was done on a case-by-case basis where factors such as the quality of the land, skill of the knights, local customs and financial status of the liege lord always played a part."

"The term Serjeanty implied that the taxes were satisfied through the performance of a personal service which could be grand or petty. Grand Serjeanty consisted of performing a personal service to the king while Petty Serjeanty involved rendering a bow, sword or any method pertaining to war. Required military service was expressed in terms of whole or fractional knights' fees. The knight system was in place until the late medieval period when it was abandoned in favor of cash payments or agreement to provide a certain number of men-at-arms or mounted knights for the lord's use to satisfy his pledge to the king."

Mike looked at me and interjected. "In other words, this was actually the basis for our current property tax and military draft systems. In America, we really don't 'own' the land simply because it's all taxed and there's a form of conscription at age eighteen."

"You got that right!" I replied as I continued in a jocular way with a god-awful imitation of an infomercial announcer. "But there's more! The tenants at the bottom of the feudal ladder were called serfs."

"The lord would allocate land to his vassals who would then allocate land to the serfs. In addition, the lord would normally retain some land for his own use in what was called a demesne or domain that distinguished what he reserved from land sub-let to others as sub-tenants. In addition, the serfs owed him a set number of days each year in which they would work the lord's fields in exchange for the right to work their own lands. Often they were required to grind their grain in the lord's mill and bake their bread in the lord's oven and use toll roads and bridges the lord built. Each time they did this, of course, they would have to pay a toll or a fee of some sort. The serfs were forbidden to set up their own roads, bridges, mills, and ovens. As you can see, the lord had a legal monopoly and would milk it for all it was worth."

"Regardless of the level - baron, lord, vassal or serf everyone had to pay the piper to the level above them, of which a portion ended up in the king's coffers. Services could vary, depending upon the need. The services by which land could be held were classified as either free or unfree, where the free was land held by religious institutions. While you wouldn't think it would be much, at its peak, the Roman Catholic Church controlled around one-third of all the productive land in England and was, therefore, a very powerful economic and political force."

"In theory, the entire medieval community was divided into three groups - the bellatores who were the noblemen who fought, the labores or laborers who grew the food and the

Oratores who represented the clergy, who prayed and attended to spiritual matters."

"As society evolved, the rank and role of the individual often became hereditary where the son of a knight or lesser nobleman would inherit the land and the military duties upon his father's death. This appears to be the case with the Terrills as there are a lot of knights in the family history and why a male heir was so important."

"Regardless of stature, the king always retained the right to decide who was to be the lord of the land and exercised these rights in what was known as 'De Prerogativa Regis', which meant 'concerning the royal prerogative'. Most importantly the king retained the right to 'primer seisin' which allowed him to take the profits of lands held for him during times of transition between a tenant's death and the formal succession of all heirs, along with the right of 'prerogative wardship' that allowed the king to determine who held title to the land when there was a dispute of inheritance."

"Sounds familiar," Mike interjected.

"When the deceased left no descendants, the hunt for heirs turned to their collaterals, such as their father's or mother's relatives, then grandparents' and so on. Within each of these lineages specific rules applied where brothers inherited before sisters, uncles before aunts, and so on. Land that had been inherited from a person's mother or father had to descend to a blood relative of that mother or father. Preference was given to males over females in tracing back these descendants where those of 'half-blood' were excluded."

"As you can see, feudalism was a working system that had one goal - the creation and maintenance of wealth and power in the hands of a few sustained through alliances and arranged marriages. When it was controlled, it worked but the addition of a system of inheritance transition had two huge effects on medieval society. First, feudalism discouraged any form of unified government simply because individual lords would divide their lands into smaller and smaller sections to give to lesser rulers and knights authority and therefore power. In turn the lesser noblemen would then subdivide their own lands into even smaller fiefs to generate even less authority for the nobles and knights."

"Feudal society was always an arrangement between individuals and not between society and its citizens. This meant that, while individual barons, dukes, and earls might be loyal to the king or a noble family, there was no strong legal tradition to prevent them from declaring war on each other. The bonds of loyalty often grew so entangled that a single knight might find himself owing allegiance to two different dukes or barons who were at war with no sense of loyalty to a geographic area but to a person, which would terminate upon that person's death."

"Second, feudalism discouraged any form of trade and economic growth simply because the land was worked by serfs. They were tied to individual plots of land and forbidden to move or change occupations without the permission of their lord, who might claim one-third to one-half of their production in taxes and fees."

Chapter 43 – Doomsday

	Born	Died
37. Seigneur de Poix Gauthier (Walter) Tyrrell III.	1 075	1 135
38. Sir Hugh Poix Tyrrell	1 100	1 159
39. Hugues de Pois Tyrell	1 159	1 199
40. Sir Roger Tyrell of Avon	1 175	1 230
41. Sir Edward Tyrell of Avon	1 210	1 315
42. Sir Galfried Lyonell Avon Tyrell	1 233	1 250
43. Sir Edmond Edward Tyrell	1 250	1 290
44. Sir Hugh Tyrell of Avon	1 288	1 377
45. Sir James Tyrell of Buttsbury	1 290	1 380
46. Sir Thomas "The Younger" Tyrell	1 315	1 382
a. Brother of Sir Walter		

Tyrell of Heron Hall		
47. Sir Walter Tyrell of Avon	1 348	1 406
48. Sir John Tyrell MP Speaker House of Commons	1 382	1 437
49. Sir Thomas Tyrell of Heron	1 411	1 476
50. Sir William Tyrell of Ockenham	1 465	1 510
51. Sir Humphrey Tyrell	1 500	1 548
52. Sir George Tyrell of Montagu	1 530	1 571
53. Lord William Edward Tyrell Lord of Bruyn & Ockendon	1 570	1 595

I reached into my satchel and pulled out another dogged-eared folder as it was time for another summary. Handing it to Mike, he flipped the page to examine all the Terrills of England who went from royalty to poverty.

I looked at Mike, smiled and continued. "In December, 1085 or nineteen years after the Battle of Hastings and establishment of authority throughout a unified England, King William decided to commission a query into the extent of his dominions to maximize taxation. All Norman lords and barons whom King William had granted land were ordered to collect information on their domains, which was to be sent to

William's advisors. Officials were then dispatched to the thirty-four shires that constituted the Kingdom of England to check the accuracy of the information and acquire more data concerning the population and productivity of the land. The officials were instructed to ask specific questions including what the particular place was called, who owned it, how many resided there and even how many cattle were kept there."

"For each landholding questions were phrased to discover how much the land was worth during the reign of King Edward the Confessor, before the conquest. The officials took evidence on oath from the sheriffs, barons and Frenchmen, along with priests, reeves and six villagers from each village. The work was rendered more difficult by the fact that most of England's population spoke Old English at the time, while William's officials spoke Norman-French. This unique survey became known as the Doomsday Book that survives today in the London Public Record Office and is an extraordinary document for its time that includes the name, address and holdings of Sir William Tiril I of Essex, England."

"What makes this so important is that it not only summarized who was who and where they were located, but it clarified the entire system of inheritance that William the Conqueror implemented begun by Charlemagne, that represented a profound, tectonic shift in the society, culture and economics of England."

"Lest we forget, William the Conqueror was not a welcomed king. He was, in fact, a dictator whose feudal structure was developed not only for the financial rewards it provided but the dominance over a conquered nation. William spent much of his time in London and built the Tower of London as his home. He never trusted the builders of London or even English stone, for that matter. His distrust was so great that he imported stone for the White Tower from Caen, France and used Norman craftsmen to do the skilled work, only allowing the English to act as laborers. William also built the first castle at Windsor and continued building around eighty more castles, as he felt they represented visible reminders to the people of England of his power and Norman authority."

"The last years of William the Conqueror's life were primarily spent fighting in Normandy as he defended his authority there as well. Amongst those opposing him was his rebellious eldest son, Robert, nicknamed Curthose by his father, due to his short legs. In a battle in January, 1079 Robert knocked William from his horse in combat and wounded him, ceasing his attack only when he recognized his father's voice. Humiliated, King William cursed his son, stopped the siege and returned to Rouen."

"On Easter Sunday of 1080, reconciliation between father and son was engineered by William's wife, Queen Matilda. The family was reunited in Breteuil in northern France for celebrations to mark the engagement of William and Matilda's 14-year-old daughter, Adela, to Stephen, Count of Blois. Queen Matilda then encouraged King William to make peace with his estranged half-brother, Odo, the Bishop of Bayeux, which William did.

"Three years later, when Matilda fell seriously ill, William rushed to Normandy to be at her bedside and wrote to Robert at Gerberol Castle asking him to immediately come to Rouen. Matilda died at Caen in November, 1083 with William at her side. In her will, Matilda bequeathed large amounts of money to the poor and her royal scepter and crown to Holy Trinity Abbey and was buried in Holy Trinity, l'Abbaye aux Dames, in Caen, Normandy."

"On September 9, 1087, William was thrown from his horse and sustained severe abdominal injuries. His condition continued to worsen and wary of the afterlife, William confessed his sins and sought pardon, directing his treasure to be distributed to the churches and the poor, 'So that what I amassed through evil deeds may be assigned to the holy uses of good men.' England was bequeathed to his second surviving and favorite son, William Rufus. Despite his bitter differences with Robert Curthose, King William bequeathed Normandy to him. To Henry, the youngest son, later destined to inherit all his dominions, William left 5,000 silver pounds. That day, he died having ruled England for 21 years and was buried in the monastery of St. Stephen at Caen in Normandy which was an abbey he previously founded as an act of repentance for his consanguineous marriage to Matilda."

Mike sat shaking his head in disbelief that I could literally rattle off the history of one of the greatest changers of life, liberty and the pursuit of happiness in Medieval times. I took a sip of my now-warm, almost-flat Sprechers root beer and added. "There's a stone slab with a Latin inscription, in the abbey Church of Caen that marks the purported burial place of the first Norman King of England. His grave has since been desecrated twice. First during the French Wars of Religion, when his bones were scattered across Caen, and, then during the tumultuous events of the French Revolution, when his tomb was again defaced and destroyed."

"After the Battle of Hastings, Pope Alexander II instructed William to build Battle Abbey on the site of the skirmish to mark his great victory and atone for the bloodshed. Peg and I visited the Abbey on one of our trips and found it not only functional but fascinating. I never let on that I'd been there when battle was raging as I didn't want Peg to know the death and destruction I'd witnessed that day."

"You were there?"

"Yup! The reason I can go into such great detail about the battle is because I saw it all first-hand."

"Whose side were you on?"

"Neither!" I replied with great pride. I'd seen enough bloodshed with Carolus and Charlemagne and learned my lesson to keep my big mouth shut as I continued. "The overthrow of the Saxon kingdom of England transformed the country in many ways, including its society, governance and culture and how it was organized and governed for over a thousand years. The changes were so profound, they even affected the language and customs and, perhaps, most visibly today, the architecture that remains from that period of time." I looked up and added. "William's system was quite a lucrative arrangement - free labor, free defense and total loyalty for all those chosen to be awarded by William the Conqueror."

"Sounds like America," Mike interjected. "We get to 'own' the land, unless we don't pay our property taxes and then boom, the government takes it back where, instead of a king, we have a court full of jesters."

It was fun listening to my sinister minister express his cynicism as I continued. "As you can see, the Tirel family relocated from France to England and seems to have gained a strong footing during William the Conqueror's rule that would last for nearly 700 years, but then that's another story and six more beers, some other day."

Chapter 44 – All the King's Horses and All the King's Men

A smile came across both of our faces as we left Joplin, Missouri and were about to enter Galena, Kansas and saw a single row of bricks painted with reflective yellow paint, with Missouri Route 66 and Kansas Route 66 roadway signs on each side. We were in Kansas and the memories of our kids getting the proverbial shit scared out of them by flying monkeys ricocheted through both of our psyches. The emotion was over in an instant, but it brought relief to two old men on yet another road trip trying to find somewhere over the rainbow.

Our smiles melted and I began again. "While my education and teaching dealt with all of Europe, my focus and passion was on England where history of the Terrills of England wouldn't be complete without referencing all the sixty-two kings and queens and how they affected people's lives, particularly in the fifteenth and sixteenth centuries, when the Terrills were at the apex of their wealth and authority and their relationship with the church."

I took a deep breath and hoped what I was about to share wouldn't offend my friend. "Humans are weak creatures by nature where the combination of wealth and authority become narcotizing and there's never enough of either until they end up hurting or even destroying the good others created. The close association of church and state, as it applies to England, is a classic example. While there were great kings and queens as well as great popes, there were the scoundrels who have sullied what should have been the awakening of mankind to the moral, ethical and social consequences that come from the four tenants Christ personified…humility, generosity, compassion and forgiveness."

"The tyrant kings include Richard II and III, megalomaniacs like Henry VIII, the mentally unsound Henry VI and the deeply troubling Edward VIII, whose engagement to the American Wallis Simpson effectively ended his brief reign in 1936 where it looks like he harbored pro-Nazi feelings.

"The entire Plantagenet dynasty, which spanned more than 300 years beginning in 1154, were violent plunderers, even by medieval standards."

"The Stuart kings, who took over in 1603, brought instability and sectarian strife."

"The Hanoverian kings who began in 1714, were simply inconsequential. The first of them, the German-born George I, never even learned to speak fluent English."

"In contrast, England has had just six sovereign queens – two named Mary, and two Elizabeth along with Anne and Victoria. All of them, except Mary I, sometimes called Bloody Mary for her heavy- handed efforts to reimpose Catholicism as the state religion, were outstanding."

"Elizabeth I is considered one of history's greatest monarchs unless, of course you happened to be black. By the time she assumed the throne, the Portuguese Crown had been selling enslaved African people for more than 100 years, first in Europe and then in the so-called 'New World'."

"England was a peripheral player in Europe's early imperial ventures, but English pirates and privateers not only plundered gold from Spanish and Portuguese ships, they also kidnapped enslaved Africans. Slavery was not legally sanctioned, but this didn't prevent many Elizabethans, including the queen herself, from treating Black Africans as slaves and, as such, simply commodities in a marketplace. There was at least one Black person in Elizabeth's household. His or her presence is recorded by a single line in an account book, which lists an elaborate coat for a 'little blak a more'. The item's detailed description suggests that this was perhaps a child who would have accompanied the queen as an "exotic" curiosity."

"On the positive side, during Elizabeth's 16th Century reign, England was transformed from a European backwater into a major power, bustling with commerce and flowering in the arts."

"Less than a century later Mary II, with her co-ruling husband, William III, helped engineer the Glorious Revolution, which shifted considerable powers from crown to Parliament. Mary's sister Queen Anne, was sickly and emotionally fragile after multiple miscarriages. Nonetheless, she was a stunningly effective monarch who, among other things, birthed a new nation by setting her minions to persuade, cajole (and bribe) the Scottish Parliament into voting itself out of existence and joining a new entity called the Kingdom of Great Britain."

"Queen Victoria, whose 19th Century reign spanned much of the industrial revolution, created the template for subsequent kings and queens trying to negotiate the buffeting winds of change.

If these sovereign queens weren't enough, English history is full of queen consorts (wives of kings), queen mothers and other women who played extraordinary roles."

"In the 12th Century Eleanor of Aquitaine pulled off one of history's most impressive acts of audacity by effectively divorcing the King of France (Louis VII) to marry the King of England (Henry II). Later in life she would also be the de facto ruler of both as regent for her son Richard I, who dashed off to fight in the Crusades. Her effectiveness was made clear when this empire, stretching from the Scottish border to the Pyrenees, came apart soon after her death."

"More than two centuries after Eleanor, a 14-year-old mother named Margaret Beaufort would go on to play an extraordinary role in the Wars of the Roses, deposing the tyrant Richard III and launching England's most consequential dynasty by persuading the nobility to back the impossibly thin claims to the throne held by her son, Henry Tudor, the future Henry VII."

"Today, Queen Elizabeth II has reigned in an era of limited, constitutional monarchy and done so with finesse and restraint. Even with the limits, she still has an enormous impact, providing for the United Kingdom a sense of continuity and tradition, even as their country underwent dramatic change. The stories of her are many and moving. As a 14-year-old she took to the airwaves to comfort the children who were being separated from their parents and sent to the countryside to avoid German bombing. On her 21st birthday she pledged a life of service and is fulfilling that pledge. It's not surprising that Elizabeth's subjects get emotional when speaking of her."

"I'm not going to outline all the popes, just those who affected the lives of the Terrills and subsequently those of us born and raised in Wisconsin."

I think Mike quietly let out a sigh of relief while driving across western Missouri as I continued "In education there's a concept called the 'theory of declining rectangles.' For all intents and purposes, it states that it's impossible to transfer all of one's knowledge to the next person and they, in turn, to the next and next. In the transfer, it's necessary to ensure that the core elements are communicated and those are represented by the rectangles. When creating a lecture, you outline the salient points and then expand from there. The smart kids quickly learn to identify the key points and remember them. I believe the same is true for the church. The disciples were profoundly dedicated and true believers. From their passion for a betterment of humanity it all began. Yet, with each generation that followed the passion and intensity became diluted and then corrupted by human nature, greed and incompetence."

"There were scoundrels," Mike offered.

"Following in the footsteps of St. Peter, the Pope is there to lead followers of the Catholic Church and act as a moral role model. Unfortunately, for St. Peter and the church, some of the 264 popes seem to have had their own ideas."

"For centuries the Catholic church has been ruled by the Pope, who was and is supposed to remain the symbol of Christlike wholesomeness and an important moral voice to some of the mankind's most pressing political and social issues. However, despite their reputation for being the righteous and ethical member in the Catholic world, this hasn't always been the case. Here are just a few examples."

"Pope Stephen VI started off his reign in 885 with a grisly show, digging up his predecessor, named Pope Formosus, and displaying his dead body to stand trial. Formosus' body was propped up on a throne as Stephen VI shouted unanswerable questions at it, accusing him of blasphemy during his supremacy. Unsurprisingly, the dead pope lost, and his body was flung into the Tiber River. Later, however, the body was recovered and given a proper burial by Formosus' followers. Stephen VI was later imprisoned and strangled by Formosus' supporters."

Pope Sergius III began his reign of terror in 904 by not only having Pope Leo V, who preceded him, murdered but also Benedict IV who had preceded Pope Leo as well. He then used his power to set up his son, Pope John XI, fathered by his 15-year-old prostitute mistress, to be Pope twenty years after him.

"Pope John XII ascended to the throne at the age of eighteen in 955. He wasn't ready for the life of a pope and soon transformed his residence into a brothel. Going further down the rabbit hole, he took part in murdering, invoking demons and even having sexual relations with his sisters. His promiscuity ended up being his demise in 964, after a husband caught his wife in bed with John XII and beat the pope so badly, he died three days later from his injuries."

"Benedict IX was pope on three separate occasions, with the first being when he was just twelve years old. He grew to be a wicked boy and ran from the position to hide when political opponents tried to murder him. In the time between his reigns, he started thieving, murdering and committing other 'unspeakable deeds' only to become pope again in 1045, which only lasted two months before someone paid him to leave. In addition to seducing young boys in the Lateran Palace, his contemporaries accused him of theft, rape, and murder where, to spice things up, Benedict enjoyed orgies and bestiality sessions. Two years after leaving a second time, he tried again, lasting only eight months before he was eventually driven out to never return again."

"While these are the really bad ones, there were obviously many good ones who attempted to eradicate the political aspect of religion and return it to its initial intent. As an example, in 1049 Pope Leo IX denounced the sale of church offices and prohibited the investiture of bishops by laymen.

"To ensure that the process of awarding roles to one's children would stop, Pope Leo IX also reinstituted the church's commitment to celibacy as a mark of dedication to God thereby eliminating any possibility that ecclesiastical offices would be inherited by the bishop's son."

"Upon Leo's demise, Pope Gregory VII was installed and insisted that he, as head of the church, would initiate and maintain a policy where the Pope had sole power to name cardinals and approve bishops. Pope Gregory VII also made it very clear that the pope, as God's vice-regent on Earth, had authority overall secular rules and the Church had the right to depose emperors and kings, release subjects from their oaths of obedience to a ruler and try all serious disputes between secular rulers. In other words, the Pope and Church were to rule the entire western world. The net result was the foundation of the divisive situations that would arise in Europe throughout the medieval and middle ages and would come to affect the Terrill lineage, as it did all others in power or with authority."

Mike interjected. "It didn't stick, did it?"

"Hardly! The rulers of Western Europe determined that Gregory's decrees would result in a profound reduction in their ability to work with bishops in controlling the masses on the local level and also result in a serious lessening of power that became known as the 'Investiture Controversy' that was finally resolved with the Concordat of Worms in 1122 between Pope Callixtus II and King Henry V. It resolved the struggle between the empire and the papacy over the control of church offices."

"Next came Boniface VIII who is famous for a horrifying quote that pedophilia was no more problematic than 'rubbing one hand against the other.' Elected in 1294, Boniface VIII established a string of statues all around Rome and even destroyed the city Palestrina over a personal feud."

"While there was a marked improvement in the moral tone of the church, on a local level priests were still often appointed by lay lords, where the rules of election were so ambiguous kings were able to navigate around them with ease."

"The Church remained the center of life until the Black Death pandemic of 1347-1352 during which people began to doubt the power of the clergy who could do nothing to stop people from dying or the plague spreading. If the Black Death wasn't bad enough, the collusive interaction of church and state from 1378 to 1418 put the last proverbial nail in the coffin where there were two and then three rival popes at the same time, supported by different countries and all living outside Rome."

"Pope Sixtus IV started his reign in 1471 and is primarily remembered for commissioning the Sistine Chapel. Despite this stunning creation, it didn't overshadow his sins, for he was known to have a large sexual appetite during his time as pope. He had six illegitimate children including one with his sister. Despite his sexual indulgences, he was quite the hypocrite, and strictly policed others by creating a tax on prostitutes and charging priests who had mistresses."

"Pope Innocent VIII wasn't so innocent! He was the first pope to openly confirm his illegitimate children, which was around eight at the time. Before his admission, they were simply known as the Pope's 'nephews.' He was also known to be a big supporter of witch hunting, blessing the act in 1484."

"Alexander VI began his papacy in 1492, only getting the position of Pope by bribing his fellow cardinals. Before becoming Pope, he was a member of Borgias, which was an Italian crime family, and his attitude did not change. During his time, multiple conspiracies and dishonesty surrounded him and he was also quite promiscuous, fathering at least nine children and famous for hosting a series of orgies, with one being named 'Joust of Whores.' He gets even worse when you see the multiple reports where Alexander VI engaged in incest with his daughter, Lucrezia."

"Pope Julius II started his reign in 1503 and was known for his domineering, manic spells. By far, his worst feature was his severe case of Syphilis, contracted from prostitutes, where it was documented that on a Good Friday, his feet were so covered by sores no one was able to kiss them."

"Pope Leo X began his realm in 1513 and is famous for his lavish spending, becoming a patron of the arts who commissioned the rebuilding of St. Peter's Basilica. After the church's wallet got a bit lighter, Leo X then convinced believers they could buy their way to heaven, selling indulgences that would reduce their sins."

"Pope Paul IV is still known as one of the worst popes for his horrific acts of anti-Semitism in 1555. Instead of being the moral symbol of the Church, Paul IV created a Jewish ghetto in a section of Rome, forcing Jewish citizens to publicize themselves by wearing yellow hats. He was so hated that, after his death, citizens celebrated by tearing down statues of him throughout Rome."

I let out a slight whiff of air, hoping that my skewering of organized religion wasn't too negative. Mike looked at me and smiled as he so adroitly stated! We all learn three ways...by seeing, by doing and by making mistakes. The initial passion for goodness became corrupted in the same way our country has, simply by coveting power and prestige and converting them into entitlement."

"When you can get away with it, you go for it. Hopefully, the years have shown that lessons were learned such that evil has been replaced by the good. Sadly, it will never be perfect simply because man is never going to be perfect. All we can do is try…try to bring peace to the world socially, politically and individually and that only comes by understanding right from wrong and good from bad and doing what's right and good, even when we know we can get away with doing what's wrong or bad."

There was a pause and if Mike were pondering how deep he should go and then inquired, "And so this is why you aren't very religious?"

I thought for a moment and then replied. "I am religious, just not in an organized way. I believe there is a God. There has to be, simply because humans are such a minute and insignificant spec in all there is. I believe that the net sum of the universe is zero and this applies to all aspects including humanity…for all the bad, there is an equal amount of good, for all the horrible people, there are those who quietly compensate in some small way. For every Hitler, there was an Oskar Schindler"

"You know about Oskar Schindler?" Mike inquired. "Everyone who studies history should know about him."

There was a long period of silence and I didn't know if the only hum was that of the tires on the road and whether it was good or bad and then Mike spoke. "After thirty years of speaking to and of God, the emotion that has stayed with me more than anything else is awe— awe of the power of love and the power of evil to infiltrate all human systems, including the church where no denomination or form of church governance is immune. The problem with organized religion is its tremendous capacity to disappoint. The gap between the behavior of religious people and our professed beliefs can be so huge that it's breath-taking. The greater our hopes for the church, the more profound our disappointment will be when they are dashed."

"My aspirations were and are lofty, namely to be a person and place that channels the best and highest human energies in one direction for the development of God's realm, 'on earth as it is in heaven.' When we seem to be failing miserably to live up to those aspirations, regardless of who we are, despair will follow."

Mike focused on the dashboard radio and added. "In an interview about the Catholic Church, NPR's moderator asked a nun if all that's challenging the Catholic Church today would be happening if nuns ran the church. Her reply was 'If you just made us cardinals or bishops in the same system, we'd probably get as arrogant as they are. This is what we have to change: the culture of arrogance.' Will, this is apropos to not only the Catholic Church, but all faiths and all levels of politics and organization. It's just part of human nature to strive to be better than the next person and superciliousness."

I'd never heard the word superciliousness and had to wait until I found a dictionary to learn it meant 'behaving or looking as though one thinks one is superior to others' and realized I'd met a whole bunch of supercilious people in my day and wondered if Mike used that in his sermons to wake up the sleepers.

We'd driven through Kansas deep in thought. While talking, we'd gone through Joplin, Missouri driven 13 miles through Galena, Riverton and Baxter Springs, Kansas and were in Oklahoma as I asked, "Should I return to the Terrills?"

Mike smiled and so I took it as the affirmative and began again. "Sir Walter Tiril II had several children including Walter Tiril III who was born in 1060 in Poix, Picardy, France. All was well until 1087 when William the Conqueror died and his lands were divided between his sons and it didn't go well. King William's son became William II or William Rufus, King of England, Scotland, Ireland and Wales, while Robert took control of his father's lands in France."

"The division of the lands presented a dilemma for those nobles who held land on both sides of the Channel including, obviously the Tiril's. Since the younger William and his brother were natural rivals, the lords worried they couldn't please both and thus ran the risk of losing the favor of one ruler, the other, or both. The only solution, as they saw it, was to unite England and Normandy once more under one ruler. The pursuit of this aim led a group of lords to revolt against William in favor of Robert in the 'Rebellion of 1088' under the leadership of the powerful Bishop Odo of Bayeux, William the Conqueror's half-brother, who Matilda had brokered the peace with."

"The Tyrells sided with William Rufus to the point that, by 1089, Walter Tyrell III, had become one of King Rufus' most trusted army commanders. By order of the King, Walter III married Adelize Alice De Clare, daughter of Richard Fitz-Gilbert De Clare of Tonbridge, Kent in 1090 and they had at least four sons: Walter Le Généraux (The General) born about 1092, Baudoin (Baldwin), born about 1095, Robert le Seigneur De Bergicourt born in 1100 and Hugues (Hugh) I, born in 1105."

"In 1091 Walter III accompanied King Rufus and invaded Normandy, crushing Robert's forces, thereby, forcing Robert to cede a portion of his lands. All was well for five years until 1095 when Pope Urban II announced the First Crusade which was a plan to wrest the Holy City of Jerusalem from the Muslims. Pope Urban justified the Crusade based on the fact that Christians in Jerusalem were increasingly being persecuted by the city's Islamic rulers, especially when control of the city passed from the relatively tolerant Egyptians to the Suljuk Turks. This was compounded by Byzantine Emperor Alexius Comenus also being threatened by the same Turks and appealing to the west for aid."

"With Pope Urban's call to recover the Holy Lands, the response by Western Europeans was immediate and Walter Tyrell III was called to represent King William Rufus. Unfortunately, beyond seasoned military veterans like Walter III, the First Crusaders were actually undisciplined and untrained peasants, most of whom met with their demise. Splitting into different parties, one group, known as 'The People's Crusade' reached Constantinople and were totally annihilated by the Turks."

"The main crusading force, featuring some 4,000 mounted knights and 25,000 infantry began moving east in 1096. Led by Raymond of Toulouse, Godfrey of Bouillon, Robert of Flanders, Walter Tyrell and Bohemond of Otranto the army crossed Asia Minor in 1097and captured the Turkish-held city of Nicaea while defeating a massive army of Seljuk Turks at Dorylaeum. From there, the Crusaders marched to Antioch that was located on the Orontes River at the base of Mount Silpius and began a six-month siege where they repulsed several attacks by Turkish armies. Finally, on June 03, 1098, Bohemond persuaded a Turk to open Antioch's bridge gate and the knights poured in, massacring thousands of Turkish soldiers and citizens while fortifying all but the Antioch Citadel or fortress that was located on top of a hill overlooking the city. Later in the month, a large Turkish army arrived and attempted to regain the city, but they, too, were defeated and the Antioch citadel surrendered to the Crusaders."

"After resting and reorganizing, Walter and the Crusaders set off for their ultimate goal of Jerusalem with a reduced force of 1,200 knights and 12,000-foot soldiers. On June 7, 1099 they reached the Holy City and, finding it heavily fortified began building three huge siege or breaching towers that allowed them to penetrate the city's walls. By July 13th the towers were complete and the Crusaders began their attack. The following day Walter and Godfrey's men opened the Gate of Saint Stephen and the balance of their army poured in. After a huge battle the city was captured as tens of thousands of its occupants were slaughtered."

"The crusaders had achieved their objectives and Jerusalem was in Christian hands – at least for a little while – as an Egyptian army marched on the city in August and defeated the outnumbered and exhausted Crusaders. The net result of all the death and destruction on both sides was the creation of five small Christian states under the rule of the Crusaders instead of a unified territory they dreamed of."
"While a hero in the eyes of William Rufus, the rest of the story of Sir Walter de Tirel III is quite different and is what he's been famous for all these years. Walter III was Lord of Poix-de-Picardie in France, and of Langham, Essex, England. By marriage, Walter III was linked to the English royal family, having wed Baroness Adeliza Ann Fitzgilbert DeClare, daughter of Richard Fitz Gilbert, founder of the House of Clare who was also with William the Conqueror at the Battle of Hastings and Rohaise de Bolebec."

"Although King William Rufus was an effective soldier, like his father, William was a ruthless ruler and, it seems despised by those he governed. According to the Anglo-Saxon Chronicle, he was, 'hateful to almost all his people and odious to God.'"

We pulled into a small café parking lot and stretched our legs and had a quick bite. I went to one of the overhead compartments, opened my case, pulled out a typed page and offered it to Mike. "Here's the 'official' report I found in my research."

'On 2 Aug. 1100, William Rufus organized a hunting trip in New Forest, Hampstead. The hunting party consisted of William Rufus and his brother Henry, Walter III, along with Walter's two brothers-in-law,

Gilbert Fitz-Richard De Clare and Roger Fitz-Richard De Clare, who all stayed at a hunting lodge the night before the hunt. William Rufus had been presented with six arrows on the eve of the hunt by his armorer. Taking four for himself, he handed the other two to Tirel, saying, 'Bon archer, bonnes fleches - To the good archer, the good arrows.'

"During the night, Rufus reportedly dreamt he went to hell and the Devil said to him 'I can't wait for tomorrow because we can finally meet in person!' Awakening suddenly, Rufus commanded a light be brought to his sleeping quarters and then forbade his attendants to leave. The following morning, the king decided to forego the hunt. However, by early afternoon, he was once again in buoyant spirits and set off through the forest.'

'The party spread out as they chased their prey, with William, in the company of Walter III, and they became separated from the others. In their search for prey, according to chroniclers, William Rufus and Walter III continued their hunt late into the afternoon and found themselves on nearly opposite sides of a forest clearing. The sun was now declining, when the king, drawing his bow and letting fly an arrow, slightly wounded a stag which passed before him. The stag was still running and the king, followed it for a long time, holding up his hand to shield them from the sun's rays. At that instant Walter decided to kill another stag and released an arrow that pierced the king's breast."

"The report went on. 'On receiving the wound, the king uttered not a word, breaking off the shaft of the arrow where it projected from his body. In so doing, the king fell forward, driving the arrow even deeper and that accelerated his death. Walter immediately ran up but found the king senseless. With that Walter III leapt on his horse and escaped with the utmost speed. Indeed, there were none to pursue him. In fact, some helped Walter's flight, while others felt sorry for him.'"

"The king's death broke up the hunting party and its members scattered to their own properties, fearing civil strife when it was learned the king had died. In his panicked flight from England, Walter III reportedly crossed the River Avon on his way to the coast at a fjord which is still called Tirilsford in Hampshire. On lands first granted to his grandfather, Walter III stopped at a blacksmith's shop near what's today known as

Avon-Tiril and had his horse re-shod with the shoes facing backward in an attempt to confuse would-be pursuers."

"King William Rufus' body was discovered the next morning by a group of peasants working in the woods. A charcoal burner by the name of Purkis placed the king's body "on a cart and conveyed to the cathedral at Winchester... blood dripped from the body all the way where the king was buried within the tower only to have the tower fall down the next year."

"To some chroniclers, such an 'Act of God' was a just ending for a wicked king. However, over the centuries, the obvious suggestion that one of William's many enemies may have had a hand in this extraordinary event has been repeatedly made. Even chroniclers of the time point out that Walter III was renowned as a keen bowman and unlikely to fire such an impetuous shot. William Rufus's brother, Henry I, was among the hunting party who benefited directly from William's death, as he went directly to Winchester, seized the national treasury and was crowned King of England, Scotland and Wales three days later on August 5, 1100."

"There's also an unconfirmed report that King Henry I actually pardoned Walter III but no reliable source has ever been found. According to some, Walter lived the remainder of his life in exile in Normandy at the castle of Chaumaît, never returning to England again. In 1116, Walter founded the Priory of St. Denis-de-l'Estrée, which existed until the 18th century. Some years later, in 1131, he established the Monastery of St. Pierre de Sélincourt as a response to a revival of religion centering around monasteries during the second quarter of the 12th century."

"Some say it was an accident, others disagree. Almost everyone said it was a reasonable end to a tyrant. King William II Rufus was loathed by the clergy in that they felt he had a soul that couldn't be saved to the point they said, 'While loved by his soldiers, the king was hated by the people because he caused them to be plundered and his demise was not wrought with tears by many.' Walter Tirel III made a pilgrimage to the Holy land in 1136 where he died."

Mike looked up and smiled and added, "So, you've got aristocracy and murderers in your past, huh? That's quite a mix."

I looked at Mike, grinned and added, "You bet, and it doesn't stop there. Sir Walter III de Tirel endeared the title of Vicomte d'Amiens 3e seigneur de Poix and was 40 and his wife, Adeliza de Clare was 31 when Sir Hugh de Tirel I Vicomte d'Equennes 4th Prince of Poix was born on November 10, 1100, in Essex, England. Sir High was the first in the family to bear the name 'Prince of Poix' as the name Tyrel became 'Tiril' in England."

"In the Pipe Roll, which were also called the Great Rolls, or the Great Rolls of the Pipe, consisting of a collection of financial records maintained by the English Exchequer or Treasury are held, Hugh is recorded as Lord of the Manors of Kingsworthy, near Winchester, Avon-Tyrrell and also owner of land at Ripley, Shirley, and Sopley, in the New Forest, England which was created as a royal forest by William the Conqueror in about 1079 for the royal hunt."

"The New Forest was created by combining more than 20 small hamlets and farms with no compensation to those former tenants and was therefore 'new' to William as a single compact area. First recorded as 'Nova Foresta' in the Domesday Book in 1086, it's the only forest the book describes in detail. All 70,000+ acres continue to exist today and remain unspoiled by the advances of humanity."

"Been there?"

"Yup! Peg and I visited and I got this eerie feeling, knowing I'd been there on one of my visits with Sir Hugh."

"In other words, the family was doing all right for themselves," Mike added.

"During Sir Hugh's life the House of Normandy was under the rule of King Henry I or Henry Beauclerc, who promised at his coronation to correct many of William's less popular policies and indiscretions. Considered to be a harsh but effective ruler, manipulating the barons in England and Normandy to his benefit, he drew on the existing Anglo-Saxon system of justice, local government and taxation and strengthened it with additional institutions, including the Royal Exchequer, charged with the collection and management of the royal revenue and judicial determination of all revenue in both England and Normandy."

"In other words, the IRS?" Mike inquired.

"You've got it!" I added as I continued. "Henry encouraged ecclesiastical reform but became embroiled in a serious dispute in 1101 with Archbishop Anselm of Canterbury, which was resolved through a compromise solution in 1105. King Henry I supported the Cluniac order who incorporated The Cluniac Reforms that were a series of changes that focused on restoring the traditional monastic life, encouraging art, and caring for the poor that began within the Benedictine order at Cluny Abbey in 910 by William I, Duke of Aquitaine."

"King Henry I was infamous for fathering a number of illegitimate children by a variety of mistresses. In spite of this, he had two legitimate offspring with his wife Matilda of Scotland, who were named William Adelin and Matilda. As the male child, William Adelin was heir apparent to the throne and was granted title of the Duke of Normandy."

"One fateful day, King Henry I, William Adelin and several other nobles of the royal court, including some of Henry's illegitimate children, were due to sail back to England from Normandy. King Henry elected to travel separately from his son who chose to sail upon a new vessel called the White Ship. The crew delayed departure until evening while a few members of the party, including two monks, chose not to sail with the group 'having left the vessel upon observing that is was overcrowded with riotous and headstrong, make that drunken youths. With three-hundred onboard and everyone drunk, the White Ship soon crashed upon the rocks and William Adelin drowned with the others'."

"When the news reached King Henry I, he was distraught and reportedly fell to the ground in remorse that many said he never recovered from. King Henry I married again but didn't have another legitimate son. King Henry initially proclaimed his daughter, the Empress Matilda, as his heir. However before naming Matilda queen, he began negotiations with his nephew Stephen of Blois to make him heir."

"Stephen had been raised by King Henry I and was awarded a great deal of land, allowing him to become extremely wealthy and powerful. In addition, in 1125 Stephen married Matilda of Boulogne, which was a major fishing port on the northwest coast of France, thereby gaining control of a major port on the English Channel and control over trade between England and France."

"When King Henry I died in 1135 the actual claimant to the throne was Matilda. Although it had been agreed that Matilda would rule with her husband, Geoffrey Plantagenet Count of Anjou, which was a French province in Northwest France that straddles the lower river Loire. However, English Barons wanted neither a female or a ruler from Anjou and the decision was made that Stephen of Blois' elder brother, Theobald, should become king. Stephen, didn't agree! He was the grandson of William the Conqueror, and like grandpa, invaded England, and on December 22, 1135, in a coup d'etat had himself crowned at Westminster Abbey instead of either Theobald or Matilda starting a period known as 'The Anarchy', as parties supporting the different sides fought in open combat in Britain and on the continent for the better part of two decades."

"During King Stephen of Bois' rein, Sir Hugh de Tirel I joined the Second Crusade in 1146 led by King Louis VII of France and Emperor Conrad III of Germany which started in response to the fall of the County of Edessa in 1144 to the forces of Zengi. Sir Hugh de Tirel I wasn't always away. He fathered at least four sons with Lady Ada Agnes d'Aumâle including Hugh Tirel II who was born in 1173 in New Forest, Hampshire, England, lived a life on both sides of the English Channel and was buried in Picardie, France."

Chapter 45 - The Angevin (Plantagenet) Kings

It was one of those rare March 17th St. Patrick's days when I wasn't in Wisconsin. Driving across the Texas panhandle we began to see billboards for a place called Mulligan's Pub and agreed to stop for 'just one pint' in Amarillo, Texas. We made it and the joint was a jumpin. I parked the bus as Mike went and asked if we could park in the lot and the bartender told us to go around in back as there was plenty of space back there. While Mike was gone, I retrieved my 'Kiss Me I'm Irish' tee-shirt and parked the bus as we sauntered into Mulligan's and ordered O'Hara's Irish Stout beer.

"You're not Irish," Mike shouted above the din of an already raucous crowd.

In probably the worst Irish lilt ever spoken I replied. "Ah laddie, that's where you're mistaken. Ya see me boy, there's a little Irish in all us Terrills" which allowed me to segue into a little bit more of the Terrill history. As the waitress placed a green plastic bowler on my head, I pulled a typed page from my shirt pocket, neatly unfolded it and handed it to Mike with the names of the eight Kings of England who affected the lives of my ancestors in England and Ireland and the duration of their reign.

· King Henry II - son of Matilda (1154-1189)
· King Richard I the Lionheart – son of Henry II (1189- 1199)
· King John I – brother of Richard the Lionheart – (1199- 1216)
· King Henry III – son of John I – (1216-1272)
· King Edward I – son of Henry III – (1272-1307)
· King Edward II – son of Edward I – (1307 -1327)
· King Edward III – son of Edward II – (1327-1377)
· King Richard II – grandson of Edward II – 1377-1399)

As I slurped what was to become one of many green beers, only after receiving permission to allow the bus to remain in the parking lot overnight, I shouted, "During this time, Henry's daughter, Matilda married and had a son named Henry Curtmantle, who was raised in France, even though he was King Henry I's grandson."

"England's greatest period of domination came under King Henry II who reigned from 1133 to 1189 and created the so-called 'Angevin Empire' that stretched from Scotland to the Pyrenees including Normandy, Maine, Brittany, Anjou, Touraine, Aquitaine, Gascony and Toulouse. In other words, literally the entire western two-thirds of today's France from Belgium to Spain. Needless to say, the French weren't too happy about English rule and every chance they had to minimize English control, they took advantage of."

"At the same time, one of, if not Rome's greatest popes came into being and that was Pope Innocent III who was, perhaps, the most powerful and qualified man to have held the papacy in history, if not the kindest or most empathetic. Despite his flaws, the Catholic Church may not have survived without him."

"Pope Innocent III was an intelligent, learned, and energetic man. Born Lotario dei Conti di Segni he took the papacy in January of 1198, and exerted a huge amount of influence over the Christian states of Europe, claiming supremacy even over the European kings." "You have to realize that the Catholic Church faced grave challenges during the 12th century, some of which threatened to dissolve it completely. Pope Innocent III, upon his election, immediately went to work taking on those challenges. One of the worst challenges lay in the Church's corruption. Innocent simply wasn't having it, and made the Church far more rigid in its policies, coming down hard on dissenters while creating an atmosphere that didn't permit corruption but also, unfortunately, didn't allow for honest and open criticism."

"What made him a candidate for being considered the greatest of all popes was his reassertion of papal rights and authority and his influence to coerce monarchs to recognize the supremacy of the Church while developing canon law, promoting administrative centralization, and expanding the Church's power that shaped the life of the Church for subsequent centuries. By increasing the strength of the church, he was able to counter-balance some of the turmoil created by generations arranged marriages within nobility."

"Henry Curtmantle matured and invaded England where he defeated Stephen of Blois' troops. Stephen agreed to a peace treaty on December 19, 1154 naming Henry as King Henry II, thereby ending the war and the House of Normandy, and establishing the House of Anjou/Plantagnent. The Plantagenet name is from 'planta genista which is Latin for yellow broom flower, which the Counts of Anjou wore as an emblem on their helmets."

Henry II married Eleanor of Aquitaine, the divorced wife of King Louis of France, and reigned for 35 years. Henry II was perceived to be both energetic and ruthless, driven by a desire to restore the lands and privileges of his grandfather. During the early years of his reign he restored the royal administration in England, re-established hegemony over Wales and gained full control over his lands in Anjou, Maine and Touraine, France."

"Henry II's desire to reform the relationship with the Church led to conflict with his former friend, Thomas Becket, the Archbishop of Canterbury, that lasted for much of the 1160's and resulted in Becket's murder in 1170. King Henry II then came into conflict with Louis VII of France as Henry expanded his empire by taking Brittany and pushing east into central France and south into Toulouse, despite numerous peace conferences and treaties. The war between England, Scotland and France finally ended with the signing of the Treaty of Boulogne with the English withdrawing from Scotland."

Before I began to slur, I added. "While most of England's interest and relationships had always been towards the Continent, Ireland remained a cluster of small kingdoms that led to the Norman invasion in 1169, which took place against the wishes of King Henry II. Hugh de Tirel's cousin, Richard de Clare, 2nd Earl of Pembroke, who was also known as Strongbow, sent Raymond le Gros along with Sir Hugh and eight other knights to claim areas for himself and those participating."

"The knights landed at a place named Dundonolf, Dundrone or even Downdonnel on May 1, 1169. Strongbow subsequently arrived at Waterford on August 23rd with twelve hundred men. Not wanting to be left out, King Henry II arrived on October 17, 1171 to establish authority over both the Norman adventurers and the Irish."

"King Henry II aimed to break the power of Richard de Clare and divide the Geraldines but quickly recognized he didn't have the muscle needed to curb their ambitions. Wishing to avoid having any one baron creating a power base that might one day threaten his own realm, King Henry awarded offices and lands of the newly created lordships to men who were also his own loyalists."

"King Henry II tried but failed to bring Ireland under the centralized control he enjoyed in England and only claimed the title 'Lord of Ireland' for himself. To ensure no one had enough power to challenge him, Henry retained control of the major ports of Wareford, Cork and Dublin, as well as a strip of the Wicklow coast in today's Northern Ireland."

"King Henry II replaced Maurice FitzGerald as 'Keeper of Dublin' with Hervey de Clare, Lord of Montmorency, who was FitzGerald's brother-in-law and Strongbow's uncle. Hervey also took command of Strongbow's forces from Raymond le gros and Miles de Cogan, who were reassigned to Wales."

"In March, 1172 King Henry II granted the Lordship of Meath to Hugh de Lacy for his service while recognizing Sir Hugh de Pois Tirel II as 'Baron of Castleknock', bestowing upon him large portions of lands, including the parishes of Killsallaghan, Ward, Cloghran, Chapelizod and Castleknock, totaling over 1,200 Irish acres. The grants were confirmed by the King in 1177 and records of the allocations are printed in 'Ware's Antiquities of Ireland,' stating that Tirel was an 'intimate friend' of Hugh De Lacy and confirmed by the King in 1177."

"So, you are part Irish?" Mike interjected.

"Aye, mate. I have a bit of Irish in me…or at least have relatives that do." I responded and continued. "Sir Hugh De Lacy built the Castle of Trim and left it in the custody of Sir Hugh Tirel II on his departure for England. The King of Connaught, Ireland sensed weakness and assembled forces to retake Trim. Sir Hugh Tirel felt the castle wasn't strong enough to resist attack and intentionally burned it. This turned out to be a mistake as the Earl of Pembroke came to Sir Hugh's support and repelled the advances of the Irish. De Lacy returned and wasn't very happy about the burned castle. Fortunately, he understood and rebuilt, making Sir Hugh de Pois Tirel II governor in 1183."

"Having learned a bit about building strong and somewhat fireproof houses, Sir Hugh Tirel elected to build his own Irish home at Castleknock and did so of stone, constructing it on two mounds of a long, narrow ridge that commanded the route into Dublin from the west. The 'Castle of Knock' had been the location of a Danish Royal residence and fortress that had been destroyed and the house Sir Hugh built remained in the Tyrell family until it fell into decay towards the end of the 1600's. The name 'Castleknock' refers to older units of land division such as a townland, civil parish and the barony of Hugh Tirel. Today, Castleknock is an affluent suburb located about five miles west of the center of Dublin."

"The Tyrrell family continued their presence in Ireland for another 400 years. During the Nine Years War, which commenced in 1594, Richard Tyrrell became a commander of the rebel forces in Leinster under Hugh O'Neill, Earl of Tyrone. In 1597 the Crown forces commenced a new campaign, involving a three-pronged attack on Ulster, aiming to link up in Ballyshannon. One force, under Robert Barnewall, and 1,000 men from the Pale were ambushed by Tyrrell and his 300 men at Tyrrellspass in what has become known as the Battle of Tyrrellspass which saw a total annihilation of Barnewall's forces resulting in cousin Richard being promoted to Colonel General of O'Neill's forces in Munster.

St. Patty's day was about to close and the Stout was getting to me. Unfortunately, I was a little disappointed that not one lovely Irish lass had given a somewhat Irish, old man a kiss. 'Oh well! Better luck next year', I thought as Mike paid the waitress and we made our way to the bus.

Still lucid enough to remember what we were talking about, I added. "While not in a direct lineage with those of us in America, Richard's still an interesting story. He was born in Spain in 1545 and was the son of Phillip Tyrrell and his Spanish wife. As head of the Tyrrell family, Richard became the Lord of Fartullagh, a barony in south Westmeath, based in what was originally called Fartullagh that became Tyrrellspass. Richard saw military service for the English-backed Crown forces in Ireland but was falsely accused in 1565 by the Earl of Kildare of the murder of Garrot Nugent, son of the Baron of Delvin. As a result, Richard subsequently allied himself with the Irish cause."

"In 1600, Lord Mountjoy was sent to Ireland by Queen Elizabeth to quell the rebellion. He besieged Richard at his headquarters at Tyrrell's Island. However, Richard escaped and joined O'Neill in Ulster. The rebels later headed south to join up with a Spanish army landing at Kinsale in County Cork but were defeated in 1601 by Crown forces in the area. O'Neill retired to Ulster and Richard elected to submit to George Carew, Lord President of Ulster, and withdrew to Cavan."

While still  having some of my wits, I went to my trusty leather satchel and found the Manilla folder with Tyrellspass labeled across the top and handed Mike a photo.

"Been there, did that?" Mike asked.

"Yup! As part of Richard's legacy, he built the castle in Tyrrellspass, which is 48 miles west of Castleknock via the M4. The building is approximately 60 feet high and follows the general pattern of the tower houses built during that period in that it's built of stone and is essentially a fort comprised a series of superimposed chambers. Unfortunately, during the Cromwellian invasion of 1650, the castle occupants suffered a great deal and many were executed and the property fell from the Tyrrell's hands.

The castle and surrounding land was acquired soon after by the Rochfort family, who became the Earls of Belvedere. It was recently converted into a restaurant and operates under the name Tyrrellspass Castle Restaurant that not only serves traditional Irish food but hosts medieval banquets as well. When Peg and I went for dinner, we saw the original spiral staircase and one of the original roof beams dating from

1280 in a part of the restaurant known as the 'lounge'. Alongside the entrance door is a Murder-hole through which intruders could be attacked."

"After King Henry II became the Lord of Ireland, he and his successors began to imitate the English system of the times as Irish Earls were created as well as Irish Parliament with seven Barons elected to represent the populous, or at least the aristocracy. The Irish Peers were in a peculiar political position. Because they were subjects of the King of England but peers in a different kingdom, they could also sit in the English House of Commons, and many of them did. In the eighteenth century, Irish peerages became rewards for English politicians, limited only by the concern that they might go to Dublin and interfere with the Irish Government."

Chapter 46: Richard the Lionheart

It was Monday and both of us had cases of the Irish flu. Neither felt comfortable driving and so Mike pulled out the checker board and began playing while peering out at the empty Mulligan's parking lot where the vestiges of St. Patrick's consisted of numerous green plastic beer cups with 'Luck of The Irish' and a shamrock on them only to remind us that we were both somewhat over-served the night before. Over a grueling three game set of checkers, I watched my red pieces erode from the board and become stacked high on Reverend Mike's side. Darn! We'd played for high stakes! I had to go pick up the empties as our way of saying thanks for allowing us to sing Irish songs and park overnight in the parking lot. With each step, and then having to bend over and pick up the dirty, dusty cups, I vowed 'Never again.'

It was ten o'clock and a lady bartender drove up dressed to the nines with three pounds of make-up on, making me wonder what she looked like underneath and whether she used one of those rubber spatulas to get off all the rouge at night. I was polite, handed her the stack of dirty cups, thanked her for the hospitality and made the excuse Reverend Mike was waiting for me. Geez, it's tough when some down-and-out lady thinks you've got money because you drive a fancy motor home!

The coffee was brewing and I vowed to get even with Mike while feeling he needed a jolt, I brewed two half-cups of espresso in one cup, which meant Mike was getting a double shot of caffeine. As he slurped his surprise, I began the treatise on one of the middle age's greatest historical celebrities.

The coffee had done its trick and I started up the bus and headed west on Route 66. Next stop, Albuquerque! With my eyes on the road, I began again.

"Upon King Henry II's death in 1189, the English throne went from King Henry and Eleanor of Aquitaine's to their two sons. The eldest was Richard, who became one of England's most famous kings as Richard the Lionheart. Born in England, Richard lived most of his adult life in the Duchy of Aquitaine in southwest France. While being England's King, Richard also ruled as Duke of Normandy, Aquitaine and Gascony, along with titles of Lord of Cyprus and Counts of Poitiers,

Anjou, Maine, and Nantes, as well as, Overlord of Brittany at various times during the same period."

"Busy guy!" Mike interjected.

"By the age of 16, Richard had taken command of his own army putting down rebellions against his father in Poitou. A natural leader and warrior, Richard was a commander during the Third or 'King's Crusade' which was an attempt by three European monarchs to reconquer the Holy Land following the capture of Jerusalem by the Ayyubid Sultan Saladin in 1187. After Phillip II of France returned home, Richard I achieved numerous victories against Saladin, which created the mystique that carried on throughout his life and history. The tie between Richard I and the Terrill family lies in the fact that Sir Hugues de Pois Tyrel II, Seigneur d'Agnieres, accompanied Richard in the King's Crusade from 1189 until 1192 and was with him in the battles against Saladin."

Sir Hugh de Pois Tirel II also participated in the Siege of Acre during the Third Crusade that represented the first major battle where the Crusaders were able to capture the city. While securing the city, Saladin's army remained largely intact and the two sides clashed again two months later at Arsuf. Once again, the Crusaders won the battle. However, with each battle King Richard's armies became more depleted and their ultimate goal of retaking Jerusalem slipped further from their grasp. For his gallantry, Sir Hugh III was known as 'The Grecian Knight' and was anointed as one of 'De Lacy's Barons' for his courage in times of battle."

"When Richard succeeded his father in 1189, he had an obligation to propagate a male heir for the throne. Even though he married Berengaria of Navarre on May 12, 1191, while on his way to a crusade, she bore him no children. In fact, Richard didn't seem to have much interest in any of the women afforded him to the point that the role of queen at his coronation was played by his mother, who was the only woman Richard ever showed any affection. Having conquered Cyprus that year, Richard arrived in the Holy Land and almost captured Jerusalem. However, he was captured, imprisoned and ransomed in Germany that caused a financial crisis in England."

"Nice honeymoon!" Mike interjected.

I continued. "Rather than regarding his kingdom as a responsibility requiring his presence, Richard has been perceived as preferring to use it merely as a source of revenue to support his armies. Nevertheless, he was seen as a pious hero by his subjects and remains one of the few kings of England remembered more commonly for his byname instead of his regnal number and is an iconic figure in both England and France."

"No story of England would be complete without mention of Robin Hood who became a popular folk hero because of his generosity to the poor and down-trodden peasants. Many chroniclers date his exploits as taking place during the reign of Richard the Lionheart with some reporting that Robin fought in the Crusades alongside the Lionheart and, therefore, Sir Hugh III before returning to England to find his lands seized by the Sheriff of Nottingham."

"The most well-known of Robin's 'Merry Men' was a man named John Little, who was reportedly a giant which motivated Robin to reverse his name to Little John. Regardless of his varying exploits, all versions of the Robin Hood story give the same account of his death. As he grew older and became ill, Robin went with his trusted friend, Little John, to Kirklees Priory near Huddersfield to be treated by his aunt. Unfortunately, Sir Roger de Doncaster had persuaded Robin's aunt to murder Robin and the prioress slowly bled him to death."

"The tale indicates that, 'with the last of his strength, Robin blew his horn and Little John came to his aid but too late. Placing Robin's bow in his hand and carrying him to a window, Robin managed to shoot one last arrow with Robin asking Little John to bury him where the arrow landed, which he did.'"

"While I'm certain the stories of Robin Hood are filled with hyperbole, there is a mound in Kirklees Park, near Leeds, England, which is within bow-shot of the house that's said to be Robin's last resting place. At the same time, the layout of Little John's grave in Hathersage churchyard in Derbyshire indicates that a very tall man was buried there."

"At one time Little John's longbow and cap supposedly hung in the church but Peg and I didn't see it. We were offered replicas in one of the souvenir stores and thought about it until I looked at the label inside the cap that said 'made in Korea.'"

"Richard the Lionheart remained King of England from 1189 until his death in 1199 when he was struck by an arrow while attacking the castle of the Vicomte of Limoges, who had refused to hand over a hoard of gold. Because Richard was always at war, in 1190 he designated his nephew, Arthur, heir to the throne of England in preference to Richard's younger brother, John, who as time would tell, was highly incompetent to the point that he has been decreed the worst English king to ever sit upon the throne."

"Had Richard not been killed the Doctrine of Representative Succession would have awarded the throne to Arthur. Unfortunately, it hadn't been accepted and sadly, world history could have been completely different. Instead, following Richard's death, brother John was invested as Duke of Normandy and in May 1190, crowned King John I, King of England."

"John was exceptionally cruel. Anyone who has read Shakespeare knows that medieval kings and nobles were forever murdering and maiming each other, either on the field of battle or more discreetly in darkened castle chambers. During the 12th and 13th Centuries, strict rules about combat and treatment of prisoners held sway where aristocrats didn't expect to die in battle, and if taken prisoner they expected to be kept in honorable captivity until they could be ransomed. King John repeatedly broke this protocol arranging for the 'disappearance' of his nephew and rival, Arthur of Brittany. When he captured his nephew in 1202, he also captured hundreds of other knights who expected to be held in honorable confinement. Yet, when their friends and families in Anjou and Brittany continued to fight, King John rounded up twenty-two of the knights, sent them to Corfe Castle in Dorset, where they were starved to death."

While twenty-two is somewhat large the venerable king killed dozens of people this way on more than one occasion, including the wife and son of his former friend, William de Briouze whom he simply placed in a cell in 1210 at Windsor Castle, locked the door and let them wither away."

"Another of King John's major failings was cowardice. While not like Henry VI or Richard II, who were averse to armed conflict. John was at war with Philip Augustus, King of France, and he didn't hesitate to invade Scotland, Wales and Ireland when he felt that the rulers of those lands had crossed him."

"When Philip Augustus invaded Normandy in 1203, John failed to confront him and fled to England, which the annals consider an act of desertion that led directly to the duchy's loss. John returned to the continent in 1206 and 1214 to try to regain lost ground. However, on each occasion, he withdrew rapidly when told his enemies were approaching and, for the first time in 138 years, the link between England and Normandy was severed. To pay for the escapades and charades, King John heavily taxed the English nobility and also quarreled with Pope Innocent III when he sold the Church offices and depleted the treasury to the point that Stephen Langton, Archbishop of Canterbury, called on the resentful barons to demand a charter of liberties to protect them from what Langton called 'the madman'."

"If starving someone to death isn't bad enough cruelty was another of John's most notable faults. Contemporaries regarded him as treacherous, remembering his attempt to seize the throne for himself while his brother Richard was in captivity and forcing himself on the wives and daughters of his barons. On top of all that, there was the generally salacious nature of his regime, where, beside the taxes, he created arbitrary fines, resulting in the greatest level of financial exploitation in England since my cousin, William the Conqueror, and the Norman conquest."

"To say that King John was inept would almost be an understatement. Like so many other rulers, any perception of weakness or inability to lead presented an opportunity for any powerful opponent to take advantage of the situation."

"You really didn't think much of him, did you?" Mike inquired. "Gee, what gave you that impression?" I replied.

Chapter 47: The Way to Santa Fe

Even though 'the bus' was ten-feet eight inches tall, eight feet wide and over twenty-eight feet long, it was agreed that 'the bus' moniker simply wasn't glamorous enough. So, Mike and I spent the next two-hundred miles discussing options. As I watched the fuel gauge slip lower and lower and lower and the reality that the fuel tank held 60 gallons, the name came to me. For forty years whenever I went to see Slick Carlson at the Mount Horeb City Service Station I'd simply say *"Slick, Fill 'er up with Ethyl"* which meant leaded gasoline, to take away the engine knock which I thought it was a great name for our travel partner. I once knew a really big lady by the name of Ethyl and so it sure made sense to me and it was certainly better than calling it Bufford Sherman Mike pulled out of his posterior simply because he thought it was one of the funniest names he'd ever heard a person called as he told me he almost cracked up when he did the poor guy's funeral.

The three of us...Mike, the newly proclaimed Ethyl and me, took the city version of Route 66 through Santa Fe. Mike looked in the AAA trip-tik that reported Santa Fe attracted artists, hikers, seekers, skiers and writers to its temperate climates and abundant scenery. AAA named it the nation's second-oldest city and highest-elevation state capital at 7,200 feet above sea level. The surrounding historic district's crooked streets wound past adobe landmarks including the Palace of the Governors, home to the New Mexico History Museum.

What can I say? The beauty of the desert wowed me. It's hard to describe the place because it's radically different from Wisconsin. Sure, the desert looks as expected. Dramatic Sangre de Cristo backdrops with rock formations that change color as the day progresses and gentle sandstorms blow over the landscape covered in two-needle pinyon trees. If I didn't know better, I would have thought I was in the Tabernas Desert in Spain's south-eastern province of Almería.

I can't quite pinpoint what was so visually stimulating. Was it the brightness and depth of the natural colors or the curved angles of the pueblos instead of Wisconsin reds and greens and sharp slants? All I knew was that it was different and profoundly breathtaking.

We both looked out the windshield in awe as I asked Mike, "How about dinner? The bus needs some gas, too. I found a Shell filling station and pulled into the pumps. The mechanic looked up, gave me a nod and a smile and came out as we both got out and stretched.

"Filler up!" I directed.

The fella wiped his hands on a rag in his back pocket and gingerly placed the gas pump nozzle into the fuel filler neck. As he stood at attention feeling the gas flow, he listened to the ding, ding, ding as Ethyl had her dinner. When all was done, the bill was $63.27 for fifty-seven gallons. Ethyl was thirsty and could have gone a few more miles if Mike wanted to push her, that is!

We went into the fella's office where cans of Shell oil were neatly aligned on the shelves, with a Shell calendar on the wall with a picture of their Indy Cars, Formula One, boats and motorcycle racing teams all lined up and ready to go. Next to the door was one of those swirly racks full of vertical rows free alphabetized, maps of Arizona, Oklahoma, New Mexico, Oklahoma, Utah and Texas all lined up and ready to go. The place was so clean, you would have thought it was a doctor's office waiting room.

I pulled out my wallet and gave the attendant a fifty-dollar travelers check, plus a ten and five in cash and told him to keep the change. I could tell by the slight smile he appreciated my generosity as I asked for directions to the nearest RV park. He replied it was only a mile away.

"Where can we get some good food?"

"Well, here in town, my favorite is the Coyote Café and their blue-corn chicken enchiladas. However, if you don't mind a little drive, go out to Rancho de Chimayó that serves traditional New Mexican cuisine and provides outside dining."

Charlie, as his shirt said, continued, "I like it because it's a New Mexican hacienda with a maze of adobe-walled rooms and tiled patios near Santuario de Chimayó.

"What do you eat when you go there? Mike asked.

"The Carne Adovada with marinated pork cooked in red chile caribe sauce is great or you can order the heavier burrito version, filled with cheese and served with refried beans and Spanish rice."

Charlie had a wry grin on his face as he added. "Don't forget to have a couple of shots of tequila. They make their own and it will knock your socks off."

After St. Patty's in Amarillo, I didn't know if I could handle the snake that bit me but then thought, what the hell, it was Santa Fe and you need to do what the locals do.

"What time you get done work?" I asked. "I own the place, why?"

"Want to be our tour guide?" "What the heck, why not?"

"What time do you close?"

"As soon as I turn off the lights and lock the door," Charlie replied.

"Really?"

"Yup!"

"What about the car you're working on?"

"That's Ed Johnson's and he's in LA and won't be back until Monday. There's no rush."

Mike had a curious look on his face and inquired. "From the accent, it doesn't sound like you're from around here."

"Naw! I grew up in New York, got burned out as a commodities broker on Wall Street, lost my family in divorce and virtually all the money I had. It was my fault and not my wife's. She found another guy who's really a great father to my kids. When it was all said and done, there's no hard feelings and I knew I needed a change of pace if I was going to ever be happy. I drove to Chicago, got on Route 66 and headed west. Like you, I made the turn, drove the six miles into Santa Fe, fell in love, took my savings and bought the gas station. One day, this pretty young thing drove up looking for directions and I fell in love again."

"Where is she?" Mike asked. "At home."

"Give her a call and ask her if she wants to have dinner with two old codgers from Wisconsin." I offered.

"Really?"

"Yup! We're pretty tired of each other's lies and would enjoy the company," Mike replied.

Charlie called home, excused himself, went out behind the office to a store room, washed up and changed clothes just as his wife, whose name we learned was Beth, walked down the hill from the small pueblo house just above the station. They both had to be in the early forties and had those pearly white teeth you saw on TV. Mike and I were smitten by the inner beauty of two people you could immediately tell were in love as it brought memories of a time gone by when Ginny and Peg filled our hearts in exactly the same way.

Beth was wearing cowboy boots and those old-fashioned, new-fangled, low-rise, skin-tight, button-fly, blue-jeans with a fancy leather belt that had a big buckle of a horse on it. Even though it was a bit cool, she had on one of those cowboy blouses with a matching set of silver and turquoise bracelets, necklace and earrings. She was a pretty girl, but then after Mike, even the blue hairs back at Heaven's Waiting Room would have looked good to me. Well, maybe not! The only thing that surprised me was the fact she had a small tattoo of a smiling sun on the back of her right hand. I don't think I'd ever seen a girl with a tattoo before in my life.

I offered to drive but Charlie said, 'No," and pulled out a pristine, silver blue 1967 Chevelle Malibu SS-396 convertible with spinner hub caps. Charlie put the top down as Mike and I climbed in the back seat. It was a bit cool but the feel of the spring air as we drove through town was invigorating.

We made it to Rancho de Chimayó and pulled into the parking lot with Charlie carefully parking away from the other cars to save from door dings as he put up the top. In we went, to a delightful night of stories told, laughter galore and the wonderment of four people who had been strangers hours before, immersing themselves as dear friends, never to be forgotten.

I went first and told of my life as a history professor. Mike went next and detailed how he was a retired life assurance salesman. When both Charlie and Beth didn't understand, Mike explained that he'd been a minister and experienced the majesty of love and could feel it in both of their hearts. Mike also made sure they were aware he wanted them to treat him as if he were just another guy whose profession simply had been trying to help people be as happy as they were.

I looked at the couple and interjected, "I call him the sinister minister."

With smiles all around Beth explained that she'd been a commercial artist in Denver for a small, struggling ad agency and when it failed, she wanted to do what she loved, which was watercolors. She'd heard about Santa Fe and the emerging artist colony and decided to give it a try. Just like we had, she'd pulled into the Shell station when this man came out with a gracious smile and took her heart away.

We each had two shots of tequila and that was enough. I don't remember when I'd laughed as hard, and as often, as that night as Mike and I poked fun at each other and our idiosyncrasies and our true depth of friendship and respect filled the table with mirth.

Charlie asked where we'd been and I told him how I'd won Ethyl and our trip to Florida. Mike then told the tale of our snorkeling trip and what we saw on the beach in a way that only Mike could tell it. I thought Charlie and Beth were going to fall off their chairs laughing about some of our shenanigans. God, it was great to laugh! It was getting late and we needed to go back to the station and get Ethyl.

"Why don't you just park in our driveway?" Charlie asked. "I'll make you breakfast in the morning," Beth offered.

"Wow! Homemade breakfast and none of Will's cooking," Mike offered.

"OK, no more Cheerios for you, buddy!" I threatened.

"He's the only person I know who can burn Cheerios," Mike countered.

We had a wonderful breakfast of some sort of burritos with eggs and sausage in them. I asked Beth what the difference was between a taco and burrito and she replied, "The main difference is the shell size. Tacos are generally a lighter snack or meal, while a larger burrito is a full meal. A taco can either be a soft or hard corn shell, while a burrito is generally a larger flour tortilla, as corn tortillas tend to fall apart more easily."

"In other words, three tacos make a burrito?" I inquired and Beth affirmed. "Well, I'll remember that the next time we drive to Madison for Mexican food. I'll tell them I just want one burrito as I don't think I can eat three tacos."

There was a pause and then a polite snicker as it seems my joke was about as flat as the taco shells. I caught Beth's glance at the kitchen clock and knew it was time to head out - Charlie to the gas station and Ed's car - Beth to her art studio and Mike and I to Phoenix. We invited them to Mineral Point as I pointed out that it was a lot like Santa Fe - filled with a lot of artists and just about as beautiful but in a different way and we'd go out to eat Cornish pasty.

With all my blubbering and Mike's incessant attempt to find a good radio station we stopped at the Santa Fe K-mart, walked into the music department and bought Glenn Campbell's cassette called 'By the Time I Get to Phoenix' even though the lyrics were backwards from our journey with Glenn leaving Phoenix, going to Albuquerque and then Oklahoma. We didn't care. All we were going to do was sing about going to Phoenix. We also picked up Dionne Warwick's 'Valley of the Dolls' cassette that had the song called 'Do You Know the Way to Santa Jose?' on it. Imagine, $9.99 each for two little plastic cases with some music in them.

I told Mike I wanted to buy a jar of pickles and he asked why. My retort was that we could also have *'volley of the dills.'* Mike almost left me in the K-mart parking lot after that one.

As we drove west Mike changed the Dionne Warwick lyrics to…. Do you know the way to Santa Fe? I've been away so long

I may go wrong and lose my way Do you know the way to Santa Fe? I'm going back to find

Some peace of mind in Santa Fe

Charlie and Beth promised to come to Wisconsin. Yet, I think we all knew we'd never see each other again. We both got Christmas cards with one of Beth's drawing on it and sent them a gift box from the Wisconsin Cheeseman. Nice people! Both of them! I still can't get over a lady with a tattoo and a nice lady at that. The world is certainly changing!

Chapter 48: The Magna Carta

Mike didn't leave me at K-Mart and we headed west for Flagstaff. With 385 miles to go, I looked at Mike and felt I needed to expand on the Magna Carta and its significance. Mike had an almost incredulous look upon his face indicating he was intrigued by what I was sharing and so I added. "I need to switch back to the Terrills so you can see how this all fits together."

Mike said "OK", making me believe the charts I'd prepared showing who followed whom to the throne were helping. I continued. "Sir Hugh's son, Sir Roger Tyrell of Avon, inherited Hugh's English lands and possessions and became the founder of the English branches of the Tyrrell family. Roger married and they had one son, Edward Tyrell (Tiril) of Avon, who was born in 1165. Sir Roger's claim to fame is that he appears to be the first person to change the Tirel name to Tyrell."

"Sir Edward Tyrell of Avon married and was probably involved in creation of the Magna Carta - Latin for *'Great Charter of Freedoms'*, that was drafted by Stephen Langton, Archbishop of Canterbury in an attempt to resolve the issues between King John and the angry barons and agreed to in 1215, at a place called Runnymeade In reality, the Magna Carta was essentially a peace treaty which promised protection of church rights and the barons from illegal imprisonment, while providing access to swift justice and limitations on feudal payments to the Crown. This represented the first time that English kingship was placed under the rule of law."

"Neither side stood behind their commitments and the charter was annulled by Pope Innocent III, resulting in the First Barons War from 1215-1217 led by Robert Fitzwalter. In the First Barons War, King John I faced a superior military force and had no choice but to give in to the baron's demands. Earlier kings of England had granted concessions to the feudal barons but these charters had been vaguely worded, issued voluntarily and easily broken. The new document forced the king to make specific guarantees regarding the rights and privileges of the barons along with freedom of the church. The net result of the concessions was the collapse of the Angevin Empire."

"I don't think anyone at that time could have imagined how profound the Magna Carta was and how it would affect not only English, but world history. The charter consisted of a preamble and sixty-three clauses that dealt mainly with feudal concerns that had little or no impact outside 13th century aristocracy. The document was remarkable however, in that it implied there were laws the king was bound to observe, precluding any future claim to absolutism by the English monarch."

"Of greatest interest to later generations was clause thirty-nine which stated 'no free man shall be arrested, imprisoned or disseized (disposed) or outlawed or exiled in any way victimized…except by the lawful judgement of his peers by the law of the land.' This clause has been celebrated as an early guarantee of trial by jury and of habeas corpus that inspired England's Petition of Right in 1628 and Habeas Corpus Act of 1679. While these clauses were designed to protect and defend the rights of both the barons and the Church, history shows there were ways around them that resulted in death and destruction decreed by future kings that allowed kings to rule with a high degree of impunity."

"Sounds like America to me." Mike commented. "The rich and famous seem to have a different set of rules than you and me."

Even though I agreed, I didn't say anything and continued. "When King John I died in 1216, his son, King Henry III, reissued the document after removing some of the more radical contents. The Barons didn't agree and the War of the Barons continued another year, resulting in re-establishment of the Magna Carta included as part of the peace treaty between King Henry III and the warring parties."

I leaned back in the driver's seat, quickly glanced at Mike and added. "We need to remember the entire feudal system had been in place for over 200 years. As time evolved, the barons grew stronger and William the Conqueror's descendants became less dominant. King Henry III reissued the Magna Carta again in 1217 confirming that, in general, the royal prerogative applied only to lands held *'ut de corona'* or 'as of the crown' and therefore as part of the crown's ancient land endowment created by Grandpa William."

"There were some really profound assertions included of which clauses 39 and 40 are most referenced: 'No free man shall be seized, imprisoned, dispossessed, outlawed, exiled or ruined in any way, nor in any way proceeded against, except by the lawful judgement of his peers and the law of the land and forbid the sale of justice and insisted upon due legal process.' From this sprang not only the principle of habeas corpus (that the accused are not to be held indefinitely without trial) but the idea of the right to trial by jury (by the accused's 'peers'). Even the presumption of innocence, pending conviction, can be traced back to the same clause."

"As important is clause number fourteen regarding no taxation without representation and with it, the establishment of a common council, duly embodied in Parliament, as a means of obtaining popular consent."

"In return King Henry III decreed that the Magna Carta did not apply to lands held 'ut de honore' – 'as of an honor', that is, of various honors that had escheated to the crown. This simply meant that any property of a person who died without heirs automatically reverted to the crown. This was justified because it served to ensure that property was not left in 'limbo' without recognized ownership. Short of funds, King Henry III reissued the charter again in 1225 in exchange for the ability to grant new taxes."

"From that point on, whenever any English king wanted money or advice from his subjects, he would order churchmen, earls and other powerful men to come to his Great Council and would generally order the lesser men from towns and counties to gather and pick someone to represent them. This practice evolved into English Parliament where, among those summoned to the Great Council, were barons and nobles, with no other title, who held feudal lands as direct tenants of the monarch. When the Council evolved into Parliament, barons and persons of higher rank formed the House of Lords. Persons summoned to the Council as chosen representatives of a larger group became the House of Commons."

"The order summoning someone to Council or Parliament was called a writ to which, the monarch provided no payment or reimbursement for the expense of attending. Councillors and later Parliamentarians, were required to vote on taxes on both themselves and their neighbors and attest to their status in the feudal system, which might cost them special taxes. In these debates, those involved risked involvement in royal politics to the point the king would request personal benevolence. Which men were ordered to Council varied from council to council. A man might be so ordered once and never again, or for all his life but his son and heir might never go. As you will later see, the Tyrrells were often in Parliament in numerous capacities, which is one of the primary reasons why their aristocracy lasted over 700 years."

"As you can hopefully see, in the Baron's Revolt and subsequent upheavals of the 13th century, the barons were acting collectively for their own interests, which was a direct threat to the entire system of feudalism. Some things stayed the same. Annual military service remained typically forty days in an effort to reduce the burden on nobles so that they didn't leave their lands unattended for too long. Normally, forty days wasn't long enough to complete a military campaign and so lesser monarchs were obliged to pay mercenaries to represent them. This dealt another blow to the tradition of feudalism and vassalage."

"Sounds like America and the military draft," Mike interjected. "Remember when men were required to serve their country and not consider it a form of employment by those who don't serve?"

I shook my head in dismay, knowing that the change of policy had been one of the key components in the deterioration of belief in American government and society. I continued, "Uses relating to lands held by the crown were subject to royal oversight because grants of such land had to take place with royal license. After 1327, if a transfer license was not obtained, the lands could be confiscated and only returned on payment of a fine. To this end, inquisitions often noted whether or not such licenses had been obtained and also contained information about whether the necessary formalities had been observed when lands were *'enfeoffed'*, which was the deed by which a person was given land in exchange for a pledge of service. If so, whether *'seisin'* - which was the term used for legal possession on the land by the inheritor, had been properly delivered and whether the new lord's tenants recognized the inheritor as their new lord."

"With this structure in place, one can look at descendants and quickly determine who got what and why. Oldest sons first, then the rest of the sons, followed by the oldest daughter and then the rest of the daughters and so on and why it was so important to be loyal to the king. Four original copies of the Magna Carta exist today, one in Lincoln Cathedral, one is Salisbury Cathedral and two in the British Museum."

"You ever see them?" Mike asked.

"I was there when they were signed," I casually replied without trying to sound self-important, as I continued. "All the royal gobbledygook had only one purpose – wealth and its maintenance – and here's what it meant to the Terrill family.

"Sir Edward Tyrell of Avon had one son, Galfried Lyonell Tyrell, who was born in 1195 in Hampshire, England."

"Sir Galfried Lyonell Tyrell of Avon, married Jane de Borgate and they had one son, Sir Edmond Edward de Tyrell, who was born in Great Thorton, Essex, England in 1225."

Sir Edmond Edward de Tyrell of Avon married Jane de Borgate and they had three sons: Hugh Tyrell, who was born in Great Thornton, Essex England in1254, James Tyrell, born in Essex, England in 1260 and his son Sir Hugh Tyrell, who was born in New Forest, Hampshire England in 1288."

"At that time, the Tyrell family resided primarily in Essex, England with some property in Ireland and other adjoining counties and had done so for over 200 years. In so doing, my ancestors played an important and integral role in governing feudal England and were known as the 'Lords of Heron Hall' in the parish of East Thornton in Essex."

"Members of the family, throughout the preceding and following generations, were called upon to serve their King who saw fit to call the Tyrells for matters of law and order, warring, maintenance of the infrastructure, economic activities, welfare of the state, record keeping, finances and even public policy. In each of these areas, members of the Tyrells were commissioned by the king to maintain the realm for the greater good of Feudal England."

"Even with the Magna Carta, things were tensions between the royals and barons. In 1265, in the midst of a civil war against King Henry III, Simon de Montfort summoned a Parliament that included representatives from all the shires and boroughs including Sir Edmond.

Edward de Tyrell of Avon, thereby initiating the House of Commons which has now existed for 500 years.

"Sir Edmond Edward de Tyrell of Avon was 46 when King Henry III's son, Lord Edward, initiated the Ninth Crusade to the Holy Land. Lord Edward was on his way home in 1272 when he was informed that King Henry III had died after 56 years of reign. Not reaching England until 1274, Lord Edward was crowned King Edward I upon his arrival at Westminster Abbey and things really began to change. After several tumultuous years, in 1297 King Edward I reconfirmed the Magna Carta."

"Sir Hugh Tyrell of Avon married Lady Jane de Flambert and they had a son named James Tyrell of Buttsbury who was born around 1300 in Chelmsford, Essex, England. Sir Hugh was appointed Governor of Carisbrooke Castle in the Isle of Wight that served as a King's summer residence and prison and was deeply involved in the Hundred Years War between England and France. Sir Hugh and the Isle of Wight played a critical role during the war because of the castle's strategic location, where any invader who landed on the island could sail up the River Solent and use the ports of Southampton and Portsmouth as bases to attack the rest of England."

"The Isle of Wight was raided five times between 1336 and 1370 and the castle was surrounded in 1377 by the French. However, as the story goes, one of Sir Hugh's archers, named Peter de Heynoe, shot and killed the French commander and the French retreated."

I paused for a moment and then added. "In 1896, Queen Victoria's youngest daughter, Princess Beatrice, became governor of the Isle of Wight. The Princess remodeled the castle, restored the gatehouse and Chapel of St Nicholas, had the great hall re-roofed and the Constable's Lodging extended. In 1913, Princess Beatrice decided to make Carisbrooke her summer home and the out buildings were converted for the Princess's servant's quarters with a tunnel dug so that the servants could get to her rooms without going outdoors. Peg and I visited there and I realized once again, we were walking on floors my ancestors had once not only roamed but defended and it gave me chills."

Chapter 49: Two Hundred Years of War

I looked at Mike and offered, "I need to backtrack a little to outline the role Scotland played in the evolution of England, if you don't mind."

Mike glanced at me as if to say, 'Tell me more' and I continued. "Having conquered Wales, the death in 1290 of Margaret, 'Maid of Norway' and claimant to the throne of Scotland, opened the way for King Edward I to manipulate the succession of the Scottish throne. Little did King Edward realize the challenge, nor the consequences, or he probably would have left well enough alone. While there were numerous battles and heroes in the Scots confrontations for independence, two have worn the time of history and they are Robert the Bruce and William Wallace, as well as the Battle of Bannockburn."

"Although I couldn't find any relation to the Tirel's in either one of them, I would be remis not to mention Robert the Bruce, who was King of the Scots from 1306 until his death in 1329 and one of the noted warriors of his generation, who eventually lead Scotland during the First War of Scottish Independence and ultimate defeat of the English."

"In 1307 King Edward I died and his fourth son, King Edward II succeeded his father. Edward II married Isabella of France, while the battle for Scotland raged on. In 1314 the infamous Battle of Bannockburn took place that saw the Scots defeat superior English forces. While being portrayed as 'the happy ending' in several movies, in reality, the fight for independence continued for another 21 years, concluding only when 'the Treaty of Edinburgh-Northampton' was signed in March, 1328."

"In 1327, King Edward II went the way of many deposed kings. He was locked up in Berkeley Castle, persuaded to abdicate and then never heard from again. 'Why?' you ask. It was due to the disasters in Scotland that resulted in a downward spiral into tyranny, none of which was more profound than what has been labelled 'the One-Hundred Years War' that lasted from 1337 to 1453."

"In 1328 the death of Charles IV, King of France, led to the succession of the House of Valis, as he died without sons or brothers. Tensions between the French and English had been simmering since the Battle of Hastings in 1066. For over

250 years English monarchs and noblemen, including the Tirel's, had historically held titles and land in both England and France, making them vassals to both kings, thereby making things quite complicated. As an example, France's King Charles's closest male relative was his nephew, King Edward III of England, whose mother was King Charles's sister, Isabella of France."

"Upon King Charles' death, Isabella claimed the throne of France for her son Edward III, by the rule of 'Proximity of Blood'. The French rejected the claim maintaining that Isabella couldn't transmit a right she didn't possess, as they had passed what was called 'Salic's Law' that disallowed female French succession. Instead, the throne passed to Charles's patrilineal cousin, Philip Count of Valois, which King Edward III protested. Philip was crowned King of France, claiming all territory, except Gascony, which was a province of southwestern France."

"Disagreements between King Edward III and King Philip came to a head in May 1337 when the French decreed that Gascony also be returned to French rule. This prompted Edward III to renew his claim to the French throne and do so by force. With battles raging in Scotland, King Edward III had to make a choice - battles on two fronts or agreeing to Robert the Bruce's terms. In 1338 England and Scotland came to terms while King Edward III maintained his claim as King of both England and France."

"Over time, the 100 Years War expanded and included factions from across Western Europe. In total there were 60 battles, where the English were considered victors in 30 and the French in 27. "Sounds like the score of one of our softball games," Mike replied as he sipped the last of his root beer. "There were five major battles.

·	The Battle of Crecy: August 1346
· 1356	The Battle of Poitiers: September
· 1415	The Battle of Agincourt: 25 October
· May 1429	The Siege of Orleans: October 1428 –
·	The Battle of Castillon: July 1453"

"Add to these, the two Naval Battles of LaRochelle that were fought in 1372 and 1419 and won by Castile, which was a domain in the central part of the current Spain. In 1385 the English also fought the alliance of France and Portugal in the 'Battle of Aljubarrota' where the English were victorious. The net result of the tit-for-tat was 116 years of war, interrupted by several truces, in which five generations of kings from two rival dynasties literally fought over nothing."

"What side were the Tyrells on?" Mike asked.

"Both sides," I responded. "When there are bullets flying and your existence is predicated on your political connections, you keep your head down and doing what you're doing. I've studied dozens, if not hundreds, of wars and they're all about strategy and planning to gain control of thoughts and emotions rather than the consequence of individual battles. From Caesar to Hiroshima, normally, the outcome of one battle doesn't decide the winner of a war simply because war is an intense conflict characterized by extreme violence, aggression, destruction and mortality."

"As you can see, Mike, the Plantagenet kings were often forced to negotiate compromises such as the Magna Carta, which served to constrain their royal power in return for financial and military support where the king was no longer considered an absolute monarch, holding the prerogatives of judgement, feudal tribute, and warfare but, now, also had defined duties responsible to the kingdom that was strengthened by a sophisticated justice system. At the same time distinct national identity was being formed by the English based on their conflicts with the French, Scots, Welsh and Irish and establishment of the English language as the primary language.

"The rivalry between the House of Plantagenet's two cadet branches of York and Lancaster brought about the Wars of the Roses, which was simply a fight for the English succession that wouldn't be culminated until 1485 and the Battle of Bosworth Field where the reign of the Plantagenets and the English Middle Ages both met their end with the death of King Richard III."

I looked at Mike and elucidated one of my most critical thoughts that came from so many years of teaching. "One cannot think of war without addressing the casualties, where just one death is large enough to impose an obligation to consider the cost represented by that number - not just one but one circle of life and the shattering bereavement it entails, to the point we must always ask ourselves, for what purpose should that cost be borne by those upon whom it falls, and whether it has been justified?"

"Amen to that," Mike responded.

Chapter 50: Sir John

While England was at war, life for the Tyrell's was actually quite good. Sir James Tyrell of Buttsbury married Margaret Heron in 1318. Margret had inherited Heron Hall in Horndon and, in so doing, began the line of the Tyrells of Heron Hall, located in Heron Essex, in the Parish of East Horndon and represented the apex of Tyrell wealth and influence."

"While the Tyrells had been an influential family in feudal England and either held or governed several pieces of land, things moved to a much larger plane with the Heron marriage. Originally the Tyrills were the hereditary Lords of Langham awarded during the Norman Invasion. The family had a base area and also held land in both Avon on the west coast and South Hampton in Hampshire, about 70 miles southwest of London."

"Heron Hall was built on a man-made island where the house existed until 1790. When Peg and I visited only the original tower bases remained, along with the moat that was still filled with water. The famous fishponds had dried up and the original house replaced by an 18th century building outside the moat, also called Heron Hall, that's still standing. For its time and place, it had to be both magnificent and intimidating."

"Sir James and Margaret saw the addition of sons James, Thomas and Walter. In the children's generation there was also Thomas Tyrell who was called Thomas the Younger, who was either the son of James or his brothers. When you're working from 'back-to- front', i.e., from the past forward in genealogy, it's really tough because each generation requires making a choice regarding which child to follow. When you're working backwards in time it's not quite as difficult. You take the son and determine the father and go back to previous generations. The missing pieces for me lie in the 1700's where Thomas Tyrell was a real stumper, as there were just too many sons named Thomas, James and John for me to figure it all out."

Mike got a smirk on his face and announced, "It's like going in the men's bathroom at Camp Randall where there are too many johns to choose from." I wanted to say smart ass but still held my tongue because of his profession.

"Along with Heron Hall and their property in Normandy, the Tyrells also held land throughout Essex and in several of the surrounding counties including farm holdings, bridges and dikes. From this land, along with vast amount of territories overseen by the family for King Edward II, the Tyrells not only became extremely wealthy but even more influential in the governing of England."

"How rich?" Mike asked.

"Several hundred million to a billion dollars in today's money," I replied.

"Wow!"

I smiled and changed subjects. "During this tumultuous period the Tyrells were assigned tasks other than commissions of Oyer and Terminer, inquisition and pardons. In many instances members of the family were lawyers or executors for those unable to appear or who died. In each of these cases, the Tyrells used their influence to respond to the needs of law and order within the realm. The Tyrell family was not only involved in defending the order but England's security at home and abroad. The king often called upon them when the realm was threatened by foreign powers. In these cases, the king often issued 'commissions of array', requiring the Tyrells to raise troops and come to his aide in times of war or against his real or perceived enemies."

"This occurred several times including, when John Tyrell was called upon to prepare for the arrival of the Spanish Armada, being sent by the kings of Spain and Aragon. Another instance occurred when the king called upon Sir John to prepare troops and accompany them to France."

"The life and career of Sir John Tyrell is a story in itself because of all he achieved. John came from the well-established Tyrell's of Essex family and his uncle was Sir Thomas Tyrell, who served as steward of the estates of King Edward III's daughter, Isabel. Sir John was named Knight of the Shire five times between 1365 and 1373. During this time, many Essex properties were acquired including Heron, Downham, Beeches in Rawreth, Hockley, Ramsden Crays and Wadden Hall in Kent, along with the Tyrell manor of Avon in Hampshire and other holdings in the New Forest."

"Sir John's first marriage to Alice Coggeshall brought him the estate at Broomfield which Alice held for life, quite likely as dower from a previous husband. Sir John witnessed the electoral indentures of 1411 which recorded his own return in the company of his father- in-law, Sir William Coggeshall. On John's father-in-law's death in 1426, the Tyrell children inherited part of the substantial Coggeshall family's wealth, as well. Upon Alice's death, Sir John married Katherine Burgate, the widow of Robert Stonham of Stonham Aspal, Suffolk and John Spencer of Banham, Norfolk, and daughter and co-heiress of Sir William Burgate of Suffolk and Eleanor Visdelou, daughter of Sir Thomas Visdelou."

"In other words, Sir John was rolling in it?" Mike interjected. "You got that right. In fact, when assessments of income from land were made in 1412 for the purposes of taxation John Tyrell was recorded in possession only of Broomfield and Heron, which were valued at £20 a year which is about $250,000 today."

"As John's career progressed along with his second marriage, so did his land holdings and they soon included property not only in Essex and Hampshire but also in Suffolk, Cambridgeshire, Hertfordshire and Norfolk. In the last-named shire, Sir John occupied manors in Banham, as well as other properties which, along with Stonham, Aspall and Burgate in Suffolk, he acquired through his marriage to Katherine."

"In April 1413, shortly before Henry's first Parliament assembled and King Henry IV passed away and was replaced by King Henry V. Lewis John provided financial securities for John Tyrell on his appointment as Master Worker of the Mints. John Tyrell subsequently assisted Lewis John in his acquisition of estates in Essex and was party with him to conveyances of property in the city of London on behalf of other vintners, most notably John's friend, Thomas Walsingham."

"All three - Lewis John, Thomas Walsingham and John Tyrell, sat in Parliament. Although the first two were members of a group closely attached to the Beauforts, John Tyrell established different connections and made the acquaintance of Sir Thomas Erpingham KG, the steward of the household of King Henry V."

"To put it all into perspective the principal purpose of the estate was to provide a source of independent income to the Sovereign that consists today regarding a portfolio of lands, properties and assets held in trust for the Sovereign and administered separately from the Crown Estate. The duchy consists of 45,550 acres of land including rural estates and farmland, urban developments, historic buildings and some commercial properties across England and Wales, particularly in Cheshire, Staffordshire, Derbyshire, Lincolnshire, Yorkshire, Lancashire and the Savoy Estate in London, which have a total value of over a billion dollars today."

"In 1414 John was party to the foundation of a chantry at Wivenhoe for members of the family of Erpingham's wife and caught the attention of the King's cousin, Anne, Countess of Stafford, who was married to Sir William Bourgchier, for whom John acted as trustee of the castle and lordship of Oakham in Rutland."

"Sir John remained in the countess service for several years and in 1415 added management of her property at West Thurrock, serving as steward of her manor of Great Waltham and was promoted to chief steward of all the estates of her de Bohun inheritance."

"During this time Sir John became the Sheriff of Exeter and Hertford and was present at The Battle of Agincourt in 1415, which was one of England's most celebrated victories and most important English triumphs in the Hundred Years' War. While VERY busy, Sir John and wife, Mary, had a son named Thomas Tyrell of Heron I'll be outlining a little later."

"Besides establishing a reputation for reliable service to local landowners, Sir John was employed by men who played important roles in government and were very close to the King. He shied away from the political battles as much as possible. However, in February 1422 Sir John once again stood surety for Tiptoft at the Exchequer and in May did likewise for William Yerde, Attorney-General to John Holand, Earl of Huntingdon."

"In Parliament, Sir John was elected Protector, following the death of Henry V and Henry's replacement by Henry VI on September 01, 1422. Beyond Parliament Sir John was appointed sheriff for the second time in 1423 and was responsible for elections in Essex and Hertfordshire and their results for the county, while sharing the joy of victory of his friends, Richard Baynard and Robert Darcy."

"In November, 1423 Sir John provided security for Lord Cromwell, a member of the King's Council. This association, along with his links to Sir's Gloucester and Tiptoft, proved to be useful that year when he married Katherine, the widow of Sir John Spencer, who had been the Keeper of the Wardrobe for Henry V. Sir John Tyrell successfully sought repayment of huge debts amounting to £2,700 owed by the late King's executors while serving as Mrs. John Spencer's executrix."

"In January, 1424 instructions were sent by the Council to the administrators of Henry V's will to award the Tyrells preferential treatment. On the other side of the coin, Sir John's election from Hertfordshire to Parliament of 1427 was determined to be irregular because it took place while he was still sheriff and running for one office, while holding another, which was prohibited. In response Parliament did what all politicians seem to do and skirted the rules by electing Sir John as Speaker. During the recess in December, Sir John obtained the prestigious and lucrative office of Chief Steward of the Duchy of Lancaster, North of the Trent, which was the post he held until his death."

"Over the years, Sir John assumed an important place in the management of the affairs of Richard Plantagenet, Duke of York, the great-grandson of King Edward III, and great-great-great-great grandson of King Edward I. Sir John rose from the rank of steward of Richard's inheritance at Clare and Thaxted to Receiver-General of all Richard's estates. It's presumed that, at the Duke of York's request in Parliament of 1433, John was one of the five men appointed to act as overseers of the administration of the effects of the late Edmund Mortimer, 5th Earl of March, who was a potential claimant to the throne of England and great- great-grandson of King Edward III and presumptive heir to King Richard II."

"Much of John Tyrell's wealth was accumulated from fees and annuities granted him by the magnates who engaged him as steward of their estates or in some other capacity. It seems likely that he received some training in law which soon made him an expert in estate management. By the time of his first return to Parliament he'd formed important local connections and begun what was to be a lifelong friendship with Richard Baynard and close association with Baynard's brother-in-law, the former Speaker, John Doreward. This was further strengthened when Doreward's son married John's sister-in-law, Blanche Coggeshall."

"In 1436 a graduated income tax was imposed on lands, rents and royal annuities where, after a lifetime of service to members of the nobility and the Crown, Sir John emerged as the wealthiest non- baronial proprietor in Essex, with an annual income of at least £396, or well over a million dollars per year in today's money. Sir John already had bequeathed an estate worth £40 a year to his son, Thomas, and leased Downham and other premises to his younger brother, Edward, whose own holdings were assessed at £135."

"Elected to his 13th Parliament early in 1437 Sir John was chosen Speaker for the third time. Sadly, on March 19th John was replaced by William Burley after being stricken by various infirmities and died on April 2nd of that year. Sir John was buried next to Mary, his second wife, in the Church of the Austin Friars in London."

I looked at Mike and stopped the expose and noted. "As you can see, Mike, Sir John accomplished a lot, made a ton of money and had friends in high places, the consequence of which were both good and bad that I'd like to share with you, if you don't mind."

Chapter 51 – Inheritance

We made it to Flagstaff as Mike pulled out the Trip Tik and read, "'Flagstaff, Arizona, is surrounded by mountains, desert and ponderosa pine forests. It's a gateway to the San Francisco Peaks and home to Humphreys Peak, Arizona's tallest mountain. Nearby, Wupatki National Monument has Native American pueblo sites and Walnut Canyon National Monument which is dotted with their cliff dwellings.'"

We fed Ethyl and, after Santa Fe, thought we'd seen enough mountain desert and elected not to spend much time in what appeared to be a wonderful high elevation town. It was "D" day. Not like World War II but a decision…did we continue on Route 66 to LA, head south to Phoenix or north to the Grand Canyon? After listening to Glenn Campbell, the decision became quite easy and so we said goodbye to Route 66 and headed south towards the Valley of the Sun.

We stopped at a rest area to stretch and pee. When we got back in Ethyl I handed Mike the binder with a drawing of the Tyrell house in Heron and began. "The key to both financial success and survival during these times was simply the consequence of the relationship between the Tyrell's and the king, regardless of who held the scepter at that moment.

"Even with the tumultuous events within the crown, the relative position of the Tyrells of Heron remained intact. In fact, the Tyrell family served numerous kings in a variety of ways throughout the history of England and virtually non-stop from 1377-1485 that included Kings Richard II, Henry

IV, Henry V, Henry VI, Edward IV, Henry VI, Edward IV, Edward V and Richard II."

"Throughout history the Tyrells, like almost all of people of feudal England, were religious. As part of their role in governing England, the family was responsible for the maintenance and upkeep of several religious locations and were members of the parish of East Horndon located in the county of Essex. The local church they attended was the All Saints Church located in Heron that still has brass rubbings of the faces of both Thomas and his first wife, Alice, on display."

"Besides *All Saints Church*, the family also maintained a family chapel known as *Tyrell Chapel* located near Brentwood, approximately twenty-two miles from London. Here, mounted high within the chapel is the helmet of Thomas Tyrell, alongside a bronze crest of the Tyrell family. Another church the Tyrells were associated was the *Church of Stowmarket* near Gipping in Sulfolk, where the remains of many of the Tyrells are interred, including those of Margret Heron Tyrell."

"The Tyrell's primary service came in the form of law and order and its maintenance within the realm. The law and order commissions fell into three main categories called Oyer and Terminer- hear and judge of all pardons and legal inquisitions that often dealt with responding to trespassers. These commissions required members of the Tyrell family to respond to a situation that threatened the order of the realm of which five such commissions were issued by King Edward III and six by Henry VI."

"As an example, in the first commission of Oyer and Terminer, Thomas Tyrell was commissioned by King Edward III to address a matter in which a number of men had trespassed on property that belonged to King Edward's daughter, Isabell. The second such commission called for Thomas to respond to the aide of Elizabeth Durant, a widow who had been assaulted and robbed. A later commission was issued to William Tyrell concerning all treasons, felonies and insurrections. As you can see, they functioned literally as judges and juries on behalf of the king."

"Another way the Tyrells were involved was through what were called 'Commissions of Inquisition' that required inquiries into events by interviewing those involved in what the King considered to be some sort of transgression. In so doing, they actually functioned as prosecutorial representatives of the king. One such commission required John Tyrell and others to enquire into complaints made by several men that undue favor was shown toward Scotland in a legal case involving the mistreatment of a Scottish prisoner."

"Other commissions required them to investigate complaints made by other nobles and landowners concerning damage to property and other trespasses. On other occasions members of the Tyrell family were required to determine who caused damage and to what extent to different properties in the King's care."

"In 1377 King Edward III died and was replaced by his grandson, King Richard II, who continued the royal relationship and reliance on the Tyrells. They remained involved in law through pardons issued to members of the area for all sorts of reasons including trespassing and failure to appear when summoned. In some cases, pardons were given for buying or selling land without permission. On the family side, a pardon was issued to Katherine Tyrell after her husband, Hugh, died and she was awarded protection by King Richard II."

"In 1381 the Peasant's Revolt broke out across much of Southern England and the mob killed the Archbishop of Canterbury and threatened London with looting. The revolt came to an abrupt halt when the rebel leader, Wat Tyler, was killed following an unsuccessful meeting with King Richard II at Smithfield."

"During King Richard II's reign the roles and responsibilities of the Tyrells of Heron remained constant as did their lives and profound wealth. Associating with the king and the royal family that included John Gaunt, Duke of Lancaster also an English royal prince, military leader, statesman (who was the third son of King Edward III and father of King Henry IV had become quite lucrative."

"Upon the death of John Gaunt in 1399 King Richard II disinherited Gaunt's son, Henry Bolingbroke, who'd been previously exiled. In response, Henry invaded England in June of that year with a small force that quickly grew in numbers. Meeting little resistance Henry Bolingbroke deposed King Richard II and was crowned King Henry IV on September 30th, becoming the first king of what was called the House of Lancaster. Henry IV's cousins disagreed and became his rivals in a group that became known as the House of York. That year Owain Glyndwr was proclaimed Prince of Wales, sparking a decade's long uprising against the rule of Henry IV."

"In 1413 Henry IV passed away and was replaced by his son King Henry V who ruled until 1422 and died at the Battle of Tewkesbury. At this time Henry V's wife, Mary, claimed the throne for her infant son, Henry VI."

"In 1431 Henry VI was crowned in Paris which wasn't well received due to the growing French distaste for English rule and the rise of Joan of Arc. When it came to domination, the reign of Henry VI and his wife, Margaret of Anjou was unstable at best and in 1450 the Battle of Blackheath led by Jack Cade, took place on the outskirts of London. While quickly suppressed, the rebellion exposed the weaknesses of Henry VI's administration and initiated a deeper crisis in the English government."

"Under Henry VI, attendance at Parliament became more valuable as did the structure to determine inheritance of authority, where descendants began to be called 'Peers' and holders of older peerages began receiving greater honor than those of the same rank that had just been created."

"If a man held a peerage, his son would succeed to it. If he had no children, his brother would succeed. If he had a single daughter, his son-in-law would inherit the family lands and usually the same peerage. More complex cases were decided depending on circumstances. Customs changed with time. Earls were the first to be hereditary and three different rules can be traced for the case of one earl who left no sons and several married daughters. In the Thirteenth Century the husband of the eldest daughter inherited the earldom automatically. In the Fifteenth Century the same earldom would revert to the Crown, who might regrant it, which meant offering it to the eldest son-in-law. In the Seventeenth Century the estate wouldn't be inherited by anybody unless all but one of the daughters died and left no descendants, in which case the remaining daughter or her heir would inherit the estate."

"What a mess!" Mike proclaimed.

I continued. "The most interesting instance of a Tyrell being called to service in the name of law occurred when both Sir Thomas and Sir William Tyrell, along with several others, were instructed to gather the King's lieges of all estates and determine whether there were traitors and rebels within Essex and adjoining counties. Needless to say, those who promised loyalty to the king weren't too happy and revolted in what was called Jack Cade's Rebellion in May of 1450 against King Henry VI, where Thomas and William Tyrell were called upon to put it down."

"Not everything Henry VI did was appreciated and just when he didn't think things could get much worse, they did. In 1453 at the 'Battle of Castillion' the French defeated the English, pushing them completely off the continent, except for an outpost in Calais, that lasted another five years."

"Perceived weakness was always met with perceived strength and Edward IV, who was a descendant of King Edward III, replaced Henry VI and became King Edward IV on March 04, 1461. Henry VI fought back and regained the throne in October, 1470. Six months later King Edward IV regained the throne and, to show his lack of respect for King Henry VI, declared that Henry, 'having lost his wits, two kingdoms and his only son, be placed in the Tower of London.' Henry died six weeks later quite possibly on the orders of King Edward IV. Life wasn't that great for King Edward IV even with the titles of King of England and Lord of Ireland, who ruled twelve more years before dying in 1483."

"On the Tyrell 15th century lineage, Sir Thomas Tyrell of Heron II was Lord of Bryn and Ockendon and husband, first of Christine Darrell and then Elizabeth Mallory, while being father of Beatrice, Jermyn, Anastasia, William Tyrrell of South Ockenham along with Hugh and John Tyrrell, who became a knight at age 35 and died in Thurrock, Essex England in 1476."

" Sir Thomas Tyrrell II (14Th Ggf, Knight Banneret of Thornton & Ockendon) was born in Little Warley, Essex, England in 1452 to Thomas de Tyrell and Lady Anne Emma Marney of Essex. Thomas had four siblings: William, Elizabeth, Humphrey and Robert and was anointed Sir Thomas Tyrrell II (14th GGF, Knight Banneret of Thornton & Ockendon). Thomas married Elizabeth Mallory Bruyn, sometimes called Ann, by whom she had two sons, William and Thomas of Heron."

"Sir Thomas Tyrell of Heron was an esquire of Edward IV's body by 1480 and transferred smoothly into the household of King Richard III. He was confirmed as an Esquire of the Body in July 1483 and, therefore, an officer in charge of dressing the king. In addition Thomas occupied the Office of Master of the Horse at King Richard III's coronation."

"While this probably doesn't seem like a big deal, it actually was. The Master of the Horse in England was the third dignitary of the court and always considered a councilor on all matters connected with the horses and hounds of the sovereign, as well as the stables and coach houses. The appointment was permanent and the Master of the Horse stood 'in waiting' on the sovereign during state occasions and remained in attendance of the sovereign and always rode at the side of the royal carriage."

"Warring was a way in which many nobles, including the Tyrells, grew in both prestige and fortune. Sir John Tyrell II was awarded a grant in 1472 by Henry VI of 100 marks a year for his service, which would be equal to around a million dollars today. The funds were granted for his participation in the French Wars and for being named Treasurer of the Household. Aside from law and war, the Tyrell families were also called upon to serve the wellbeing of the realm. One such way was to maintain the infrastructure. In order to do this the Tyrells received several other commissions and requisitioned supplies for the building of palisades to protect towns from attack."

"The area of governing the realm also required the Tyrell family to maintain economic order where commissions were granted by the king to hold markets, purchase goods and manage other areas of England's economy. In one instance, King Edward III required Sir Thomas to seek out those who were withholding grains from market and arrest them. Another commission required Sir Thomas to purchase wheat and malt in Essex. In extreme cases the Tyrells were required to protect and escort goods during times of war. There were also cases when the Tyrells were required to make sure that certain goods arrived when the king granted a special license to allow them to enter the country without duties and customs."

Chapter 52: Families of the Realm

"Throughout the middle ages groups of families were designated by their social rank or 'realms.' The best-known system was the French Ancien Régime (Old Regime), which consisted of a three-estate system made up of clergy which was considered the First Estate, nobles which represented the Second Estate, peasants and bourgeoisie who were grouped in the Third Estate. In England a two- estate system evolved that combined nobility and clergy into one lordly estate with 'commons' as the second estate."

"The Tyrells were considered Families of the Realm and, therefore, ranked with other nobles and the clergy and fundamentally one step below royalty. In this position they were often responsible for the welfare of those in their stead including maintaining hospitals, caring for the poor, maintaining the spiritual needs of the people and taking care of both the widowed and orphaned when a lord died and left no heirs of age. The first instance of this for the Tyrells dealt with a commission from King Edward III for Sir Thomas and others to visit the King's Hospital of Neuton in Holdernesse, which the King's daughter, Isabell, had recently been bestowed ownership. Their job was to check the condition of the hospital because there had been reports of negligence."

"The king also relied upon the Tyrells for the spiritual needs of the people. For this the king asked Sir John Tyrell II to help develop a chantry, which was a special area reserved for the performance of *'chantry duties'* which today, we call funerals. John did so at the Chapel of St. John and provided funds for the income and maintenance of the chaplains. Sir Edward Tyrell and the Darcys, who were longtime friends, employed a chaplain for the chapel of St. Mary the Virgin in Danbury, Essex, while Sir Thomas Tyrell provided patronage for the parish of East Thorndon that permitted the family to celebrate certain divine services there."

"One of the major ways in which the Tyrells were involved in the maintenance of the realm was through record keeping and land transactions. These were often in the form of 'inspeximus', which was confirmation and reaffirmation of one or several royal grants made in the past, which were official copies issued to people by order of the king. Other dealings with land dealt with grants of property to people."

"In many of these instances the Tyrells found themselves as either the grantees or grantors of property. Often, however, the records reflect the changing of property ownership from one hand to the other that needed to be approved by the king. Occasionally the Tyrells bore witness to documents requested in inspeximus and conformation. Other dealings the Tyrells had with record keeping were commissions of inquiry to determine who owned or occupied land, where they helped settle disputes."

"The king's finances were often left in the hands of the Families of the Realm and it was to them the king turned when he needed financing for public works and, most importantly, war. The Tyrells found themselves involved in this process through the collection of debts and taxes and determining loans. Sir William Tyrell was particularly involved in the collection of debts, as can be seen in the patent rolls where people were ordered to make a payment to Sir William."

"Sir John Tyrell was involved in the many of the decisions to make loans to the king and collection of taxes. After the Magna Carta it became increasingly difficult for the king to finance his wars without the permission of his people. By ordering the Families of the Realm to discuss the matter, the king was able to gauge support for and encourage his men to support the defense of the realm."

"On April 9, 1483 King Edward IV was technically replaced by twelve-year-old King Edward V who was de jure of England and Lord of Ireland until June 26th of that year. Edward V was never crowned and his brief reign was dominated by the influence of his uncle and Lord Protector, the Duke of Gloucester, who deposed him to reign as King Richard III confirmed by the act entitled Titulus Regius, which denounced any further claims through his father's heirs. Edward V was placed in the Tower of London, along with his younger brother and both simply disappeared. There's more to the story, and I'll get to that when I talk about the Tyrells of that time."

"Instead, King Richard III replaced King Edward IV but things weren't that great for Richard, either. After his coronation, he ruled for just two years and two months until he was killed in 1485 at the Battle of Bosworth, I mentioned earlier. No one knew where King Richard III was buried until they dug up a parking lot next to a church in Leicester, in the East Midlands of England and found his remains. For centuries he'd be walked upon, stomped upon and driven upon and I guess it was God's way of getting even."

I leaned back in the driver's seat, randomly felt my shirt pocket for my long-gone pipe that hadn't been there in nearly forty years and concluded. "As you can see, the Tyrells were an important and active family in maintaining the governance of the realm. Through the different forms of service, the Tyrells left their imprint on feudal England, which evolved into colonial America, which established a great deal of the jurisprudence regarding real estate and inheritance we use today. While their biggest impact was in the field of law, they also provided substantially for the welfare of the populace by providing the means for spiritual guidance and stewardship of the widows and orphans in their domain."

Mike looked at me and inquired, "How do you remember so much?"

I replied. "Mike, not only did I study this and do my Doctoral Thesis on the role the Tyrells played in European history, I taught classes at the undergraduate, graduate and doctorial levels for forty years. I learned what I have by studying and remembering it and through repetition and also because I experienced a lot of it on my 'trips' to the past."

"Still, it's amazing that you know so much." "Thanks!" I replied, considering it a compliment.

Chapter 53 – Sedona

Mike flipped to the next section of map in the Trip Tik and was engrossed in reading the back. Without looking up he asked, "have you ever been to Sedona?"

"Nope" I replied, still gazing out the front window, watching the bugs meet their demise.

"Sounds pretty neat. Can we take a detour and go there?" "Why not?"

Mike instructed, "Take Highway 89A South" and so I did. We drove a few miles and all of a sudden, we were in a large stand of Ponderosa Pines. A sign by the side of the road read 'Oak Creek Canyon Vista Point' three miles. 89A began winding down until we reached the bridge crossing Oak Creek with its shimmering waters. We'd only gone 28 miles from Flagstaff but it seemed like we were in a different world.

We stopped at the vista point and got out with our mouths open in disbelief. Now I've dreamt that heaven was going to be like Wisconsin but boy oh boy, what we saw had to come in a close second. Now I've been all over the world and this was really something with breathtaking red rock monoliths enveloped in soul- enriching serenity and towering canyon walls seeming to reach all the way to the sky.

Mike looked at me and softly smiled. Neither of us could fully express the beauty and tranquility we shared. We focused our attention on the sign that explained it all. 'Millions of years ago, the area now known as Sedona was covered with sea. Ever so slowly with the gradual withdrawal of the waters combined with the earth's powerful forces of upheaval, this masterpiece of nature was created. Sculpted by wind and erosion, the crimson monuments of vividly colored mesas were formed. Today Sedona is brightly adorned with panoramic beauty so unique it doesn't exist anywhere else in the world.'

We simply gazed at the majesty until the spell was broken and climbed back into Ethyl and headed into town, only to realize we weren't the only one discovering the town and finding a parking place for Ethyl really became a challenge. Round and round and round we go until we finally found a parking lot that charged a dollar to park Ethyl. Mike and I found a restaurant called Sedona Memories and walked in to an almost full house.

"Table for two?" the hostess inquired.

"Sounds good to me." I replied as she escorted us back near the kitchen.

Water was served and menus provided. I opened the menu up and almost gagged. The price of a sandwich was more than a full day's meal back home and I had to remind myself "Will, you're not in Minnie Point, anymore."

The somewhat harried waitress arrived and took our orders asking if we wanted anything more than water to drink. Mike asked for lemonade and that sounded good to me as I replied "make that two" meaning I wanted the same. The harried one thought I wanted two glasses for me and that's what I got. At a dollar each, I almost gave one back. Imagine, a dollar for a glass of lemonade.

We'd come right at the end of the lunch rush and so, as we were eating, the place started clearing out and the pace slowed. The harried one came back and asked if we needed anything else. I looked at her name badge and it said 'Alice'. Sure enough, the first thing in my mind and then out of my mouth was Arlo Guthrie's 'Alice's Restaurant'.

Alice finally broke a smile and noted I was the first person THAT DAY who mentioned it.

I replied how beautiful Sedona was and Alice, who by the way, didn't own the restaurant, replied that after a while you got so used to it you never enjoyed it anymore. Then, as an after-thought she said, "most of us don't have time anyway. It's so expensive to live here that we all work two or three jobs just to make ends meet." I thought for a moment and realized that there's a cost to living in heaven and even there, I guess you'd get so used to it that it wouldn't be special anymore.

With that, Alice was gone as she slapped the bill on the table. Imagine twenty-five dollars for two sandwiches, some potato chips and three glasses of lemonade. Mike offered to pay and placed a twenty and ten on the table as we sauntered out into the masses walking the streets, looking for mementos of Sedona that probably were made in Korea or Taiwan.

Chapter 54 – Wars of the Roses

It's 150 miles from Sedona to Phoenix and so, as I started up Ethyl, I looked at Mike and inquired, "Do you want more history?"

"Sure, why not?" Mike said with a smile.

I smiled at Mike's enthusiasm and began. "I need to divert from the family for a few minutes and talk about Kings Henry IV, V, VI and VII, along with Edward the IV and V, with Richard III thrown in."

"OK," Mike replied.

I continued. "You need to remember there was no 'common ground' or singular loyalty amongst any of the lords of England. They were simply in it for themselves, all the way up to who was running the country. One group who was loyal to one descendant would pit themselves against another group loyal to another descendant. Historically, the most famous 'argument' was called the Wars of the Roses which pitted the House of Lancaster versus the House of York and was based completely on the challenge of patrilineal versus matrilineal inheritance."

"One quick question," Mike inquired. "How did the Wars of the Roses get its name?"

I smiled, realizing the question asked had been part of my lectures on English history for four decades and answered. "The wars were actually named several years after their end based on the supposed badges of the contending parties where the white rose represented those attuned to the House of York and red to those of the House of Lancaster."

"Weren't they a little wilted by then?" My smart-ass minister inquired.

I simply shook my head and retorted that several of my students had asked the same question and they all flunked, too. Instead, I stated. "I need to backtrack a little bit in terms of who's who and what's what, as the period from 1422 to 1471 is critical to both the history of Europe and the Tyrrell family."

Mike shrugged his shoulders realizing I was going to do it anyway, so why not go along for the ride. "The House of Plantagenet held the English throne from 1154 to 1485 and included King Henry II, Richard the Lionhearted, King John, King Henry III, King Edward I, King Edward II, King Edward III and King Richard II."

"King Henry IV was the grandson of King Edward III and Queen Philippa, who seized the English throne from King Richard II in 1399. Henry IV was the first king in the House of Lancaster and reigned without question from 1399-1413. He married twice, first to Mary Bohun, who gave birth to a son who became King Henry V and, second, to Joanna of Navarre."

"When King Henry IV died in 1413 King Henry V attempted to marry King Richard II's widow Isabella. However, that didn't work out and he ended up marrying her sister, Catherine of France, who was heir to the throne of France. King Henry V sired a son named Henry VI, who thereby inherited the thrones of both England and France in 1422 when his father and grandfather died within months of each other. The problem was King Henry VI was only a year old when it happened."

"King Henry VI's early youth was dominated by two uncles - Cardinal Beaufort and Cardinal Humphrey, Duke of Gloucester. Both Cardinals opposed each other on various social, political and financial matters, while attempting to sway young Henry in their favor. Henry's power base was maintained due to the strength of his uncle, Sir John of Lancaster, the 1st Duke of Bedford, third son of King Henry IV and brother to King Henry V, who was regarded as a prince, general and statesman who commanded England's armies in France during a critical phase of the Hundred Years' War and acted as regent of France for his nephew Henry VI."

"When Sir John died in 1435, the combined Duchy of Burgundy, located in Northeastern France, broke their alliance with England, which led to the collapse of English rule in that area. At the same time, the dual monarchy proved too difficult for both King Henry VI and England to maintain. This was particularly due to the successes of the Dauphin of France and Joan of Arc and their battles with Burgundy."

"OK, you've got me stumped, what's a Dauphin?" Mike inquired.

"The term Dauphin of France was originally Dauphin of Viennois, and was the title given to the heir apparent to the throne of France from 1350 to 1791 and then again from 1824 to 1830. During King Henry VI's realm, France's Charles VII was dauphin, who defeated the opposing forces in Burgundy and then the English as he unified France. The net result was the weakening of England's influence in France to the point that Normandy which had been under England's rule since William the Conqueror, was all that was remaining of English control after 400 years of dominance."

"Henry's personality was not nearly as dynamic as those who preceded him. However, his lack of personality was replaced by his cultural patronage and genuine interest in education. While debasing the strength of England, King Henry VI left a legacy of educational institutions, having founded Eton College, King's College, Cambridge, All Souls College and Oxford. His focus completely outweighed his limited interest in administration to the point that England's failures in France resulted in several demonstrations. Included was the Cade Rebellion of 1450, protesting King Henry VI's ineffectiveness as a leader, along with over-taxation of the working classes, the crown's failed attempts to secure French territories as well as corrupt bureaucrats and church officials who combined to encourage factionalism throughout all levels of English society."

"That's all?" Mike lamented in a sarcastic way.

I continued on. "On the York side, Richard Plantagenet married Cecily Neville and, as the Third Duke of York, was the most prominent duke in England. Being of royal descent, Richard was a leading English magnate who inherited vast estates and served in various offices of state in Ireland, France and England, whose finances were managed by Sir John Tyrell. Richard ultimately governed as Lord Protector during the rule of King Henry VI and became the most powerful nobleman of his day."

"For several years Richard had been increasingly opposed by King Henry VI's court. After open warfare broke out between the two factions and King Henry became his prisoner, Richard laid claim to the throne but lacked sufficient support. Instead, an agreement, known as the 'Act of the Accord,' was made such that Richard would become King Henry VI's heir, thereby displacing the succession of King Henry and Margaret's seven-year-old son, Edward, Prince of Wales."

"In 1460 the Yorkists claimed Richard's descent which was through the senior female line from Edward III, to be superior to that of Henry VI's Lancastrian title. The Lancastrian lineage was through the junior male line and therefore, it was their belief that the Duke of York should have been designated heir to the throne when King Henry V died." "The Act of Accord, resulted in the Battle of Wakefield in December, 1460, led by nobles loyal to King Henry VI and his Queen Margaret of Anjou against Richard of York's army, during which Richard of York was killed

With Richard's death, one would have thought it would mean the end of the challenges and, perhaps, the fighting. However, this setback was simply challenged by Richard's son Edward, who decisively defeated the Lancastrians in February, 1461 in the Battle of Towton, where 120,000 men fought and 28,000 died and Edward assumed the title King Edward IV."

"In other words, four times more than died in the Battle of Gettysburg?" Mike asked.

"Yes," I replied and continued. "London opened its gates to King Edward IV's forces and King Henry VI and Queen Margaret fled to Scotland, only to be captured and imprisoned in the Tower of London in 1465. Henry regained the throne in 1470 through an alliance between the Earl of Warwick and Queen Margaret. However, his brief period of freedom ended in the spring of 1471 when King Edward IV returned from the Low Countries and defeated the Earl of Warwick at the Battle of Barnet. Edward then defeated the troops accompanying Queen Margaret and her son, Edward, Prince of Wales, at the Battle of Tewkesbury, in which the Prince of Wales was killed and King Henry VI was subsequently put to death in the Tower of London."

I stopped for a moment to catch my breath, sip my soda and let all that I'd reported settle in while adding. "This entire escapade represents a very critical period in the lives and times of the Tyrell family. While all this conflict between the House of the Lancaster and the House of the York might seem like just one more episode for the kings of England, what personally comes into play is the fact that the Tyrell family had deep financial associations and commitments to both sides, to the point they would both win and lose regardless of who won the Wars of the Roses."

Chapter 55 - Choosing Sides

We were getting into Phoenix traffic which consisted mainly of license plates from California, Minnesota, Wisconsin and Illinois. After all my blabbing my emotions were drained. Even though the story was about to get really interesting I thought we should call it a day in the history department. A slight smile of gratitude pursed my lips as I thought of the man who had become my friend who was kind enough, patient enough and decent enough to let an old man share his life, passion and love of the past one more time.

I had no idea where we were going as Mike was playing navigator and directed me to 2400 E Missouri Ave. In front of us was the Arizona Biltmore Hotel and Mike told me to pull in. I shivered to think what a night was going to cost. I looked at Mike and I think he perceived my chagrin.

"Did I ever tell you what my son does for a living?" Mike inquired.

"No."

"He's the Vice President of Government Relations for Hilton Hotels. Kevin lives in Virginia and works with the government and politicians to acquire and keep their business and is on the fast track to move to their corporate offices in California."

"OK." I replied, still not getting the connection.

"Will, he's a big cheese. This means he gets some benefits including allowing me to stay at any Hilton property twice a year for free and this is one of them. I wanted this to be a surprise."

"We're going to stay here for free? Holy chamomile! The Arizona Biltmore?"

I looked at the gorgeous building as Mike offered. "This is my favorite hotel in the world. It opened in 1929 and was tailored after your cousin Frank's prairie style of architecture. It's been a private retreat for some of the most influential powerhouses of the past seventy years and tonight, my friend, that includes you."

I didn't know where to park Ethyl when the valet came out and I inquired. Mike told him who he was and the valent almost kissed Mike's feet and assured us that Ethyl would be parked in the back lot for our duration.

Mike queried, "Behind Terrace Court, East and Garden Wings or over by the cottages?"

"Behind the cottages, if that's OK." The young man offered. "Sounds good," as Mike slipped him a ten-dollar bill.

As we walked into the lobby Mike filled me in on the stained- glass design as he noted. "The property was once owned by the Wrigleys from Chicago, who sold it to the Talley's who intended to remodel the property. Just after the sale, a devastating six-alarm fire ripped through the resort during renovations and it looked like the end was in sight. Instead, the Talley's promised to reopen for the holiday season and hired all the students from Taliesin West and a construction crew who worked 24 hours a day for 81 straight days to save the season. In celebration of the 1973 grand reopening, Olgivanna Lloyd Wright, who was Frank's third wife, donated "Saguaro Forms and Cactus Flowers" as a stained-glass gift.

Mike was turning into the historian and I was loving it as he added. "Frank originally created 'Saguaro Forms and Cactus Flowers' as a pencil drawing for a series of covers for Liberty Magazine. The magazine said they were too radical and never published them. Olgivanna found the drawings and commissioned an artist from Mesa to put them into stained glass."

"It's gorgeous!" I exclaimed.

Mike checked us in and we were escorted to the Citrus Club Cottage Suite. As we were being escorted, the host, as she was called, noted, "Each cottage and suite at the Arizona Biltmore is individually designed to reflect our warm and authentic desert spirit. The cottages are the picture of old-world glamour with a contemporary twist, with beautiful restored interiors, curated art touches, cozy king or queen beds and a private patio for extra space to relax after a day exploring the surrounding Sonoran Desert."

She opened the door and I whispered, "Holy shit." What lay before me was like a dream as she continued. "Most guests enjoy the view and, with our current spring weather, feel free to open the floor- to-ceiling windows." Pointing to the bookshelves, she added, "There's a complete collection of vintage board games and also a mini-library at your disposal."

As she waved her hand towards the living room she noted, "Please admire the hand-curated art reminiscent of the surrounding desert and the artisanal tea set, imported from France. For exercise and activity, we have the golf course, seven different pools and horseback riding, if you so desire. Your personal firepit will be ignited each night, if you so desire, and your favorite beverages have been stocked in your bar. If you need anything else, we're on call 24 hours per day."

I looked at Mike and he simply smiled. "Twice a year! Kevin goes all out and this is his way of saying 'Thank you' to you."

For the next seven days, we got the road film off our bodies and our minds and never once thought of home or Heaven's Waiting Room or even Ethyl for that matter. We did everything except golf. Seven days wouldn't have been long enough for me to play 18 holes, and they don't make four-digit golf counters.

Finally, and reluctantly, it was time to go. Mike called the front desk and a young man with a golf cart took us directly to Ethyl.

"Don't we need to check out?" I asked. "Already did," Mike replied.

"Can I pay my share?" "OK."

"How much do I owe you?"

"Half of nothing is still nothing."

"You mean it was all free?"

"Will, he's the Executive Vice President of the corporation. He's works a ton of hours each week and this is one of his perks. Trust me, he earns it and knows I love it."

"Can I send him a thank you note?"

"He gets one every time I mention that we're going somewhere in Ethyl and you won't even let me chip in for gas."

Ethyl seemed awfully plain after the Biltmore as we reluctantly made it out of Phoenix and began backtracking to Flagstaff and the Grand Canyon on I-17. It seemed strange to be driving on the Interstate after Route 66. We weren't in a hurry but everyone one else was. Even in the right lane, people were upset when I was only driving five miles over the speed limit. I'd taken a week off from the history lesson and asked

Mike if he wanted to hear more about the Terrills, to which he sort of frowned at me and said "Of course."

"Ok, but I need to backtrack a little bit so that everything makes sense."

"Go for it!"

"The Tyrell family was caught between a rock and a hard place. The Wars of the Roses meant they needed to choose sides. Did they choose Henry VI, who'd treated them well, or King Edward IV, who had the power and stamina to win?

"As I explained earlier, the Tyrell family was quite well off. Beyond the legal stuff, Sir Walter Tyrell was also knighted for his efforts during the Battle of Ardes that took place in June 1351 between French and English forces during the Hundred Years War so they had money and prestige"

"Sir Walter and Lady Jane had two sons including John Tyrell of Heron who was born in 1382 and Edward Tyrell. As I summarized, Sir John Tyrell had been involved politically on both sides where picking sides in a pissing match only meant the Tyrell family was about to get their pants wet."

"Sir John and Alice Coggeshall had several children including Thomas Tyrell of Heron who was born in 1410. Thomas became Sir Thomas and married Anne Marney in 1431 and inherited Sir John's business and position, being named a Knight of the Body in 1452. With the outbreak of the war, Sir Thomas' sympathies remained with King Henry VI and the Lancastrians. In 1460, Sir Thomas was among the supporters who held the Tower of London when the Yorkists entered the city and, fortunately, appeared to suffer no recriminations after the Yorkist victory.

With his wife being the daughter of Sir William Marney of Essex, Sir Thomas had four sons of which the eldest was William Tyrell, who died before Sir Thomas did and was buried with Sir Thomas' first wife, Alianore Darcy at the Church of the Austin Friars in London, alongside Sir John and his stepmother. Sir Thomas's second male heir was Sir Thomas Tyrell of Heron II, who was born in 1430, and really got caught in the cross-hairs of the Wars of the Roses."

"Sir Thomas had a son named James Tyrell who was born in Gipping Suffolk England in 1455 and married Anne Arundel in 1469 who bore four children including James Tyrrell. James fought on the Yorkist side at the Battle of

Tewkesbury in May 1471 and was knighted by King Edward IV."

"Sometime during the next decade Sir James Tyrrell became associated with Richard of Gloucester and was made a Knight Banneret in 1465 for his service in Richard's wars in Scotland, after which Richard became King Richard III. Upon King Richard's coronation, Sir James was named Master of the Royal Henchmen and appointed High Sheriff of Cornwall in 1484. Sir James Tyrell was also in France in 1485 but played no part in the Battle of Botsworth Field, which signaled the end of the Yorkists and the start of the Tudor Dynasty."

"The Tyrrell genealogical trail has a whole lot of crossroads and it's been tough trying to figure out who's who. The one thing I do know is that they were all related and were either brothers or cousins. As an example, Lord William Tyrell, Lord of South Ockenden was born in 1468 and married Elizabeth Bodley in 1495. They had four children including Sir Humphrey Tyrell Lord of Great Thornton Hall Manor who was born in 1500, Thomas, John and William Tyrell of South Ockendon, Essex who was born in 1522."

"Sir Thomas Tyrell of Heron II had several siblings including Robert Tyrell; Humphrey Tyrell, Esq., of Heron; Ambrose Tyrell; Edward Tyrell; Anne Darcy; William Tyrrell and Elizabeth Isabel Darcy. Most of the family laid low and didn't get involved in the turmoil. However, Sir Thomas II's brother, William Tyrell, was beheaded at Tower Hill, along with Sir Thomas Tuddenham, John Montgomery, John de Vere the 12th Earl of Oxford and John de Vere's eldest son Aubrey, after the discovery of an alleged plot to murder King Edward IV in 1462."

"For seven years, there was relative peace and then the war resumed in 1469 when George and Richard Neville, the 16th Earl of Warwick - who was called Warwick the Kingmaker or Warwick for short - temporarily captured King Edward IV, seized control of the government and succeeded in reinstating King Henry VI as King of England in 1470."

"Through marriage and inheritance, Warwick emerged in the 1450s at the center of English politics. Originally, he supported King Henry VI, however, a territorial dispute with Edmund Beaufort, Duke of Somerset, led him to collaborate with Richard, Duke of York, in opposing the king. From this conflict he gained the strategically valuable post of Captain of Calais, a position that benefited him greatly in the years to come."

With royal approval and definitely not on his own initiative, Richard, Duke of York, may have helped kill both Prince Edward of Lancaster and King Henry VI. However, due to his dedication to King Edward IV, Richard earned the king's gratitude while marrying Anne Neville, widow of Edward of Lancaster, thereby earning him a share of the Warwick inheritance in both Wales and the north of England, where he was warden for the defense of the western marches toward Scotland."

The political conflict turned into full-scale rebellion. At the Battle of Wakefield, Yorkshire, Richard, Duke of York was slain, as was Warwick's father. However, Richard's son later triumphed with Warwick's assistance and was crowned King Edward IV."

"King Edward IV initially ruled with Warwick's support but the two disagreed about foreign policy and also the king's choice to marry Elizabeth Woodville. After a failed plot to crown Edward's brother, George, Duke of Clarence, Warwick helped restore Henry VI to the throne.

"So that's how Henry VI regained power," Mike concluded, making me realize he was actually paying attention.

I added. "However, the triumph was short-lived and on April 14, 1471 Warwick was killed by King Edward IV at the Battle of Barnet."

"Elizabeth Woodville's later conduct confirms that she took a strong role in politics. Following Edward IV's death, with the aid of members of her own family, she attempted a coup to enable herself to act as regent for her young son. But in 15th-century England, regency powers were always assigned to the senior living prince of the blood royal and not to the mother. Thus, when Edward IV died, according to English custom, power belonged in the hands of his surviving brother, Richard, Duke of Gloucester, who would, of course, go on to become King Richard III."

"It's amazing the complexity of power back then."

"That complexity remains today. However, back to the family! Sir Thomas Tyrell was never 'attainted', which was a good thing. In England a Criminal Law Attainder was the metaphorical "stain" or 'corruption of blood' which arose from being condemned for a serious capital crime such as a felony or treason. In extreme cases the penalty not only resulted in losing one's head but property and hereditary titles as well, along with the right to pass those rights on to one's heirs. The decision was up to the king who could determine any degree of punishment he so desired."

"Sir Thomas Tyrell Sr. co-operated with the new regime, at least to the extent of serving on the commission of the peace, from 1463 until his death from natural causes in 1476. However, in 1478, Richard Neville's compliance in charges of treason against Sir Thomas' brother, George Tyrell, resulted in George's execution from which Neville was the principal beneficiary. Although Richard Neville made himself more dominant than King Edward IV planned, King Edward accepted the position once he realized it would enhance his own power base."

"Overriding the opposition was Edward IV's former chamberlain, Lord Hastings who enlisted Richard Wydevilles as his ally. Wysdeville was an English landowner, soldier, diplomat, administrator and politician whose son married an aunt of King Henry VI, while he was father-in-law of King Edward IV."

"After a brief illness, on April 9, 1483, King Edward IV unexpectedly died and was succeeded without question by his eldest son, Edward V, who was only twelve years old and became King Edward V, followed in line by Edward V's brother, Richard of Shrewsbury, Duke of York, who was just ten years old at the time."

"Edward's uncle, Richard of Gloucester, followed in succession and was designated Lord Protector of Edward V in the late king's will. Richard of Gloucester swore allegiance to the future king. However, the royal council, dominated by Queen Elizabeth, spelled Widville or Woodville's, family, decided to immediately crown Edward V king, thereby rendering the protectorate of Edward unnecessary, enabling Queen Elizabeth to rule on Edward V's behalf." "Sir Wydeville mistakenly believed that Richard of Gloucester was his friend and had the queen's brother, Earl Rivers, arrange to meet with Richard and the Duke of Buckingham. At the meeting Richard seized the twelve-year-old future king, dismissed his household and placed Rivers and

Edward's half-brother, Lord Richard Grey, in custody. Asserting his loyalty to Edward V, Richard escorted him to London and was re-recognized by the royal council as Lord Protector and therefore head of the government."

"Twelve-year-old, Prince Edward was originally placed in the Tower of London in May, ostensibly to prepare for his formal coronation. On June 13th Uncle Richard had Lord Hastings executed, allegedly for treasonable conspiracy but probably to remove Edward V's most devoted supporter. On June 16th Uncle Richard secured Edward V's ten-year-old brother Richard of Shrewsbury on the pretext of ensuring the boy would attend Edward's coronation which was set for June 22nd and then moved to June 25th."

"June 25th arrived and the coronation was postponed indefinitely. Events took a dramatic turn when Edward IV's marriage was declared bigamous, thereby making Edward's children by Elizabeth illegitimate as young Edward and his brother, Richard, simply vanished."

"While Uncle Richard, who became King Richard III, has been blamed, some historians identify the culprit as Sir James Tyrell, who acted on the king's orders simply because, Sir James Tyrell implicated two accomplices named Miles Forest and John Dighton, who purportedly murdered the boys in the Tower in late summer of 1483."

"The famous English historian, Sir Thomas More did extensive research and stated that 'the princes were smothered with the pillows on their beds by Sir James Tyrell, John Dighton and Miles Forest. Sir James is reported to have confessed to the crime in 1502 when under sentence of death for treason.' Although no bodies were produced at the time, two small human skeletons were found under a set of stone stairs in the North Tower in 1674. However, there is no conclusive evidence that these were the princes as two more bodies were found in 1789 at Saint George's Chapel in Windsor Castle."

"King Richard III was never formally accused of the murders. His successor, Henry VII, simply made general accusations of 'unnatural, mischievous and great perjuries, treasons, homicides, and murders, in shedding of infant's blood, with many other wrongs, odious offenses and abominations against God and man.' Other possible culprits included Henry Stafford, 2nd Duke of Buckingham, Richard

III's right-hand man and even, Henry VII, himself to strengthen his claim to the throne."

Mike interjected, "If your ancestor was involved, who gave the orders to Tyrell and his accomplices?"

I shook my head and replied. "King Richard III is the name most associated with the mystery as he had the greatest motive, that being their right to the throne that was stronger than his. Shakespeare certainly decided that he had given the order for the boys to be killed. However, Henry Tudor, who later became Henry VII, had an even shakier claim to the throne based solely on the right of conquest!"

"With both princes missing, Richard publicly declared his claim to the throne and on June 26, 1483, seized it while being backed by the northern army from its camp at Finsbury Fields. This allowed Richard of Gloucester to become King Richard III with he and his bride, Queen Anne, crowned at Westminster Abbey on July 6, 1483." "The Wars of the Roses had become a vicious encounter between the two houses that extended across England during the latter half of the 1400's that took the lives of aristocracy including George and James Tyrell. Across the English Channel, Henry Tudor, a descendant of the diminished House of Lancaster, realized Richard's difficulties and laid claim to the throne. Henry invaded England in August of 1485 on the southwest coast of Wales. Marching inland Henry gathered support as his army aimed for London. King Richard III assembled his troops and intercepted Henry's army at Bosworth Field."

"The deciding Battle of Bosworth was fought on Monday August 22, 1485. King Richard divided his army, which outnumbered King Henry VI's Tudor's alliance of Lancastrians and disaffected Yorkists into three groups with one group allocated to the Duke of Norfolk and another to the Earl of Northumberland, while King Henry VI kept most of his force together."

"Richard's frontline attacked but struggled even though some of Norfolk's troops fled the field. Northumberland took no action when signaled to assist his king. Henry Tudor assisted King Richard as they gambled everything on a charge across the battlefield to kill Henry and end the fight. Seeing the king's knights separated from his army, Henry's allies intervened and came to Henry's aid, surrounding and killing King Richard III, thereby, marking the end of the House of York, where Richard III represents the last English monarch to die in battle."

"Fellow historians consider the Battle Bosworth Field to mark the end of the Plantagenet dynasty and the historical period known as the Middle Ages, making it one of the defining moments of English history. The Wars of the Roses, literally extinguished the male lines of both dynasties leading to the rise of the Tudors of Penmynydd, who were a noble and aristocratic Welsh family and very influential in Welsh and English politics."

"What happened to James Tyrell?" Mike asked.

I didn't think you'd ask. However, if you get us a couple of cans of pop, I'll fill you in"

Mike made his way back to Ethyl's galley as the brochure called it and returned with two cans of Seven-Up as I added. "As you might remember James Tyrell was born in 1445 and was the eldest son of Sir William Tyrell of Gipping, near Stowmarket in Suffolk, and Margaret Darcy of Maldon. Sir William Tyrell was Sheriff of Norfolk and Suffolk under King Henry VI and most decidedly a Lancastrian. Due to his loyalty, Sir William Tyrell was executed in February, 1462 for treason against King Edward IV."

"So much for public service!" Mike interjected as the empty Seven-Up cans hit our recycle bin.

Chapter 56 - Cornwall

We made it to the Grand Canyon and the obligatory, "Holy shit!" was said as we admired one really big hole in the ground. We stood for over an hour before reciting "Been there, did that," as we watched the colors change with the movement of the sun and knew it was time to head for Vegas.

"Do you want more history?" "Sure, why not?"

I smiled and began. "Sir James Tyrell was 22 when he served as elector for Suffolk in 1467 and was called esquire by 1469. In that same year he married Anne Arundell, heiress of Sir John Arundell of Cornwall, and they sired four children including James."

"Quite possibly in these early years, James Tyrell assumed various minor duties for John de la Pole, Duke of Suffolk, brother-in- law to Edward IV, whose principal seat was less that ten miles away from Gipping. Sir James was knighted by Edward IV on the battlefield at Tewkesbury in May 1471 and shortly thereafter, entered the service of the Duke of Gloucester."

"In 1474 Sir James was one of the challengers at the ordination of King Edward IV's infant son, Richard, as Duke of York. The following year Sir James was with the King's army during the abortive war in France, probably in the retinue of the Duke of Gloucester, as he continued to ascend in power and authority with appointments as a commissioner in Suffolk in 1475, Sheriff of Glamorgan in 1477 and member of Parliament for Cornwall in 1478." " Sir James was made Knight-Banneret by Gloucester during

the Scottish campaign in July, 1482 and in November, James was appointed Vice-Constable, of Gloucester's office of Constable of England along with Sir William Parr and Sir James Harrington. After the summary execution of Lord Hastings and the arrest of the suspected co-conspirators, King Richard III temporarily placed Archbishop Rotherham in Sir James' custody."

"I've shared the tale of Sir James involvement in the disappearance of the young princes but must note he was listed among the knights at the coronation of King Richard III and made Master of the Horse, as well as Master of the King's Henchmen."

"In November, 1483 Sir James evidently played a role in arresting the Duke of Buckingham and transporting him to Salisbury for execution. Three days later he was made commission of array for Wales, given by English sovereigns to officers or gentry in a given territory so that they could *muster and array* residents to ensure they were trained for war or military service. Before year's end he was also appointed Steward of the Duchy of Cornwall for life."

"Tell me about Cornwall," Mike requested.

A pleasant smile crossed my face as its 'home' to so many of us in Mineral Point. I looked at Mike and began. "Throughout history little has been written about Cornwall. At the southwestern tip of today's island of Great Britain, it was sparsely populated with continuous occupation starting around 10,000 years ago. As a source for copper and tin, those who did venture to the almost forgotten land, came for the metal that made its way back to Rome and developing nations in Europe and the Mediterranean."

"When recorded history started in the First Century BC, the spoken language was Common Brittonic that would develop into Southwestern Brittonic and Cornish. Cornwall was part of the territory of the tribe of the Dumnonii that included modern- day Devon and parts of Somerset. After a period of Roman rule Cornwall reverted to rule by independent leaders and continued to have a close relationship with Brittany and Wales as well as southern Ireland, its neighbor across the Celtic Sea."

"In the middle of the Ninth Century, Cornwall fell under the control of Wessex but kept its own culture. In 1337 the title Duke of Cornwall was created by the English monarchy to be held by the king's eldest son and heir."

"Cornwall, along with the neighboring county of Devon, maintained some local control over the production of copper and tin, which was its most important product and with it, it's independence from the follies of England. For some it was simply a distant place where no one wanted to go. For others, including the Tyrell's, there must have been a sense of peace and tranquility, away from the challenges of the political lives of England."

"Anne Tyrell's half-brother, Thomas Arundell, was attainted after Buckingham's rebellion and King Richard

III's Parliament awarded Arundell's property to the Tyrells. In February, 1484 Sir James was granted the stewardship of Buelt in South Wales for life and in September designated one of the Chamberlains of the Exchequer assigned to serve in the treasury."

"Is that where the word check comes from?" Mike asked. "You got it," as I continued. "In January of 1485 Sir James Tyrell assumed command of the garrison at Guisnes Castle, which was one of two English fortresses guarding Calais, France and did so by replacing Lord Mountjoy. In June James was appointed Constable of Tintagel Castle. In spite of the anticipated invasion by Henry Tudor and the fact that Sir James was Commissioner of Array for Wales, King Richard III didn't recall him to England in the spring and summer of that year. Instead, Sir James remained at his post at Guisnes, even as the Yorkist dynasty ended on August 22, 1485 at Bosworth Field."

"Surprisingly for one so worthy of King Richard III's trust, Sir James suffered very little under Henry VII. Sir James wasn't at Bosworth and wasn't attainted by King Henry VII's Parliament. However, he did lose the sheriffdom of Glamorgan and Morgannok, as well as many of his other offices in Wales. King Henry VII seemed content to allow him to continue his command at Guisnes Castle to the point that, in February, 1486 Sir James was restored as Sheriff of Glamorgan and appointed Constable of Cardiff Castle."

"On June 16, 1486 King Henry VII granted Sir James a pardon for unspecified offences and then issued a second pardon on July 16th. One pardon erased all challenges and indiscretions for those officials who had served the previous government and, to this day, it seems odd to have been awarded the second pardon."

"Sir James continued to rise in authority and was officially restored to his post as Lieutenant of Guisnes Castle in December, 1486. That same month, he was sent from Guisnes Castle on behalf of King Henry VII to Maximilian, King of the Romans and also attended the coronation of Elizabeth of York in November, 1487. In 1489 Sir James fought at the Battle of Dixmude and, as Captain of Guisnes, took part in the negotiations leading to the Peace of Etaples in June 1492."

"Unfortunately, Sir James' Yorkist sympathies proved to be his downfall. In 1501 he protected Edmund de la Pole, Earl of Suffolk, who had fled to Guisnes to escape criminal charges and encourage opposition to Henry VII. The news reached King Henry, who demanded Sir James return to England. Evidently, Sir James decided it was safer to stay where he was and a stalemate ensued. King Henry VII sent troops to besiege the castle. Lured out by promise of safe passage, guaranteed by the Privy Seal, Sir James was arrested along with his eldest son, Thomas, and forced to surrender the castle."

"Sir James Tyrell along with Thomas, Christopher Wellesbourne, Sir John Wyndham and 'an unnamed sailor' were charged with treason. Sir James Tyrell and Sir John Wyndham were tried at the Guildhall, convicted and beheaded on May 6, 1502. Sir James Tyrell was either not allowed or declined to make the customary final speech from the scaffold. Thomas Tyrell and Christopher Wellesbourne were imprisoned, while the unnamed sailor was hanged, drawn and quartered. Sir James' body was interred in the Church of the Austin Friars, in London."

Chapter 57 - Vegas

We made it to Vegas with all the lights. While advertised as glamorous, the sad reality was all the people simply walking the strip trying to find the joy and excitement others had bragged about. As we walked north, I saw the barkers offering anything and everything one could imagine and felt embarrassed in suggesting we visit sin city. Mike noted that Las Vegas had the highest per capita population ratio to churches in the United States. I thought that was good until Mike corrected me and noted that the higher the number, the fewer the churches and the fewer the churches, the fewer numbers who attended regularly.

"Too many other important things?" I somewhat sarcastically uttered and was then surprised by Mike's answer.

"There's a lot in life other than being religious and life doesn't need to be centered around organized religion."

"What do you mean?" I asked in earnest.

"Will, religion is a structure and an organization. It has specific messages based on the interpretation of a few, intended for the many. The tough part are the hypocrites."

"Hypocrites?"

"Yup."

"What do you mean?"

"The Bible thumpers who think they're closer to God than others simply because they have a deeper level of belief and feeling."

My thoughts went to those I'd met who felt that way.

Mike added. "There's a thing called 'false piety.' This is when a person wears a religious disguise of devotion and outwardly abides by rules while being inwardly unkind, uncharitable, and exclusive. Those exhibiting false piety try to control others by using the pretense of love."

"The Pharisees were consistently criticized by Jesus and were prime examples. Thinking they were superior to others, they foolishly believed they were better positioned with God and, therefore worthier of God's attention."

"Those with false piety believe they're in an exclusive 'club,' who divide things between 'mine' and 'yours' and 'us' and'them' as they quickly criticize and point out flaws and errors in other's thinking. Conformity becomes their first commandment and control is the game's name."

"The requirements for 'club membership' are clear: *do what we do, think what we think, and believe what we believe*'. Attempting to control others using the lure of 'status', they seduce others into thinking conformity is the only way to holiness. Clinging to *'my beliefs'* and *'my way of thinking,'* they fail to see the more significant relationship with God that's veiled in the lure of 'status' or 'salvation,' as they seduce others into thinking that conformity is the only way to holiness."

Mike continued. "Clinging to *'my beliefs,'* and *'my way of thinking,'* these people fail to see the more significant relationship with God veiled in all of the important virtues of justice, mercy, faithfulness, and forgiveness. Sparkling clean on the outside but dirty on the inside, spiritual arrogance is a grave sin that alienates and hurts the little ones and those considered *'least'* in God's kingdom."

We stopped walking for a moment as Mike looked into my eyes and continued. "I sincerely believe God knows no favorites and everyone belongs *'to the club'* regardless of whether you're an official, bona fide member. Sometimes membership may be a detriment to actually living if someone joins the team for the wrong reasons. The genuinely humble ones may not appear to be overly 'pious' but they know they're broken and need mercy. There's no shame in being broken. In fact, many things need to be broken in order to be what they truly are! There's a reason Jesus told us to pray in private. Simply because it's only between you and God and nobody else's business."

Wow! This was getting pretty deep. My friend was letting his hair down and removing the last vestiges of reservation that stood between two people accepting each other for what they really were, simply two individuals, both with strengths and weaknesses, who now had inherent trust in each other and therefore had become brothers.

It felt good - really, really good!

I was actually embarrassed for having judged others when I, in fact, was a lot like them. Vegas was another one of those *'been there, done'* that' experiences and I knew it was time to head for home.

Chapter 56: All the King's Horses and All the King's Men

· King Henry VII – (grandson of Edward III) 1485-1509
· King Henry VIII – (son of Henry VII) 1509 – 1547
· King Edward VI (son of Henry VIII) 1547 -1553
· Lady Jane Grey (wife of Henry VIII) 1553
· Queen Mary I – (daughter of Henry VIII) 1553 – 1558
· Queen Elizabeth I (daughter of Henry VIII) 1558 - 1603

After seeing all the 'sinners' it matched perfectly with the next part of my dissertation on the Terrill family and with Trip Tik telling us the best driving route from Las Vegas home was via I-70 East and then I-80 East, I shook my head 'no' as the majesty of the Rockies lured my senses, beckoning me physically, mentally and spiritually.

Realizing the trip was going to be around 1,500 miles I hoped Mike could handle the rest of the Terrill story and wasn't just being polite. I paused for a moment and asked Mike, "I'm not boring you, am I?"

"God no! First of all, the narrative is incredibly interesting. Second, to be able to detail names and dates and consequences like you have is mind blowing. If it wasn't for your history, we'd be listening to me sing. So, please continue."

There was relief. I think he really was interested in what an old man had to say and so I continued. "Due to the Wars of the Roses and no patrilineal inheritance, King Richard III's successor was King Henry VII, who descended from John of Gaunt, fourth son of King Edward III, and the first king of what became known as the House of Tudor who ruled England from 1485 until 1603."

"The Tudor name came from King Henry VII's grandfather Owen Tudor, who married Catherine of Valois widow of King Henry V, and grandfather of King Henry VII. Owen was a Welsh aristocrat who declared himself king by 'title of inheritance and judgment of God in battle', and did so after slaying Richard III at the Battle of Bosworth Field. His position was accepted and was crowned on October 30, 1485, while securing parliamentary recognition early in November of that year."

"Bet you were there!"

"Yup" as I added. "It was tough watching one of my ancestors beheaded, knowing I couldn't do anything but watch, as my involvement could have changed history or even resulted in my own demise."

"King Henry VII's reign lasted until his death in 1509 from consumption, which we call tuberculosis, at which time Henry VII's son, King Henry VIII, was coronated. So much has been written about Henry VIII, who was the second son of Henry VII and Elizabeth of York. Not planning on being King of England, Henry VIII became heir to the English throne when his elder brother Arthur, died in 1502."

"Henry VIII had excellent schooling, learning both French and Latin and loved music. He actually wrote pieces for his wives. While some historians and he, himself, give credit for writing the classic 'Greensleeves' it's official title - 'A Newe Northen Dittye of ye Ladye Greene Sleves' - was actually registered by Richard Jones at the London Stationer's Company in September, 1580 and is referred to in several late-16th-Century and early-17th-Century sources, such as Ballet's MS Lute Book and Het Luitboek van Thysius."

"In 1505 at the age of fourteen, Henry VIII became King. In 1509, Pope Julius II gave permission for Henry to marry Catherine of Aragon at Greenwich Palace of which the legality of the marriage was in question because Catherine had been married to Henry's elder brother, Arthur, who died in 1502."

"Henry was intensely dedicated to the continuation of his lineage and coveted a son. This profound obsession played a distinct role in the marital, social and religious history of England that began on January 01, 1511 when Catherine gave birth to a boy who died in February of the same year."

"The friction between France and England continued and in June of 1513, twenty-two-year-old Henry invaded France at the Battle of the Spurs and Fall of Therouanne which was named due to the speed of the French retreat from the battlefield. The town of Therouanne fell to the English two weeks later, where the English entered the town and simply destroyed it. After the victory at Therouanne, Henry turned to Tournai and it, also, fell. However, this time an English garrison took control and was stationed there."

"On September 9th, King James IV of Scotland's invasion of England came to an end at the Battle of Flodden where he was killed. At the same time a peace treaty with France was negotiated by Thomas Wolsey where one of the terms was that Louis XII of France would marry Henry VIII's younger sister, Mary, after Louis XII wife, Queen Anne, died in hope that she might yet have a son. Queen Anne died, Princess Mary was betrothed to the elderly Louis XII and hope was in the air. Mary, however, was described as a youthful beauty whose fast-paced life, 'wore down her aging and weakened husband who died less than three months after their marriage.'"

"Were they related to Nelson Rockefeller?" Mike inquired.

I just shook my head, put a wry smile on my face and continued, thinking it was funny my friend was actually the sinister minister I'd called him. "All of Henry VIII's sons died. His daughter, Princess Mary, was born in February of 1516."

"While proud to have an heir, later activities indicate Henry would have been much happier, along with several abruptly deceased wives, to have a son. The Treaty of London or Universal Peace was signed in 1518 between England, France, Burgundy and other states in an attempt to produce a peaceful Europe. The treaty stated that the countries would not attack one another and if they did, the other countries would come to the aid of those being attacked."

"In other words, the precursor of NATO" Mike interjected. "Yup!" I concurred. "However, within the treaty was the agreement that two-year-old Mary would marry the French dauphin." "In 1521 the Treaty of Bruges was signed in secrecy in Bruges,

France between Thomas Wolsey, representing King Henry VIII and King Charles V who's titles included, Holy Roman Emperor, Archduke of Austria, King of Spain, Lord of the Netherlands and titular Duke of Burgundy. In the treaty, Wolsey promised King Charles V that King Henry VIII would join with him in a joint campaign against France and King Francis I. The meeting was held in secret because England was supposed to be a mediator in the dispute between Charles and Francis. That year at a ceremony at Greenwich Palace, Henry VIII was bestowed with the title Defender of the Faith, which was conferred by Pope Leo X in recognition of the book Henry wrote against Martin Luther."

"The failure of Queen Catherine to produce a male heir began Henry's search for someone who would. Anne Boleyn, sister of Mary Boleyn, who was Henry's mistress, came to his attention. To end the marriage between Henry and Catherine of Aragon, Thomas Wolsey set up a secret tribunal where Henry had to answer charges of having an illegal marriage. The court was held in secret so Catherine didn't know. The plan was to present the facts to the Pope who would then annul the marriage. Problems occurred when Rome was attacked by Catherine's nephew Charles V, Holy Roman Emperor where Pope Clement VII was captured, thereby eliminating any chance the Pope would annul the marriage."

"Henry simply informed Catherine of Aragon that their marriage was invalid because she'd been married to his brother, Arthur. Anne Boleyn, who Henry had become infatuated with, wanted Henry to divorce Catherine and marry her. Thomas Wolsey was sent to France and the court of Francis I to secure the release of Pope Clement VII to get the annulment between King Henry and Catherine of Aragon."

"In 1532, England's financial needs were growing to the point that Parliament passed a law which prevented the Pope from receiving Annates, which was the income received by the bishop in the first year after his appointment. Henry VIII had a clause added that allowed him to postpone the act, hoping this would persuade the Pope to annul his marriage to Catherine. Needless to say, this caused quite a stir in English politics to the point that Sir Thomas Moor resigned as Chancellor because he believed this would separate England from the Catholic Church and he couldn't accept King Henry VIII becoming the leader of the Church."

"Traditionally, when an ecclesiastical position was filled, the first year's income and one-tenth of the income from then on had to be paid to the papacy. Henry VIII had a statute passed that meant the payments went to the English Crown instead of the church and was probably done to force the Pope to annul Henry's marriage to Catherine of Aragon. When that didn't work, in November of that year, the Act of Supremacy was passed denoting the King as supreme head of the Church of England. This act was so broad that it was to be recognized by the clergy that any and all errors, heresies and other abuses in the past, present or future for the king and his heirs were to be accepted and forgiven. If that wasn't enough, Henry VIII had the Act of First Fruits and Tenths passed that changed the financial dynamics of the relationship between Church and state, making King Henry exulted king and ruler. To this day, the Church of England remains under the auspices of the sovereign and not a separate entity as is the case of the Second Amendment to the US Constitution."

"The monasteries, abbeys and nunneries had in the past played an important role in the fabric of English life. Not only had they acted as a place of worship but were also a center for education, refuge for travelers and provided food for the poor. Instead, Henry

VIII obtained much needed money by suppressing hundreds of religious houses across the country and selling off their lands and assets."

"Henry and Thomas Cromwell directed surveyors to report on the state of each religious community, starting with the smaller houses first. Those houses that were badly run or where discipline for the religious order they followed had become slack, were shuttered immediately and their lands and assets taken. The abbots were offered pensions or money to surrender their houses but also threatened with violence if they didn't. Several abbots were executed for not surrendering, while the inhabitants of the houses were sent to larger abbeys or just abandoned. A second round of suppression followed that concentrated on the larger religious houses. The suppression didn't come without a cost. Several revolts were sparked by the Dissolution of the Monasteries."

"Oliver Cromwell had been one of the most powerful proponents of the English Reformation, and creator of true English governance. He helped engineer an annulment of the King Henry's marriage to Catherine of Aragon so that Henry could lawfully marry Anne Boleyn. Henry failed to obtain the approval of Pope Clement VII in 1533 so Parliament endorsed the king's claim to be Supreme Head of the Church of England, giving him the authority to annul his own marriage. Cromwell subsequently charted an evangelical and reformist course for the Church of England from the unique posts of Vicegerent in Spirituals and vicar-general."

"On January 25, 1533 Henry VIII married Anne Boleyn at Whitehall Palace. Anne was expecting a child which Henry and Anne hoped would be a boy. This caused yet another stir, while on May 23rd Sir Thomas Cranmer declared the marriage between Henry VIII and Catherine of Aragon illegal and it was annulled."

"On June first, Anne Boleyn was crowned Queen of England at Westminster Abbey by Thomas Cranmer, Archbishop of Canterbury and ninety days later, Anne Boleyn gave birth to Elizabeth, a healthy girl, at Greenwich Palace much to the dismay of King Henry." "By the order of Henry VIII, his eldest daughter Mary's, title of Princess was removed in 1534 and she was taken to Hatfield to be a servant in the household of Princess Elizabeth, her younger step- sister. Mary was around eighteen years old at the time and certainly not happy with this arrangement and would not accept that Elizabeth had a better claim to the English throne than she did."

"To ensure that King Henry VIII's wishes were retained, a statute was passed by Parliament called the 'Act of Succession' that declared Mary Tudor as illegitimate and not the heir of King Henry VIII. The marriage between Henry and Catherine of Aragon was deemed null and void, thereby making the children of Henry and Anne Boleyn true heirs to the English throne."

"Catherine of Aragon died on January 07, 1536 at Kimbolton Castle. Some say she was poisoned. Others believe she had cancer. Three weeks later, on January 29th, Anne Boleyn had a premature birth resulting in a stillborn boy. The failure to give Henry a son meant the end of her marriage to the king. Henry needed a new wife who could give him a male heir and he had his eye on Jane Seymour."

"On May 2, 1536, Anne Boleyn was arrested at Greenwich after the May-Day jousting tournament and on May 19th beheaded for treason and adultery at the Tower of London. Four weeks later, Henry VIII married his third wife, Jane Seymour, the former lady-in-waiting to both Catherine of Aragon and Anne Boleyn at York Palace, now the Palace of Whitehall. In July, Parliament declared that Elizabeth, like her elder step-sister, Mary, was illegitimate, allowing the yet-to-be- born son of Henry VIII to become the heir to the English throne."

"Henry's decisions regarding the Church were extremely unpopular and following a year of demonstrations, assurances were given that the complaints would be heard. Instead, Henry summoned the leaders to London where the rebels believed they would discuss terms with the King as they had been promised free pardons. Instead, Henry had the rebels arrested and sent back to their homes where they were tried and executed."

"King Henry was quite the guy and, depending on how he felt, determined how you died. The fastest was beheading - chop, chop and it was over which he did an estimated 57,000 times. Next came being drawn and quartered, where you were hung until almost dead, pulled down. had your entrails removed and burned before you as your appendages were attached to four horses who slowly walked away in different directions and literally pulled you apart. When he was really in a bad mood, Henry would have you locked in one of the dungeons such as at York Castle and simply left there to die of starvation."

"Nice guy!"

"Jane Seymour gave birth to a son named Edward at Hampton Court on October 12, 1537. The birth had complications and Jane became ill, died and was buried in St. George's Chapel, Windsor Castle and the monastery at Gloucester that was surrendered to Henry VIII as part of the Dissolution of the Monasteries."

"During his rise to power Oliver Cromwell made numerous enemies including Anne Boleyn, due to his fresh ideas and lack of nobility and actually played a prominent role in her downfall. On January 6, 1540 Henry VIII and Anne of Cleves were married. Although Henry was disappointed that Anne didn't resemble her portrait, the marriage went ahead as planned until July 9th of that year when Henry had the marriage annulled. For this *lack of judgement*, Oliver Cromwell fell from grace and was arraigned under a bill of attainder and executed for treason and heresy on Tower Hill in July 1540. The king later expressed regret at the loss of his chief minister and his reign never recovered from the loss."

Waiting three weeks Henry married Catherine Howard on July 28th of that year. Once again, things didn't work out too well and on February 13, 1542, Catherine was beheaded on Tower Green within the Tower of London after being found guilty of adultery and therefore treason."

"In 1543, the Succession to the Crown Act was passed by Parliament specifying the order of succession to the English throne after the death of Henry VIII, naming Edward as heir instead of Mary and Elizabeth."

"In July of that year the Treaties of Greenwich were signed by the Scots with King Henry VIII swearing peace between the two nations and stating in the agreement that Mary Stuart, or Mary Queen of Scots, should marry Henry's son, Edward. Although these two treaties were initially agreed to, they were rejected by the Scots by the end of the year. King Henry initially demanded that Mary be brought to England but both sides agreed she should remain in Scotland until her tenth birthday."

"On July 12, 1544, Henry VIII was 53 years old and married Catherine Parr, his sixth and final wife at Hampton Court Palace. Henry was busy constructing Southsea Castle at the entrance to Portsmouth harbor to protect against French invasions and was also building Hurst Castle, which was another of his chain of gun-fort fortresses on the south coast of England designed to defend England from a French invasion."

"In May of that year, the Treaties of Greenwich collapsed and Henry VIII tried to get another agreement by sending the Earl of Hertford to Scotland where they attacked and destroyed Edinburgh. This was the first military action in a series of engagements between England and Scotland now known as the Rough Wooing."

"On Jan 28, 1547 Henry died at Whitehall Palace and was buried in St. George's Chapel Windsor next to Jane Seymour, said to be his favorite wife. Later that year, Yarmouth Castle on the Isle of Wight was completed as the last of the gun-forts Henry built to defend the south coast of England."

"Was Henry VIII buried in a coffin?" Mike inquired. "I think so, why?" I asked.

"How could they find six friends to carry it?" Mike sneered, showing his distaste for one of the most famous kings in European history.

I shook my head, smiled and continued my dissertation. "Well, it wasn't safe being a monarch. Seventeen or nearly one-third of the sixty-one who had been monarchs between 1066 and Henry VIII, were murdered, assassinated or executed away from the battlefield upon which there would be a willing replacement. In Henry VIII's case it was Henry's son, Edward VI, who was crowned at the age of nine, upon which a Regency was created. Although he was intellectually adept and fluent in both Greek and Latin, Edward VI was not physically robust and therefore considered a 'weak' ruler dominated by nobles using the Regency to strengthen their own positions. Edward's brief reign saw the foundations laid for one of the great transformations of English society, namely, the English Reformation."

"The King's Council, which was previously dominated by King Henry VIII, succumbed to profound factionalism. Upon Henry's death, Edward Seymour, Earl of Hertford, soon to be Duke of Somerset and King Edward's eldest uncle, became Protector, helping transition the Church of England to be more Protestant. To this end, the Book of Common Prayer, which replaced Latin services with English, was introduced in 1549 and several Roman Catholic practices including statues and stained glass which were removed, while marriage of clergy was allowed."

Chapter 58: Peaks and Valleys

We were driving through the Rockies when Mike expounded something I'll never forget. "Will, isn't it amazing that the mountain peaks would have no meaning if it weren't for the valleys below?"

Without really thinking about it, I simply agreed as Mike continued. "It's a lot like life. We all have peaks and valleys in our lives, loves, hates, happiness, sadness, joy and sorrow… achievements and disappointments… they're all there. When we're standing on top of the mountain, we should never forget that being there is temporary and is only provided meaning by the valleys below."

"When we're down in the valley of despair, we need to remember what it took to reach the peak and expect that the day will come when we are finally atop the mountain again. It's truly sad when a person assumes things will always be great and takes things for granted instead of relishing the view. It's also tragic when another is down in the valley and believes their life in nothing more than sadness."

"God gave us the ability to see the peaks and the valleys. We as humans, must take it upon ourselves to recognize both and realize they're simply fleeting moments that can have so much more meaning if we recognize them and accept their existence."

Wow! I didn't need to go to church, Mike brought God to me as we wove our way through the peaks and valleys of Colorado.

In Denver we connected with Interstate 80 and just as the Trip Tik said it would, once you left Denver and the Rockies, you were in the flatlands that seemed to go on forever and ever and ever. We stopped and gave Ethyl a drink, stretched our legs and focused on heading home.

As we pulled back onto I-80, I began again. "In June, 1553, learning that the fifteen-year-old King Edward VI was in the throes of tuberculosis and not long to live, Lord Guilford Dudley, son of the Duke of Northumberland, married Lady Jane Grey, one of Henry VII's great granddaughters. Edward VI re-wrote his will, naming Jane and her male heirs as successors to the Crown. Edward did this in part because his half-sister, Mary, was Catholic, while

Jane was a committed Protestant who would support the reformed Church of England. The will removed Edward VI's half-sisters, Mary and Elizabeth, from the line of succession on account of their illegitimacy, thereby subverting their claims under the Third Succession Act."

"On July 6, 1553 Edward succumbed and four days later Lady Jane was proclaimed as the first Queen of England and awaited coronation in the Tower of London. However, support for Mary grew quickly and most of Lady Jane's supporters abandoned her."

"On July, 17th the Duke of Northumberland and a militia of some 3,000 men travelled to Cambridge in an attempt to stop Mary Tudor. Moving on to Bury St. Edmunds, the Duke came up against a much larger army supporting Mary. Accepting defeat, Northumberland was arrested and taken back to London to be held in the Tower of London."

"The Privy Council of England changed sides and proclaimed Mary as queen on July 19, 1553, thereby, deposing Lady Jane after a grand total of nine days as monarch. Queen Mary became the first woman to rule England in her own right, rather than through marriage to a king. Mary's first proclamation as queen was the Act of Parliament where she validated her mother's marriage to Henry VIII. This resulted in both Mary and her sister, Elizabeth, becoming legitimate daughters of a king."

"On August third, Mary Tudor arrived in London to a huge welcome. Entering through Aldgate, Mary was met by Elizabeth, Anne of Cleves and many others. Mary quickly ordered the release of her supporters that had been locked up at the Tower of London while the Duke of Northumberland and his supporters were placed in the Tower to await trial and execution."

"On September eighth, Elizabeth agreed to attend a mass but when the day came she pretended to be ill and only took part under protest. Elizabeth had refused to attend any Catholic ceremony including the one that Mary had arranged after the death of Edward. Mary and Elizabeth disagreed strongly over religion. Needless to say, religion and the challenges imposed by Henry VIII, in terms of the Church of England versus the Roman Catholic Church played a huge role in the social, political, aristocratic structure and direction of England and appears to all stem from Henry VIII's sense of inadequacy regarding providing a male heir for which tens of thousands of people lost their lives, not only during his realm but, as you will quickly see, those of his heirs."

I stopped for a moment to let it all soak in and then began again. "Queen Mary actually accomplished a great deal. She led the only successful revolt against central government in 16th Century England, eluded capture, mobilized a counter-coup and, in the moment of crisis, proved to be courageous, decisive and politically adept. The conflict was so overwhelming that Mary realized providing a male heir would move her sister, Elizabeth, who was a Protestant, a step down in the line of succession. Mary, being a staunch Catholic, began searching for a Catholic suitor and it was suggested she consider Prince Philip II of Spain, who was the son of her first cousin, the Holy Roman Emperor Charles V. Unfortunately, this suggested marriage was met with such hostility that Wyatt's rebellion broke out based on the fear that England would become subservient to Spain."

"Mary reinstated Catholic Mass in 1553 and the Pope's authority was reinstated the following year. The title of Head of the Church, which her father had taken, reverted back to the Pope and Roman Catholicism was re-established as the official religion, officially supported by Mary's sister Elizabeth, who adhered to Mary's Catholicism during her reign."

"Queen Mary's father-in-law, the Duke of Northumberland, was accused of treason and executed while Lady Jane and Lord Guilford Dudley were held prisoner in the Tower and convicted of high treason in November, 1553. Mary initially spared Lady Jane's life. However, Lady Jane was perceived to be a threat to the Crown when her father, Henry Grey, 1st Duke of Suffolk, became involved in the Wyatt's rebellion and both Lady Jane and her husband were executed on February 12, 1554."

"Mary's reign wasn't that much longer than Edward's as she died in 1558. During her five-year reign, Mary had over 300 religious dissenters burned at the stake in what are known as the *Marian Persecutions*. While, most remembered for the burnings and the moniker Bloody Mary, her accession changed the rules of the game and the nature of new, feminized politics that were yet to be defined."

"However, in many respects, Mary proved more than equal to the task. Decisions over the details of the practice and power of a Queen Regnant or female monarch, equivalent in rank to a king who reigns in her own right, as opposed to a queen consort, who is the wife of a reigning king, or a queen regent, who is the guardian of a child monarch and reigns temporarily in the child's stead became precedents for the future."

"In April of 1554, Mary's parliament passed the Act for Regal Power that stated that queens held power as 'fully, wholly and absolutely' as their male predecessors, thereby establishing the gender-free authority of the crown. Mary also restructured the economy, reorganized the militia, rebuilt the navy and successfully managed her parliament. By securing the throne, Mary ensured that the crown continued along the line of Tudor succession including her sister, Elizabeth."

"Elizabeth I was crowned Queen of England and Ireland from November 17, 1558 and reigned until her death in 1603. Sometimes referred to as the Virgin Queen, Elizabeth ruled as a devout Protestant and was the last of the five monarchs of the House of Tudor. As one of England's greatest rulers, movies have depicted her sacrificing her life for the good of the realm. While resistant to being married and childless, Elizabeth had numerous male friends including Robert Dudley, Sir Walter Raleigh, Francis Drake and Robert Devereux, as well as many prominent suitors, including many of the crown rulers of Europe and their heirs. She nearly married Thomas Seymour, brother of Lady Jane Seymour and husband of Henry VIII's final wife, Catherine Parr."

"Mary's husband, Philip II of Spain, proposed to Elizabeth after Mary's death. Mary and Philip were cousins, and Elizabeth's father, Henry VIII, had divorced Mary's mother in part, because he became convinced it was wrong for a man to marry his brother's wife. Philip apparently had fewer qualms about creating a parallel situation with Elizabeth. Elizabeth turned Philip down and eventually fought a war against him and the Spanish Armada. Elizabeth's intellect was quite well known due to her extraordinary leadership qualities, noted academic brilliance, financial acumen and the fact that she fluently spoke English, Welsh, Greek, Latin, Spanish, French, and Italian by the age of eleven and continued to learn the basics of languages such as German as she grew older."

"No Cornish?" Mike retorted. "What a lout!"

I shook my head at the wise guy and continued on. "One of the key issues during Henry's, Edward's, Mary's and Elizabeth's reign dealt with the relationship each had with the Catholic Church. Henry created the Church of England for both financial and personal reasons. Edward didn't rule long enough to affect the relationship. Mary reverted back to the Catholic faith and then Elizabeth redirected England back to Protestantism."

"If these changes had been peaceful transitions, it would have been one thing but each shift was not only a change in religion but a change in the social, political and ethical basis of a society and culture that resulted in one thing – death! Death to those whose beliefs were contrary to those of the person in power."

Chapter 59: The Terrill Split

We stopped for dinner at a Bennigan's and, as we got back into Ethyl, I opened my leather satchel and handed Mike yet another chart. As we pulled back onto I-80 I began again. "England's sovereign system continues to this day. However, the direct effect and relationship to the sovereigns by the Terrills became less and less and less, not due to the lack of authority of the rulers but, the decline in wealth, power and subsequent authority of the Tyrells. For this reason, I've stopped researching how the Terrills interacted with those in high places but did create a grid that shows how complex the entire situation became."

"William's brother, Thomas Tyrell was born on February 21, 1478 in Gipping, Suffolk, England and married Margaret Willoughby in 1494, when he was sixteen years old. They were the prolific parents of seven sons and seven daughters including Sir Hugh and Sir William Tyrell."

"Thomas Tyrell eventually received a King's pardon in April 1504 by King Henry VII. Unfortunately, Sir James was officially attainted in 1504 by Parliament for treason and his lands forfeited to the King. In 1507 Thomas successfully appealed the attainder and the estate at Gipping was restored."

"It doesn't appear the Tyrells had much to do with Henry VIII and probably laid low from his eccentricities simply to save their heads. What did happen was the family lineage 'split' and so we need to follow two different families."

"Lord William Tirrell, Lord of South Ockenden, was born in 1465 and was half-brother of Charles Brandon, 1st Duke of Suffolk who was married to Mary Tudor, King Henry VIII's younger sister. William Tirrell married Elizabeth and they sired Humphrey Tyrell, John Tyrell of South Okenden, along with Thomas, William, Anne and Mary Tyrell.

"Humphrey Tyrell was born in 1500 and married Jane Ingleton in 1519 holding the title of the Manor of Bryun. Jane Ingleton was an heiress and they lived in Thornton Hall after her father's death. Humphrey was educated at Eaton and Cambridge. They had one son, named Sir George Tyrell Of Thornton, who was born on May 16, 1519 in Thornton, Yorkshire, England."

"After Humphrey's death in 1548 Jane married Alexander St John. She died on April 24, 1557 and was buried in the Church of St Michael and All Angels, Thornton, Buckinghamshire. Throughout my studies I was never able to learn much about the Tyrrell residences until Thornton."

"Sir George Tyrell of Thornton married Lady Eleanor Montagu in 1550 in Thornton, Buckinghamshire and they were the parents of six sons and four daughters - Sir Edward Tyrrell born in 1551, Thomas Tyrell of Rushton born in 1552, Francis Tyrell born in 1554, Emma born in 1556 and died that year, another female born in 1559 and died that year, a son born in 1562 who died that year, Jane Tyrell of Thornton, Robert Tyrell, Sir William Terrell Lord of Bruyn born in 1565 and Eleanor born and died in 1566."

"Here is a summary of Thornton parish that I found in an old summary of the family."

'The Tyrells of Thornton rose through a combination of careful estate management and marriages. By the mid-sixteenth century, a compact estate situated north-east of Buckingham covering Leckhampstead, Oakley and Thornton, had been assembled. George Tyrell, the Member's father, was apparently an enclosing landlord and, despite later claims, consolidated his estate before he died on May 10, 1571. George Tyrell himself was twice married, and fathered 12 children. His second marriage, to the daughter of Thomas Aston, made him a relative of Sir Roger Aston who was the master huntsman to King James VI.'

'George was a politically significant figure in Buckinghamshire by the 1590s and wealthy enough to have spent about £3,000 on building a house called 'The Toy' at Thornton by 1603. He served as the county sheriff in 1594-5 and was knighted by King James at the Charterhouse in May 1603. His estate's closeness to Buckingham probably explains his appointment as a magistrate for the borough in 1603 and its decision to choose him as one of its Members in 1604.'

'The Thorton parish comprised an area of 1,347 acres of which seven are covered by water, 129 acres of arable land, 1,033 laid down in permanent grass and sixty-one of woods and plantations upon which wheat, oats, barley and beans are grown. The River Ouse formed the parish boundary for some distance that widens out into a small lake that flows past the lawn of Thornton House.'

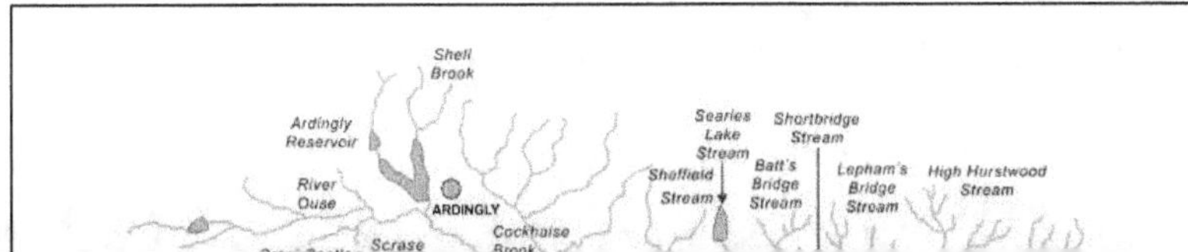

'The Sussex River Ouse is a beautiful and fascinating network of over 750 miles of rivers, streams and brooks which collect water from just over 250 square miles of the surrounding countryside. The main River Ouse begins from springs near to Slaugham in West Sussex before flowing south east to Haywards Heath before meeting its main tributary, the River Uck, at Isfield. Feeder streams for the River Uck come from the north-east and south-east of Uckfield before meeting the main river. From their confluence (meeting point) the River Ouse flows southwards through Barcombe Mills to Lewes and finally meets the sea at Newhaven.'

'There was no Thornton village proper but a few buildings, among them the Home Farm, lie on the eastern outskirts of the park with one or two houses further south. The country is very open and chiefly given up to pasture for grazing; the only woods of any size are Great Wood on the west boundary and Cowpen Wood in the south-east of the parish. The open common was the cause of a dispute in the 16th century between Humfrey Tyrell, the lord of the manor, and the tenants, who accused him of having destroyed all the growth on the common. The commissioners heard the case in 1535, when the tenants declared that they had always felled furze and blackthorn by license of the lord but were fined for felling whitethorn. The green, as parcel of the manor, had been formerly enclosed with a stone wall by George Ingleton but it had lain common for forty years or more; houses had been built on it and stones from the wall taken to repair the manor-house. Nevertheless, Tyrell had encroached upon the tenants' rights by inclosing with a hedge in the autumn of 1529 2 acres of land used as common for beasts. They admitted, however, that the stone wall at the mill had been injured by the wives washing there and by the course of the common kine, and had also heard that one of Tyrell's servants had been thrown into the water by Robert Wilson's wife and her maid.'

'Thornton Manor descended to George Tyrell in 1550. He made a settlement of the manor in 1571 and died that year. His son Edward, was sheriff of the county in 1595-96 and member for Buckingham borough in 1604. Edward died in January, 1605 leaving the Thornton property, including the mansion-house, to his son and heir, Edward Tyrell, while Edward's widow Margaret, received an estate in Nast End, Great Leckhampstead, and Oakley Manor.'

Mike looked at me and noted that 1604 was a very important year in religious history. Being curious I inquired "Why?"

Mike responded. "In January 1604 King James convened the Hampton Court Conference, where a new English version of the Bible was conceived in response to the problems of the earlier translations perceived by the Puritans."

"King James gave the translators instructions intended to ensure that the new version would conform to the ecclesiology, and reflect the episcopal structure, of the Church of England and its belief in an ordained clergy. The translation was done by the leading biblical scholars in England who divided the work between them: the Old Testament was entrusted to three panels, the New Testament to two and the Apocrypha to one. In common with most other translations of the period, the New Testament was translated from Greek, the Old Testament from Hebrew and Aramaic, and the Apocrypha from Greek and Latin."

"The final version was published in 1611. There are 80 books of the King James Version include 39 books of the Old Testament, an intertestamental section containing 14 books of what Protestants consider the Apocrypha and the 27 books of the New Testament. Noted for its 'majesty of style' the King James Version has been described as one of the most important books in English culture and a driving force in the shaping of the English-speaking world."

Loving history, I now had another spec to add to my maelstrom of significant and insignificant facts as I reverted back to the family notes.

"Edward was Sheriff of Buckinghamshire in 1612 and joined with his wife, Elizabeth, and younger brothers, Timothy and Thomas, in making a settlement of Thornton in 1626. He had been knighted at Windsor in 1607 and was appointed a baronet in October 1627."

"Edward's eldest son, Robert, joined his father in restoring the manor in 1632 but did not take part in a further recovery six years later. Robert was disinherited by his father in February of 1638 when George obtained a new baronetcy for his two younger sons, Toby and Francis, leaving Sir Edward in possession of Thornton until his death in 1656."

"Edward's son, Toby, succeeded to the title and estates before dying in 1671 at which time Thornton Manor was passed to his son, Thomas. Thomas resided at Thornton Manor until his passing 1705 when Thomas's son, Harry, inherited the estate."

"Harry died three years after his father, probably from the plague, leaving three sons, one of them posthumous, of whom his eldest, Thomas, inherited the manor and died a bachelor the following year. The second son, also named Harry, died unmarried two years later and Thornton passed to the third son Charles, who lived there until 1749."

"Harry left a daughter and heir, Hester Maria, under the guardianship of his mother, Hester Lady Tyrell, with the Baronet title passing to Thomas Tyrell. Hester Maria, to whom Sir Charles Tyrell left property at Thornton and Leckhampstead, became the wife of the Rev. William Cotton. She died in 1778 while her husband survived until 1782 but it doesn't appear they held Thornton after her death. This is because Elizabeth Cotton, who was Hester and Rev. William's daughter, and her husband Thomas Sheppard, appear to have sold the manor."

I glanced at Mike as yet another eighteen-wheeler zoomed by and added. "When King James I created the hereditary Order of Baronets on May 22, 1611 for the settlement of Ireland, he offered the dignity to 200 gentlemen of good birth, with a clear estate of £1,000 a year, on condition that each pay a sum equivalent to three years' pay to 30 soldiers at 8d per day per man (total − £1,095) into the King's Exchequer. To be recognized as a baronet it was necessary to prove a claim of succession. When this has been done the name was entered on The Official Roll. There have been over 1,300 Baronets based totally on descendance, where the title was classified as either active or dormant if, five years after the death of the previous incumbent, no heir came forward to claim it. Due to the fact there were several Tyrrell lineages, those of Thornton were called Baronet Tyrell of Thornton and those of Springfield were called Baronet Tyrrell of Springfield. Due to the 'break' in lineage in the 1700's that made the name untraceable, I've chosen to first follow those of the Thornton's and then those of Springfield."

"I need to outline the consequence of the laws of primogeniture as it affected the destiny of the Terrill family. William's older brother, Sir Edward Tyrrell first Baronet of Thornton, was born in 1551 married Mary Lee and had five children - Edward, the eldest surviving son and heir, born in 1573, Francis, Cassandra, Herbert and Maria, who married William Tyrell, and Charles, as a result of which Mary died. Edward evidently re-married within two years as further children are baptized at Thornton."

"I've been trying to keep the lineage going with the oldest son. However, it's really necessary for me to talk about two brothers, William and Edward Tyrell. Lord William Edward Tyrrell of Bruyn was born in 1570 and was the second son of Sir George Tyrrell and his first wife Eleanor Montague. Eleanor was the daughter of Sir Edward Montagu, Chief Justice of England under King Henry VIII. The family was an old Anglo-Saxon aristocratic surname whose historic seat was in County Essex but expanded into Buckinghamshire early in the 16th Century."

"In keeping with the laws of primogeniture, William Tyrell's older brother, Sir Edward Tyrrell, who was born 1551, inherited most of their father's estates and titles upon their father's death. Lord William became Lord of the Manor of Bruyn in Berkshire and also possessed land in Reading, Berkshire that he inherited from his mother. In the 1570's he alienated the Manor of Bruyn and settled in the city of Reading, England. Around 1587 he married Margaret Richmond Webb in Stewly, Buckinghamshire. The couple lived at St. Giles, Reading, Berkshire, England, and had three sons – David, born in 1588, Francis, born in 1592 and Robert Tyrell, born in 1594."

"Both William and Margaret died in August, 1595, possibly of the plague, leaving their three young descendants to be raised by relatives. Robert, their youngest son, is said to have had a son named Richmond Tyrrell who emigrated to Virginia, thereby founding the large and prominent colonial Virginia Terrell family."

"In 1595 Sir Edward Tyrrell was made Sheriff of Buckinghamshire and Bedfordshire, was knighted in 1603 and elected as a member of Parliament for Buckingham. The achievement of arms can be seen in window glass at Thornton Hall which is now the Convent of Jesus and Mary, that includes the families of the Tyrrells of Essex who had intermarried, in addition to the Ingletons of Thornton."

I wiped my brow with the back of my hand and looked at Reverend Mike and simply exclaimed… "Whew!"

Chapter 60: Cornwall 1595 – 1834

After spending the night in a RV park outside Omaha, Nebraska, we hit the Iowa State line and were heading home. It was a little over 300 miles and so I directed Mike to open the satchel and remove a file entitled 'Chronology of the Terrill Family from 1594 to 1846' as we headed for Iowa City, where we'd connect with US Highway 30 up through Dubuque, the scary bridge and into God's country.

Mike opened the file named 'Tyrells of Thornton'.

	B orn:	D ied:
54. Robert Tyrell	1594	1643
55. John Terrill	1615	1700
56. George Terrill	1665	1731
57. Stephen Terrill	1712	1774
58. Stephen Terrill of Troon	1749	1831
59. Stephen Terrill of Troon Moor	1776	1846

I asked Mike if he'd mind reading what was written as it was simply too much to remember. However, before he could start I thought I'd better outline what a baronet was. "The term baronet is believed to have been first applied to nobility who, for one reason or another, had lost the right of summons to Parliament. The earliest mention of baronets was in the Battle of Barrenberg in 1321. There is a further mention in 1328 when King Edward III is known to have created eight baronets with more created in 1340, 1446 and 1551."

"The current hereditary Order of Baronets dates from 1611 when it was erected by King James I who granted the First Letters Patent to '200 gentlemen of good birth with an income of at least £1000 a year'. His intention was two-fold. First, he wanted to fill the gap between peers of the realm and knights so he decided that the baronets were to form the sixth division of the aristocracy following the five degrees of the peerage. Second, and probably more importantly, he needed money to pay for soldiers to carry out the battles in Ireland."

With that information and, in his loquacious 'preacher voice' Mike began. "Sir Edward Tyrell created a baronetcy in 1627, naming his first son, Robert, as heir and then in 1638 took out a second patent naming to his second son, Toby Tyrrell, as heir."

"Sir Edward had two wives, both of whom were named Elisabeth. The Buckinghamshire Tyrell pedigree states that his first wife, mother of all his children, was Elisabeth Kingsmill. The Thornton Church records indicate the names of all the offspring born, but only three were baptized which probably means the others died at birth - Toby, Francis and Mary, where his wife's name was also given, though it states that the mother's name 'Elizabeth' does not help to clarify matters."

"Sir Toby Tyrrell, Second Baronet of Thornton was born in 1617. He first married, Edith, the daughter of Sir Thomas Windebank, on December 1, 1638 at St. Giles in the Fields who was presumably of child as both died in 1643."

"Toby's second wife, Lucy, was the daughter of Sir Thomas Barrington and widow of William Cheyne of Chesham Bois, Buckinghamshire, who survived Toby by 20 years. Sir Toby Tyrrell and Lucy Barrington had a son named Thomas. Looking at the dates of the other children suggests that Thomas was born between 1643 and 1646, in which case, he could be either Lucy's first child, or possibly born to Edith before her death."

"Sir Thomas Tyrrell, Third Baronet of Thornton married Frances Blount in 1665, the daughter of Sir Henry Blount of Tittenhanger, Hertfordshire. They had six sons and four daughters including their eldest son, Harry Tyrrell, who was born in the late 1660's and died in 1708, Thomas born in 1693, Harry born in 1695 and Charles born in 1708."

"Sir Harry Tyrrell, Fourth Baronet of Thornton married Hester, the daughter of Charles Blount, Esq., in1692 who gave birth to Thomas Tyrrell, their eldest child, in 1693, Harry in 1695 and Charles in 1708."

"Sir Thomas Tyrrell, Fifth Baronet of Thornton, was the eldest son of Sir Harry, who was born in 1693 'about a quarter of an hour afore noon' who matriculated at Oxford in November, 1710, died December 25, 1718 and was buried January 1, 1719 at Thornton."

"Sir Harry Tyrrell, Sixth Baronet of Thornton, graduated from Oxford in 1711 and died in November, 1720."

"Sir Charles Tyrrell, Seventh Baronet of Thornton was the third son of Sir Harry and was born 1708. In 1726 he married Jane Elisabeth Sellon of Geneva, by whom he had two sons, who both died young along with James, Henry, and one daughter, Hester Mafia. Their daughter and heiress, Elisabeth, married Thomas Sheppard of Littlecote."

"Sir Thomas Tyrrell was titled the 'Eighth Baronet'. His cousin, Thomas, was the son of Charles Tyrrell and also brother of the first Sir Harry and was the family heir at Thornton who lived at Thornton and was buried there in 1755. The register refers to him as Sir Thomas Tyrell Bart and the memorial placed on the church wall by his sister, Elisabeth Forrester, states 'In memory of Sir Thomas Tyrrell Bart.' It's said that he claimed the title but was not recognized by the College of Heralds, though it's difficult to understand why this should be, unless there was some doubt of his paternity."

Mike paused and so I asked him to read the contents of the file named 'Tyrells of Springfield' and Mike began again.

"The Springfield line includes "Sir John Tiril First Baronet of Springfield, who married Lettice Coppin, daughter of Thomas Coppin and had a son, Charles Tyrell II, born in 1660. John gained the title of First Baronet of Springfield on October 22, 1666."

"Sir Charles Tiril, Second Baronet of Springfield, married Martha Mildmay in 1682 at Woodham Mortimer, Essex. Their children were John Tiril, born in 1685 and a daughter who married Colonel Windham of Earlsham, Suffolk. Dame Martha Tiril died on March 27, 1690 followed by Sir Charles Tiril on February 3, 1714. Both are buried at East Horndon, Essex."

"Sir John Tiril, Third Baronet of Springfield, was husband of Elizabeth Cotton who was the daughter of John Cotton Esq. of the Middle Temple and of East Barnet, Middlesex/Hertfordshire, and Elizabeth Wright. She was the second wife of John Tiril, the son of Sir Charles Tiril 2nd Baronet, and Martha Mildmay, and they had three sons: Sir Charles Tiril - 4th Baronet, Sir John Tiril - 5th Baronet, as well as an unknown son."

"Sir Charles Tiril, Fourth Baronet of Springfield, became the 4th Baronet Tiril of Springfield on the death of his father in 1729 but died on July 27, 1735 at the age of age 11."

"Sir John Tiril, Fifth Baronet of Springfield was born in East Horndon, Brentwood, Essex, England in 1728. Sir John Tiril became the fifth Baronet of Springfield who married Mary Crispe and had one daughter before passing away in January 1766 in Heron Manor, East Horndon, Brentwood, Essex, England."

Mike took a deep breath as I instructed him to pull out the sheath marked 'Tyrells of Bryun' that I had referenced previously and he began again.

"Sir William Tyrrell of Bruyn's had a son named Robert Richmond Terrell of Reading who became Counselor of Borough Guardian and married Jane Baldwin in 1617. Jane was the daughter of Robert and Joan Pigeone Baldwin and they had three sons: Robert, Richmond and William Tyrrell. It must be noted that, none of the three were knights and represent one end of the aristocratic Tyrrell line in England."

"The third brother was Thomas Tyrrell of Gipping, who first married, Margaret Willoughby, daughter of the tenth Baron Willoghby de Eresby, and then married Mary Grey in 1554, in Gipping, Suffolk, England and became parents of Vincent, Charles, George, John, Vincent, James and Thomas."

"Sir John Tyrrell of Gipping was born in 1597 and married, Elizabeth Munday, daughter of Sir John Munday Lord Mayor of London, and they had two sons James and William and a daughter Anne, who married Sir Richard Wentworth of Nettlestead, by whom she was the mother of Thomas Wentworth, First Baron Wentworth."

"Sir John Tyrrell was a landowner and politician who sat in the House of Commons from 1661 to 1676. He was educated at Wadham College and awarded a BA in 1620. He was a student of the Inner Temple One of the Four Inns of Court, which were professional associations for barristers and judges in London and was knighted in 1628 becoming a Justice of the Peace for Essex until 1641. Sir John married Martha

Washington and they had four children: Lawrence, Thomas, Charles and Sir John Tyrell II, who was born in 1630."

"In 1643 Sir John went to see the king regarding eight-hundred pounds in back taxes on land he inherited from his uncle at Heron. Unable to pay the taxes, the estate was confiscated in 1648, thus ending the Heron lineage. In 1655 Sir John was imprisoned at Yarmouth after Penruddock's Rising, which was a Royalist revolt launched in March of that year, intending to restore Charles II to the throne of England."

Mike paused for a moment, looked at me, and inquired, "In other words, this is the point where your family when from aristocracy to commoner?"

I replied. "It seems so. It's a long way from owning an estate to copper mining in Cornwall, yet this is what appears to have transpired."

I thought I had the answer and so I continued. "The Baronetage of England comprised all baronetcies created in the Kingdom of England before the Act of Union in 1707 where the Baronetage of England and Nova Scotia were replaced by the Baronetage of Great Britain. There were five baronetcies created for persons with the surname Tiril or Tyrrell, of which all five creations are extinct, as is the Tirell baronetcy from Hugh Tirell descendant of Sir Walter Tirell, the accidental killer of King William II, which simply disappeared from the rolls."

"In our patrilineal ascendancy, the consequence of not being the eldest son resulted in a completely different path. Robert Terrell was the third son and therefore not privy to the inheritances of his brother who was born in Reading, England in 1594 and appears as the first 'commoner' after twenty generations of aristocracy. Robert married Jane Baldwin on June 29, 1617 at St. Giles in Reading, Berkshire and they had eleven children of which their second son was named John Terrell, born on June 25, 1618, of which I believe I am a descendent."

"Robert's will is quite interesting as it indicates there is no mention of land or title – just money that makes me assume that the decision by the King to take back Heron in 1648 ended not only the wealth, but the prestige and power that came from land ownership. There's a copy of Robert's will in the satchel under that name indicating a profound change from the genteel to the working class. Please take it out and read it"

Mike began. "Robert Terrell, of Reading in the County of Berkes, Clothier, hereby wills, to the poor of St. Giles, Reading, 30 shillings. To my son, Robert Terrell, 150 pounds. To my sons, Richmond William, and Timothy, at the age of twenty-one the like sums of 125 pounds. To my daughters, Mary and Margaret Terrell, 150 pounds each, at age of twenty-one. To son, John Terrell, my racks, furnaces, shears, handles, and other shop stuff, and implements of clothing, and also my great gilte bowl. To son, Robert, silver beer bowl. To William and Timothy, the silver spoons that were my children's. To Mary silver and gilt salt. To Margaret trencher salt. My wife, Jane, to have custody of the plate during her widowhood. Residue to said wife, Jane, and son, John, executors. Overseers: Brother-in-law, Mr. Thomas Baldwin; friend, Mr. Richard Stamps, and brother-in-law, Richard Hunt. Signed, Robert Terrell. Witnesses: Richard Stamps. Richard Hunt Thomas Warner.'

Mike concluded. "In other words, it appears that Robert Tyrell was a clothier, which I believe means a tailor."

I nodded and added. "Perhaps, but there was and remains a profound difference between a tailor, clothier and apparel and what are called true clothing, or Bespoke Experiences. A tailor takes existing clothing and fits it to your body. A clothier measures the suit and has it custom made by another person. To have a Bespoke Suit, the person who does the fitting actually sews the item."

"Savile Row in London is the birthplace of what's called Bespoke Clothing, at places such as Henry Poole & Co & the Huntsman. Today, even the Row's famed custom houses who offer true custom apparel, rarely offer bespoke clothing due to price sensitivity and the time frame needed to complete true bespoke garments. Peg and I visited Henry Poole & Company on a lark and found out that a true bespoke suit started at about 5 quid or $6,500 US dollars."

"How many did you buy?" Mike inquired.

"Well, after I cleaned out the pants I was wearing, I said, 'Thank you very much and walked out. I don't think my Terrill ancestor was in that business based on the tools he bequeathed and it appears he was a long way from being the knight or lord that his uncle and twenty-one generations before him had been."

Chapter 61: Ch..Ch...Changes

We made it through Iowa, *where the tall corn grows*, and the mesh bridge where I paid twenty-five cents to cross because we had six wheels. We were just fifty miles from home when Mike asked, "What happened to all the power and wealth?"

I came out of my introspection of giving money to those Hawkeyes, caught myself and began again. "Profound change began in the 1600's that saw three major events have deep impact on England's political and social life, with a permanent consequence on all the former aristocratic families. These included the English Revolution, Restoration of the Stuarts and the Glorious Revolution when James II was deposed and constitutional. monarchy established under William III and Mary II.

"Prior to the 20th century, the English Revolution was generally applied to the 1688 Glorious Revolution. However, Marxist historians also began using to describe the period from 1639 to 1651 that saw Wars of the Three Kingdoms and the Interregnum, or the period between the execution of Charles I in January, 1649 and arrival of his son Charles II in London in May 1660 England was ruled under various forms of republican government. Charles II return marked the start of the Restoration and a return to the status quo in many areas. This eleven-year void of titular power from royalty to representation allowed for social changes as people demanded less authority and more freedom from the rule of a royal family."

"After King Charles execution, the Restoration of the Stuarts also began, where the efforts of Oliver Cromwell's son Richard, who was Lord Protector of England, Scotland, and Ireland, failed and simply enhanced the strength of Parliament. Cromwell lacked his father's power and authority when he attempted to mediate between the army and civil society and this allowed Parliament to increase their presence at a time that contained a large number of disaffected Presbyterians and Royalists."

"Richard Cromwell's main weakness was that he didn't have the confidence of the army when he summoned Parliament in 1659. Instead, the Republicans assessed Cromwell's rule to be 'a period of tyranny and economic depression' and attacked the increasingly monarch-like nature of the Protectorate. The net result was that Richard was unable to manage Parliament and control the army and, on May 7th, a Committee of Safety was formed on the authority of the Rump Parliament displacing the Protector's Council of State that was in turn replaced by a new Council of State."

"Another piece of the transitional pie was The Glorious Revolution, also called 'The Revolution of 1688' and 'The Bloodless Revolution' that ultimately changed how England was governed by giving Parliament more power over the monarchy and planting seeds for the beginnings of today's political democracy and theoretical concept of representation."

"At that time, there was also an upsurge in interest regarding the intent of the Magna Carta. Lawyers and historians contended there was an ancient English constitution, going back to the days of the Anglo-Saxons that protected individual English freedoms. They argued that William the Conqueror's Norman invasion of 1066 had overthrown these rights while the Magna Carta had been a popular attempt to restore them, making the charter an essential foundation for the contemporary powers of Parliament and legal principles such as habeas corpus. Although this historical account was badly flawed, jurists such as Sir Edward Coke used the Magna Carta extensively, arguing against the divine right of kings propounded by the Stuart monarchs."

"Both James I and his son, Charles, attempted to suppress discussion of the Magna Carta, until the issue was curtailed by the English Civil War of the 1640's and the execution of Charles I. The political myth of the Magna Carta and its protection of ancient personal liberties persisted after the Glorious Revolution of 1688 until well into the 19th century. Research by Victorian historians has shown that the original 1215 charter was about the medieval relationship between the monarch and barons, rather than the rights of ordinary people, which is similar to the US Declaration of Independence, that was actually about the rights of a nation and not the people as misinterpreted in the second sentence. However, the charter remained a powerful document, even after almost all of its content was repealed in the 19th and 20th centuries. The Magna Carta still forms an important symbol of liberty, often cited by politicians and campaigners and held in great respect by the British and American legal communities with Lord Denning describing it as, 'The greatest constitutional document of all times - the foundation of the freedom of the individual against the arbitrary authority of any despot'."

Mike looked at me and smiled. "You really did your homework. How many times did you go back in time and space?" Mike asked.

"Fifteen, so far!" "So far?"

"Yup, I'd like to keep going back but the frequency and duration keep getting less and less."

"Other than history and genealogy, what else have you learned?"

"I learned not to make changes. When I'm there, I'm concerned those changes will alter history and could have profound effects.

"Sounds like the movie 'Back to the Future'.

"I met Bob Gale who wrote the book a few years ago and told him he was spot on. I didn't share with him that I was actually doing what he created, but without the Delorean."

"All I can say, is this is incredible," Mike replied.

I responded with a proud smile. "Thanks, but you have to realize this is what I did for a living. I know it's wrong to only follow the patrilineal side and only those with the Terrill name but it gets really complex when you either go back or come forward for so many generations, simply because there are so many permutations. I estimate there are well over ten-thousand people who could have been researched. I readily admit and accept that there are errors in terms of a direct linkage to our family. I took names that had stories behind them and hope no one minds."

"Why do you think there might be errors?" Mike inquired. "Because my great, great grandfather mentioned that he and his father and grandfather worked in the Queensland mine. Assuming 23 years between generations and George leaving Cornwall in 1826, one would think there had to be at least a fifty-year gap between aristocracy and humility."

Mike looked at me, gently shook his head and added. "The one thing you've taught me that I will always remember is that the feudal system was predicated on power. Power of the king to give and take land, power of the barons who 'owned' the land, power of the knights to sublet the land and the powerless serfs who worked the land and paid taxes to the knights, barons and king."

I plastered a great big smile on my face, realizing my student understood. I added, "I taught my students that the decline of feudalism needed to first identify where the nobility's power came from so they could understand why the changes that happened ended up weakening the nobility's power. Nobility really stemmed from land ownership in the early medieval period. Land was really the main source of wealth. So, in that period, being noble really wasn't particularly different from being wealthy. As time went on the responsibilities of the nobles increased as feudalism developed, and more importantly, the idea of nobility became more than just economic class distinction but a social one, as well. You could no longer marry into nobility and even purchasing land if you weren't a noble was difficult, if not impossible in many parts of Europe. Nobility became this powerful idea that became intertwined with the economic, social, religious and familial statuses of its members."

Mike just shook his head and said, "The have's and have not's. Nothing's really changed!"

"Here's some more on the family. John Terrill was christened on June 25, 1618 in Reading, England. He died on March 13, 1661 in Reading, which is southwest of London. Little is known about John in regards to whom he married and the children he had, except one son, George Terrill."

"John's will was dated March 1, 1661 that names his sister Margaret and her husband, Thomas Warner, as executor and executrix and also names his brothers (Robert, William, and Richmond) and sister Mary, his Uncle Richard Hunt of Reading and cousin Robert Terrell of Reading."

"We saw the beginning of the transition in the will of Robert Terrill that indicated he was not a man of wealth. In the period between 1618 and 1640 something happened and the family emigrated from Reading to Camborne, Cornwall. Perhaps it was the fear of religious persecution. Perhaps it was to escape financial tyranny. Perhaps it was for love and not the merger of two families. No one knows why a wealthy family with over 500 years of power would move to a little town in Cornwall, but they did."

"George Terrill was born in Camborne in 1643 and married Christian Bray on August 8, 1663 and they had four children including George from whom, the patrilineal heritage of the Terrills of Mineral Point, Wisconsin runs through that I call, George II. George I died in 1700 and was buried September 22, 1700 in Camborne."

I continued. "From the late half of the 17th Century to the end of the 18th Century, in essence, was the height of noble power except for our part of the Tyrell family. Political and social influence matched this economic hold, so that, in some regions, aristocrats and gentry enjoyed a near monopoly on high positions in the church, army and administration. To a significant extent these intertwining forms of domination and the social, political, economic and ideological justifications that accompanied them defined England and Europe's social order."

"Parliament was composed almost exclusively of nobles at this point, even if they weren't title holders. Whether one was in the House of Lords or Commons, this period saw the complete rejection of the absolute monarchy where nobility was literally stripped of all real power. Then something happened in the 19th Century that brought another change and the power moved away from the nobility to the commoners, namely the industrial revolution and colonialism." "During the Age of Discovery in the 15th and 16th Centuries, Portugal and Spain pioneered European exploration of the globe and, in the process, established large overseas empires while planting European customs throughout the world. Envious of the great wealth these empires generated, England began to establish colonies and trade networks of their own in the Americas and Asia. A series of wars in the 17th and 18th Centuries with the Netherlands and France and the 1707 Act of Union with Scotland, had a significant impact on the governmental and political structure of both England and Scotland. By joining the two countries into a single kingdom with a single Parliament, it allowed England to focus on it colonialism and become the dominant power in North America as well   as   the Indiansubcontinent after the East India Company's conquest of Mughal Bengal at the Battle of Plassey in 1757."

Chapter 62: Expansion and Contraction

I told Mike to open the satchel and find the file that said 'Colonial English Territories' on it. Mike did and examined its contents as I noted. "The countries with the thicker borders around them were under British control. As you can see, they had a lot of ground to cover to the point that they virtually circumvented the globe."

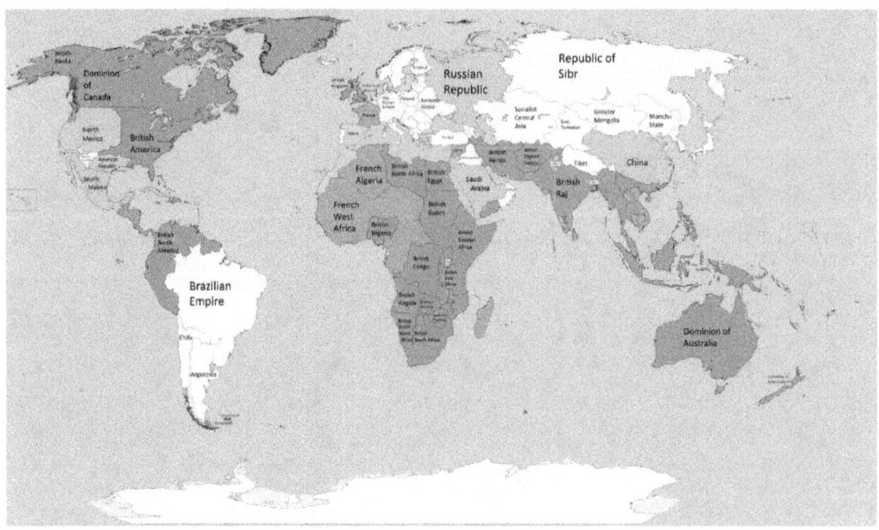

"The American War of Independence resulted in Britain losing some of its oldest and most populous colonies. By 1783. British attention then turned towards Asia, Africa, and the Pacific. After the defeat of France in the Napoleonic Wars that lasted from 1803 to 1815, Britain emerged as the principal naval and imperial power of the 19th century and expanded its imperial holdings. There was a period of relative peace from 1815 to 1914 during which the British Empire became the global hegemon described as 'Pax Britannica" or 'British Peace."

"Alongside the formal control that Britain exerted over its colonies, its dominance of much of the world's trade meant that it effectively controlled the economies of many regions such as Asia and Latin America. Increasing degrees of autonomy were granted to its white settler colonies, some of which were reclassified as dominions. With global expansion, all the areas required resources in order to function in terms of British soldiers and government officials to sustain order and compliance."

Mike inquired, "So how did the industrial revolution erode noble power?"

"You need to remember that medieval feudalism was essentially based on the relationship of reciprocal aid between lord and vassal. As that system became more complex, the relationship weakened. Lords came to own multiple estates and vassals could be tenants on various parcels of land so that loyalties became confused and even conflicting, with people choosing to honor the relationship that suited their own best needs."

"Another blow to the system came from sudden population declines caused by wars and plagues, particularly the Bubonic or Black Death Plague of 1347, that changed all of Europe socially, politically and economically, as well. While there had been other plagues during the previous 1,000 years, most were localized or not in Europe, while the Black Plague represented a major European outbreak."

"From 1347 to 1350 the Black Death killed 25 million people, representing one-quarter of the population of Europe and another 25 million in Asia and Africa. Just when Europe began recovering, a second major epidemic occurred in 1361, called the pestis secunda, in which another 10% to 20% of Europe's population died.

By 1430 Europe's population was lower than it had been in 1290 and wouldn't recover the pre-pandemic level until the 16th Century, only to be decimated in the 20th Century by two world wars. The combined plagues created tremendous social, political and economic upheaval where whole families were wiped out and villages abandoned. Crops couldn't be harvested, travelling and trade became curtailed and food and manufactured goods became in short supply."

"Due to a labor shortage, the surviving villagers demanded exorbitant wages from the remaining aristocratic landowners. In so doing, they prospered and acquired land and property of their own as the plague broke down normal divisions between the upper and lower classes and led to the emergence of a new middle class."

"With labor supplies short, demands for change by those remaining resulted in the English Peasants' Revolt of 1381, that was also named 'Wat Tyler's Rebellion' or 'the Great Rising,' that had various causes including the socio-economic and political tensions generated by the Black Death, as well as extremely high taxes resulting from the conflict with France during the Hundred Years' War. These were all exacerbated by the instability within the leadership of London. The situation reached a flash point with the intervention of a royal official named John Bampton in Essex in May, 1381. Bampton attempted to collect unpaid poll taxes in a village named Brentwood. This attempt ended in a violent confrontation, which rapidly spread across the southern part of England, where the rebels demanded a reduction in taxes, an end to serfdom and the removal of King Richard II's senior officials and courts."

"Another key factor was the increase in commerce and the greater use of coinage that changed the way the feudal system worked. Money allowed feudal lords to pay their sovereign instead of performing service. In so doing, the monarch's use of mercenaries meant military service and, thus, the barons themselves became less important to the defense of England. Conversely, a monarch could now distribute money instead of land in his system of rewards. Finally, a rich merchant class developed with no ties or loyalty to anyone except their sovereign, suppliers and customers. Even serfs could buy their freedom and escape the circumstances into which they were born. All of these factors conspired to weaken the feudal system based on land ownership and service, even if feudalism would continue beyond the medieval period in some form and places."

"If that wasn't enough, the plague continued to occur in small epidemics throughout the world with a major outbreak of the pneumonic plague in Europe in 1665 and 1666. The epidemic reached its peak in September, 1665 when 7,000 people each week were dying in London alone. In two years, one-fifth of London's population died, representing around 100,000 people. How bad was it? Remember the nursery rhyme Ring-Around-The Rosie? It was about the plaque. Here are the lines and then what they were really all about..."

Ring, a-ring, o'rosies, (a red blistery rash)
A pocket full of posies (fragrant herbs and flowers to ward off the 'miasmas')

Atishoo, atishoo (the sneeze and the cough heralding pneumonia)
We all fall down. (all dead)

I looked at Mike and continued. "If all that wasn't bad enough, as farming became less profitable, the government stepped in to artificially support the elite where the *Corn Laws* were an example of the nobility's effort to counter the devaluation of crops simply because the nobility had less capital to maintain their estates and couldn't pay their taxes."

"Throughout history money is, was and will always mean power, simply because those who have the money are the ones holding the government purse strings and, therefore, the government itself. All this was compounded by taxes that favored the rich and punished the rest. We see it today in America where the special interest groups, representing big industries, literally control what our government does or doesn't do."

I realized this was a pretty basic answer and I'd gotten off track and so I added. "We also have to look deeper into what that money meant. Money alone doesn't suddenly make a thousand years of feudal social stratification disappear, despite efforts by those capitalists to the contrary. Indeed, some of the new rich even bought estates from pauper lords whose only assets were their titles and mansions in an attempt to essentially buy their way into status. This procurement wasn't enough to break the noble's hold on power. Many nobles were still quite wealthy and more than a few moved past the stigma of being capitalists and opened their own mines, factories and more. I sincerely believe this is what happened to my ancestors. They were quite happy with their estates and growing crops and then poof, the entire structure they lived under for nearly seven hundred years crumbled."

"Concurrently, there was another profound shift continuing to take place that was the most important key in ending the nobility's hold on power and that dealt with the demographic shifts. With the shift to a manufacturing economy instead of an agrarian one, money was not being spent building factories on rural farmland. It was being spent building factories in cities and ports where the products could be shipped to a global market and labor was plentiful. England,

Wales and Cornwall experienced a huge shift during the 19th Century. Even though the total population of the country was growing, the rural population was shrinking. This put even more pressure on farming as a viable industry. More to the point, it meant that a huge number of people were no longer under the power of one of the nobles. People who once lived in villages on the noble's estates, moved to cities dominated by the newly wealthy, 'common' industrialists."

"The primary cause of the demise of the estates lies in inheritance taxes. While those living were secure, their death meant the inheritance was required to pay a huge sum to the government they couldn't afford. Instead, they began selling off parcels to pay the government. When that wasn't enough, they became indebted to the government and, in many cases, including our family, when they couldn't pay the inheritance tax, they lost all the land and with it the title, prestige and power to control their own destiny. While all this was happening, my ancestors had begun making a living as copper miners in Cornwall and living their lives without all the trappings their relatives and ancestors enjoyed.

"By the mid 19th Century, cities were becoming the dominant economic forces in England and Wales, yet, political power still resided in the rural areas and was still dominated by the lords. Some rural areas were so depopulated that they might only have a handful of people living in what were called the 'rotten boroughs' that could literally be bought! At this point people started to get angry and demanded changes. The House of Commons was supposed to be a representation of tax paying communities, yet, the majority of representation was for underpopulated, underpaying counties."

"Nothing has changed, has it?" Mike offered.

"Nope!" I replied. "While the US Constitution established two legislative houses, where the House of Representatives is based on population, the Senate is based on two Senators per State. This means that those Senators in lesser populated states have equal say to those in more populous states and truly affect the balance of power and, therefore, the need for compromise. As an example, California has as many people as the 23 smallest states combined. This means that the two

California senators have forty-six others who have the equal interest of their own constituents and re-election to worry about and why nothing gets done in Congress."

I switched back to the past and continued. "At a time in world history when monarchies and feudalism were giving way to self- governance and/or socialism, the aristocratic way of life in England became increasingly difficult to maintain. A myriad of factors contributing to the unsustainability of the aristocracy were at once both complex and uncomplicated. Conscription to the military and wartime casualties created a labor shortage. Rationing exacerbated the already hardscrabble subsistence of the working class. The costs of the war landed the country in debt and the national debt resulted in crippling taxation. Particularly devastating to generational wealth were inheritance taxes. On its face, this convergence of economic drivers seemed complex, but at the root of everything, a much simpler fuse had been lit."

"The overwhelming majority of the population was less well- off than the aristocrats. That fact was not new. What had changed was society's tolerance for the magnitude of the differential. It's not difficult to imagine feelings of resentment welling up as tenant workers – who spent their days raking hay – looked up at the warmly lit windows of the manor house and listened to violins or watched guests leave in their gilded carriages after lavish dinners in white tie and tails. Eventually, those without declared enough was enough. Unlike France or Russia, disruption in England was evolutionary, not revolutionary. It took decades, and nearly everyone could eventually see it coming, though some took much longer than others to open their eyes."

"As the saying goes, 'no taxation without representation,' and the rest of the story is fairly obvious. Through a series of reform acts, power was gradually redistributed to the cities where the nobles held little influence. Rural voting areas were gradually consolidated as urban areas, gaining more and more power, until, by the early 19th Century the power of the nobles was broken."

"Ultimately, the power of the nobility rested on their near monopoly of land ownership and the wealth that created. When land was the primary way to generate money, there were few forces that could challenge them. However, once they no longer had the monopoly on wealth and the people who depended on them moved on, their power began to fade. That was somewhat delayed by tradition and stubbornness but eventually it was inevitable."

Mike sat and shook his head as if for the first time he really understood what happened to Europe and England and what was happening to America.

Chapter 63: Coming to America

I had Mike pull out yet another Manilla folder that summarized the family as I continued. "George Tirrill II was born in 1665 and was married in 1690 to Elizabeth whose last name is unknown and they had eight children – Eleanor, Richard, George III, Eleanor, Christian, John, Johnson, Stephen Terrill born in 1712, Dorothy and John."

"Stephen Terrill was the patrilineal great, great grandfather to the Terrills of Mineral Point who was baptized on May 17, 1712 in Camborne and married Jenifer (Jane) Courtis on March 31, 1746 in St Hilary, Cornwall. They had eight children including Stephen Terrill of Troon who was born in 1749 and passed away in 1774.

I directed Mike back to the satchel for one last file simply called 'Family Photos' and continued. "Stephen Terrill of Troon was the patrilineal great grandfather to the Terrills of Mineral Point and married Temperance Jeffrey on June 17, 1775 in Camborne, Cornwall. They had nine offspring that included Stephen Terrill of Troon Moor.

"Stephen Terrill of Troon Moor was born in 1776 and was the patrilineal grandfather to the Terrills of Mineral Point who married Elizabeth Osborne. Of their children, John Terrill was born in 1803 and, with his wife, Elizabeth Vivian, whom he married in 1831, emigrated to Mineral Point, Wisconsin in November 1835 with their two oldest children, John Henry was born 1834. Stephen was born 1836 but died in 1838. John and Elizabeth not only had this photo taken, but added six more children…Steven who was born in 1839, Francis in 1842, the first William, born 1845 who died in1848, another son, named William, born in 1848 and finally Samuel in 1850."

"John and Elizabeth chose Mineral Point because John's brothers Stephen and William were already here. Stephen owned the establishment known as Stag Inn Hotel and land on High Street where the Sweet Shop was, while William built the City Hotel and was also the builder and original operator of the Mineral Point Brewery. John and Elizabeth, cleared 300 acres and built a log house out on Townline Road with 160 acres purchased later by the sons, which, after over 150 years, is still called the Terrill Farm."

Mike stopped looking at the old photos and asked "Why did people emigrate from Cornwall?"

I replied. "A devastating collapse of the economy in Cornwall resulted in a massive exodus of much of the population, often referred to as the Cornish Diaspora. It wasn't until 1971 that the population of Cornwall returned to about 350,000, which is what it had been in the mid-19th Century. The emigration was caused by a number of factors but was mainly due to economic reasons and lack of jobs, when many Cornish people or 'Cousin Jacks' as they were known, migrated to various parts of the world in search of a better life."

"A driving force for some emigrants was the opportunity for skilled miners to find work abroad, later in combination with the decline of the tin and copper mining industries in Cornwall. It's estimated that 250,000 Cornish migrated abroad and these emigrants included farmers, merchants and tradesmen but miners made up most of the numbers. There's a

well-known saying in Cornwall, 'A mine is a hole anywhere in the world with at least one Cornishman at the bottom of it!'"

26, 1870."

"They had seven children Estella J (Terrill) James, William John Terrill, Henry Willis
Terrill, Mabel (Terrill) Harris who's in the back row on the right, Hazel Terrill Harker and Montgomery E Terrill.

We were heading for Mineral Point when I added. "The second photo is William Terrill who was born November 30, 1848, in Mineral Point and married Mary Ann Thomas on December

William passed away in 1925 and is buried in Graceland Cemetery in Mineral Point."

Mabel married George Orville Harris in February, 1905 in Mineral Point and bore three daughters, Eithel, Hazel and Dorothy."

Mike looked at the fourth photo as I added, "This photo was taken in 1914 and included all the Terrill cousins at that time. Eithel is the second from the left in the first standing row, Dorothy is second from the right in the first row with Hazel right behind her.

"Initially, the family lived on a farm if Fayette, Wisconsin until moving to Waldwick in 1910 and residing there until the late 1920's when they relocated to Mineral Point. Mabel died on September, 1958 of a stroke in Dubuque and was laid to rest in Graceland Cemetery."

We were 'home' and the stories were over. Imagine A deep sigh of relief filled my lungs as I pulled the bus into Heaven's Waiting Room parking lot. We opened the door to let in the fresh spring air, stepped out onto the parking lot, as I looked at Mike and then down on the ground, as memories of the entire family rushed through my veins and into my heart. "These were kind, honest, decent people who loved each other as much as they loved to laugh. The family get togethers were always the best. So much food! So much fun! So much to laugh about! God, I miss those days!"

I wanted to minimize what I'd expounded and so I added a caveat. "My research took me back in time and provided a look at what it was like so long ago. While I've had the luxury of tracing the Terrill name to before the birth of Christ, all people are special and this means, actually no one is special."

"If you're of European extraction, you're probably the fruits of Charlemagne's prodigious loins as he sired at least 18 children by five different wives and concubines and that's why I call him the King of Hearts and why today, he remains on each and every deck of playing cards. On and on and on and on, generation after generation of lives lived, loves lost, dreams created and then destroyed. Yet, here I am wondering who will follow in our footsteps and whether the life they live will be as wonderful as ours have been. As important, will they understand, respect and honor the past? Without it, there is no understanding of the future."

We unloaded our suitcases and walked into the lobby. Nothing had changed and the warmth of familiarity enveloped us in a cloak of goodness. While traveling can open one's eyes and sometimes one's heart, coming home to what's familiar also has a warm glow that can't be measured.

Mike and I got on the elevator and stopped at second floor. Mike turned and gave me a big hug as he whispered, "Thank you my friend."

"No, thank you," I replied. "For listening to an old man relive what, other than Peg and the kids, has been a part of his life."

I made it to my apartment and everything was as it had been. The soft clicking of the mantel clock reminded me that the only thing that had changed was time. Time had moved on, as it always does and all we can do is ride along until it too will come to an end for each of us.

Chapter 64: Reflections

Mike and I agreed to dinner at 'home' and so we met in the lobby at six. We had spaghetti and meatballs and I looked out west at the fields and pondered. "I wonder if what I've studied is accurate and realize it's probably pretty close, simply because genetic history is merely a numbers game. You had two parents, four grandparents, eight great-grandparents, sixteen great-great grandparents and so on. But this ancestral expansion is not borne back ceaselessly into the past. If it were, my family tree when Charlemagne was Le Grand Fromage, would harbor more than a billion ancestors and represent more people than were alive back then."

I turned back, looked at Mike and continued. "What it does mean is that pedigrees begin to fold in on themselves where a few generations back become less linear and more web-like. Consanguinity, or sharing common ancestors, results in the marriage of related individuals of which about ten-percent of the world's population is married to a second cousin, or closer, and that's about 800 million people."

"Marriage between cousins wasn't always prohibited and so, not too far back, someone in my family tree actually married someone else from the same roots where geneticists Peter Ralph and Graham Coop showed that all Europeans are descended from exactly the same people. Basically, everyone alive in the ninth century who left descendants, is the ancestor of every living European today."

"With today's genetic sequencing, the deep, intimate history of everyone can be revealed as we carry traces of our ancestors in our cells and now you can have your past unscrambled that will match parts of your DNA with people from all over the world. The results are beguiling but won't necessarily show your geographical origins in the past. The neat thing is that it will show with whom you have common ancestry today. The truth is that we're all a bit of everything and we come from all over. If you're white, you're a bit Viking, Celt, Anglo- Saxon and even a bit Charlemagne. Done right, DNA testing can be an immensely powerful tool for studying families that can disclose unknown cousins or parents. Further back, the past becomes dimmer but not invisible."

"Often genetic ancestry relies on the Y chromosome, which is inherited only via the paternal line, or via mitochondrial DNA, passed from mothers, which was how the Terrill lineage was traced from my grandmother. These make for persuasive, but often simplistic, analyses of ancestry. These two chunks of DNA only make up 2% of your genome. What about the other 98%? It has to come from somewhere, too, and that's how we all guess about the rest of our ancestors."

"Each subsequent generation, the contribution from an individual from our lineage, becomes less. Genetic inheritance works in a similar way. Half of our genome comes from our mother and half from our father, a quarter from each of our grandparents. But because of the way the DNA deck is shuffled, every time a sperm or egg is made, it doesn't keep halving perfectly as you meander up through your family tree. If you are fully outbred, where all our ancestors came from outside a particular family or tribe, we would have 256 great- great-great-great-great-great-grandparents. But their genetic contribution to us isn't equal. Before long, we all will find ancestors from whom we bear no DNA. They're still our family and blood relatives but their genes have been diluted out of our bloodline. Even though we are directly descended from Charlemagne, we may well carry none of his DNA."

Mike asked. "So, what does this all mean?"

I replied. "Ancestry is messy. Genetics is messy, but powerful. People are horny and that's why we have nearly eight billion people consuming Mother Earth and all she provides. While we think we're special, it's estimated that over 107 billion people came before us. Today, around 385,000 babies are born each day and 185,000 people die who had hopes and dreams, goals and aspirations who are now arriving or are now gone. Life is complex and the ability to dig deep and recreate a history, a legacy and a past has been and will always be something very, very special."

I looked at the recently plowed fields and pondered in retrospect, aware that where I'd been and what I'd done could have had profound consequences. I looked at Mike and stated, "After my visit with Charlemagne, I'd matured and came to realize that any change I made could potentially change the history of the world and the Terrill family and that was never my goal. I only wanted to be an observer."

"Were you able to do that?"

"I tried. I truly wanted to leave well enough alone."

I continued. "In all the historical reports I've read about marriage, even when women were under discussion, no study has ever examined their behavior over a long chronological period. If they had, I'm certain they would have seen that, like the Terrill family, the goal for an aristocratic woman was to make 'a good marriage', which was simply a fitting match of wealth and status, religious affiliation and age where the bonus consisted of less easily defined qualities such as temperament and moral qualities. You can quickly see that, in numerous instances, the explicit purpose of marriage among the upper classes was to advance the political and economic interest of the patrilineal family. During our family's time it's estimated that more than 95% of all surviving aristocratic daughters eventually married, while today in America that figure is around 30%".

"Why?" Mike asked, as I continued.

"If we go back to Martin Luther's time, we see that, after the Reformation, there were no nunneries in which to place daughters as a reasonable alternative to marriage. This limitation of what a family could do with their daughters happened in a time when it was a moral obligation on the part of families to see that their daughters married their social equals. Marriage at this level was a very complex affair in which the needs and desires of the couple were subordinated to the needs of the family as a whole. Fulfilling this obligation frequently cost families a great deal of money and resources."

"Elite families had to consider many factors when arranging appropriate, profitable matches for their daughters. My examination of the marriage strategies of aristocratic families over five centuries revealed three paramount concerns. First, the continuation of the male line. Second, the preservation of inherited property. Third, the acquisition of more property and prestige. You can see it in the charts of my ancestors and royalty by whom they married and their offspring. It isn't until the last generation in my summary that a son wasn't born and, yet, the Terrill name showed up when they left Cornwall and came to America."

"The importance of a good marriage was largely a point of agreement between children and their parents. Socialization had seen to it that British noble children, on the whole, looked for the same type of benefits from marriage that their families wished for them. Making a good first marriage was crucial to elite women as it could set the entire tenor of their adult lives. On a personal level, the success or failure of the marriage influenced their emotional happiness. On a more practical level, marriage determined their standard of living and often their family's access to patronage, political influence and the royal court. The union could also determine the level in which a woman could expect to re-marry, should her first husband die or they divorce where a wealthy, well-connected widow was always someone widowed men sought after."

"Do you think of the women as victims?" Mike inquired. "Somewhat," I responded before adding. "Aristocratic women understood the benefits they stood to gain from the status of their husbands and generally agreed with the larger goals of their families. The importance of familial status was paramount in determining marriage choices that continued right up until the end of our aristocratic lineage. The concern of the family often was not so much personal happiness of the man and woman but, rather, to facilitate the attainment of social advantages for the family. The system served this end with remarkable effectiveness and there's no question that a young woman of the aristocracy aimed to marry and marry well. She had few if any alternatives and failure to marry meant a lifetime as an old-maid, living in the households of family and friends. The importance of marriage to a mate of good rank and fortune consistently concerned noble women across the centuries."

"The real issue, beyond the merger, was the high mortality rate amongst women when giving birth. It's estimated that one-in-five women died during this event and this is the primary reason why you see so many instances where a man was married multiple times."

Mike inquired. "In other words, women were not only bartering chips for the sustenance of the economic wellbeing of the family, they carried the risk of giving their life for its succession, if and only if they could produce a male heir?"

"That's about the way it was," I replied. "When did things change?" Mike asked.

"You mean, when did the system begin to fall apart?" "Yup!"

Chapter 65: Changing Times

I paused and hoped I wasn't being too basic for a man of the cloth as I continued. "Arranged marriages, particularly amongst aristocracy, were the norm in Britain until the 18th century. In England, marriages of young people aged 16 or 17 required parental consent by law and were not legal below the age of 16. Although it's now considered old fashioned, it's not unheard of for one partner, usually the male to ask the parents of the other partner, usually the female, for their hand in marriage. What's amazing is that arranged marriages are still the norm in many cultures around the world and are not illegal in the U.K. if the couple consents to be married. Forced marriages are completely different and are outlawed by the Antisocial Crime and Policing Act, even when marriages occur outside the Britain."

"So, things changed in the 1600 and 1700's?" Mike asked.
"Yes."

"Why?"

I continued. "In seventeenth-century England, marriage and morals played a much more important social role than today. A family was centered around a married couple and represented the basic social, economic and political unit of England. In the Stuart period from 1603 to 1714, a husband's 'rule' over his wife, children and servants was seen as an analogy to the king's reign over his people. In other words, it was an indicator of a hierarchy constituted by God. A woman was regarded as the 'weaker vessel' and a creature physically, intellectually, morally and even spiritually inferior to a man, therefore, the man had a right to dominate her."

"Given its social significance, marriage was considered a matter of a larger community, not only to the couple themselves, but their entire family. Although the number of purely arranged marriages was decreasing, as opposed to the previous centuries, young women were expected to consult their choice of a partner with their parents and relatives, especially with those who intended to bestow some property on them. Generally speaking, the poorer a girl was the greater freedom she had in choosing her future husband. But even the children of the poor were expected to ask their parents for their blessing, even though money played a small part here."

"The relative position of women in the seventeenth-century English marriage was dictated by the patriarchal nature of family relationships, with an emphasis on the subordination of women. Common law was strongly biased in favor of the husband/father and a married woman had no financial rights independent of her husband. The man also had a right to beat his wife, which was, sadly, a rather common practice."

"Closely connected with matrimony was the issue of sexuality. Marriage provided the only space in which the seventeenth-century woman was allowed to express her sexuality and even this space was not without limitations. Married life was perceived as a parallel of Christ's bond with his Church, so passionate love between husband and wife was regarded as undesirable. Infidelity in marriage was severely punished where the Rump Parliament even imposed a death penalty on it."

"As has been suggested, the main purpose of marriage was having children and, particularly, a male descendent. It was not only ensuring an heir that was significant. The husband couldn't act as the head of a family until his marriage had produced an offspring, so it was also a matter of social prestige. For a woman, the whole thing was even more serious. Infertility was perceived not only as a social defect but a downright punishment by God. Therefore, women were under enormous pressure to have children beginning with their wedding day. An important ritual was the christening of babies - a way of letting the community know that the marriage fulfilled its purpose." "Traditional Church law placed great emphasis on the sacredness of marriage and on its inseparability. Divorce in the modern sense of the word was not recognized. A substitute option was declaring the marriage invalid simply by stating that the bond had never been a proper marriage. To do this, it had to be proven that the marriage was defective in some way. The most common reasons were the infancy of the couple at the time of the spousals, permanent impotence or frigidity or the discovery that the couple were in fact relatives. Declaring the marriage invalid gave both partners an opportunity to remarry. However, the wife lost all inheritance rights and the children were proclaimed illegitimate."

"Another method of escape from an unhappy marriage was a legal separation 'from bed and table.' This procedure was possible in cases of proven adultery or extreme cruelty. Contrary to the previous option, the separation did not affect the wife's inheritance rights nor the legal status of the children. However, the disadvantage was that the marriage bond remained undivided and the separated partners could not marry again."

"The third option was a procedure called divortium a vinculo matrimonii, an act very close to divorce, which could only be achieved upon the decision of the Parliament. Needless to say, it was a very protracted and expensive procedure. By the mid 1800's only 200 people attempted it and only six of these were initiated by women, with legal divorce not established until 1857."

"Seventeenth Century England still saw no targeted effort of women to achieve better social conditions. However, it can be said that the position of a married Englishwoman underwent a slow but steady, improvement, especially regarding her choice of a life partner. Also, the Puritan emphasis on mutual love in a relationship was a positive development in changing the roles and responsibilities of husband and wife and then entire concept of marriage."

"Things were a lot different back then but what happened is still in play today where the only big difference is there are a lot fewer arranged marriages and few if any 'mergers.' There's still love and hate, dreams and nightmares, aspirations and failures where what seemed so important back then seems so trivial today and the purported debauchery was really the consequence of the increased mortality rate, particularly of women giving birth."

"One of the key elements that affected English values was the Puritan movement that began in the 1530's when King Henry VIII repudiated papal authority and transformed the Church of Rome into the Church of England. To Puritans, the Church of England retained too much of the liturgy and ritual of Roman Catholicism and needed to eliminate ceremonies and practices not rooted in the Bible which they believed allowed the Puritans to have a direct covenant with God in terms of enacting their reforms. As Puritans attacked the established church, their principles gained popular acceptance, especially amongst lawyers and merchants of London who saw in Puritanism, a reflection of their growing discontent with economic restraints families were forced to contend with that accompanied the beginnings of a market economy where supply and demand and the direct production of goods and services was coming into play."

"In the English society of that time, strongly influenced by Puritan values, sexual integrity and the status of a married person provided a woman with respectability and social prestige. This, together with the fact that it was very difficult for women to find ways of making an independent living, meant securing a husband was a matter of great importance."

"The initial, 1620 Pilgrim migration was based on the Puritan beliefs that a new world would allow them to mold a society and culture devoid of the dogma, history and limitations being carried over from the rapidly eroding feudal system that had permeated life in England for hundreds of years. Interestingly, Puritans felt they were still part of England. It was only due to English taxation that the thought of breaking free from the standards, customs and laws of England finally took hold."

"As one examines the basic structure of America we see so many things that were inherited from England from the rights established for barons in the Magna Carta to forms of taxation and foundations of law and order. America's social, political and legal foundation virtually comes the basic philosophies established by the Greeks, enhanced by the Romans, incorporated by Charlemagne, sophisticated by William the Conqueror and implemented in medieval Europe."

Chapter 66: Checkmate

The next morning, I arrived in the quiet room as we agreed to resume our Wednesday cribbage game and to my surprise, Mike was sitting there clutching the written summary of my ancestry, while propping his elbows on the empty chess board in front of him. I thought it was odd as I looked at him, realizing he had some sort of message he wanted to share.

"I've been thinking about your heritage," Mike offered. "I mean all the kings, dukes and barons and how power and prestige usurped love and affection and, then, all the battles and beheadings. If I counted right, there were 27 generations before Charlemagne and 37 after which means that you were able to trace a total of 64 different generations. While most of us can't get beyond grandma and grandpa, what's amazing is that you've gone all the way back and tied them all together."

I think Mike could sense my frustration and that was the reason for the chess board as I inquired, "Why the board?"

Mike looked down and then up at me and continued. "Will, your family history is one filled with love and war, happiness and sadness, honor and deceit, just like everyone else's and that's why I've got the papers and the board in front of me."

I must have frowned as Mike continued. "The ancestors you summarized all had several things in common. First, they were all born and died. Second, they were all married and had the children you traced. Third, they came from aristocracy that was handed down from generation to generation and so I'd like to outline how I think it all fits together, if that's all right with you."

I glanced at the board as Mike began. "The board in front of me, represents life, where we all start with the same set of circumstances. We are born! For some it's a glorious occasion. For others, nothing more than a consequence of the physical interaction of two others. Around us are those in our early years who protect us, defend us, nurture us and, hopefully, make us feel wanted, needed and loved. As we progress, we are actually moving towards the other side of life, which is our demise. For some this will happen before they reach their natural end because of calamity or illness. In life, no matter where we end, there will always be those forces trying to impede our transition and hinder our objective, which is simply to progress to the opposite end of the board in the best possible way."

"I once read a psychosocial treatise created by a gentleman named Erik Erikson that addressed the eight stages of development across the entire lifespan, just like there are eight rows to a chess board where there are then eight options in terms of which square to visit. At each stage individuals deal with conflicts that serve as turning points in their development. When the conflict is resolved successfully, the person is able to develop the psychosocial quality associated with that particular stage and become ready to move to the next stage as they learn about the conflict confronted and the major events that occur during each point of development."

"The first stage is called *'trust versus mistrust'* and is the earliest psychosocial stage that occurs during the first year or so of a child's life. During this critical phase of development, an infant is utterly dependent upon his or her caregivers. When parents or caregivers respond to a child's needs in a consistent and caring manner, the child learns to trust the world and the people around him."

"The second psychosocial stage involves the conflict between *'autonomy and doubt'*. As the child enters the toddler years, gaining a greater sense of personal control becomes increasingly important. Tasks such as learning how to use the toilet, selecting foods, and choosing toys are ways that children gain a greater sense of independence."

"The third stage is known as *'initiative versus guilt'* and occurs between the ages of about three and five. This stage is centered on developing a sense of self-initiative. Children who are allowed and encouraged to engage in self-directed play emerge with a sense of strong initiative, while those who are discouraged may begin to feel a sense of guilt over their self-initiated activities."

"During middle childhood between the ages of about six and eleven, children enter the fourth stage known as *'industry versus inferiority'*. As children engage in social interaction with friends and academic activities at school, they begin to develop a sense of pride and accomplishment in their work and abilities. Children who are praised and encouraged develop a sense of competence. Those who are discouraged are left with a sense of inferiority."

"The fifth stage is centered on *'identity versus role confusion'*. At this point in development, the formation of a personal identity becomes critical. During adolescence, teens explore different behaviors, roles, and identities. Erikson believed that this stage was particularly crucial and that forging a strong identity serves as a basis for finding future direction in life. Those who find a sense of identity feel secure, independent and ready to face the future, while those who remain confused may feel lost, insecure and unsure of their place in the world. To be named a knight or baron in your ancestor's times assisted in creating identity."

"The sixth stage is centered on *'intimacy versus isolation'* that focuses on forming intimate, loving relationships with other people. Dating, marriage, family, and friendships are important during the intimacy versus isolation stage, which lasts from approximately age 19 to 40. By successfully forming loving relationships with other people, individuals are able to experience love and enjoy intimacy. Those who fail to form lasting relationships may feel isolated and alone and to me this is the most important stage of all."

"Once adults enter the seventh stage of *'generativity versus stagnation'* occurring during middle adulthood, the psychosocial conflict becomes centered on the need to create or nurture things that will outlast the individual. Raising a family, working, and contributing to the community are all ways that people develop a sense of purpose. Those who fail to find ways to contribute may feel disconnected and useless."

"The eighth and final psychosocial stage is known as *'integrity versus despair'* that begins around the age of 65 and lasts until death. During this period of time the individual looks back on his or her life. The major question during this stage is, 'Did I live a meaningful life?' Those who have a meaningful life will feel a sense of peace, wisdom, and fulfillment, even when facing death. Those who look back on life with bitterness and regret will have feelings of despair and that's one of life's tragedies. You can only imagine what all the people you referred to were thinking when they were about to die. It wasn't about wealth and power, it wasn't about prestige, it was about whether they sincerely felt wanted, needed and loved."

"With each stage, or square, all of us have made decisions that make us either happy or sad, satisfied or dissatisfied, powerful or powerless and with each progression, there was a risk to our overall wellbeing, just like there was for all the people you have outlined who preceded us and just as it is today."

"Sure," I replied as I leaned back and took a sip of my coffee. Mike began again. "You and I were blessed. We both met wonderful women who filled our lives with significance so that we feel that our lives have been filled with integrity and our only despair is that Peg and Ginny are no longer here with us."

A bit of sorrow went through me as Mike continued. "I did hundreds of weddings and they almost all boiled down to the same components that evolved during my tenure, ranging from some couples 'having to get married' because the woman was pregnant, to today, when people get married for all kinds of reasons and from a lot of different perspectives. Sadly, less than half of all marriages end up 'forever' and the pain and suffering couples go through is immense, let alone the cost of divorce on not only the couple but the children they bring into this world."

Mike followed my lead, leaned back and continued. "If we look at the time you outlined in your genealogical summary and the immense wealth and power your ancestors once had and then look at who married whom, you begin to see that amongst your ancestors, in many instances, it wasn't love and marriage, it was a business merger for financial growth or stability and that's probably why you find your once aristocratic lineage ending up in a hole in the ground digging for copper – somebody said, 'Screw it', I'm not merging. I'm getting married for love and not for money'."

I concurred, indicating that Mike was spot on, as I chimed in. "Members of not only the Terrill aristocracy but all aristocracies of the time, belonged to the genteel set largely by virtue of their birth. During the time of the Terrill British history, family politics consumed a great deal of their attention simply because it correlated to wealth and subsequent power and prestige to the point that families took great care in arranging the marriages of their children."

"So nothing has really changed, has it?" Mike asked.

I thought for a moment and realized Mike was spot on as I continued. "Historians have examined aristocratic marriage patterns, and, like me, have done so by focusing on men, feeling somewhat inadequate for not following matrilineal heritages."

Mike glanced at the chess board once again as I added "Interestingly, the basic requirement for a legally valid marriage was not a formal consecration in a church but the completion of a marriage contract, commonly called 'spousal'. Spousal's were an act in which the bride and groom said their vows in the present tense. In a majority of cases, this procedure was accompanied by a church ceremony. However, if the marriage was concluded without witnesses and was not consecrated in a church, it still had the same legal validity. This practice existed in England from the twelfth century until 1753 where not having to go through a church ceremony made it possible for secret lovers to marry without the knowledge of their parents, thereby escaping the dynastic scheming of their families."

With that Mike handed my genealogical summary back to me and shared that he'd performed over 150 marriages during his career and could normally tell if the marriage was going to last or not. He didn't believe that any of his marriages had been arranged.

I looked at him and questioned how he could tell. He said it was easy because there were seven different criteria for a successful marriage and those who understood and worked at the relationship succeeded, while those who didn't never had a chance.

"In small towns, a minister has to be more than just someone who preaches, he needs to also be a marriage and grief counselor and someone to turn to in times of trouble. This means if you're going to be effective you need to understand the dynamics of marriage, the stages of life and the consequence of death."

"My Bachelor's Degree was in Counseling Psychology." "You mean clinical psychology?"

"No, there's a big difference. Clinical Psychologist work with a broad range of psychopathology and clinical diagnoses and receive more extensive clinical training with serious psychopathology and major depressive disorders. Counseling Psychologists focus more on emotional, social and physical issues that arise from typical life stresses and more serious issues associated with school, work or family settings concerning relationship issues, substance abuse, careers, and difficulty of adapting to life changes."

"While I was starting on my Masters, I had some personal issues and found myself needing answers I couldn't find in any books. One day as I was walking down State Street in Madison, I saw that the door of St. Paul's Catholic Church was open and went inside. It had been years since I'd gone to church. What I found was peace…peace of mind, peace of spirit and a pervading sense of oneness that I hadn't felt before. For some reason, all the issues that had been building up inside of me seemed insignificant as tears streamed from my eyes."

"I considered turning Catholic and becoming a priest but the more I looked into it, the more I realized that, while it's a noble calling for some, it was too singular for me, as I needed someone to love and share my life with. I examined all the possible alternatives and the more I looked into the Congregational faith, that allows greater freedoms than others, the more I felt it was the right fit for me."

Mike looked down at the ground and then back at me and I knew what he was about to say was coming from the heart as he added. "An inward transformation occurs in a person who decides to follow Jesus Christ. Things change! They see the world differently and understand their journey more deeply and profoundly where they have their sights fixed on eternity and union with God and hold themselves to higher standards and virtues. Trust me, there were things I did that I'm not proud of and things I did that I regret and, yet, I hope and pray that I've made up for them without being unrealistic about what to expect in others."

Mike took another deep breath and continued. "Turning to Christ requires a conscious choice and takes dedication. While the basic premise of Jesus' message may appear straight forward in terms of the love of God, neighbor and self, the implications of doing so are really challenging where the true disciple is called to live radically and often finds themselves at odds with society, the world and even others within their own homes."

"It meant literally starting over in terms of my education and I earned a second Bachelor's Degree in Religious Studies with courses in the mystery of God, world religions, religious ethics, marriage and the Church, and the Old and New Testaments. Next, I earned a Master's degree in divinity that taught me about the rigors of being a church leader and how to handle the responsibility to my congregation and community, including how to write and deliver sermons, transformational leadership, theological aesthetics, conducting worship services, and political theology."

"In so doing, I learned that I needed to hold myself to higher standards, which comes with a price where we have to leave other things behind. Trust me, it's difficult to be a person of faith, hope and love in a world often fixated on its own fulfillment and self-absorption. What really hit home was to realize that God's ways are not ours, which became crystal clear if you have enough courage to stand against the tide. I began calling it 'putting love in motion,' which required that I challenge all the accepted modes of doing business and fighting complacency without going overboard and isolating myself from reality. Few people like Bible thumpers and that was the one thing I never wanted to be. I'm a long way from being a saint and, yet, hopefully, like them what has made me different and a better person is that...like the saints, I persevered."

"I hope I'm not pontificating, Will. People don't want to be told they're sailing their ships in the wrong direction. Clinging to their insistences and need to be correct, people become defensive when challenged. We were asked by one of our professors to tell him what love looked like. I thought about it and remembered what Saint Augustine had written...'Love has the hands to help others. It has the feet to hasten the poor and needy, the eyes to see misery and want and the ears to hear the sighs and sorrows of men.' I responded and then added. 'Love also has the courage and honesty to tell people what they may not want to hear but need to and model without wavering a life of humble, loving and faithful service simply because we want to and not for any other form of reward."

I stood in abject silence. The man before me had opened his heart and let me in. I stood bathed in a profound sense of humility, both in affirmation and respect until the deafening silence of respect was broken as Mike added. "I finally took both my written or oral examinations, became ordained and received my license to practice in Wisconsin."

"License?"

"Heh, it's Wisconsin."

Mike looked at me and sort of shook his head. "I had opportunities to become an associate pastor in Milwaukee or Pastor in Mineral Point. I was 28 years old, in debt up to my ears and married with a kid on the way. I asked Ginny which she preferred and she asked if we could take a ride to Mineral Point. We came into town and both knew we were 'home' and we never left. Everything we dreamed about was here…the right people, the right heritage, the right everything. We rented the apartment above the Red Rooster and moved in and the rest, they say, is history."

"While the demands of giving a sermon every week seems to be the biggest challenge for most ministers, for me it was quite simple. I'd read the Bible passages applicable to the time of year and speak extemporaneously. They told us in school to always remember K-I-S-S which meant 'Keep It a Short Sermon' and I became famous for my 'six-minute wonders.'"

"Six-minute wonders?"

"The congregation would wonder what I said in those six minutes. Never did I say this is what 'God said.' Never did I criticize or chastise. My goal was to preach about the four points – humility, generosity, compassion and forgiveness and then, at the end of services, always leave them laughing."

Mike shrugged his shoulders and continued. "It didn't take too long until we realized that building a parish meant reaching out beyond the four walls and so we got involved in anything and everything until people began to realize that I was just another guy."

I must have had a look on my face that questioned Mike's words as he added, "Religion is assuring a sense of satisfaction with who you are and how you fit in this world, in other words, life assurance."

I smiled at the thought as Mike continued. "I began to realize that our little town really didn't have a person for someone to share their problems with and so I began opening my doors to anyone and everyone who simply needed someone to talk to. As my reputation grew, so did the number of people who made appointments to see me simply because they knew what we talked about was between them, God and me. After a while I think I'd heard it all and quickly learned the criteria to a successful marriage that I shared with more people than you can imagine."

"What criteria?" I asked.

"Attraction, association communication, understanding, trust, compromise and forgiveness," Mike rattled off as he had probably done a thousand times as I simply smiled at his concise simplicity. He had the answer to what most married couples look for their entire lives as I urged him to explain what he meant.

"We come into this world programmed to do one basic thing… sustain our genetic heritage. We have primal and learned behaviors that transcend that single objective, namely, propagation of the species. As mankind became socialized the period of bonding became extended and with it the entire spousal concept."

"No one should ever expect it will be easy! Marriage is a very difficult task, and, yet, it's one of, if not the most important, job in a person's life if they expect to be happy and satisfied."

"Part of my job as a minister was to be a counselor where all my years taught me that a long-term marriage is NOT easy!"

Mike drained the last of his coffee, gently smiled and said. "One of my classes in how to give sermons hit it right on the head when the professor said, 'Through words, you can communicate not only thought and ideas but feelings and emotions. You can excite and anger. You can make people laugh and cry, chortle or frown. You can make them pull within themselves and truly think about all that they are and all that they want to be. You can paint pictures that rile even the weakest of imaginations. You can stimulate the senses and make one move beyond 'now' into a world they might never have pondered before. With this you can help them become alive, as it moves them away from their 'now' and induces them to think, dream and ponder - to meet others and make both parties think, act and respond, mentally and intellectually'."

"People have asked me why I became a minister and I tell them it happened because of one word - caring. Caring is a critical part of life and its happiness. Without caring we would all be indifferent and there would be no peaks, only valleys. Caring could, in its purest form, be classified as 'passion' - a passion for life, a passion for love and a passion for other beings, both animate and inanimate. While many people would call passion for others compassion, I don't! To me, that word sounds didactic, elitist and condescending."

"Passion is a degree of caring where there becomes greater value and, therefore, the chance of a greater loss and sorrow. Perhaps this is why so many people remain passion-impaired. With passion comes risk, where the loss can become greater, the disappointment more profound and the emptiness even deeper. When something for which we have passion suddenly dissipates and we feel pain and today's plastic world tries to minimize it so that we are never allowed to be sad."

"Will, I sincerely believe one MUST be passionate, caring and enthusiastic. Without these attributes we are only a shell, walking, interacting, functioning in a world like some plastic snowman sitting on a neighbor's lawn at Christmas. There but not really. Glowing but not really. Dynamic and three dimensional but only as what they represent and not what they truly are."

"Caring is part of our self-concept. It's a segment of our inter- personal definition that gives us personal dimension. We care because we want to fully integrate ourselves with other people and other beings - to make ourselves better and to hopefully make them better, too. To think, feel and act in such a manner as to then walk away from one of life's intersections better, more positive and in some way moved. Equally then the nirvana we all aspire to will flow like a torrent upon the landscape enveloping all those who witness and experience the true bonding of two people based on a profound acceptance of each other."

I stood in awe of the man who had become my friend. We'd laughed together and shared so much and in the void of singularity created by my Peg departing, I was once again filled with the joy of friendship and the peace that comes from sincerely feeling important to another.

We headed for the elevator and when we got to Mike's floor I held out my hand only to be pulled in with another great big bear hug from someone I knew really cared about. At the same time, I provided what I always called an inside-out smile, where the joy from within radiates to the smile on the outside, that is there simply because you're happy —

happy to have someone to listen to, someone to laugh with and someone to share this thing called life.

Chapter 67: Waldwick

Summer came and summer went. The warmth of the days slowly eroded like soft sand at the edge of the sea. Mike's knee had healed and he was not only walking without a limp but confident of his ability to drive long distances. He indicated he wanted to go visit his son and grandkids and told me he was going to be gone for nearly a month. Needless to say, my card playing, beer drinking buddy was going to be missed.

I dillydallied around doing this and that and got the urge to go out to the Forest. The weather gods were being good to us. It was early November and we hadn't had the first frost yet. I drove out to Waldwick, parked my car and made my way down into the Forest, stopping at the remains of the school foundation to reflect on all those who'd matriculated through its confines with dreams of grandeur in their heads. After my pause, I slowly made my way down the deer path to the springs with hopes that 'He' would be there. It had been a long time since I'd seen my four-legged friend.

To my pleasant surprise the big buck was standing there as if waiting for me. Our eyes met, if only for an instant. The obligatory nod took place indicating I was to follow him. Being obedient and familiar with the routine, I traversed the stream and entered the bog, slowly following behind the grand master as he nonchalantly led me to the spot where steam rose from the ground, creating the fog I knew would take me elsewhere.

I willingly stepped upon the moss and was enveloped in the mist. For a moment it seemed as if nothing had transpired and yet my senses told me I'd once again traversed time and space. As had been the case so many times before, I didn't know where I was going or even when.

I paused to catch my breath and then exited the shroud to find myself in a low valley, surrounded by rocky outcroppings, covered by sturdy moss that had the gumption to exist where little else could survive. I looked left and right and caught a glimpse of the roiling sea upon which the waves of winter had begun their never-ending assault.

Slowly making my way from the valley, I saw a path leading both north and south. The area looked familiar and the familiarity bred comfort within my soul. Perhaps I'd only traveled in space and nottime. As I stood there I saw a cart with large wooden wheels approaching, drawn by a single horse hauling a load of thatch of Norfolk Reed from the sea marshes beyond the cliffs.

In our travels Peg and I had traversed Great Britain numerous times and, based on the topography, I began to deduce I'd been relocated to Cornwall with the shore of the Celtic Sea before me. In other words, I was where it all began in terms of how, when and where the Terrill family last lived before coming to America. I hoped my journey was intended to finally tell me why.

I made my way to the path and realized that it was simply worn stone. It was then I realized I'd traveled in both space and time as the path was simply the predecessor of the road Peg and I had driven before. It all seemed so…comfortable and I felt as if I'd come home. A slight smile crossed my face as I recognized the outcroppings that told me Waldwick, Cornwall, England was nearby.

I followed the cart path, turned left or southwest and headed for where it all began. I was on my way to my last English ancestor's home as my heart filled with a profound sense of excitement and joy. After all my travels, after all the ancestors I'd met, after all the events and experiences I'd encountered, I sincerely felt I was finally nearing that point in time and space that was no longer ancient history but a direct connect with my ancestors who'd come to America.

The walk wasn't far, in fact, just over the second hill. A smile creased my lips as I came to a site that made the entire journey worthwhile. Before me, standing proud and erect in all its glory, as it had for nearly a thousand years, was the entrance to the Queensland Mine. Made of cobbled stone from the bowels of mother earth herself, the adit level stood as a reminder of the many souls who'd gone below, some of which had never returned.

George Terrill, my great, great grandfather had worked in that very mine as had his father and his father and his father before him. Perhaps I could finally put links in the chain that trailed back to Carolous de Menapii, so many stories before. George described Queensland as matching that of Cornwall's greatest mine, Botallack, in terms of size, intensity and misery and it appeared that his description was quite accurate. Queensland's primary shaft reached 1,700 feet in depth then stretched out like fingers of an empty glove for distances of nearly a mile in all directions, including beneath the cold Cornwall shore.

When Peg and I visited, the absence of function had taken its toll and entering any of the winzes below was simply unsafe, even for a young man, and not for an old geezer like me. However, with my new visit, I observed men coming and going, hauling the ore away in ox carts for smelting near the sea. From the garb the men were wearing, the ox carts and the condition of the adit level, I calculated I'd come to Cornwall in the 1700 or 1800's. I guess I could explain it but George did a much better job than me in his memoires as he stated.

'We labored, dripping our salty sweat into the soft, moist ground, the waves of the ocean pounded above us, beating out a never-ending rhapsody to which pick and shovel sustained their cadence, like so many heartbeats within. Each day, I became buried, as if dead. Each night, I was resurrected, gasping for the sweetness of life."

In a time of relative peace, in a land so wrought with war that plowshares were beaten into swords three times within my first twenty years, we were still conquered … not by soldiers but by the system. In a period of a few brief years, in a time of our great- grandfathers, the bounty had been lean and, in place of a free worker, what had become known as the factory system had been born … developed at first as a temporary structure. But, after nearly four generations of existence, the system had been finely honed, like the finest of watches, where every piece neatly fit together, and all parts moved in unison, against the call of freedom.

The Company owned the mine. All that was taken belonged to the Company. We knew the system, and yet still we played the game—too dumb, too fearful, too ignorant to move on. Hoping, hoping, hoping that it would be different. Praying, praying, praying that we would be the lucky ones. Knowing, knowing, knowing that all was against us. Aware, aware, aware that what we dug was our own grave into which we would someday fall.'

A little later, George wrote…'We grew up within the shadow of the mine. While it was simply a dark hole in the ground, you never felt free of its presence, you never escaped the threat that it could one day take your life, and you had a constant fear that your destiny was never more than one bad decision away. The mine was where all boys were trained to work, and by the age of thirteen, I already knew the 'game,' as my father called it.'

'There were four points to this 'game'. First was what we were paid for our labor or, as we called it, our 'tare'. From our tare, we paid for the despicable roof under which we and our families ate, slept, and dreamt, along with the few victuals we could put on the table to feed our lot. Nothing fancy like meat, mind you but a few eggs, flour, and what vegetables we couldn't grow. Finally, we paid what we could to send our children to school … a school I might add, owned by the factory … hoping that at least they could escape our self-inflicted misery but knowing all too well that someday the boys would end up beside us, while the girls married them to keep the cycle going.'

'What we were paid was a simple matter. Each month, the estimator would work his way down into the mine and check the progress, measuring each vein of ore to see whether it was thick and full, like some small stream after a spring rain, or whether it had narrowed and become thin and sparse as the hair on an old woman's head.'

'When the vein was thick and full, the estimator set the tare low. It would be easy pickings, and no one was allowed to earn his keep without paying his due. To do that would be to allow someone to climb above the hole into which he had fallen, and that was simply not the plan.'

'When the vein was thin and narrow, the estimator would raise the tare. Work was still difficult but the carrot on the end of the stick would dangle there, begging you to pull the sweat from your brow and dig, dig, dig to keep the mine and your life going.' 'I remember my childhood in bits and blabs as it blurred before me. And yet,

there are points as sharp as that of a needle that stick within my brain. We played sea captain and dreamt of sailing away, fresh air in our lungs. We played soldier and dreamt of marching away in clean, bright uniforms, believing that bullets were only meant for others and none for us. We dreamt of tomorrow but quietly, oh so quietly settled for the confinement of today.'

'I was two and twenty and had nine years within the shafts. This is when most things seem to have come into focus. It was the year when so much began to happen to change what followed.'

'The years had made me strong of back, and I only prayed that I could breathe the freshest of air every day, sweet with the nectar of freedom. At eighteen, I had married Sarah Lawrence, a pretty girl of fourteen. We had known each other our entire lives, and it was meant to be. We lived with my parents, sleeping behind an old blanket that served as our privacy ... listening to my father's raspy breathing, measuring each sleeping breath as if it were his last.'

I walked past Queensland and continued down the pike and into the tiny hamlet I already knew. I was home! Home to where it all began! Home from where my ancestors fled! I was in Waldwick and the joy of seeing it as it once was made me flush with gratitude.

Wearing a wrist watch and 'funny' clothes, unlike anything the folks of Waldwick had ever seen as had happened in my past visits, I was prepared for the curiosity I'd generate as I made my way to the pub, sauntered in and ordered a beer.

It was mid-afternoon and the pub was nearly empty. Working men were still down in the mine and ladies back then, never entered a pub alone, if at all. The matron behind the bar looked up and frowned.

'Strange clothes! Strange man!' Probably cascaded through her mind. I looked at her with her unkempt gray hair pulled back, ruddy cheeks from the winter's wind that had taken what had probably once been a lovely young girl and bathed her in loneliness and forsaken sadness, while adding more than enough girth that could no longer be hidden behind her now-dirty white apron. She smiled a sad smile who'd rinsed her mouth in too much beer that yellowed the few teeth that were still remaining.

"What'll it be?" the matron asked, as she gave me the once over.

"A mug of beer, please."

With that, she poured the beer and said, "That'll be two-pence."

I must have had a strange look upon my face as I realized all my currency was American paper from the 20th century. I pulled out a dollar bill and placed it on the bar.

"What's this?" the matron asked. "American currency," I replied.

"American? You can't expect me to take a piece of paper for a glass of beer?"

Reality was striking home as I offered. "Tell you what, how about me trading this fine Timex watch for food and lodging for seven days?"

I took off the watch and handed it to the matron who had a perplexed look on her face as she inquired, "And what do you suppose I'm to do with this? What does it do?"

"It tells time," I replied. "For what?"

I then realized it was before 1868 and I certainly wasn't talking to Countess Koscowicz of Hungary who had the Swiss clock manufacturer, Patek Philippe, create the first wristwatch.

I was perplexed when this quite rotund man who'd been sitting at one of the tables approached. "My name is Charles Fitzgerald and I'm manager of the Queensland mine," Fitzgerald offered as he stuck out his hand.

A thought rushed through me. "My God! It's the hated Fitzie George had written about". The question then became 'Is this before or after Sarah's episode with this pig?" As I stuck out my hand and returned the gesture, I was feeling the cold, damp sweat that only comes when a heart is made of stone.

"Let me see the contraption," Fitzie requested.

I slid the Timex and handed it to Fitzie as he peered at the face.

"In other words, you've taken the clocks from our homes and made them so small you can wear it on your wrist?"

I shook my head in agreement as Fitzie slid the Timex on and inquired, "Where's the pendulum?"

"It uses a spring located inside. You simply wind the small wheel each day and it will keep time." I offered.

"Anyone else have one of these?"

I thought, 'Not for 60 years if my guess is right'.

"Tell you what. You can stay here for one week and eat, as well, and I'll keep the watch."

"Include four pints a day and it's a deal."

Fitzie shook his head no and said, "How about three?"

The Timex cost $14.99 at the Ben Franklin on High Street in Mineral Point. I agreed as Fitzgerald and I shook hands on it. With that, the bombastic, bloated windbag was gone as

Alice, the bar maid, hotel hostess and, as I learned later, lady friend of Fitzie, led me to my room.

Settling in is quite simple when you've got nothing with you and so, after showing me my room, pointing out where the privy was and explaining that no women were allowed for 'cavorting' as she called it, I was set free to go. I decided to go for a walk and realized that little had changed since Peg and I had visited. Once again, George described it better than I.

'Our house was owned by the mine. It was a row house, simply one large room with a fireplace for both heat and cooking. It was but twelve paces wide and nine

paces deep. The roof was thatched, and there was one small window made of glass so distorted that the light that shone through meandered upon the floor, drunk with the disdain of neglect, muddied with the tears of those who had lived there, died there, and cried there before us. Within the room sat one table and four chairs. Beside the table sat one bed with a rope that reached from post to post upon which a curtain had been sewn. The privy was out back and was shared with the seven other families who called this ramshackle arcade home. There was always some sort of noise…people laughing, people crying, people arguing, people fighting, people taking their innermost frustrations and spewing them into the air for everyone to breathe.'

'Late at night, the sounds would subside. Silence would envelope our existence and smother humanity in solitude. When all was still, I could hear my mother's tears. She knew that my father's time upon this earth would be short, and soon she would join the others … alone, afraid, angry … wondering what each day would bring for a woman of forty-three … young in years but old in body and, more importantly, ancient in spirit.'

'When the moments were right, Sarah and I would have our time together, quietly enjoying each other. We would whisper our secrets and smother our laughter, knowing that our actions, thoughts, and hopes were bouncing off walls and ears so very near.'

'In our third year, Sarah became expectant. It was time, and we felt ready. From the first day, all was not right. She was sick and frail, and soon she began to bleed down under. As Mother would later say, "It was God's way." When Sarah got her strength back, she became expectant once again. For the second time, God chose a different way than we had intended. After nearly five years, we had no children. Perhaps it was a blessing for what was to come. I don't really know but that's the way it seems to me now.'

'For all those years, I had watched my father grow old and then the fallow set in. At first, it was a little stoop in his back, and then the cough was more intense. Soon his strength was leaving him, and the foreman was on his back. Either dig harder and deeper or get out of the mine. There were others waiting to take his place ... younger, stronger, more willing. My father endured as long as he could, the cold sweats of night filling the bed with his misery.'

'My father was a common man, with only simple dreams ... a roof above his head, a meal upon the table, someone to love him, and every now and then a pint and a laugh to make him forget his lot. Even with such a common thread, he had his wisdom that he would share with me and my brother. "Get away," he would say. "And never tarry another breath for another man beneath the earth. A man is only a total man when it's his land and all the sweat and tears are simply for himself.'

'I thought my brother was the lucky one. He was never of the mind to work within the mines. Instead he made his way to sea until one day he sailed for America and jumped ship, taking with him only the shirt on his back and a head filled with dreams of all that could possibly be. He settled in Virginia, and those dreams ... many of them... came true. But I'll speak of that a bit later, you'll see.'

'I remember that cold sixteenth day of March of my twentieth year as if it were yesterday. A deafening silence arose from beyond the blanket. My father's staccato breath no longer beat out its rhythm. Silence overtook our home. Father had succumbed at age forty-eight. Our moans were such that the neighbors on the other side of the wall came rushing over. They knew that his time had come, and they were there to comfort. Like so many others who lived in the row houses, attached side by side, soul by soul, life and death were an everyday occurrence that you hoped and prayed would stop at someone else's doorstep and not your own.'

'It was a workday like so many others, and the grief in my mother's eyes fell as tears that burned her cheeks with desolation. My heart pounded with sadness. The stillness of my father's face beckoned me to look deeper at the man who had always been there for me.'

'Though surrounded by others, I sat somehow feeling all alone, seeking answers to all that was and all that had been. How I wanted to stay with him, to say my goodbye, to tell him how much I loved him, to listen to his whispers one more time. And yet, the mine called, and I knew that it was me who was being beckoned. My sadness turned to anger. My anger turned to fear. Now I would have to carry on. Death did not stop Mother Earth's calling.'

'As I stopped in the doorway, one last time, I remember looking back over my shoulder trying to memorize the image of all that there was. I slowly, quietly, reluctantly, walked towards the shaft to take me down to my purgatory. I prayed to God to let me escape from the Hell within which I lived. By the time my shift had ended and the sweet nectar of life was upon me again, my father had been buried. Forever, he was in the ground he had learned to hate.'

"I stopped and looked down the lane to at my ancestor's home and smiled. It was just as it had been when Peg and I visited. The narrow cobblestone lane was the same, protected from progress simply because it was too narrow for cars. The thatch on the roofs was still in place but probably a few generations newer than what we'd seen. Gone were the satellite dishes, telephone lines and electric wires that had punctuated the sides of the stone buildings. It was as if time stood still, except the houses weren't filled with the gift shoppes, candle stores, fudge factories and linen emporiums enticing the tourists to take a bit of Cornwall home with them when Peg and I were here."

"As it was nearing late afternoon, I made my way back to the inn and sat at the bar nursing my next mug when the miners began arriving. They were a jocular group, simply relieved to be above ground and breathing fresh air. Normally, they'd have a pint, swap rumors and head for home. It was as it was and always had been until the mines petered out and folks moved on to different dreams that, in many cases, became just another nightmare."

"I was sitting at the bar minding my own business when two miners began talking about George and Sarah. While Sarah thought her clandestine rendezvous with Fitzie had been totally secretive, Fitzie's housekeeper was aware of the circumstance and word spread throughout the village with comments such as 'whore' associated with Sarah and talk of whether she offered herself to others became part of the conversation.

Further on in George's story, he speaks of the indiscretion. 'Old man Fitzgerald had been with the mine since before my time. He was a rough, crude brute. He had a reddish complexion that matched his hair, and he always had a snarl upon his face. The mine had been good to him and his wife. They lived in the big house upon the hill and had all the fineries of life. Fitzgerald's wife was an ugly, old hag. When we were upset or felt that we had been shorted, we'd make fun of her … crooked nose, crooked teeth, and crooked spine is what Henry would say. But then they deserved each other.'

'Sarah had shown Fitzgerald that she could do the numbers, and he took it upon himself to make her an apprentice in the payroll office. He made quite certain to all that he was doing this out of sympathy for my father and the fact that we had taken Elizabeth in and all. Everyone knew that Old "Fitzie," as we called him, liked to keep his eye on pretty lasses, and my Sarah was certainly one of those.'

'At first, Sarah's place was simply to construct the weekly tare sheets. She would add up the totals and make certain that they were correct. Old Fitzie told her that any mistakes would come from her pay. She wasn't paid enough as it was to afford any deductions.'

'It wasn't long before Old Fitzie realized that Sarah could do much more and had her figuring pay and deductions owed. It always broke her heart when a woman would show up to claim her husband's pay only to find out that the total of the rent and food was greater than what they had earned and they got nothing but the knowledge that they would go further into debt to the system.'

'Old Fitzie had developed a way of keeping track so that he knew who was near the breaking point … that point where a man would give up and risk debtor's prison to spending one more day digging in the mine. At that point, Old Fitzie would call in the tare master and foreman and make certain that the team was given the richer veins so that they could get closer to the top of the hole. How strange that a man so heartless could play God, and yet he did, day after day, week after week, year after year … making certain that no one could ever escape.'

'Every now and then, someone would try and sneak off and head for the ships and to America. The problem was that Old Fitzie had an agreement with all the sea captains, and he would give them a bounty simply for turning someone in. When they were caught, they would either be sent to debtor's prison or come back and lose all privileges, working the worst part of an already terrible job.'

All conversation ceased when George walked in as the uncomfortable reality he was the subject quickly took hold. Right then, I knew when it was. I'd arrived right before Sarah, Elizabeth, baby Henry and George would begin their ill-fated journey to America.

George ambled up to the bar and stood next to me and ordered a pint. Alice couldn't look George in the eye as she slid the mug in front of him, while the former laughter of others turned to whispers behind George's back.

As George's pint began to empty, I glanced at Alice and told her to put it on my tab. George looked at me in wonderment. Why would a stranger offer to buy him a pint?

"Do I know you?" George inquired. "No," I politely replied.

"Yet, I feel I do. That's strange!" George replied.

How do you tell someone they're your great, great grandson? How do you explain that you've come from the future? George examined my attire while I noted I'd come from America as if he couldn't tell by my accent and had purchased the clothes in New York City. I would have said Chicago but the city was simply a couple of ramshackle houses back then. George accepted my answer and the routine of where are you from and why are you here took place. I detailed that I was a retired college professor who'd come to Cornwall to better understand the people and the culture.

George accepted my response as I ordered yet another pint for the two of us. As Alice placed the beer in front of us she offered. "The gentleman here, came with American money. If it weren't for Fitzie, he'd been sleeping in the cold tonight. You see, he traded some sort of fancy wrist clock for a week's stay."

The mention of the name Fitzie virtually made the hair of George's arms raise up. You could tell there was bad blood between them.

Alice continued. "I'm certain, George, that your wife will be coming down with the pay for your pints as Fitzie agreed to pay for room and board but only three pints per day."

"George looked at me with a quizzical expression on his face and I could tell he wanted to say something as he looked around the pub before offering, 'Can we go for a walk?"

I agreed, knowing that what he was about to share was critical. We downed our pints, turned to face the stares and walked outside. When we were a few feet from the entry, George offered. "I don't know who you are or why you're here but I've got this feeling I can trust you.'"

I felt likewise as George continued. "I hope it's to help make things right for all of us. You see, my wife's been keeping the books for old man Fitzie and discovered he's cheating us miners. Now, my Sarah is an honest soul. She wouldn't cheat anyone. I guess that's why we're so poor. As the months have gone by, she's realized that the numbers simply don't add up. Not only are there adjustments to the amount paid for the tare but figures are short, as well, and Old Fitzie is pocketing the difference."

"Sarah makes the numbers correct and then, when it was time for pay, they're changed again. Those poor, stupid bastards sitting in the pub, who've given their souls to the mine aren't receiving their fair share and don't even know they're being cheated. When you have no way with numbers and can't read, how can you ever really know?"

George looked at the ground and then at me as we kept walking. "Sarah knows she can't speak of what she knows. To do so will be the end of her job and that will put my life and what little we have at risk. She's kept it to herself, except when it comes to figuring my tare and is always certain to let Old Fitzie know she's double- checked the numbers. I guess that's been the reward for keeping her mouth shut."

We stopped walking as George looked at the entrance to the mine and continued. "My best friend was a man named Henry. He and I worked as a team down in the mine until we got careless and had a cave-in and Henry died. Henry was married to Elizabeth who was expecting at the time of the accident. The cave-in was my fault! No one else! I should have been more careful!"

George looked at me while adding, "Last April, little Henry was born and Sarah and I offered to let Elizabeth stay with us. With Henry, our little house changed again. The sound of a child made Sarah and me want our own all the more but so far it's not to be. With the baby, our lives now have a routine. Sarah and I work while Elizabeth stays home and takes care of the house and the baby and makes certain that all is as good as it can be."

George had a forlorn look on his face as he admitted. "We owe the mine money. However, the fact that my pay is all mine and Sarah's working has helped us get closer to reaching ground level than ever before. It's still a hard climb but we've secretly begun hiding money for the four of us to leave for America."

I let George share what I already knew as he continued. "For about six months, things were going along quite smoothly, and all seemed well, then one day, Old Fitzie called Sarah in and told her she was dismissed. He said that he thought she was stealing from the company; something there wasn't a shred of truth to. My Sarah was taken aback. She denied any wrongdoing. She begged Old Fitzie to double-check her work. But he would have none of it. Our dreams are on hold as our funds have begun to slowly disappear."

George looked me in the eye, leaned in and whispered. "I learned that the four of us can book passage from Ireland to America for half the fare they're charging from Liverpool. All we need is some way to get to Ireland. We're still short of funds. We still owe the mine. We're still as far from tomorrow as ever and, yet, we can almost sense seeing the sun rise when it's always been so dark."

My God, I wanted to share what I knew but knew better as it could change history.

George continued. "I did some figuring and learned that we can skip across the sea by ferry from Wales and then, if need be, walk to Cork and the ships. The problem is that Old Fitzie has us and he knows it. I'm working harder I've ever worked in my life. I dig and dig and dig until my body aches, and, yet, without Sarah in the office to check the numbers, I have no way of knowing whether we're getting my fair pay. Sarah knew to the shilling how much it would take for all of us to escape. For Elizabeth, Henry, her, and me to leave Cornwall forever."

George splayed his fingers for expression as he noted. "It would take a pound to reach Ireland and then another nine pounds, sixpence to travel from Ireland to America. Each week, Sarah count's what we have and keeps track of how much more we need."

"Two days ago, a boy came to the door. He had a message for Sarah that Old Fitzie wanted to see her. Sarah thought he had need for her in the office again and went quickly. It seems Old Fitzie had learned that we've asked about Ireland and is afraid others will realize they can escape that way, too. Old Fitzie is also anxious that Sarah will begin to tell people about his pay scheme and there will be trouble. Old Fitzie knows about how much money it'll take for us to escape from this hell hole and he's going to make certain that any effort on our part will require more than we'd ever be able to pay.'"

We stopped walking and George looked out at the sea. "The boys in the mine don't think I know what's happened and, yet, I know everything. Yesterday Sarah made her way up to the mine office, thinking she was about to get her job back. Instead, Old Fitzie told Sarah his other bookkeeper had audited her work and found she'd stolen fifteen shillings intended for pay and that she'd been stealing from the miners. He threatened to let the miners know it was her who'd caused all the problems."

"'Sarah's of sharp wit and had the correct answer. She told Fitzgerald it wasn't true and it would be her word against his. She told him that no one, including me, knew of the pay adjustments and any accusation of wrongdoing would only open up a whole mess where everyone would begin to question each and every pay stub ... where every single week there would be doubt in the miners' minds as to whether they'd been cheated.'"

"Losing a miner every now and then is one thing, to have all the miners stop working at once would be a totally different matter, that would not only threaten the mine but Fitzgerald and his way of life.'"

"Sarah's outsmarted Old Fitzie and he knows it. She's much smarter than he thought. He needed some form of leverage to make certain she never breathes a word of what's going on to anyone while getting rid of her along the way."

"We stopped again and George looked me straight in the eye and continued. "Yesterday, while I was down in the mine, something happened. I can feel it. You see, when I entered the cottage, I could tell something was wrong. Sarah's eyes had a blank stare, unlike anything I'd seen before. Her face was flush as if bitten by the winter's wind, and her hair, normally so much in place, was askew. I'd learned not to ask too much and so last night I kept my mouth shut."

"'Elizabeth spent the night taking care of Henry and she avoided meeting the eyes of either Sarah or me. How strange it was to have the three of us under one roof and, yet, it was as if we were worlds apart. As we pulled the curtains closed and lay down for sleep, Sarah turned away from me, and I could sense that she was crying."

"I don't know why. Nor in my wildest dreams would I ever had imagined. Slowly, the darkness of night pulled down the lids of my eyes and I fell asleep, unaware that the person lying next to me would not close her eyes, nor share in any of her solitude, for fear that her living nightmare would play out within her head"

I looked at George and offered my condolences. I didn't know what I could share or how to tell him what I knew. All that mattered was to make certain the four of them left Waldwick for America as I added. "George, I've come to be of assistance. I've come to help you leave Waldwick. What needs to happen is there must be closure to what has transpired."

We shook hands as George headed for home and me to the pub. George to Sarah, Elizabeth and baby Henry. Me to the thoughts that rattled in my brain, not knowing what to do, what to say, what to feel. I'd vowed to never alter history and, yet, my soul told me I had no choice and needed to risk the consequences.

Chapter 68: The Duel

As I entered my room and was about to go to bed, there was a soft knock on the door. I opened it and it was George. He'd come to inform me that he'd elected to settle the matter with Fitzie once and for all. Either he or Fitzie needed to die and do so by what was called a 'Judicial Duel' that was formally introduced by King William I in the 11th Century that allowed two men who had a legitimate quarrel to settle it once and for all. The reason for George's visit was he wanted me to be his second.

While teaching European history I'd lectured my students on the nature of duels and their rationale and knew that, while simply a commoner, George and Fitzie's aristocratic heritage meant they were entitled to determine the terms and conditions of the duel. Dueling had been the way officers and gentlemen settled matters of honor for centuries. Up until the mid-19th Century there were certain situations where a meeting with pistols or swords was seen, not just a possible response to a perceived insult, but the only honorable one. Men risked being ostracized from society for not issuing a dueling challenge in response to an insult.

One of the reasons for the decline was that the definition of what constituted an insult requiring 'satisfaction' became so broad, men were dying over trifles and a hasty word or two, where the pettiest of quarrels could lead to pistols at dawn. By the time of the *last duel'*, duelists were likely to be condemned, ridiculed or both. The attitudes of society and those in positions of power had changed. It became so hard to arrange a meeting without it being discovered and intercepted by the authorities that adversaries were having to go to ever-greater lengths of secrecy and subterfuge. Queen Victoria made her displeasure of the practice known. Prince Albert called it 'barbarous' and was a prime mover in putting an end to it. Wellington, the iconic military figure of the day, worked with Prince Albert in changing attitudes. Ironically, Wellington himself took part in a duel that was one of the nails in the practice's proverbial coffin.

At first, I did everything I could to stop George but he was insistent. Having studied duels throughout European history, I outlined what was called Code Duello, first crafted in Ireland in 1777, who's goal was to instill a sense of order and pragmatism in dueling and minimize the probability that either party could somehow cheat. In addition, Code Duello afforded the opportunity for either party to apologize with no bloodshed. However, when your wife has been prostituted and it's the talk of the town, apologies didn't seem apropos, even though the written code stated, 'The first offense requires the first apology, though the retort may have been more offensive than the insult.'

What made the duel even more probable was Code Duello stated 'Any insult to a lady under a gentleman's care or protection to be considered as, by one degree, a greater offense than if given to the gentleman personally, and to be regulated accordingly.' That night, the rumors about Sarah had reached George ears.

Adultery was considered the ultimate lie upon which many duels were fought. Under the Code Duello rules, if the duel came as a result of a lie, the liar could choose to apologize, shoot or both. 'When the lie is the first offense, the aggressor could either beg pardon in express terms, exchange two shots previous to apology, or three shots followed by explanation or fire until a severe hit was received by one party or the other.'

In my lectures I would talk about the fact that during the 17th and 18th Centuries duels were most often fought with swords consisting of the rapier, or espada ropera, which was a type of sword with a slender and sharply-pointed two-edged blade that was popular in Western Europe and seen on most military officers of the time. Later a smaller or 'court sword,' called a claidheamh beag or claybeg in Gaelic, was developed that was a light, one- handed sword designed for thrusting which evolved out of the rapier. I noted to my students that any man - civilian or military - with pretensions to gentlemanly status would have worn the small sword on a daily basis but common folks wore neither and were rarely proficient in their use."

After my agreement to act as George's second, George went to Fitzie's house and challenged him to the duel. George reported he told Fitzie he knew about his indiscretions and it was time to put an end to the tyranny that had seeped into the lives of so many or die trying. At first Fitzie thought it was a lark, never believing George was man enough to risk his life. Instead, George outlined all that he knew about the wage scheme and the women who'd been bedded simply to save their way of life. George vowed that either he or Sarah would share their knowledge with the men of the mine and assured Fitzie he would see the end of a rope if he failed to meet George's challenge. Fitzie realized he had no choice and accepted the challenge that was set for sunrise two days hence.

Fitzie chose his foreman, who was a man named Oliver, as his second. Oliver and I met at the pub the following afternoon and realized that the first cut would be the deepest and there was little that could be done to stop the pending bloodshed.

In Cornwall, at that time, only men of wealth and status were technically allowed to duel - or at least, only men of wealth and status dueled using the Code Duello. So, if you had a backup, they needed to be honorable enough to fight in the first place. In this case, neither Oliver or I came from wealth or power and were simply friends of the two who reluctantly came to make certain death was fair and square. We'd agreed to do anything and everything we could to stop the nonsense.

In the case of George and Fitzie, both were somewhat aware of their family's aristocratic heritage and, quite honestly, I don't think it would have mattered as their anger and disdain for each simply grew exponentially. With a sneer, Fitzie took it upon himself to detail what had transpired between he and Sarah to the point that the challenge was presented not only in the name of George and his honor, but Sarah, Elizabeth, baby Henry and all those who'd suffered under his intolerance that none of us believed would end any other way than with one man dying.

By selecting Code Duello, Fitzie had a lot of say regarding how the duel was to take place and where. He chose the cliffs at Parranporth with a starting distance of twenty paces. Fitzie and Oliver fixed the time at sunrise while Oliver and I met again to review the specific rules of engagement.

With neither George or Fitzie being proficient with the sword, it was agreed to use matched pistols. On Wednesday, November 12, 1823 the four of us slipped out of Waldwick and made our way to Parranporth.

Fitzie had the choice of weapons and selected a set of dueling pistols while Code Duello rule number two allowed George to administer the first shot towards Fitzie. George's shot missed as the toothy grin of the lecherous pig punctuated his disdain. In defense of George, smooth-bored flintlock pistols firing round balls weren't the most accurate weapons, so this was hardly surprising. It was Fitzie's turn as he took aim and shot, also missing.

Oliver and I loaded the second set of pistols in the presence of each other and George was allowed to choose his weapon. This was done to make certain there was a fair and equitable chance for both parties. Depending on the skills of the two people, the dueling rules could be adjusted, where they could opt to fire at a rapid pace or a slower rate. With both men now seething, the rapid pace was selected while Oliver and I were charged with reloading the pistols and directed both men that the shooting wouldn't stop until it was over.

The case with George and Fitzie was neither side was willing to back down. The anger from George and disdain from Fitzie was simply too great. After the first shots were fired, per Code Duello, George was required to explain why his feelings were hurt, at which point Fitzie could have apologized and the duel would have stopped. The rules stated, 'If the parties would rather fight on, then, after shots by each - but in no case before - Fitzie was allowed, once again, to explain and apologize. If accepted, the duel was over.' If Fitzie apologized, the duel could have been delayed. Had Fitzie's apology been accepted, the duel would have been over. Instead, Fitzie graphically spoke of his pleasure with Sarah, which did nothing more than incite more anger in George to the point he was too angry, too embarrassed and too hurt to accept any apology, let alone the diatribe evoked by Fitzie.

In Code Duello, violence could only be remedied with more violence and once someone was hit, there was no turning back. After the first round, Fitzie could no longer apologize and the two had to just keep shooting. When no apology was offered, both parties took five steps closer and were now only fifteen paces apart. For the third round, they were allowed to choose their weapon with Fitzie receiving first choice."

Code Duello noted, 'In all cases a miss-fire was considered equivalent to a shot while a snap or non-cock was considered a miss- fire as well.'

The men took their places and Oliver gave the command for Fitzie to fire but nothing happened. It seems when Fitzie selected his pistol it had been at half-cock and therefore incapable of discharging its ball. An experienced second would have realized his man was about to receive a shot without being able to return fire and alerted him. Being unaware, Fitzie took aim and when no shot rang out, he stood motionless as George's shot hit him in the right shoulder.

By the accepted principles and etiquette of dueling, the duel should now have been halted. George had fired while Fitzie's misfire also counted as a shot and both men could have left with their honor intact. In retrospect, Oliver and I could have and should have intervened. Instead, George and Fitzie chose pistols for the fourth round as George demanded they shoot again and Fitzie agreed.

Perhaps Fitzie's simmering hostility towards George was such that neither of us could impose our will on him. For whatever reason, Fitzie and George went to their marks once more, now just five paces apart, turned and waited for the word to shoot as they faced each other. Fitzie was first and attempted to raise his arm but the initial hit to his shoulder had shattered his collar bone and he was unable to aim.

Fitzie shot and missed again. This time, George accurately returned fire. Because of the sideways stance adopted by both men and Fitzie's girth, the ball entered Fitzie's right hip, passed through his lower abdominal wall and exited through his left groin. Blood from the wound splattered a distance of three feet, signifying an arterial bleed, Fitzie crumpled to the ground while George simply uttered, "That's for my wife".

Rule 23 stated, 'If the cause of the meeting be of such a nature that no apology or explanation can or will be received, the challenged takes his ground, and calls on the challenger to proceed as he chooses; in such cases, firing at pleasure is the usual practice but may be varied by agreement.' George, simply chose one of the dueling guns, pointed it at Fitzie's chest and pulled the trigger.

Bam! It was over! For an instant, the shock of death and its consequence overwhelmed us. Killing someone in a duel was the same as killing them under any other circumstances – against the law. I stood, simply shaking my head, as we rolled Fitzie's body to the edge of the cliff and it plunged down into the churning sea. Later, a witness reported seeing three men dressed in black, with faces hidden, pushing something into the ocean, as we desperately made our way back to reality.

George went to the mine and crawled beneath mother earth for what would be one last time. I went back to the inn and slipped in the back door as if I'd been in the privy. At noon George was called to the surface believing he'd met his demise. Instead, it was a message from Sarah to come home immediately. George did and the rest of the George's story remains true and now I know why my ancestors really came to America.

Chapter 69: Reality

I walked back to the spot whence I'd come and stood in the spot of moss as a soft breeze blew in from the bay that settled around me. In an instant, I was back in the Forest and I thought it was 'today' except the gray November skies and empty oak trees had been replaced by soft white summer clouds and the trees had leaves upon them. I walked back to my car and felt the only thing that had changed was the fact that my Timex watch was missing.

I drove back to the apartment and saw the crowd out by the pool. I hadn't returned to 'now'. I'd come back to when I first moved into the apartment. The faces of what had once been strangers all looked familiar and yet, there wasn't that softness that comes from knowing someone that had been there when I left that morning.

I joined the group and was handed the name tag Hank and Kat had prepared with our room numbers printed on them as Hank served as MC. As he went around the group, each of us had to stand and he introduced every person without using a single note card, telling the ensemble who we were, which apartment we were in and where we came from. Hank announced that it would be an annual event and indicated there was an open bar which are two of the finest words spoken in Wisconsin. The elderly herd wandered towards the two bartenders where I once again, expected cheap booze. Wrong! I glanced at all the top shelf stuff including Korbel brandy, Crown Royal whiskey and Spotted Cow beer. Once again, I was in Badger heaven! As I stood in line, the fellow behind me tapped me on my shoulder and said "Hello, neighbor". I turned around and saw Jack and Jane Arnold who'd just moved in. "You just get here?" I asked.

"Just moved in. We had to wait until we closed on the house and that was Thursday," Jack replied.

Jack had been an insurance salesman in Mineral Point and knew everyone. I think he did all right for himself as he always drove a new Cadillac.

I looked at Jack's name tag and his apartment number said 319, which was Reverend Mike's. I inquired, "Are you sure they've got your apartment number, right?"

Jack looked at me as if I was nuts and replied, "Sure. We're all moved in."

Something wasn't right, but I didn't say anything.

Now I was getting 'up there' and yet I thought I still had all my faculties and so I didn't say another word and waited another week for Reverend Mike to return. I went out alone for dinner and checked his parking stall with Jack's Cadillac sitting there.

After one more week, I went and wrapped on door number 319. Jane opened and inquired why I'd knocked. "Is Reverend Mike home?"

"Who?" "Reverend Mike."

Jane just shook her head, "Who's Reverend Mike?" "Reverend Mike Thomas," I replied.

"Never heard of him."

"This is his apartment," I countered.

"Will, are you OK? We're the first ones to rent this apartment.

There's never been anyone named Reverend Mike living here."

I shook my head in disbelief. "Mike was the Minister of the Congregational Church in town. He and his wife Virginia, were at the Church for over 40 years and built it up by making it an integral part of Mineral Point, participating in virtually anything and everything to help the community."

Jane looked at me as if I had a screw loose. "Will, there hasn't been a Congregational Church in Mineral Point for over fifty years. I've never heard of Reverend Mike or his wife and I've lived here my whole life."

I stood in shock. I really didn't know what to think. I apologized and made my way to the quiet room. It was Wednesday and that had always been our cribbage day. I entered the room only to find two others sitting where Mike and I always sat. I simply shook my head, put my hand to my mouth, turned around and headed for Shirly Chalmer's office, who was managing the complex. I knocked on the door, stuck my head in as Shirly looked up and smiled, inquiring, "What can I do for you, Will?"

"Has there ever been a resident living here by the name of Reverend Mike Thomas?" I inquired.

"No!" Shirly confidently replied as she'd been with the apartment complex since the day it opened.

"Have I been playing cribbage with anyone, every Wednesday morning for the past two years?"

"The past two years? We've only been open three weeks and most of the time you've either been in your apartment or out at the family farm."

"No Mike and Virginia Thomas?" "Not here."

I knew I needed to find out more and went back to the Mineral Point library and looked at all the old Democrat Tribune newspapers and found nothing. Finally, I went to Madison and the Historical Society and looked up Charles Fitzgerald, Waldwick, Cornwall, England and stood completely dumbfounded as the article spoke of Fitzie as the third son of James FitzGerald, First Duke of Leinster, and Lady Emily, daughter of Charles Lennox, Second Duke of Richmond, brother of William FitzGerald, Second Duke of Leinster, Lord Henry FitzGerald and Lord Edward FitzGerald. Through his mother, Fitzie was the great-great-grandson of King Charles II· There were 19 children in his family and he became manager of the family-owned Queensland mine, disappearing in 1823, leaving behind a wife named Susan and a daughter named Emma.

The article noted that, upon his death, Fitzie's unscrupulous dealings became known, while his wife was considered a witch for wearing some sort of timepiece upon her wrist. It was also noted that Mrs. Fitzgerald, their daughter Emma Thomas and Emma's son, Michael, perished when the Fitzgerald home was 'set ablaze' by an angry mob of miners who wanted compensation for the thefts Fitzie was accused of taking.

The Thomas name burned into my soul...Reverend Mike Thomas? Could it be? Was he actually a descendant of Fitzie? A chill went through me. I'd altered time and circumstance. With it, I'd lost my best friend. Had I not left the watch! Had I not intervened, Mike would have existed and all the good he and Ginny did for Mineral Point would have taken place. Them it hit me, without the duel, George might never have left Cornwall and I wouldn't even exist. I vowed never to travel through time again. I'd seen enough, done enough and affected enough and learned a very big lesson - leave well enough alone and let nature take its course.

When I retired and lost my wife, Peg, I began to examine my own mortality and that led me to ponder what death is really like. Is it simply to cease and desist or is there really a hereafter, where our soul goes and we continue on for eternity? Perhaps that's what's kept me going all these lonely years. During my life I spent my time and energy learning about people who lived and died and how they existed and what the consequences were of their lives on those who followed in their footsteps.

Soon it will be my turn to be spoken of in the past tense and I wonder what people will say of me. Was Will a good man? Was he kind, honest and generous? Will I be fondly remembered and truly missed until I, too, am nothing more than a name on a page who evokes no emotion from those who come across William Terrill, born in 1917 and died when he did.

My trips to the Forest have become infrequent and the journey more difficult as the consequence of age has crept within my soul. I still yearn to travel down the deer path and cross the little stream to stand at the spot that took me back so many times and have my eyes meet those of the buck as we look into each other's eternity. I think of Carolus de Menapii and Charlemagne, William the Conqueror and Sir Thomas Tyrrell of Heron. I yearn to learn more about so many Tyrells and what they thought and how they felt, to hear their laughter and see their tears, yet I now accept that it won't ever happen again.

Somewhat selfishly, I long to stand in the spot of transcendence with just one wish – please to take me back - not to a distant place or past but to the 'ranch' Peg and I called home, so that I could hold her one more time and tell her I love her.

Dedicated to my wife and our years together, with the hope that her last wish was the same as mine.

The Waldwick Series: The ten-book series spans nearly 200 years and are independent yet intertwined in several ways including, characters, location and thematic objectives that examine current social issues from different perspectives. Regardless of the time period or the characters in question, the core component - judging people by who they are instead, of what they are, remains paramount.

Waldwick addresses the subject of physical, social, economic and political oppression in the 1800's. Set in Cornwall, England, Virginia and Southwestern Wisconsin, *Waldwick* frankly discusses what one family was willing to do to overcome oppression, as told through the eyes of the narrator, George Terrill. *Waldwick* then summarizes what happens when the oppression is removed and opportunity arises. Integrated into the story line are actual events and people and how the main characters are affected by their existence and their interaction with these people and events. Above all else, *Waldwick* is a love story … love of the land, love of one another and the love of freedom, woven in a tapestry of acceptance, tolerance and justice. *Award Winner*

War of My Brothers examines America of the early 20th century and how and why it changed as seen through the eyes of Hank Terrill, great grandson of George Terrill from the original Waldwick. Ride along as Hank witnesses World War I, the Spanish Flu, the 19th Amendment, that gave women the right to vote, the Great Depression, World War II, Korean War and Viet Nam and how life changed, people changed and those who govern changed, as well. Experience the traumas of life and the joys of the living as you thank God that it didn't happen to you.

The King of Hearts has been reviewed as *"ambitious, extensively researched and deeply engrossing"*…a story that traces the actual Terrill family through 60 generations as it learns the consequence of wealth, power and prestige over 700 years only to have it all collapse around them. Using a blend of magic realism, lyrical prose and imagery *The King of Hearts* weaves a complex tapestry of a family's history from 65 BCE through sixty generations. Beneath it all, the book is about friendship and the deep, mutual bond between people based on trust, support, and genuine connection that goes beyond just companionship—it's about understanding, loyalty, and being there for each other through life's ups and downs.

Little Spirit Based in contemporary Wisconsin, *Little Spirit* examines the concept of eminent domain and the taking of land and dignity, first from the Indian's perspective and then today, as seen through the eyes of George Terrill IV a descendant of the original George Terrill. Using flashbacks through a 94-year-old, blind, Ho- Chunk Indian elder, named Great Grandfather, George learns about the feelings and challenges of the Ho-Chunk nation and the taking of their land and also how contemporary America hasn't changed that much in terms of citizen rights.

Driftless revisits George and his wife fifteen years into their marriage. Reflecting on the challenges they face when their marriage becomes mundane while examining the profound question of which is worse… having nothing or everything. As the mystery of the Forest is revealed *Driftless* examines the consequence of technology and the power of special interest groups to control the status-quo for their financial gain, while addressing the issue of individual rights in time of personal need, where the one thing all people have in common is … time!

The Hayflick Limit addresses the challenges of parenthood, while discussing a person's rights to live and die. When affected by an incurable malady the question becomes *"Would you choose five-to-seven years of normal mental acuity, at which time you would abruptly expire, or risk everything and allow for the slow, gradual decline with hope that a different, longer-lasting cure might come along?"* The Hayflick Limit addresses the role of government in establishing the validity of the Hippocratic Oath?

Let Go examines the consequence of bullying as Melia Terrill is affected by the verbal onslaught and her commitment to the only friend who has shown her the beauty of acceptance for who she is. The books examines the perks and perils of extreme wealth, the solitude of loneliness and frustration of achieving one's goals only to realize that all dreams can become nightmares when one risks everything for perhaps nothing as it delves into thoughts, emotions, joys, sorrow and consequences of being a captive of one's own past and fleeting fame.

Survivor...How Death Saved My Life looks at the consequence of an altered set of priorities and how it can take a near-death experience to "right the ship". Totally immobilized for six days, George Terrill examines his life and it's mistakes and vows, if he survives, to make things right. *Survivor* addresses the psychology of fear, the challenges of being told you have less than a 5% chance of living three hours and what you think about when you sincerely believe you're going to die.

Greed is a thought-provoking literary tale of ambition gone awry, exposing how the pursuit of wealth can fracture family relationships. This intense novel, explores the intricacies of human nature and the pursuit of meaning. It serves as a critique of modern society's obsession with wealth and status that challenges readers to reconsider what success truly means, making this book not just an exhilarating journey but a profound reflection on the human condition.

And/Or Using Newton's Third Law as a lens to explore relationships where every action sets off a chain reaction, *And/Or* journeys in ways no one can predict or control while asking difficult questions about resilience, identity, and redemption. As such, it ponders deep philosophical reflections and existential questions by drawing sharp connections between science and human nature, asking such profound questions as...Is it possible for a person to truly recover from betrayal? Can love survive after it's been broken? And when one loses everything, what's left? *And/Or* is a gripping, thought-provoking read that will linger long after the final page.

Disclaimer

This book and all the Waldwick Series books are works of fiction. Some of the events and experiences detailed herein are true and have been faithfully rendered as researched by the author to the best of his abilities. The information contained in this book is intended to provide helpful and informative material on the subjects and events addressed and written as an interpretation of his learning. No part of this text may be reproduced, transmitted, downloaded, decompiled, reverse-engineered, or stored in or introduced into any information storage and retrieval system, in any form or by any means, whether electronic or mechanical, now known or hereafter invented, without the express written permission of the author.

The author is a descendant of miners from Cornwall. There is a town called Mineral Point, Wisconsin, where his childhood was filled with magical moments and marvelous memories. There is a village called Waldwick that remains nearby and is the birthplace of his grandmother and mother. There are many Terrills living in the area who are his relatives, and he hopes and prays that he's done the family name justice by what he has written, for they are the kindred spirit upon which our country was created. There is no reality to the names used as they are all of consequence.

If the tale he weaves meets your fancy and your interest is piqued, he highly recommends visiting the wonderful area just southwest of Madison, Wisconsin. The scenery is spectacular and is only exceeded by the honor, dignity, and warmth of the people who reside there.

He's written this book as a tribute to his grandmother who was a Terrill and from whom, he learned the value of integrity and honesty and the joy of acceptance that only comes from an open heart and a profound sense of decency that she emanated with each breath.

WWW.WaldwickBooks.com